Praise for Alexander C. Irvine:

"Irvine's prose is rich and evocative…" — *The Washington Post*

"Aexander C. Irvine is one of our finest new fantasists… a very versatile writer, fluent across the entire range of SF, fantasy and horror" — *Scifi.com*

"The first time I read a story by Alexander Irvine, I thought, here is a writer with a devious and logical mind…Irvine['s] stories rewrite history, or rather write the strange truth behind a history we think we know." — Theodora Goss, *Strange Horizons*

"Alexander C. Irvine has gathered quite a bit of well-deserved notice for his short fiction over the last couple of years." — Rich Horton, *SFSite.com*

"Exciting, spooky and wildly inventive…" — Sean Stewart, author of *Perfect Circle*

"…quirky and grotesque… you can think of Tim Powers's books for a touch-stone, but Alexander Irvine definitely has his own, individual voice." — Charles de Lint, author of *Widdershins*

"Boisterously imaged… everything a reader cold hope for…" — Karen Joy Fowler, author of *Sister Noon*

"Irvine has a good-natured fondness for his characters that serves him well." — Jeff VanderMeer, author of *Shriek: An Afterword*

"Irvine zeroes in on America's religiosity, commercialism, know-nothingism and other lovable quirks… rely on Irvine to ultimately make everything clear, and make the confusion enjoyable, accomplishing this through prose that's zesty and vivid" — Paul Di Filippo, author of *The Emperor of Gondwanaland and Other Stories*

"The rich emotional coloration of Irvine's prose, coupled with his remarkable sense of place, familiar and exotic lends his stories a deeply felt vividness. And on the basis of the wide range of genre boundaries crossed… his extreme creative versatility cannot be doubted." — Nick Gevers, *Locus Magazine*

"…although there are times we may rather wish Irvine had kept some of his balls in his pocket, there are also moments when, suddenly, the density of depicted reality increases…" — John Clute, author of *The Encyclopedia of Science Fiction*

"That Alex Irvine is one of contemporary fantasy's more challenging authors is, of course, his strength. Anyone doing his part to bring originality and skewed perspectives to a genre far too beholden to formula is someone you should be reading." — T. M. Wagner, *SFreviews.net*

Pictures from an Expedition

Other books by Alexander C. Irvine include:

A Scattering of Jades
Unintended Consequences
One King, One Soldier
The Life of Riley
The Narrows

Pictures from an Expedition

STORIES BY ALEXANDER C. IRVINE

NIGHT SHADE BOOKS
SAN FRANCISCO

"The Lorelei" © 2005 by Alexander C. Irvine. Originally published in *The Magazine of Fantasy & Science Fiction*, January 2005.

"Green River Chantey" © 2000 by Alexander C. Irvine. Originally published in *Alfred Hitchcock's Mystery Magazine*, May 2000

"The Fall At Shanghai" © 2003 by Alexander C. Irvine. Originally published in *Alchemy* no. 1, October 2003.

"The Golems of Detroit" © 2005 by Alexander C. Irvine. Originally published in *The Magazine of Fantasy & Science Fiction*, May 2005

"For Now It's Eight O'Clock" © 2004 by Alexander C. Irvine. Originally published in *Strange Horizons*, March 2004

"Clownfish" © 2006 by Alexander C. Irvine. Original to this collection.

"Gus Dreams of Biting the Mailman" © 2003 by Alexander C. Irvine. Originally published in *Trampoline*. edited by Kelly Link, Small Beer Press, 2003.

"Pictures From an Expedition" © 2003 by Alexander C. Irvine. Originally published in *The Magazine of Fantasy & Science Fiction*, September 2003.

"Reformation"© 2003 by Alexander C. Irvine. Originally published in *Live Without a Net*, edited by Lou Anders, Roc, 2003

"The Uterus Garden" © 2003 by Alexander C. Irvine. Originally published in *Polyphony 2*, edited by Deborah Layne and Jay Lake, Wheatland Press, 2003

"Volunteers"© 2004 by Alexander C. Irvine. Originally published online on SCI-FICTION, July 28 2004

"Peter Skilling" © 2004 by Alexander C. Irvine. Originally published online as "Retroactive Anti-Terror" on *Salon*, Feburary 19 2004; this title originally published in *The Magazine of Fantasy & Science Fiction*, September 2004.

"Shepherded by Galatea" © 2003 by Alexander C. Irvine. Originally published in *Asimov's Science Fiction*, March 2003

First Edition

ISBN-10 1-59780-049-X
ISBN-13 978-1-59780-049-5

Night Shade Books
Please visit us on the web at
http://www.nightshadebooks.com
Printed in Canada

CONTENTS

THE LORELEI

The Lorelei is gone now. Where she stood is now a bare promontory of stone, overlooking the Rhine under a moon whose light hides more than it illuminates. Where once I saw her, languid and deadly, trailing an arm in the shallows, there is now a stunted bush struggling to cast a shadow. Another time Ryder painted her behind a gaunt and broken oak, peering down at a lone fisherman. The fisherman's net dangled forgotten in his hands, and he gazed enraptured at her while his boat drifted toward the rocks that would be his death. But Ryder, knowing he was the fisherman, nearly always painted the Lorelei alone.

I knew Albert Pinkham Ryder for twenty-one years, long enough that I can tell you the story of the Lorelei from the beginning. I do not know where it ends.

When the acid in my stomach keeps me awake, I leave Martha sleeping and go upstairs, to watch the moon mark the passage of the night. On these nights I think of Ryder, and when I think of Ryder my remembrances gather the Lorelei up from that part of my soul that was once romantic, once able and yearning to believe in an invisible world not our own. Often daybreak, and the sounds of my dear Martha rising, letting the dog into the yard, making breakfast—all of this draws me back into the present, this abominable, apocalyptic year of 1943 in which I am a poor man who once was wealthy, a man of seventy who once was young. It is all because of Ryder, because his unflagging pursuit of art drew me into its wake, and because I failed to meet the example he set.

* * *

MY NAME IS CHARLES PELLETIER. I came to New York from Bangor, Maine, in 1896, with a degree from the Maine State Teacher's College folded in the briefcase my uncle Philip had presented to me as a graduation gift. Both of my parents passed away when I was young, leaving Uncle Philip as my sole benefactor; it was my good fortune that he owned three sawmills in Millinocket and Old Town, so my schooling was a burden he assumed willingly and with ease. My desire for a career in New York was less palatable to him, but he himself had abandoned the place of his birth when he came to Bangor from Wolfville, Nova Scotia, so perhaps he attributed my wanderlust to an inherited family trait. In any event, he questioned me sharply, ascertained the strength of my commitment, and at last agreed to furnish me with a small allowance during my first year in the city. At the end of that period, it was understood, I was either to stand on my own two legs or return to Bangor, where I would take up a place in Uncle Philip's business.

My real reason for wanting to come to New York, of course, was to paint. I would put my degree to good use only until the income from my art enabled me to free myself of Uncle Philip's largess—and from the onerous life of the grammar-school teacher. In the city I intended to meet Homer and Eakins and Chase Whistler and everyone else I could find, to learn from them and put their acquaintance to good use. Commissions too cheap or jejune for those established figures would, I imagined, begin to come my way once I had demonstrated my ability; and I felt certain that I would more than match up to the task.

On April the seventeenth I stepped off a train and was swept away in the mad crosscurrents of Manhattan. I found lodging in a rooming house near Washington Square, on Macdougal Street; my single room had large windows facing south, and before I'd even eaten a meal in the city I purchased a new easel and several canvases from an artists' supply house on Eighth Street. Walking through the park with my goods, I felt firmly at home in a way that is only possible when you find yourself actually doing something that for years has been the material of dream. Two boys played with a dog; couples walked slowly around the fountain; the afternoon sunlight caught the steel frame of a water tank over a row of buildings on Fourth Street.

I noticed the old man slouched before an easel scant seconds before he spoke to me. "Are you a student, there?"

I stopped and set my roll of canvases on the stones of the path. "No sir," I said. "I intend to be an artist."

"So you're a student," he said, and scratched at his wild beard. His fingers left streaks of yellow and red in the gray. With the same hand he gestured at his easel. "You can take this as your first lesson if you like."

Stifling an arch remark, I stepped around him to look, and saw that his subject was the same line of rooftops over which I had remarked the water tank. The tank shone like a lighthouse beacon, gathering the scene to itself and casting carriages and passersby in the colors that stained the artist's whiskers. The effect was of such violent energy that I was physically shaken; I had never painted anything remotely like it, had no idea in fact that the artist's brush could transform paint into fire too bright to look at. I thought of my own canvases, carefully rolled and stored in Uncle Philip's attic. Once I had slept outside on the shores of

Chimney Pond so that I could capture Mount Katahdin at dawn; but my dawn was the pinched wick of a candle next to the incandescence I now beheld. My first lesson indeed.

"Marvelous," I said, though I wasn't sure I liked what he had done. It was too much, perhaps, an excess of color, overdone as a drawing-room sonnet—but so compelling! I looked a while longer, and my teacher took up his brush and went back to work. Shadows grew, and the sky took on the pallor recognizable to any man who has ever seen a smokestack. At some point I stopped observing and began analyzing, and just as I became conscious of the change the old man put down his brush and said, "You've seen enough for one day."

Startled, I wondered how long I had stood watching him. "Would you mind if I came to see you again?"

He turned to look at me from beneath the brows of an Old Testament prophet. "You can come back when you have something to show me," he said, and went back to his work.

* * *

THE EVENING AND THE NIGHT PASSED without my notice. I was consumed, living only for the rising of the sun so that I might take up my brushes and fling myself into the creation of light. In the morning my trunks arrived from Bangor, but instead of furnishing my room I left them where the teamsters set them down and went back to painting. It all seems impossibly naïve and romantic now, this violent awakening, but if it had not been that old man in the park it would have been someone else. I had come to New York as a disciple looking for a master, and like a baby bird I took the first painter I saw for that master.

For weeks I rose with the dawn to paint the line of Lower Manhattan roof-tops I saw out my window. Uncle Philip's money went straight into oils and turpentine and canvas, and enough food to keep me going. Before I knew it I'd been in New York for a month, and seventeen canvases of my room's southward prospect curled in the corner, unmounted. It was time to go back to the park. I had something to show.

On a rainy morning, freed by weather from my compulsion, I selected the best of my work and spent the day carefully reworking it. Then I left it on the easel and slept. The next morning, buoyant, I went downstairs and out into the street. I bought a bottle of wine and a cheese from a store on Thompson Street, and since the rain had cleared by then I took a turn through the park in hopes of seeing my accidental master.

Washington Square Park was a sea of easels, but the streaked beard of my unknowing mentor was nowhere to be found. For the first time it occurred to me that he might not return. Perhaps he typically painted elsewhere, and had come to Washington Square on a whim. In all likelihood he had forgotten our brief conversation; it was even possible that his brusque dismissal had been intended to ensure that I never bothered him again.

My optimism curdled as quickly as it had appeared. I went home despondent, crashing back to earth after my monthlong fury of optimistic ambition. The bottle of wine I'd meant to share went instead entirely down my own throat, and when it was gone I stormed out into the windy night and walked, neither knowing nor caring where I went. After some time I found myself in Battery Park. The late-spring wind growled up from the Verrazano Narrows, cutting through my inebriation as well as my thin coat. I turned up my collar and walked more slowly, acutely aware of my vulnerability to any one of New York's legion of robbers. I could imagine the exasperation and disappointment on Uncle Philip's face when he heard that his nephew had been beaten and robbed while wandering drunk along the Manhattan docks. No doubt he would terminate my allowance and demand that I come home. It was even possible that he would come to New York to fetch me, letting me baste in his disapproval as he surveyed the chaos of my room and hired men packed my possessions for their return to Bangor. My canvases would dry and crack in Uncle Philip's attic, and one day he would dispose of them without telling me. As an old man I would recall my month in New York with embarrassment, perhaps even shame; I would realize that men such as myself were meant for safe careers close to home. I was no adventurer, nor fortuneseeker. Nor artist.

A piece of paper blew flapping past me and out over the water. Roused from my self-pity, I looked upwind and saw a figure slouched on a bench facing the tip of the island. He appeared to be writing, but he made no move to chase after the sheet that had escaped him. I looked after it, but it was gone into the darkness; doubtless the Hudson had by now claimed it, and its words were now bleeding into the dark water.

I took a few steps in his direction. When he did not look up, I regarded him more carefully, debating whether to approach him. Perhaps he did not know he had lost part of whatever he was writing—and how could he see to write in the lampless night, lit only by the stars and a waning sliver of moon?

Just then he lifted his hand and a second sheet of paper fluttered from his lap. It caught briefly on the arm of the next bench, then tumbled out of sight after its predecessor.

"I don't know many writers," I said, "but surely most of them don't put their work to so sudden an end."

He laughed, and then looked at me. Now that I was closer to him, I could see that his hat and coat were tattered, his dark beard unkempt. One of his shoes was untied, and the skin of his leg showed palely through a hole at the knee of his trousers.

"Ha," he said. "More of them should."

"What is it you're writing there?"

"Poems."

Dressed like a vagabond, writing poems and feeding them to the waters, he seemed a mystical figure, a character from a fantastical story whose inexplicable actions hid a kind of wisdom. I was drawn to him.

"Why throw them away?"

"Because they're terrible. Nobody has ever written poems this bad. Fish are all the audience they deserve."

His candor emboldened me. "If they're so bad, why do you keep writing them?"

He gave an exasperated snort. "You don't know much about it, do you? If you have to write poems, you write poems whether they're good or bad. Once in a while I write a good one. And I'm not a poet. I'm a painter."

Of course, was my first thought. Every strange bearded man I speak to in this city is a painter. Alcohol and frustration opened my mouth again and I said, "I hope you treat your paintings better then your poems."

This seemed to make him angry. "I treat them as well as they deserve."

"Beg pardon," I said. "I'm new to the city. I didn't mean to offend."

"Too many people complain about how I treat my paintings," he said, and began to scribble another poem. After a few lines he let it go, and it rose away.

"I'm an artist," I said. "Or rather, I mean to be."

"Have you any talent?"

"Yes, I do," I said, though I wasn't sure.

He stood and flung his remaining papers to the wind. "All right then," he said. "Let's go see."

This was very likely the last thing in the world I had expected him to say. For a moment I couldn't respond.

"Well?" he prodded. "Are you an artist or aren't you?"

"What's your name?" I asked him, to avoid answering his question.

"What's it matter? If I was Rembrandt or Titian, would that make your decision for you?"

"No," I said. "I'll show you. But I'd like to know your name."

"Pinkie," he said, and as an afterthought extended his hand.

* * *

AND THAT WAS HOW I MET ALBERT PINKHAM RYDER, though I had never heard his name at the time. The art classes I had taken in Bangor, from a sulfurous Scot named Craig MacTavish, had focused on the traditional; to him Turner was a wild-eyed savage and American art not worth mentioning. I had seen Homer, Eakins and Bierstadt and some of the other Americans one could see at exhibits in Boston—or, rarely, Portland—but of the living art circle in New York I knew next to nothing. I had come to the city out of some vague feeling of dissatisfaction with my teaching, and a nebulous conviction that I wanted something I would never get from MacTavish or the conservative curators of New England museums. My chance encounter in Washington Square Park, wrenching as it was, had felt like a validation of those hopes; and when in the grip of pessimism I stumbled across Ryder, again I felt as if leaving Maine had been the right thing to do.

But that came later. The night I met Ryder—or I should say, the night a purported artist calling himself Pinkie invited himself to my room to look at my work—I felt only that his very oddness made him worth cultivating. If that sounds strange, recall that I was twenty-three years old, drunk, and yearning after some reason to avoid taking a job teaching children things they didn't want to know.

We walked north in silence. I tried a few conversational sallies, but they blew away on the wind like one of Pinkie's stillborn poems. When we got to my house, he nodded and said, "The right place, anyway."

"What do you mean?"

"This part of the city is crawling with people who call themselves artists. Some of them actually are."

"Do you live nearby?"

Pinkie hesitated. "In Chelsea. Eighteenth Street."

I didn't press him. We entered my room and he went directly to the canvas I'd left to dry that afternoon. For a long time he stood looking, and I exerted all my energy not to interrupt him.

At last he turned away and looked at me. "Keep at it," he said, and walked past me to the door. I watched him go, paralyzed by conflicting impulses: to thank him, ask him to elaborate, suggest we meet for a meal or so I could see his own work. In the end I did none of those things, and when his footsteps had faded down the stairs I mechanically closed the door, undressed, and sat on my bed looking at my best canvas by the light of a lamp that soon dimmed and went out.

* * *

As did I. When I woke up the next day, it was past noon. The sight of easel and canvas exhausted me. I set about cleaning and putting my things in order, and when night fell my room looked like the abode of a civilized man. I took the satisfaction of this work with me on a long, nocturnal walk up to Madison Square and back down through the streets of Chelsea. I hesitated when I crossed Eighteenth Street, wondering if I might turn down it and encounter Pinkie again, but thinking about it I realized that he might have been an impostor, no artist at all, just a tattered insomniac willing to pander to a young stranger's enthusiasm. The thing to do was find out.

Over the next weeks I began to discover the city's galleries and museums, mostly (I admit this with some chagrin, but later it will become clear that I was directed by an intrinsic trait of my character) to eavesdrop on conversations about who was meeting where, and in this way I gathered information about where New York's artists took their leisure. Pinkie had said that Washington Square harbored numbers of artists, but Greenwich Village had enough taverns and restaurants that I might drain Uncle Philip's allowance before ever finding the salon I was certain must be there.

Fear of embarrassment kept me from making more direct inquiries. My experience thus far of artists in New York had been enough to encourage me, and I still spent most clear mornings putting the light through my window to the best use I knew. My encounter with Pinkie, though, had spent my reservoir of boldness; I couldn't imagine asking someone whose work I'd seen hung at the Art Students League to come and see whatever I was currently daubing on Macdougal Street.

Also I spent quite a bit of time considering whether to obtain legitimate employment. Uncle Philip wrote frequently to ask how I was getting along, and I answered regularly, suggesting that I was still learning the lay of the land. It went without saying—or so I implied in my letters—that I would soon be settled in a teaching position.

Apparently my vagueness dissatisfied Uncle Philip, for one day in November a letter arrived from him enclosing a note of introduction to the headmaster of a private boys' school on Thirty-third Street. It seemed that Uncle Philip had contracted the building of a summer home for this man, a Doctor Philbrick, in Kennebunk, and Doctor Philbrick had suggested that Uncle Philip's promising nephew might be glad of an interview. *It is quite a prestigious institution*, wrote Uncle Philip, *one with which you would be proud to associate.*

This was a conundrum. If I failed to pursue this doubtless fortunate opportunity, Uncle Philip might well be angered to the point of revoking his support. If, on the other hand, I took up teaching, I would spend my mornings initiating the scions of Manhattan's merchant class into the mysteries of Shakespeare and the pluperfect—instead of painting.

As had quickly become my habit, I took a walk to clear my head and consider the problem. With the benefit of hindsight I have no doubt that I made my way intentionally to Eighteenth Street, but at the time I found myself on the corner of Sixth Avenue as if I had fallen there from the sky. And there, shambling away from me with a loaf of bread protruding from the pocket of his coat, was Pinkie.

I hurried after him, calling as he turned into a doorway and fumbled for a key.

He looked up and frowned, his gaze darting as if he suspected I was part of a gang. "Who are you?"

"We met in Battery Park," I said, trying to catch my breath. "You were writing poems and—" I flung my arm out in imitation of his gestures that night.

"Ah," he said. "Still imitating?"

"Imitating?" I said dumbly. "Imitating who?"

"Your sun," Pinkie said. He inserted his key in the lock. "What good is the form and color of a sun if it doesn't burn you?"

I could form no response. Hadn't he encouraged me? Had I misremembered our entire interaction?

"You're still painting what you see. Imitation. Paint instead what you feel about what you see."

"I am," I said. "I do."

One corner of his mouth quirked. "I doubt," he said, and gestured for me to follow him as he shouldered the door open.

A lamp was burning in his room as we entered, and I marveled at his carelessness. I would no more leave a flame when I left my room than I would strike a match to my paintings myself; indeed, I have more often considered the latter than the former. That pedestrian surprise, though, was soon washed away by what I can only call awe at the squalid chaos of Pinkie's studio. Canvases lay everywhere: leaning against walls, stacked atop one another, half-buried by heaps of rubbish. A small, clear space on the floor provided an approach to his easel, and on a small table next to it clustered tubes of paint, buckets of varnish and turpentine, brushes piled like fallen sticks, even candles whose melt spilled over the table's edges to spot the floor. The odors of all these things, in addition to the indelicate aroma emanating from Pinkie himself, overwhelmed my senses, but even through the involuntary tears that blurred my vision I could see enough to be staggered by the power of his work.

* * *

No ONE WHO HAS SEEN RYDER'S PAINTINGS since his death can have any idea of their impact. His pursuit of particular effects was absolute and in the end self-annihilating; to achieve his wondrous lusters, his inhuman colors, he piled paint upon varnish upon wax upon paint upon whatever else he thought might bring to life his singular vision. While these canvases lived, there was nothing like them in the world. Even now, when he is twenty years in the grave, Ryder's work is a gate it does not do to approach too closely. This may sound melodramatic—but I have not yet spoken of the Lorelei.

* * *

"I WENT TO EUROPE A FEW YEARS AGO, four or five," Pinkie said. "Twice, now that I think about it. Something seized me there. I paint differently now."

The canvas I beheld on his easel was dominated by a fierce sweep of yellow-green light, arcing from the top left of the frame across and down to the bottom right corner, where it hung on the fingertips of a stooped, almost a Blakean, figure straddling the uppermost crag of a mountain. The rock seemed real enough to sweat, and the tiny female figure bathed in the great demigod's light was obscure and faceless and compelling as the beloved of a dreamer. No art is well described in words, and I have done poor justice to this work of Ryder's, but let it be entered in my defense that Ryder's art is utterly incommensurable with written language where the work of most his peers is merely difficult to talk about. Certainly he could not talk about it without resorting to gnomic aphorism.

"Who is she?" I breathed.

Ryder shrugged. "These fantastical scenes, they capture me now. I feel sometimes as if I've been noticed, as if a slow eternal gaze has fallen upon me, and having brought me into focus has surrounded me with a world of magic and danger and…" He trailed off, grew a little sheepish; licked his thumb and rubbed at one of the mountains in the background. "Feel like I'm getting close to something, or something's getting close to me," he mumbled. Licked and rubbed again. "Well. Hm." Just like that Pinkie forgot I was there, swept away by some interaction of his saliva with whatever he had slathered on the canvas earlier in the day. I looked away from him, was equally overwhelmed by everything else I saw, and foundered. I struggled to find words.

The sound of a young woman's voice drifted in through the open door. I tore my eyes from the canvases arrayed—well, scattered—around the room and looked at Pinkie, only to see that he looked every bit as stunned and overwhelmed as I felt. A question flashed through my mind: How could he bear it? How could he bear to feel this way every day? Surely it would destroy a man to experience such a consuming passion every moment he stood before his easel; and was it this that drove him down to Battery Park in the darkest hours, to create things for which he cared nothing and fling them away on the unlettered winds?

This reaction surely betrays the fact that although I might have been a painter—and a successful one, in a certain way—I was never an artist in the way that Ryder was. My own work never moved me except insofar as it hinted that I had absorbed some of the reflected brilliance of my betters.

And in any case, I had completely misapprehended the source of Ryder's rapture.

He opened his mouth and paused as if he had forgotten what he meant to say. Then, softly, he said, "Has ever man heard a more beautiful sound?" And rushed from the room.

I followed him down the hall, and caught up to him as he knocked heavily on the last door before the stair. His body trembled before it as before an altar, and when it opened Pinkie knelt and said, "Was it you who sang to me?"

A young woman, ordinary in face and dress, her sleeves rolled to the elbows, stood in the doorway. "I beg your pardon, sir?" she said. Looking from Pinkie to me, she frowned.

"Your song," he begged. "I heard your song."

"Aye, sir, I did sing," she said. Again her gaze flicked to me as if I might interfere—or, alternatively, explain; but I could do neither.

"It was a song to save a man's soul," Pinkie said. "I cannot be without it. Without you. Will you be my wife?"

Plain shock smoothed the lines on the girl's face. "Who are you?"

"I am he for whom you sang," said Pinkie. "When we are married, I will paint your voice. Please." His hand disappeared into his coat pocket, and he spilled a handful of papers onto the floor by his knees. Bank drafts, a dozen or more, some of them for sums greater than Uncle Philip had proposed as my year's funding. Who was this man, that he lived in squalor, crumpled his commissions in a pocket, and proposed to marry a washerwoman half his age for a verse of song?

The girl's eyes widened at the sight of the drafts scattered on the grimy wooden floor. I could see her performing the calculus every poor unmarried woman has worked through a thousand times, and coming to the expected solution.

"Mister Albert Ryder," she said, "I will be your wife."

He closed his eyes and reeled back. "What is your name?"

"Frances Mulrooney."

Pinkie—Albert Pinkham Ryder—stood and took her hand. He bent to kiss it, courtly as a duke, then straightened again. "Frances, I will return tomorrow. Think of me tonight, as I will think of nothing but you."

"Good night, Mr. Ryder," said Frances, and shut the door.

I wondered where her mother and father were, and what they would say when she announced her betrothal to the eccentric artist down the hall. Their astonishment would turn to speculation when she described the handful of uncashed checks I was even then rushing to collect, as Pinkie stood and walked entranced back toward his room. The drafts in hand, I was about to call out to him when another voice pre-empted my own.

"Pinkie! Come to dinner!"

The speaker was a hale and mustachioed man midway in age between Ryder and myself. He strode around the railing at the top of the stairs and past me to follow Ryder into his room. I trailed after, and entered Pinkie's studio in time to hear him say, "Stanley, I have met my life's companion tonight, my muse and helpmeet. We will be married tomorrow."

"Good God," said Stanley. "Who?"

Pinkie was rummaging through the heaps of abandoned paintings, flinging aside whatever junk came to hand. "A nightingale, an angel, at the end of the hall. I had never known she was there, and today—just now—I heard her sing. I cannot be without her. She is all that matters now." He banged into the pot of stew bubbling on coals in the middle of the floor. Brown sludge lapped over the edge. For a dazed moment I envisioned him dipping a finger in it and then smearing it carefully onto one of his canvases, where the browns weren't quite viscid and runny enough.

Stanley turned to me. He noted that I held in my left hand a large number of bank drafts. "Don't tell me he gave you those."

"No, he offered them to the girl," I answered. "I picked them up when he walked away."

He extended a hand and I gave him the checks. He set them on a bureau near the door, but made no move to clean up the spilled stew. "She didn't take them?"

I shook my head.

"So she rejected his proposal."

"No, she accepted it all right. But she left the checks where they were."

This clearly disturbed Stanley. "Who is she?"

"A girl. Frances something. Mulrooney. Dressed like a domestic. She was singing some kind of ballad, and when Pinkie heard it he rushed off like she was a mermaid."

Stanley turned to Ryder. "Pinkie, this is absurd."

Ryder ignored him. He'd found the canvas he was looking for and now he dipped a dirty rag in a bucket of dirtier water and ran the cloth across its surface. I couldn't help but wince; Stanley's lack of reaction indicated he'd seen it all before.

"For years I've felt her getting closer," Pinkie murmured. He looked at me. "Wasn't I just telling you that, Charles? Now at last I see her."

His fingers trailed across the canvas as he set the easel's previous occupant against the wall and put this new one in its place. I looked more closely at it, and felt an odd twinge at the memory of Pinkie saying, *Feel like I'm getting close to something, or something's getting close to me*, for here on this canvas was the same crag of rock, this time looming over a forbidding valley. In the sky at center, the life of a pale moon bled out into thin clouds; below, a curve of river, and in the bottom right corner a man in a boat, indistinct, outlined and hinted at. Perhaps because of Pinkie's words and the moment, the image seemed to me fraught with expectation and longing, emptiness deepened by false hope.

But now I am confusing experience and memory. In truth, the canvas was scarcely more than a sketch, crude lines and savage angles, bleak and muted colors. Still Pinkie caressed it as if he might draw something from it to explain his behavior—and still, I tell you, the composition was the same.

"Pinkie," Stanley said sharply. "You can't marry a girl you've never met just because you heard her singing down the hall."

" 'Who ever loved, that loved not at first sight?' " Pinkie quoted.

"For God's sake. We're not talking about first sight, are we? Shakespeare never said anything about first sound. And even if he had, this isn't a play, and Romeo and Juliet ended up dead."

"Go away, Stanley," Pinkie grunted. He still hadn't taken his eyes from the sketch.

"I am, next week. Remember? London? Might be a good idea if you came with us."

"Tomorrow I will marry her."

Stanley turned to me. "Apologies for my discourtesy. Stanley Terrell."

"Charles Pelletier." We shook hands. When Stanley said something in French, I added, "From Maine."

His smile was mostly devoid of malice. "And how do you know Pinkie, Charles?"

"I'm new to the city. I met him in Battery Park and he came to my room to look at my paintings."

Stanley's left eyebrow raised a practiced half-inch. "You're a painter as well. Do you know Ryder's work?"

Again I felt a little unsteady, as the recent memory of walking into this room flooded over me. "Just today," I said. "It's extraordinary."

"It is that. But if I may be permitted another borrowing from the Bard, Pinkie is a bit of a stranger in this world. We—his friends—occasionally have to look after him, and this is one of those occasions. I hope I won't offend you if I suggest that he and I need to address this issue in private."

"No," I said. "I understand perfectly." And I did, though I could barely stand the excitement and curiosity the previous half-hour had aroused and I wanted nothing more than to be in on whatever happened next. It was the stuff of legend, the artist saved from himself by the intervention of friends, and I was witnessing it firsthand. It was very hard to nod and take Stanley Terrell's card as he shut Pinkie's door in my face, leaving me alone and exhilarated by proximity to the man who is still the only genius I have ever known.

* * *

PINKIE'S FRIENDS DID TAKE HIM ABROAD for a little while, and when they returned there was no more talk of marriage. The girl moved out and disappeared, and Pinkie, as long as I knew him, never spoke directly of her again.

Which is not to say that he never spoke of her. The unfinished canvas he'd excavated from the wreckage of his studio that day became his voice for her. I am sure of it. I am sure, too, that when he said he had felt her coming closer to him he was right. Too many things are otherwise inexplicable.

The first of these is his sudden engrossment in a strange poem of Heine's that Stanley Terrell later (years later, when Pinkie was dead and Terrell and I had come to an understanding) told me Pinkie had heard for the first time on that London trip.

> Ich weiss nicht, was soll es bedeuten
> Dass ich so traurig bin,
> Ein Märchen aus alten Zeiten,
> Das kommt mir nicht aus dem Sinn.

I know not why it should be that I am so unsettled; a fable from olden days will not leave my mind. How many sleepless nights I have passed with these lines rolling through my mind, wondering if what I know to be true is in fact the truth. Ryder's art was always about the pursuit of the unknowable, the unreachable; and knowing him I came too close to things I myself should never have known and could never reach. This doomed us both, and in different ways we each chose this fate.

I remember an argument among two portraitists (we were all portraitists, but these two had settled into it and did little else) about the correct translation of *traurig*. *Distressed*, claimed the first, but the other argued that was too faint, that there was a power of sadness in the German which the word "distressed" failed to capture. "I mean, really," he said. "Dis-tressed? Losing your hair?" *Unmanned* was that party's preference, and then the conversation grew vulgar and comical. Where this dispute took place I do not recall, nor the names of those involved—the only other recollection I have of the evening is of Ryder himself, watching the exchange but not participating, a smile of what might have been condescension playing at his lips. He knew something they did not, and they did not know the difference: this was one thing that marked him as an artist while they painted portraits.

As did I. My part in the story is yet to come.

Apart from moments like that one, Ryder betrayed no sign that he longed for the girl at the end of the hall. The only reason I knew is that he took me into an oblique confidence over the next years, as he painted and repainted the Lorelei. It had begun as a commission from a businessman who collected contemporary Americans and wanted to add Ryder to his Blakelock and Homer; when I first saw it he had been working on it for some time. Years. This was not unusual. Ryder often worked on a single painting for years, and more than once his exasperated buyer would suggest having his funeral procession stop by Ryder's studio—to which Ryder unfailingly replied, *If it is ready.*

The Lorelei, though. She occupied him from sometime in the early Nineties until his death in 1917. The canvas grew gnarled and ridged from coats of paint and layers of whatever else he worked into it as he sought the woman whom he could never have.

Periodically Ryder would appear in my doorway and invite me to his studio, where he would either groan or exult over the progress he'd made on the Lorelei. By this time I had abandoned the pursuit of teaching—my skill with oils meant that I could make a careful living as a portraitist and painter of opulent homes. Occasionally my work appeared in the corners of New York's smaller galleries, but I attained neither fame nor notoriety, and certainly not wealth. All three came later, and not together.

I could never visit Pinkie without the feeling that he was trying to tell me something. He hovered at the edge of my field of vision, and more often than not other lines from Heine's poem found their way to his lips.

* * *

It's often been remarked that Ryder did little new after the 1890s, spending his time dithering over commissions and reworking canvases from earlier parts of his career. This is true. The Lorelei had claimed him by then.

It would be years before she claimed me, and then only because Ryder gave her the strength. In the interim, events conspired to test me, and enough time has now passed that I can admit I failed the test utterly.

In the spring of 1897, Uncle Philip discontinued his support and demanded that I return to Bangor. I had expected this since my failure to pursue the teaching opportunity he had created for me, but it was nevertheless unsettling. For perhaps the last time in my life I demonstrated a backbone, and refused my uncle's order. He wrote me a curt letter, and I rededicated myself to making a life for myself in New York City. It cost me quite a bit of pride, but I made inquiries among the circle of artists and patrons who orbited Pinkie's studio, and eventually I was able to eke out a subsistence livelihood painting portraits and landscapes. My talent was unexceptional, but I can claim for myself a certain competency, and later I was to discover unexpected reservoirs within myself. Or perhaps I should say that the Lorelei made me aware of them. Or bestowed them upon me.

Die Luft ist kühl und es dunkelt,
Und ruhig fliesst der Rhein;
Der Gipfel des Berges funkelt
Im Abendsonnenschein.

The air is cool and it's getting dark, and the Rhine flows quietly; the mountains glow with the evening sun. A loose translation, but it will do. Ryder's *Lorelei* is also a loose translation, especially since the nymph herself has vanished from it.

Die schönste Jungfrau sitzet
Dort oben wunderbar,
Ihr goldenes Geschmeide blitzet,
Sie kämmt ihr goldenes Haar.

Sie kämmt es mit goldenem Kamme,
Und singt ein Lied dabei;
Das hat eine wundersame,
Gewaltige Melodei.

No wonder Ryder responded so powerfully to these lines. *The most beautiful girl sits over there, wondrous, showing her golden treasure, combing her golden hair.* The Jungfrau is a mountain and a woman, and her golden hair is at the same time the sunset on the peak. Ryder's landscapes were always alive, always so much more important than whatever human figures inhabited them—and after his death, his Lorelei faded into the mountain overlooking the Rhine. *She combs with a golden comb, and sings a song meanwhile, that has a strange, powerful melody.*

This poem! When I should be painting, I find myself reciting its lines under my breath, in German even though I know not a word of that language save enough to parrot Heine's lines. The first time I remember doing so was sometime in 1907, I think. Ryder's health was already beginning to fail; his kidneys gave him terrible trouble, and the strange aura of wise naivcté that once accompanied him faded. During the last ten years of his life he was almost literally a shadow of his younger self—a shabby, unwashed, ill recluse who painted and painted but finished almost nothing. My financial health paralleled his physical decline. After the turn of the century, my small niche in the New York art market grew even smaller, until I was faced with losing the room I had by that time inhabited for nearly twelve years. I was thirty-three years old, with no prospects, relying on a circle of more successful acquaintances to keep me in bread and paint. The shame of this time in my life has never quite left me, although my most shameful behavior was still to come.

I will avoid it no longer. On a fall evening in 1907, I stood before my easel, gazing with loathing at a series of sketches I had executed in preparation for a portrait of a ten-year-old daughter of a Yonkers automobile whiz. Father and daughter were both gaudy and soulless, but their commission meant another three months' rent, and I had no other paying work. Circumstances had degenerated to the point that I had begun to consider teaching work again. To put the thought out of my mind, I started to mutter under my breath, and it was Heine's lines that came from my mouth. I do not remember beginning to paint, but I have a confused recollection that everything around me grew in intensity—became more *there*, is the only way I can articulate the experience. Colors, the sensation of breath in my lungs and the slight drag of the brush as I drew it across the canvas, the sound of rote German repeated endlessly, unconsciously, as the night flew. At last the mundane intervention of my bladder brought me out of this fugue, and when I had relieved myself I returned to the easel and with profound shock realized that I had not painted a daughter of the as-yet-unnamed Gasoline Aristocracy at all. I had painted a marvelous Albert Pinkham Ryder.

The Lorelei was near.

* * *

I THOUGHT TO SPEAK OF THIS TO RYDER, but the next time I saw him he was consumed with deranged optimism. "I am finding her again," he assured me as we regarded his latest work. "You see, Charles, what has become of me these last years. My reputation grows; everything I paint sells if I wish it to; but it's a Faustian bargain, because what I wish to paint is lost to me. Until now."

The canvas before me was—and this pains me terribly to say, because I have never admired any man the way I admired Pinkie Ryder—a miserable failure. Muddy, without any sense of composition, lacking even Ryder's typically casual approach to the human form. Stick figures against a background that might have been heath or ocean or sky. Ryder was then sixty, and would never paint anything of any significance. At least part of this sad denouement is my fault. At the time I had an inkling of what was happening, and was idiotic enough to welcome it; only later would I understand what I had done. Again it would be Heine's lines that pulled back the veil.

Den Schiffer im kleinen Schiffe,
Ergreift es mit wildem Weh;
Er schaut nicht die Felsenriffe,
Er schaut nur hinauf in die Höh.

Ich glaube, die Wellen verschlingen
Am Ende Schiffer und Kahn;
Und das hat mit ihrem Singen,
Die Lorelei getan.

The sailor in his little boat is gripped with wild sighs; he doesn't see the reefs, he only looks at the sky. I believe the waves will fling both boat and man to their end—and that, with her song, the Lorelei did.

The night Ryder heard the Lorelei sing—through Frances Mulrooney if you will—he was painting himself bringing light to a tiny woman. In her voice he understood that he had gotten the situation exactly reversed, and turned to this old canvas, barely scratched upon, provoked by a spooky poem he had heard on a tour of Europe, to understand that he in fact was the fisherman, and the Lorelei—wherever she was—called him to a golden, melodic doom.

The Lorelei was his Galatea, and he a Pygmalion with brushes instead of chisels. He brought her to life. Before Ryder thought to paint her, she was a legend, a Rhineland Siren palely copied from whatever bastardized Homeric stories seafaring Teutons brought back from their Mediterranean adventures. His initial faltering starts on the painting brought her close enough to life that she could force herself the rest of the way. I pity Frances Mulrooney sometimes. What must it be like, to pledge yourself to a strange artist in the hall outside your apartment and then never see him again? Did she feel that she had been part of something larger even than love? Did she feel the Lorelei briefly alight on her as if she were an oasis in the desert between fantasy and the sensual world?

I romanticize this, but at the same time I believe what I write here. Part of it is an attempt to justify myself, yes, but I was a little bit in love with him as well. An admiring, courtly kind of passion. Even had I mustered the nerve to speak of it nothing would have happened. Ryder was a childlike Petrarchan when it came to women, and a lover of good cigars and wine more than either sex. Perhaps this accounts for the Lorelei he created. One of the modern painters would create a Lorelei more like Rosie the Riveter than Homer's sirens, but Ryder and I were men of our times, and the Lorelei a frightened idealization of Woman and Art and the Unknown. Which for us were three different ways of saying the same thing.

Ryder's reefs were made of the Lorelei herself, or perhaps of his pursuit of her. The rocks on which I was to founder were composed of less rarefied stuff.

* * *

THE YONKERS AUTO MANUFACTURER REVOKED MY COMMISSION when the deadline had passed and I could not even show him a study. I was desperate, and in my desperation made a decision that brought me tremendous success—and taught me how bitter success can be.

An artist knows no shortage of shady characters. We are a naïve lot, and where there is money and naiveté will be found all manner of swindlers and genteel criminals. One such was a man widely understood to be a trader in art of dubious provenance. I will call him Bruce Cleaves, since it would be petty of me to expose him after he did so much for me. I called Cleaves to my apartment and showed him the Ryder. He looked it over, and just like that I became a forger.

Cleaves demanded a canvas per month from me, an inhuman schedule but a necessary one given that sooner or later buyers would catch on. He sold my Ryders in places where Ryder was known only by reputation: Oregon, California, Texas, Colorado. Mostly California; to this day there are movie moguls who proudly show their latest leading men and ladies my paintings on their library walls. Cleaves took care to broker some of my own work as well, primarily uninspired dockside scenes for tourists and others who want nothing more from art than a recapitulation of their own memories. As a result of this legitimate success, moderate though it was, I was able to court and marry Martha Van Pelt, the third daughter of an old New York family. Her father and aunt were devoted to Ryder's work, and I believe that I was granted her hand because I brought them both to his studio once in 1913. Ryder was then, at sixty-six, a kind of peripheral darling of American art; at the epochal Armory Show that same year, he was the only native artist hung in the central gallery. By bringing the two elder Van Pelts to the omphalos of this strange genius, I secured the hand of the woman I had come to love.

I also turned Ryder into a sideshow curiosity, but this was not my worst transgression against him. Without doubt the vilest deed of my life was stealing the Lorelei. He gave her life, and when he weakened through the best intentions of his friend, I led him further astray.

* * *

SOMETIMES IN LIGHTER MOODS PINKIE WOULD SET Heine's words to the tune of a popular song, and lilt around the catastrophe of his studio as he dabbed at the Lorelei. At other times the sight of the perpetually unfinished work brought out a grim determination in him. As he grew more eccentric, he began to ask me to observe his progress on the painting, and God help me I did everything I could to prolong his agony of conception. If the Lorelei was at the riverside, I suggested she perch on a rock; if she reclined, I suggested a standing posture; if he gave her blond hair, I remarked on the deep reds and oranges of sunset. For years I was able to tell myself a dual lie: that I was preserving myself and not injuring him because he would never have finished the painting on his own in any case, and that his financial well-being inured him against his periodic fits of Lorelei obsession. Only the part about self-preservation is true.

As long as I kept Pinkie heading down blind alleys, the Lorelei stayed with me. To this day I don't know whether I actually summoned her by murmuring Heine's lines while I stood at my easel, but after her annunciation in my room in 1907 I never dared alter the routine. Did she know Ryder had lost the initial force of genius that created her? Perhaps. I believe now that she battened on me because I was there when she sang in Frances Mulrooney's voice, and because

Pinkie trusted me. She might have found a thousand more talented artists in New York, but I have had years of long nights to consider this, and I think she simply left master for disciple. Created by Ryder, she turned to a secondhand Ryder when the original began to fail her. When the creator fails the creation, what then?

All of this is an attempt to forge the numinous into a chain of logic. Foolish. In any event, it doesn't matter. In 1915, Ryder's health collapsed. He was hospitalized for some time, and upon his release he had to leave New York for the house of Charles and Louise Fitzpatrick, patrons and friends with a house on Long Island. He died in 1917, and the next year was given a one-man show at the Met. His death made my trade immensely lucrative; Cleaves once told me that there were at least five times as many ersatz Ryders as genuine, and I have done more than my share to fatten the ratio.

The Lorelei was found in his studio, nearly destroyed by his twenty-year obsession. Well-meaning admirers attempted to restore it, but she had been fading, and soon was entirely gone.

As was my career when, a year after Pinkie's death and soon after the Met show, Bruce Cleaves ran afoul of a sharp-eyed dealer in—of all places—Tulsa, Oklahoma. He took himself off to Europe, where I hear he is still in the business, mostly with Picassos and other contemporary pieces that are easy to slip over on a public with more money than taste. With the war, his fortunes took a turn for the better; Nazi confiscations increased demand for European art and made buyers less conscientious about determining provenance.

I was not so lucky—or perhaps it would be more accurate to say that after staving off my just desserts for eleven years, I was forced to take account of my life. At forty-four years old I was suddenly a glorified amateur landscape painter with a house far beyond my means and a childless marriage. As an act of penance I told Martha everything, and only then, abased and contrite, did I realize how magnificent was the woman Pinkie Ryder's acquaintance allowed me to marry. She was angry, of course—she is still angry, and twenty-five years have passed. In the midst of her fury she took hold of our financial affairs, sold the house and established us in more modest circumstances. Then she told me to paint. Since then she has never failed to give me space to work, and she has never failed to hold things together with iron competence and a good deal of financial acuity. We survived the difficulties after the Great War, and then the much worse collapse after Black Monday. Now we even own modest shares in General Motors, which makes me chuckle when I think of the Yonkers commission I neglected when the Lorelei appeared to me. Dear Martha. As in art, in marriage I have done much better than I deserved.

I have never tried to paint a Ryder, never whispered the maybe-incantation of Heine's lines, since Pinkie himself died. That last year before Bruce fled to

Europe, he was selling off work I had completed while Pinkie lay bedridden at the Fitzpatricks'. I do not know if I could paint Ryder now, but I have my doubts. My suspicion is that the Lorelei has moved on.

I will be seventy in three months, Pinkie's age when he died. Here is my small penance.

During the past six months, I have put a good deal of effort into growing a beard. I think I will take my gray whiskers and I will go down to Washington Square Park. I will sit. In the darkness…well, it is difficult to find darkness in New York in this age of electric light, despite the wartime blackouts. I will sit in the park, and I will paint what light there is to find, and if a young man or young woman with eager eyes and an armful of canvas should happen by, I will try to find words to speak of the violence of feeling.

Green River Chantey

On March 18, 1929, the day after his twelfth birthday, Ray Cady Junior sat shivering on a fallen tree that sloped down into the smooth waters of the Green River. He'd been outside two hours now, and the night air was sucking the heat from him. At least winter was over, and hints of cave-country spring were starting to show up in garden plots and on tree branches.

The fat, bright face of the moon reflected in the still water, along with a few stars that disappeared at any tiny ripple caused by bug or fish. Behind Ray Junior a narrow tributary stream led to Echo River Spring, where water from the lower levels of Mammoth Cave drained into the Green River on its meandering way to the Ohio. All that way, he thought, from here to west of Owensboro where the Green meets the Ohio, then down to Cairo, Illinois, where the Ohio meets the Mississippi, then all the way to New Orleans and out to sea. How far was that? And that was just the water on the surface; Ray knew there were at least two rivers in the lower levels of the cave, Echo and River Styx. Nobody knew where they went, and if you could go from Mammoth Cave to New Orleans on the surface, maybe you could do it underground, too. Maybe you could even go as far as Gloucester, Massachusetts, where Grandma Ware had come from.

The names of all those places fascinated Ray, who had never been to any of them. But he'd seen them all on the big map at the school in Rowletts before Dad said he had to stop going and start working around the house and over at Floyd Collins' Crystal Cave. "You're a tall one for twelve anyway," Dad said. "Tourists'll think you're older than your age." Ray didn't have much use for the cave; Floyd Collins' glass-topped coffin and the crystals shining from the walls and the faint drip of water back among the dark rocks made him wish for the deep, soft green of the hills in daylight.

He shifted on the tree trunk, leaning into the upturned tangle of roots that served as a chairback, and the harmonica in his pocket poked him in the hip.

Ray's feet dangled above water on either side of the tree. The river had risen with early spring and they hadn't yet released the water through the dam downstream at Brownsville. He looked around carefully even though he knew nobody would come looking for him. Pa was stupid drunk at home and Ma wouldn't leave while he was in such a condition, at least not while there was a chance he would wake up so she could holler at him. She'd stay up all night reading Bible verses out loud, then kick Pa out the door in time to make the first tour in the morning.

So nobody would have noticed that the harmonica, which Pa had gotten for Ray Junior's birthday and Ma had thrown away amid a storm of Baptist righteousness, had found its way back into the pocket of Ray Junior's dungarees. Neither would they have noticed that Ray Junior had found his way out of the house and into his fallen-tree chair by the river.

He pulled the harmonica from his pocket and brushed lint away into the shadowed water under his feet. The moon shone almost bright enough to read the engraved HOHNER as Ray Junior traced the letters with his fingers. He brought the harmonica to his mouth and blew into it, savoring the reedy tones. An actual musical instrument, and it was his. The thing was to keep it hidden from Ma.

Ray tried to think of a tune to play, one that he knew all the way through. Not a lullaby, nor a hymn neither. He was stumped until he looked up into the night sky and remembered a tune that Grandma Ware used to whistle while she hung out the laundry or quilted by the stove next to Grandpa's wooden leg. He'd never learned the words, but Grandma Ware had told him the tune was a sea chantey about watching the stars. In the song, you picked a star when your man went to sea, and if the star went behind a cloud while you were looking, it meant your man wouldn't survive the voyage. Ray wondered why the sailors' women hadn't just not sung the song on cloudy nights.

He had always meant to learn the words to the chantey, especially since Grandpa Ware had actually been lost at sea, but Grandma Ware had died three months ago without ever teaching him.

Ray fitted the harp to his mouth again and picked the notes out one by one, gradually stringing them into a mournful line as he watched the stars on the surface of the river. As he played the line all the way through for the first time, he saw a ripple break the reflected stars into a million dancing slivers, and then something seized his ankle and jerked him off the tree into the dark water.

A weird, gurgling laugh echoed in the water as Ray struggled to get his feet under him. He stood up in the waist-deep water, shaking with fear and the shock of the cold river, and grabbed hold of a tree branch to haul himself up onto the bank. Then he noticed a pale knobby hand thrust out of the water. Holding his harmonica.

The laughing stopped as a head appeared next to the hand, its eyes shrunken away into empty sockets, its nose eaten away. "Good thing I caught the harp, lad," spoke the head. "I don't know how well they work wet."

A salty, fishy stink assailed Ray Junior as he stood gaping at the head. Spots covered the mostly bald scalp, and a few strands of hair straggled into the water around a face that was wrinkled and swollen at the same time. Like a prune, Ma would have said.

"Take it, lad," the head urged. It smiled, exposing three teeth and a long strand of river grass stuck to pale gums. The hand moved toward Ray, who made no move to take the harmonica.

"Go on, I kept it dry for ye." Somehow that made sense; Ray reached gingerly to take the harp from the bony hand. He started to put it back in his pocket, then remembered he was still standing in the river. As he stood wondering what to do with the harmonica, the hand disappeared and the head leaned back, barely keeping its face above water.

"Ha. So there it is," it said, and the hand reappeared holding a sodden wool cap.

It was hard to be afraid of an apparition that lost its hat while dragging you into the river. "Is the water a lot deeper where you are?" Ray asked.

The head didn't answer until, with the aid of a second hand, the cap was adjusted at a jaunty, crooked angle. "No," it said then, "the water ain't any deeper here. I just have a bit of trouble standing up. Give a hand, will ye?" it finished, holding out both hands.

"I don't know," Ray said doubtfully.

"Come on, Ray," the head cajoled. "Yer name is Ray, ain't it, after yer drunk of a father?" It squinted at him, an unnerving effect in the absence of eyeballs.

"Well, yessir," Ray said. "But I don't guess you need to talk about my daddy that way if you're asking me to help you up."

"If he's my damned son-in-law, I guess I can," the head answered petulantly. "Come on, boy, now that yer grandmother's dead I need to get my leg back."

It all finally dawned on Ray. He looked at the harmonica, then up at the thick canopy of stars, then back at the walking—well, swimming—ghost of his Grandpa Ware. "Grandpa," he said as he hauled the one-legged apparition upright, "that might not be too easy."

* * *

JEWEL BREEDLOVE HAD BARELY POURED HIS MORNING COFFEE and gotten his feet up on Sheriff Knox's desk when Edwina Cady came thrashing in out of the rain in a raincoat several sizes too small and told him that someone had stolen Floyd Collins' leg.

"Just his leg?" Jewel asked, taken aback by the sight of Edwina wearing Ray's raincoat. It was like something out of Barney Google. Edwina outweighed Ray by a good fifty pounds, all put on since she'd married. Jewel wondered what she would have looked like if she'd married *him*.

Edwina's entire body puckered into a threatening scowl, the air of menace even spreading to the drooping flowers in her hatband as she transfixed him with a gaze of hemlock-pure contempt. "No, Jewel, they took all of him from the coffin," she said. "But when we found him this morning, he was missing one leg."

The clock on the wall of the Edmonson County Sheriff's Department read nine thirty-three. "You found him this morning?" Jewel repeated.

Edwina straightened, tugged at the soggy remains of her hat, and emitted her most forbearant and patronizing sigh. "Must really be comin' down out there," Jewel remarked. It wouldn't hurt to be civil, and she sure wouldn't take the trouble if he didn't.

Then again, Jewel thought, if it was me married to Ray Cady, I wouldn't be sweetness and light either. It was a damn shame; when he'd sparked fifteen-year-old Edwina Ware before the war, he'd been sure they'd end up together. But then the war got in the way, and Jewel had come back in the spring of 1918 to find Edwina with a baby and a new last name.

He'd been hurt about it, and told her so, and then they hadn't spoken for a while. But now Jewel mostly just felt sorry for her. Ray Cady hadn't started out mean and he hadn't been a drunk, but he'd always been lazy, and he'd picked up the rest when he found out that his new wife was smarter than he was and not afraid to let him know it.

"Jewel," Edwina said, snapping him out of his woolgathering. "Do you plan on asking me any relevant questions, or should I wait for Knox?"

"Guess it'll have to be me. Knox is visiting his people in Detroit, and he'd just make me do it anyway." Jewel flipped open his notebook and found a pencil in his shirt pocket. He gnawed on the pencil's eraser, resisting the urge to light a Lucky—as he normally did when taking a deposition—out of fear of Edwina's Baptist-whetted tongue.

"All right. When was the body found?"

"I told you, this morning. And I guess it'll be gone again by the time you get around to doing anything."

"Edwina, the man's four years dead and he only has one leg. I don't reckon he'll go far. What time this morning and who found him?"

"Do you mind if I sit?" Jewel looked up. The hostility had drained suddenly from Edwina's face, as if she no longer had the energy to maintain it. He indicated the chair in front of the sheriff's desk and she sat.

"Ray found the casket empty at about five this morning, I guess," Edwina began, but Jewel interrupted.

" 'Scuse me, Edwina, but what was Ray doing in the cave—hell, anywhere awake—at five in the morning?"

"He went in early to work on the tourist trails," she said icily. So much for civility, Jewel thought. He wrote RAY 5AM in the notebook, circled it, and surrounded it with question marks. Ray getting up early to work on Crystal Cave's trails was about as likely as Floyd Collins walking back from wherever they'd found him. The only reason Jewel could see Ray up and around that early was to raid one of his guides' liquor caches back in the cave somewhere.

"So Ray saw Floyd's body was gone. Where did he find it?"

"He didn't. I did, down by—by Echo River Spring." Edwina fluttered a hand under her chin, indicating a catch in her throat.

"Minus a leg."

"Minus a leg."

"How about his tooth?" Floyd Collins had sported a gold front tooth. It was the only reason Jewel could think of for outsiders to actually steal the body. But with all the caves in the area fighting over the same tourist dollars ... hm. Jewel made a note to talk to the Mammoth Cave people, and the new folks running Horse Cave and Onyx Cave.

"I couldn't tell. His mouth was still sewed shut."

"And you didn't find the leg?"

"No, Jewel, I didn't. I thought that was your job."

Here we go again, thought Jewel. "All right, so Ray found the casket open, came and told you, and the two of you went looking for the body?"

"Yes. Ray Junior came, too, so there was three of us."

It was five minutes by car from the Cady house to Crystal Cave. If Ray had gone down at five o'clock, he could have discovered the theft and been back by five-thirty. But it was three miles from Crystal Cave to Echo River Spring, over hills and through forest in the dark, and you couldn't search woods from a car. Then back to the cave, back to the house, and eleven miles on the state road to Brownsville, and all of this in time for Edwina to be sharpening her tongue on Deputy Breedlove by nine-thirty. Jewel thought about the edge in Edwina's voice and filed all of it away for later.

"Did the thieves leave a trail?" he asked. Best to play it formal until he had a better idea of what was going on; on the other hand, though, he was starting to think he had a pretty good inkling right then.

"They did, one you could follow in the dark." Point for you, Edwina, Jewel thought. "It went as close to straight as it could, all the way to Echo River Spring."

"Was the body in the water?" Did embalmed bodies sink? Jewel didn't know.

"No, on the bank with just its feet—foot, I mean—in the water," Edwina said.

"Lord, Jewel, you could see it yourself if you'd bestir your lazy backside from Knox's chair."

* * *

THE RAIN HAD MOSTLY LET UP, but the sky was still lowering as Jewel held the car door for Edwina and preceded her down the narrow trail that led from the Mammoth Cave Ferry turnoff to the edge of Echo River Spring. Looking around the spring's banks, he saw a displaced blindfish and large quantities of churned-up mud, but no body. He turned to face Edwina, trying to keep the suspicion off his face as she puffed her way down to join him.

"I don't see no body, Edwina," he said mildly. She made a show of squinting up and down the tributary stream that drained the spring into the main flow of the river, but finally she just stamped her foot in the mud and said, "I swear on the Book, Jewel, it was here. You can believe me or not." Without another word, she spun on her heel—slipping a bit on the muddy trail—and lumbered back up the trail.

Jewel took a careful look around before following after her. If she was telling the truth, the body might have slid into the spring. Then again, he couldn't see any kind of marks and he strongly doubted that it had rained hard enough to obliterate every skid and footprint, especially under heavy tree cover. So why was the mud so frothed up? Indians covering their tracks came to mind, the way you read in a Zane Grey novel; but the only place to go was into the river.

"Damn," he said. "Wish I knew if embalmed bodies sink." He didn't want to have to drag the river, not for a man who'd been dead four years, and if the body had been sucked into the cave by a backflow from the river, things could get really complicated. Was the river that high? Didn't look that way, but then he wasn't an expert. "Damn," he said again, and started up the trail, wanting a smoke and wishing Knox was back from Detroit.

* * *

THE CADYS, EDWINA, RAY, AND RAY JUNIOR, lived in a clapboard shack down a dirt trail east of Floyd Collins' Crystal Cave. The land was owned by Dr. Thomas, the local dentist who also owned the cave and who had bought Floyd Collins' body from old Lee Collins after Floyd died trapped in a twisty tube in Sand Cave. Thomas exhibited the body under glass in the Grand Canyon, Crystal Cave's spectacular entrance room. Ray worked as a guide in the cave, giving tourists the rigmarole about Floyd being "the world's greatest cave explorer" while they gawked at the waxed body in the black suit. Crystal Cave's discoverer had become its greatest tourist draw.

Jewel frequently had to fight down urges to point out to the tourists that the world's greatest cave explorer had died because he got his foot wedged under a rock that weighed less than thirty pounds in a tunnel eighteen inches wide, and that the reason the body wore gloves was because he'd torn the flesh from his fingers trying to get himself free, and that the reason his head rested so deeply in the satin pillow was that by the time rescuers could get him out, he'd been dead two days and cave crickets had eaten off his ears. But usually Jewel was in a better mood than that.

Today, however, any tourist might have gotten an earful, because Jewel was out in the rain following a bloodhound's receding behind through the dripping woods north of the Cadys' home. He was cold, wet, hungry, and possibly out of his jurisdiction, as the line between Edmonson and Hart counties was just east of Crystal Cave and took a sharp turn near the riverbank. Not to mention the fact that he was searching *upstream* from the spot where the body might have fallen into the river; everybody seemed to have convinced themselves that Floyd Collins could hop on his one embalmed leg. Jewel decided that if the body was found in Hart County, he was going immediately back to Brownsville no matter what anybody said. The only reason he'd come along was because Lon Bricker, Hart County sheriff, had begged him to act as a buffer between Edwina and everyone else.

"Lon, are you serious?" Jewel had said. "Have you ever heard her speak to me?" He'd had to raise his voice over the baying truckload of hounds, and he hoped Edwina hadn't picked up on the conversation.

"Y'all have some history, Jewel. She'll listen to you. You think her tongue's sharp with you, you should hear her talk to my deputies." Lon spit out his chaw and picked lint off his plug before biting off a fresh chunk. He shook his head and drops of water bounced from the ends of his handlebar mustache. "Or Ray," he added. "Jesus. I got a call and went out there in January, brought Zeke Allison 'cause I hate goin' to houses myself. Never know what someone'll do." Lon spit and scuffed the brown splotch into the mud as the dog handler went around to the back of the truck.

"So we get there, the kid's nowhere in sight and we can hear Edwina screaming in the car a hundred yards off. Zeke knocks and calls in, 'cause he and Ray drink together and I don't know either of the Cadys to talk to. She stops hollerin' and opens the door about three inches. 'I didn't call no one,' she says.

"'Well, someone called us,' says Zeke.

"'Well, I didn't,' she says, 'but since you come all the way out here I'll explain. My no-good shine-soaked bastard of a husband burnt up my daddy's leg for firewood last night because he was too lazy to go twenty feet to the woodpile. I think you will agree that was uncalled-for.'

"'I certainly do, Edwina,' said Zeke, 'but we don't want no one to get hurt.' Then we hear something break inside and Ray says, 'Damn, bitch, open the door. Who is it?'

"Edwina's eyes just get winter-cold when she hears that. 'I think this is something to be discussed between man and wife,' she says. Then she shuts the door in our faces."

"Good Lord," Jewel said. "He really burnt up the old man's leg?" It was the only memento they had of him, Jewel knew; he'd been sunk by a storm in 1906 off Massachusetts and his leg had washed up in Gloucester two weeks later. Francis Ware, Edwina's mother, had come to Hart County that year to stay with cousins, and Jewel had heard the whole story on the banks of the river when he and Edwina were teenagers, him hoping she'd shut up long enough to get kissed and her talking to see how long he'd wait. He had no trouble envisioning her reaction to losing the leg so soon after Grandma Ware's passing last Thanksgiving.

"Yup," said Lon, "he did. Now we all know Ray Cady *is* a drunken lazy bastard, but this time I was worried he might really get hurt."

"So what'd you do?"

Lon spit and wiped his mouth. "Shit, we left. Better him than us."

So here Jewel was, being dragged by this maddened hound down the rippling hillside that defined the northern edge of Flint Ridge. The dog's baying went up an octave, and Jewel slipped on the incline, skidding several yards on his right side as he fought desperately to keep from being pulled around headfirst. Well, Lon had told him not to hold onto the hound when it got the scent. But he didn't know either if embalmed bodies sank or not, Jewel thought as he scraped across a mossy rock, so what would he know about dogs?

Then the dog stopped, just as Jewel was tumbling to a halt at the bottom of the hill and realizing what ridiculous thoughts he'd been having. He wondered if he'd hit his head and not noticed, but was distracted from finding out by the dog's digging at the underbrush. Jewel got his bearings; he was less than a thousand yards from the entrance of Crystal Cave, at the base of the bluffs that stood along this part of the Green River's southern bank.

Had the hound found the leg? Jewel scooted forward, clots of mud and rotted leaves dropping from his pants, and peered into the brush.

"Well, I'll be damned," he said. He dropped flat on his stomach and wriggled under the bushes, pushing the dog away as he got hold of an oblong shape wrapped in a gunny sack. He yanked, the sack tore, and Jewel could see a stiff hand in a soggy, stained glove.

He wriggled backward out of the brush and fired two shots from his revolver. Immediately every dog within a mile began howling with renewed and maniacal vigor, the one at his side included. "Shut up, you crazy hound," he said.

"I'm half-tempted to shoot *you*." He holstered the revolver, lit a Lucky, and sat down to wait for Lon.

* * *

RAY CADY JUNIOR WAS A CURIOUS AMALGAMATION of his parents, somehow seeming to have acquired only the best qualities of two people who annoyed Jewel profoundly. He had his mother's lively intelligence and quick wit combined with the easygoing charm that had been Ray Senior's best feature before too much sour mash had pickled it out of him. Jewel wondered if liquor would do to the boy what it had done to the man; in the cave country, fruit never seemed to fall far from the tree.

For just a fraction of a second, he caught himself wondering how things might have turned out if he had been the man to father a child on Edwina. But the boy who sat before him, staring between his knees and looking as if he needed a drink, brought his attention back to the here and now.

Jewel wouldn't have minded a nip himself, notwithstanding the fact that Edmonson County was dry and that he himself was charged with enforcing that dryness. The trick to being a good lawman, Jewel felt, was knowing which laws needed enforcing and which were just intended as guidelines. It was kind of the difference between the Ten Commandments and the Golden Rule; some laws were laws, some were more in the line of fatherly advice.

"Thou shalt not lie to an officer of the law," Jewel said. "Ain't that one of the Ten Commandments?"

Ray Junior didn't look up. "No sir, I don't believe it is."

"Well, son, it is one of the commandments of the Penal Code of the Commonwealth of Kentucky, and you have been lyin' to me like I was your second-best girl. Now you and I both know that Floyd Collins didn't walk three miles up the Green River on one leg in a gunny sack. Correct?"

Ray nodded. "Yes sir."

"So," Jewel went on, "someone must have put him there. But your mama and daddy both swear that they found him by Echo River Spring, and they say that you were there, too."

"Yes sir."

"And they say that the one leg he had left was hanging in the water."

"Yes sir."

"And they say that the thieves also pulled Floyd's gold tooth out of his head."

"Yes sir."

Bingo. Jewel stood up behind Knox's desk. "Ray Junior," he said, "I can always tell when somebody's lyin' to me, and usually it's because they start saying 'sir' all the time. Now I'm going to take you home and speak to your mother one more time, and while I'm speaking to her I want you to think about that Penal Code I mentioned. Particularly the parts about grave robbing, body snatching, hindering an investigation, and taking the fall for something you didn't do."

Ray Junior kept his head down. One hand briefly fiddled with something in his shirt pocket before jerking back into his lap.

"What you got there?" Jewel asked.

"Nothing. Sir."

"Come on, kid, I ain't trying to make trouble for you. You want to know what I think happened? I think someone offered your old man more than he could turn down to steal the body for the attention it would draw. And if you want to know who I think it was, I'll tell you: I'll bet it was that damned dentist Thomas. Am I getting warm?"

Ray Junior said nothing, but Jewel could see that some of the tension had gone from his face. "If you ain't careful, kid, you'll crack a smile," Jewel said. "Come on, lemme see."

The boy tugged a harmonica out of his pocket and handed it to Jewel. The deputy turned it over in his hands, noticing the streaks of corrosion that marred the shiny surface in a rough handprint. "Looks like someone with a handful of battery acid got hold of it. Is it yours?"

"Yes," Ray Junior said. "Can I have it back?"

Jewel handed the harp back and opened Knox's office door. Gesturing theatrically, he clicked his heels together. "After you."

* * *

HALF AN HOUR LATER, JEWEL PARKED IN FRONT of the Cady place and told Ray Junior not to get out of earshot. As he got out of the car, the elder Ray came limping out of the house.

"Sweet Jesus, Ray," Jewel said. "What happened to your leg?"

Ray Senior watched his son disappear inside his house before he answered. "Jewel, you'd be doing me a kindness if you didn't curse so much around here," he said, keeping his voice low. "Edwina's so deep in the Good Book nowadays, she don't tolerate much." He shifted his grip on the crude crutch and scratched at the bandage swathing his bony thigh under the cut-off leg of his overalls.

Jewel couldn't help himself. "Is that what happened to your leg, her not tolerating?"

Ray surprised him by neither glaring nor spitting on his shoes. Instead he just shook his head like he was too tired to respond—like Edwina had, earlier in Knox's office. "No, it ain't. I just had me an accident."

"I'm sorry to hear that, Ray." Jewel decided to let it go. "Is the lady of the house available?"

* * *

THE LAST RAYS OF SUNLIGHT WERE TRICKLING in through the thin curtain that covered Ray Junior's window as he slumped on his cot and rubbed a hand across his bristly scalp. Deputy Breedlove was sure to get them in trouble, Ray thought, because even if he did find out what really happened, he wouldn't believe it.

He was glad he finally had his own room, even if it was just an attached shed that Ma had moved his cot into. It was his, and he and Pa patched up an old stove that Dr. Thomas had thrown out so Ray Junior could stay out here even through the winter—"Long as you cut your own wood," Pa had said. That was fine with Ray. He reckoned he was old enough to have his own room, even though the walls of the house were so thin a body couldn't sneeze without someone on the other side saying bless you.

But that had its good side, too, for instance now when he could listen to the conversation between Ma and Deputy Breedlove. They had sparked when they were not much older than him, Ray Junior knew from gossip among the cave guides, and he waited breathlessly for something improper to happen, some chink to appear in his mother's fearsome Gospel armor.

"Jewel, how many times have we gone around about this? Put that thing out," she said. They were out on the front stoop. Ray Junior reckoned his father was somewhere within eavesdropping distance, too.

"Edwina, I'm investigating you for a felony. You can damn well stand up-wind."

"Investigating? Harassing, more like, and when we done most of the work for you. We reported the crime, we found the body—"

"You stand to benefit from the crime. Did you think I wouldn't notice that? The Louisville papers are full of it, 'Famous dead caver's body snatched in dark of night' or some such. And you think people won't come see Floyd Collins' Crystal Cave now that there's been a grave-robbing? Shit. I ain't got any dumber since I asked you to marry me, just older."

Ray Junior had to concentrate to keep from whooping. She'd been engaged! Ma had been engaged to Deputy Breedlove before Pa!

"And I ain't got any dumber since I said no." Ray Junior sagged back onto his cot. The situation was not so scandalous as he had hoped. Still ... he perked up again as Jewel went on.

"Well, then, a few things must seem strange to you. Take the itinerary you fed me this morning: Down to Crystal at five a.m., back here, back down to Crystal, searching all the way to Echo River Spring and back, then getting into Brownsville in time to interrupt my coffee at nine-thirty. The Army Corps of Engineers don't move that fast, Edwina, and that's ignoring the fact that I wouldn't believe Ray Cady getting up sober at five a.m. if I saw it myself!"

Ray Junior was a little hurt. Deputy Breedlove didn't have to talk Daddy down that way.

"And then you tell me Ray Junior was with you. Bald-Faced Lie Number Two. Three, if you count early-rising Ray Senior, but I'm willing to let that slide because I wasn't there." Ray Junior felt sick to his stomach. What had he done to give them away? He fiddled with his harmonica, fitting his hand into the corroded handprint Grandpa Ware had left on it.

"If I understand you correctly, Jewel Breedlove, you are calling me a liar." Ma's voice was actually trembling, and Ray Junior trembled along with it; he couldn't remember ever hearing her this angry. "I said the boy was there, and he was there."

"Is that so? Well, I fed him a ringer when I was talking to him an hour ago. I told him that you'd said the thieves had pulled Floyd's gold tooth out, and he said yes they had. But you never said that, and Floyd's mouth was still sewed shut when we pulled him out of the sack." Ray Junior heard Deputy Breedlove's boot scrape on the porch as he crushed out his cigarette. "The only conclusion I can reasonably come to is that Ray Junior was instructed to agree with whatever account you gave. Now isn't that true?"

There was a long pause. Ray Junior sat shivering, thinking of the many tortures he would undergo before his parents were carted off to jail and he was sent to the Home for Wayward Boys. Deputy Breedlove was mean as a snake to trick him like that, and acting nice all the time, too.

"You want the truth, Jewel?" Ma's voice had calmed. She even sounded a bit smug.

"I would appreciate it."

"All right. Monday night, Ray Junior was down by the river—"

Ray Junior didn't stay to hear any more. He was out the door like a shot, sprinting down the narrow trail that snaked west along the river toward Echo River Spring.

* * *

JEWEL CUT THE COUNTY AUTO'S IGNITION and let it rattle to a halt in the turnoff at the Mammoth Cave Ferry landing. It was only a couple of hundred yards or so to the spring.

If I find Ray Cady Junior sitting by the spring talking to the walking ghost of his grandfather, Jewel thought, I am going to turn in my badge and become a preacher. And if I find him feeling sorry for himself on account of having two

certifiable gooney-birds for parents, which is much more likely, then I will realize what a fool I have been for ever listening to anything Edwina Cady said. He
was not looking forward to either event.

Jewel shut the door of the county car softly even though he doubted that
the sound would carry far through the trees. He hesitated for a moment, then
reached back through the open window and found his revolver. Its holster had
split in the morning's rain, so he tucked it into his belt at the small of his back,
wriggling in his pants until it rested comfortably and wouldn't slide down one
of his pantslegs. The big old Colt was an annoyance, but after seeing the hunks
gouged out of Ray Senior's hip and thigh, Jewel wanted to be prepared.

The trail was broad and easily negotiable despite the dark. Stars gathered in
rich clusters above the canopy of trees, winking as he crept around the spring
itself and left the trail at the turn that led back up to the Mammoth Cave Hotel.
The spring was close, and Jewel moved carefully in case the boy—or, for all he
knew, the haunt—had unusually acute hearing. He had barely taken ten steps
when he heard Ray Junior's voice and caught a sharp stinging odor of salt and
mud and weeds and something dead.

"I appreciate you not taking Daddy's leg," the boy said.

A different voice replied, a thin bubbling wheeze that gave Jewel a shivery chill
from his stomach right down into his balls. Lord Jesus, he thought. I don't want
to be a preacher. Don't make me see this.

"I should have, the useless bastard," the voice said, and Jewel's chill deepened
as he recognized the New England accent he'd noted in Grandma Ware. "This
damned lump is stiffer than the wooden one ever was."

There was a long silence, awkward even from where Jewel stood. "You ruint
my harp, Grandpa," Ray Junior finally said.

"Let's have it, lad." A quick glittering scale flashed from the rusty harmonica,
and then a long, patient wail drifted across the river, a melancholy line that Jewel
hadn't heard since the time before the war when he'd sparked a sharp-tongued
brunette named Edwina Ware. It was the melody she'd hummed while she
stroked his hair and watched the river go by, the old sea chantey she'd learned
from her mother.

"You learn that song now, son," said Old Man Ware. "That harp works fine."
Water slapped softly downstream, and a few seconds later there was a quiet wash
against the bank at Jewel's feet. He held his breath until the wash receded, then
let it slowly out and began making his way back to the trail. Behind him, he
heard Ray Junior painstakingly working out the notes on the harp, false starts
and bright sad lines following Jewel all the way back to the county auto at the
ferry road turnoff.

He sat in the car, thinking too hard even to move the Colt from where it dug
into his kidneys. The leg was gone, that was damn certain. Floyd's body was

back, and Dr. Thomas would find a way to turn a profit from the whole thing. Ray Senior and Edwina would go on being persnickety at each other, and the boy would work on the harmonica and have something to think about other than his gooney-bird parents.

"I can't see the harm in any of it," Jewel said out loud. Knox would be back in the morning, and he could go deal with Edwina if he wanted to; Jewel planned on spending a few days with his feet up on a desk. Guess I don't have to be a preacher after all, he thought as he started the car and headed back to Brownsville. And maybe I ain't that much of a fool either.

It was like he always said: the trick to being a good lawman was knowing which things to pursue and which to let be.

THE FALL AT SHANGHAI

T he olive-skinned man with a fresh haircut and a new suit lounges at the broad windows of the journalists' club, here on the top floor of Broadway Mansions, the tallest building in Shanghai. He is not a journalist. Nonetheless his interest in the view is keen, for he knows that today is the day that Shanghai begins to fall. He would not be there if that were not so.

The conversations in the bar revolve around women, cricket, and war. Casually eavesdropping, the man smoothes his hair down over his forehead and studies his ghostly reflection in the window.

"Sun never sets on the bloody British Empire, my arse," exclaims a bespectacled Englishman at the bar, his jaw jutting toward his placidly seated companion. "Well, it's about to, isn't it, thanks to Neville bloody Chamberlain." He drains his drink and pounds on the bar, bouncing ice cubes across the polished mahogany. "I'm telling you, this war that's coming—and make no mistake about it, war is coming—is going to be curtains for the Empire. Every other bloody empire, too," he adds, glaring darkly out the window. "Fifty years ago, who cared what the Japanese did? And now look at them: 'Asia Sphere of Co-Prosperity,' my arse. They're out to own the bloody Pacific Ocean. You can be damn sure they'll kick us out of here. And the Chinese, if they ever learn to feed themselves, God help us all."

"Seems to me the Germans are the more immediate worry," the companion interjects.

"The Jerries, fagh. They've always been trouble when they weren't distracted by philosophy. What we should be worried about is these new bastards with big ideas like the Japanese and the Reds. You think the Yanks are going to jump in on our side against Hitler if they've got bloody Hirohito to worry about, too? You're fooling yourself; they'll stay home unless someone is stupid enough to throw the first punch and draw them into it. And if we're counting on the Yanks in the first place, then the bloody Empire doesn't count for much, does it? No," he says, shaking his head, "it'll all be different. Yanks have ideas about bloody atomic power, cobalt reactions, and whatnot, probably blow up the sodding world anyway." He sweeps all of the ice cubes off onto the floor and sits brooding.

The man in the suit shakes his head, thinking, *If only it were that easy*. He hopes it is, for he intends to go no further. The necessary ache of mourning vies with the restless, impatient dissatisfaction that has been his companion since the beginning of his wanderings. He longs for a moment of peace, for a taste of the placid certainty that knowledge is said to bring. It is four twenty-five in the afternoon of Saturday, August thirteenth, 1937, and four million inhabitants of the doomed city are plunging ahead through their lives. He sees the Whangpu River through his faint reflection in the window, watches the ruffled wakes of junks and steamships streak its yellowish muddy waters on their way to the sea. Sixteen stories above the Bund, he watches the chaotic jumbled flood of people that is Shanghai, hears the crackle of gunfire to the north and west as the Imperial Japanese Marines grind inexorably toward the city. Four million people. He remembers a time when there were not so many on the earth.

"Unique view, *ne*?" The man turns at the sound of the voice. At first he does not see anything except the milling crowd of journalists; then he realizes that the voice has come from the chair next to him. The speaker is a Chinese man of indeterminate age, his skin the translucent parchment of too few meals and too many hits on the opium pipe. A pink flash at the wry corner of his mouth is either tongue or one of the opium lozenges Shanghai is famous for. There is a look in his eyes, a set to the wrinkles around the corners of his mouth, that makes the man in the new suit run nervous fingers downward through the black hair that curls over his forehead.

"Unique. Yes it is," the Chinese continues, the lozenge making a brief appearance on his rolling tongue. His presence here in the British-run club is odd, his casual use of Japanese slang even odder. The Japanese are the real power in Shanghai, everyone knows it, but the British still command enough respect not to be openly flaunted and the Chinese themselves maintain a hemlock-pure hatred of all foreigners who don't spend money and most of those who do. The lazy-eyed man in the plush chair is either drugged into carelessness or supremely confident, and if he's that confident he's working for the Japanese. "What's your name?" he says, and winks, one eye disappearing behind a profusion of wrinkles. "I'm Wang."

He tells Wang his name and Wang grins, a broad grin exposing tombstone incisors and an expanse of empty gum as he makes a great show of appraising the man's face. "Kane, right," he says through the grin, rolling the diminishing lozenge through the spaces between his teeth. "More likely Cohen, *ne*?"

Immediately he raises a placating hand, the grin moderating conspiratorially. "No problem here. Suzuki-san says Jews okay, and it's his opinions that butter my bread. Too expensive to have any of my own, especially in this whore of a city."

Suzuki-san? Butter my bread? Slang. The gist of it was clear, but slang moved too fast. Language moved too fast. It was easier when there was no one to talk to, when he was walking. Wandering. Waiting with his thoughts until he was called to witness another fall.

Wang drops his hand and tugs at the razor crease of his trousers. He winks. "You're an Iraqi, I'm a Chinese barbarian. To Suzuki-san, it's all the same."

The man in the suit allows himself an inward smile at the misconception regarding his name. Cohen he will be, then. And as for his ancestry, well, Iraq isn't too far off, and it's a natural assumption for the Chinese to make. The four Iraqi Jewish families in Shanghai control a considerable percentage of its assets. They and their associates are among the few Jews allowed into places like the journalists' club.

He lights a cigarette as the clock behind the bar chimes once. The coarse Turkish tobacco burns deeply into his lungs and he holds it for a moment as he sees four of the American-built Northrop airplanes drone north over the Whangpu. They are near enough for the insignia of the Chinese Nationalist Army to be clear as they each drop a single bomb over the Bund, nerve center of Shanghai's International Settlement and banking center of the Far East. Conversation in the lounge falls away to a lone British voice murmuring, "Jesus Christ."

Two of the bombs fall harmlessly into the river, rocking the moored junks and throwing up misty yellow plumes in the afternoon sunlight. The third crashes onto the roof of the Palace Hotel, jewel of the International Settlement. A pillar of black smoke shot through with dirty orange flame erupts through the roof and the top-floor windows of the majestic hotel; shards and blocks of masonry tumble into the teeming street among a million gleaming splinters of glass.

The fourth bomb explodes on the sidewalk at the lobby doors of the Cathay Hotel directly across the Nanking Road, and the renowned avenue of shopping and pleasure is transformed into an abattoir. The rippling shock wave crushes every window in the hotel's facade, and the fragments add their glittering cascade to the smoking chaos in the street. Cohen—he has decided to adopt the name for the time being— stands at the window and absorbs it all, every detail and texture branding itself on his memory. He gazes intently, as if reading, at the sweeping crescents of blood daubed across storefronts; his ears fill with distant booms and frantic, tinny screams. It has taken him centuries to get to Shanghai.

* * *

THE BLOOD CRIED OUT FROM THE EARTH; that much was true. And he stood and wept in fear and sorrow and rage.

"Am I my brother's keeper?" The words wrenched free of his throat before he could stop them, and their echoes mocked him from the depths of the still-young heavens, the blood on his hands and arms and face twitching and leaping in thick droplets to the heaving earth. Great rents yawned in the anguished ground, swallowing the blood and the body of his brother, and the voice of the earth thundered to darken the sun. He remembered stars visible through gaps between his feet, remembered the voice and droplets of blood falling away to infinity.

The sentence pronounced upon him bore him to his knees, his tears falling to the trembling earth and leaping up again as if scalded. "It is more than I can bear," he whispered, and the long grasses died around him and the leaves fell from the withering trunks of trees.

To walk upon the earth that cursed him in his brother's voice. To be killed by no man, but neither befriended. To have murdered his brother, and have that bloodlust the last thirst he would ever quench. Neither blood nor woman nor power would sate him ever again.

Death would have been easier. He felt a feather-light touch on his bowed forehead and screamed into the starlit cracks at his feet, wailed like an infant despairing at the moment of its birth.

* * *

HE TRACES A LAZY FINGER ALONG THE BACK of the girl's neck, the moon providing enough light for him to see the fine, dark hairs at her nape and the subtle ridge of her spine curving down to disappear under the tousled sheets. He has forgotten the dream—or, more accurately, he has allowed himself to believe it was dream rather than memory, and has then forgotten it. Over time, this pretense has accumulated some of the weight of truth. Outside, the Garden Bridge connects the International Settlement with the French Concession, now ceded to the Japanese. The single guard at the bridge has a group of young Chinese lined up in front of him and is walking up and down the line, viciously slapping each one in turn. A group of British bank clerks passes unnoticed, their laughter punctuated by *slap slap slap*, pause, *slap slap slap slap*. The girl whose spine Cohen's finger is now tracing is deaf in one ear as a result of a sentry's blow which burst her eardrum. She is not a whore, yet.

He gets up and pads across the bare wooden floor to the window facing away from the bridge. The narrow, crooked streets of Shanghai's industrial district wind away from him, a peculiar mix of brick Victorian row housing and mud-floored huts with thatched roofs, all scarred black from airborne embers. Huge gaps loom darker than the surrounding buildings, the few remaining timbers of bombed or burned factories visible only as a lessening of the darkness that seems more complete here than anywhere else in the city. For it is here that the Chinese themselves live, here that the weary certainty of conquest settles its dulling embrace. The foreigners, after all, can leave. To the south, the hungry glow of fires along the Avenue Edward VII is reflected in the placid waters of the Whangpu, and the chatter of machine-gun fire stutters sporadically out of the burned-out corpse of the old city.

At moments like this, he remembers that all cities look the same in their dying.

He wonders how long it will be before the final collapse. The bombing of the Bund by the Guomindang was a last-ditch effort to draw foreigners into the war; everyone knows that despite Chiang Kai-shek's insistence that it was all a horrible accident. Before the first ambulances had arrived to carry away the dead, the journalists in the Broadway Mansions club were already discussing how they'd play it for their respective papers. But the British in the International Settlement will continue to conduct business as normal, blithely certain that their citizenship renders them invulnerable until the Japanese center them in the crosshairs. And the Jews, the Kadoories and Sassoons and the other families who have made their fortunes in the city, they will still be there, joined by an increasing tide of refugees from Europe who have somehow decided that Shanghai will be their haven. The Japanese seem inclined to let them come, perhaps only to annoy the Germans, but that will change when the Japanese feel more confident or the Germans insist, and then the Ezras and Hardoons will be lucky to escape with their lives. When the city finally dies, the only people who will be there by choice will be the Japanese, who will have everything, and the Jews, who will be grateful that they are not in Germany.

Is this the city, he wonders, where it will all finally come to an end? Is this the time?

The girl stirs on the bed, rolling into the space he has vacated. He envies her sleep more than anything, the simple release to not be anywhere, not watch anything, not have to relearn the lesson that has been scarred into him since Jericho and Troy. Rome. Alexandria. Constantinople. And on and on and on. Weary and unsatisfied, he presses his aching forehead into the cool pane of glass, wanting the girl, knowing that it will make no difference at all.

* * *

ONLY THEMECH WAS FAITHFUL TO HIM, wandering beside him until the birth of his first son Enoch brought them to rest. Still foolish, thinking himself beyond the eyes of God, he settled and fathered his sons Olad, Lizaph and Fosal, his daughters Citha and Maac. Then Themech his wife grew old in years and died, leaving him to watch as his children followed her one by one. But they bore children of their own, and his seed spread his ideas to all men. It was he who first set boundary stones around a field, he who built a wall around the city he named for his firstborn, he who conceived of weights and measures that all of his children should partake equally of the meager bounty they wrested from bitter soil. How was he to know that his inventions would be misused? How was he to know, and why was he responsible?

Enoch begat Irad, and Irad Mehujael, and Mehujael Methuselah, and Methuselah's first son was Lamech.

* * *

THE MOON SHINES HUGE AND DIFFUSE through the tapestry of fog, limning the placid Whangpu in milky distant light. It is three o'clock in the morning, and even the soldiers have gone to bed. He has left the girl in the room, to walk here alone. Alone, aching and sorrowful, a needful man taught by thousands of years to suffer without averting his eyes.

"It was ever thus," he says quietly, listening to the words as they slip from his mouth into the enveloping darkness. The fog plays tricks with hearing: the slap of water against a piling could as easily be the cautious footstep of burglar or beggar. He sees the first of the six men in front of him, beads of condensation on his bare shoulders catching the tenuous light in a thousand delicate winks. The form of the second resolves out of the fog behind the first, and two others wait patiently on each side.

They are silent, a bad sign. A thief would have demands—money, jewelry, a wallet. He stands watching them, watching the fog gleam in their hair and the shadows deepen in the creases around eyes and mouth as the moon slowly settles into the river. He fingers the short curved knife, blade and handle carved from a single horn. Its presence comforts him even though he knows he will not use it.

"You will understand if I address you as Mr. Cohen, will you not? I have no other name for you." The voice, Wang's voice, comes from behind him. He does not turn.

"I believe I told you my name." Even as he speaks he knows it is useless, knows as he always has what will come next. Always the wrong man sees him, a blind and malicious man ignorant of whose work he does.

"I believe you were lying. I believe that your name is Kadoorie, or Ezra, or Sassoon. It is stamped on your face and in your voice, *ne*? And if I don't know you, it must be because someone doesn't want me to. Well. I get what I want around here, see?" As in the journalists' club, Wang's voice drops sporadically into the cadences of American gangster movies. "We'll see who gets what they want." Quiet footsteps behind him, the voice fluidly dodging through the fog to arrive at his ears with no clue of its beginnings. The six men take a step forward, the fog shifting around them, and he sees that they are Japanese. His bowels tighten with fear, not for himself; *visited sevenfold upon them,* he thinks.

"And I don't care which family you belong to," Wang continues. "The message will get to all of them that matter. Nobody hides from Wang. Nobody tries to hide from Wang." The six men step forward into a tight circle.

* * *

THE ARROW HAD STRUCK WITH THE FORCE of the finger of God, driving him to the parched earth and severing the mark from his forehead in a splash of blood onto the bitter earth. It was written that he had died of the wound, but much of what was written was wishful and much else simply erroneous. The archer bore the name of Lamech. He might have been the same Lamech at the end of Enoch's line. If he was not, perhaps it was enough that they were all insane in those days, and bore each other's beliefs the way they bore each other's names.

He lay blinded by the pain, listening to the sound of the thirsty soil drinking his blood as footsteps shuffled to a stop near his head. "Father," shouted a young voice, "you have shot a man with a horn on his head!"

"Alas!" came the answering cry. "I have killed my ancestor Cain!" *Old blind Lamech,* the bleeding man thought wryly, *it seems the boy spotting for you on your hunt sees no better than you do. He is named for me, is he not? A pity he will not live so long.*

And then came the earthquake, and great chasms opened in the earth. Again, everything again.

* * *

ONE OF HIS EYES IS SWOLLEN SHUT, or perhaps stuck shut by blood leaking from the fissured lump of scar tissue on his forehead. *No, no pity,* he thinks. *No pity at all.*

He is filled with sorrow, a deep burden of helpless knowledge. For the pronouncements of the Father endure far beyond their usefulness. The predawn sky is the uncertain gray of cigarette smoke, and thunderheads lurk to the west and north like the unruly pointed skulls of giants hunched over the horizon. *There were giants in the earth in those days.* He smiles at the remembrance, his lips cracking as he murmurs to himself, fumbling through his disordered thoughts for an idea that hides behind endless galling regurgitations of guilt.

It is becoming harder to focus on the now. *The past of giants and patriarchs was so much easier to understand,* he thinks. This time of machines and money has passed him by, left its creator lying bloody in the street, wondering, *Am I truly the cause of this*? Another invention soon, child of another mind to be abused, distorted.

A boot nudges him sharply in the ribs, pushing him deeper into the past, echoing like the blows that fell on the head of his brother Abel. He does not move as he is dragged to the edge of the wharf and pitched into the stinking dark waters of the Whangpu.

Please, Father, he thinks as he falls, *shall even this be visited seven times upon them*?

* * *

EVEN THE GIANTS KNEW FEAR WHEN THE skies did not lighten and the rain did not stop, for had not God told Noah what His wrath would bring, Noah his descendant, Noah chosen in his humility to start it all again?

And as the water crept over the valleys and lowlands, people fled to higher ground, and from the naked tops of hills and ridges they spotted the great rounded belly of the Ark and the busy figures of Noah and his family struggling to drive the animals into the safety of its hold. "If we can be on that boat," they said, "we can be saved instead of the animals." And they armed themselves and came in a horde shouting down into the valley after the Ark. But Noah had planned well. The Ark rested on the bank of a river, and as the rabble advanced, the angry waters swirled over the banks and lifted the Ark into its current. In desperation, men swam out into the torrent, some managing to scrape their fingers bloody on the Ark's rough sides before they were beaten under by Noah's faithful sons.

And he had watched with them as the waters sluiced through the villages and freed the bones of the patriarch Adam and the blind murderer Lamech to dance and skip through the drowning yellow grass. He had only to stand on the hill and watch the Ark bob away until the waters covered his guilty head. Then would the rejuvenated race of man be free of him, of his borders and measures and walls.

But as the waters covered the hill and heaved him off his feet, he swam, pulling himself across the backs of the weak and dodging the clubs of Shem and Ham and Japheth until he could bury the carved blade of his knife in a seam at the bow and hunch under the curve of the great vessel, out of reach of their blows. And as he clung grimly to the bone handle, the waves crashing over his head, he tried to justify his choice, tried to justify the future he had caused.

* * *

HE SPLUTTERS TO THE SURFACE, THE BLIND WILL TO live overriding the desire for release as it always has. Pain flares through his sides, his back, his head. Watery blood trickles stinging into his eyes. There is still mist on the river, and it seems he can hear things moving just out of sight, things that whicker and murmur in a language he might once have known. Something smooth and sinuous coils through his legs, brushing against him in what feels like welcome, the insistent greeting of a neglected pet.

I thought they were all dead, he thinks. But it all happens again, it all creates itself again.

Choking on the rainbow film of gasoline on the water, he flails blindly in what he hopes is the direction of the wharf. His hand strikes something hard and cold, a link in a huge metal chain. He seizes it, but it is slick with scum and oil; his grip falters until he thrusts one arm through a link and grasps his hands together. As he rests, his arms already beginning to quiver with chill and strain, the rim of the sun appears over the wide bend of the river.

* * *

THE SEA CREATURES HAD COME QUESTIONING HIM as he clung to the prow of the Ark, twisting their great bodies in front of him and pausing to regard him with great, luminous eyes. Their gaze seemed an indictment: *Was it the sea beasts, the fishes, the creeping things who created borders and walls and murder?* they asked. *Why then must we perish?* And they turned their bellies up and dove for the last time into the limitless deep, until on the third day after the last mountain was covered Leviathan rose and looked on him, and the weight of its gaze nearly loosened his grip from the horned handle of the knife. Its call echoed in the waters and trembled in the timbers of the Ark, and it too turned onto its side and fell from sight into the depths.

On the deck of the Ark, Noah and his sons watched in wonder at the gathering of the great sea creatures. They leaned over the side of the vessel, astonished at the sight of dying Leviathan, and saw the man clinging like a barnacle to the underside of the bow. "Bring him before me," commanded Noah. "I would know who has the strength to defy our Father's will."

Shem and Japheth held the rope as Ham slid down to seize the stranger and bear him up to the deck. He clung silently to the knife as he was brought before the patriarch, and would not relinquish it even when struck across the wrists with Noah's staff. Noah looked at the bone blade more closely, studied its ugly blunt curve, then stepped forward and held the man's dripping hair away from his face. "See the scar of my ancestor Lamech's arrow," he said to his sons. "This is Cain the fratricide, who was made stranger to the earth and all who walk it. If you would seek the cause of the deluge and the cleansing of man from the earth, look to him. It was he who first lived in wealth and luxury, he who crushed the good nature of man beneath boundaries and measures and walls. The blame for wars in the Father's name may rest upon the shoulders of the fratricide, for it was he who taught men to envy and guard and covet."

Noah raised his hand to the clearing heavens, and the face of the waters grew still. "I say this to you, ancestor Cain, murderer of Abel: as long as there be wars fought over boundaries and riches, as long as walls are broken and cities plundered, you shall be there to see. You shall not avert your eyes from the sack and ruin that you have caused in your defiance, and know you this: had the deluge covered you and drowned you in its waters, men would have been free of the stain of you. By your life, you condemn unknowing multitudes to die. This is the curse of the Father upon you."

"There is no law and no judge," he had responded, and was pitched over the side.

* * *

THE MISTS WILL NOT BURN AWAY under the heat of the rising sun. They fall back from the river into the city, shrouding the jumble of brick and wood and the four million people who live within. He has slipped lower on the anchor chain, his hands clasped around one link and his head lolling to one side in exhaustion, his chin and one ear underwater. He can still dimly hear the calling of Leviathan and its smaller kin, questioning him.

A booming clang echoes through the hull of the ship, sounding different in each ear, and he realizes abruptly that the pall hanging over the city is not mist but smoke. Burning, the city is burning in a hundred different places, its poor starving and brutalized, its businessmen broken, its citizens murdered and imprisoned and cast out of their homes. Shanghai is dead.

Another city is dead.

Cain is not dead. He is about to fall once again, but he will not die. Not as long as there is another city at whose end he can bear silent witness. And how many there will be during the next few years. Their names tumble through his mind: Nanking, Warsaw, Prague, Manila, Dresden. Hiroshima. He has no idea what he will see, except that he will have already seen it at Tyre, at Carthage, at Tenochtitlan. At Jerusalem.

A second clang shivers down the length of the chain, and it slowly begins to rise. He holds on desperately as he is pulled higher, his arms straining against his own weight. The ship, he sees, is British: HMS *Bonny*. A refugee ship, casting off with its cargo of tourists and foreign businessmen, leaving the Japanese and the Jews to pick over the corpse of the city and take what living from it they can. An urge to strike out overcomes him, to leave his own mark on this city whose death rattle is all around him. The knife is in his hand. *Had I not laid down borders and built walls*, he thinks, *someone else would have. Had I not murdered, someone else would have.* He strikes at the ship with the knife, a weak thrust that glances away from the iron hull, unbalances him, leaves him kicking like a dying man at the end of a noose. He grunts and thrusts again, and the knife cracks into long thin shards that fall tumbling into the murky water. Again this happens. Again he shatters it over the death of another city and its freshly doomed multitudes. Without it he gains a moment of respite. Until he falls, he can believe—as old Lamech believed—that he is someone else.

The blood trickling from his forehead freshens into a steady stream as his feet are raised from the river. "There is no law and no judge!" he cries in a broken voice. On the Bund, heads turn and fingers point; on the *Bonny*'s deck, sailors look quizzically at one another. Knowing what will happen, he still has voice to refuse it: "There is no law and no judge," but this time it is only a whisper, and his grip loosens and he falls like a stone into the opaque waters of the placid Whangpu.

The Golems of Detroit

Midnight in the golem factory. Sweat and clay and blisters. Twitching pains in the wrist and the small of the back. The door to Moises' sanctum opens and closes. The motion of Moises' passing bangs the row of hanging platforms together, as if the unlivened molds were thrashing in whatever nightmares afflict clay that knows it must be born.

Twenty-eight men work in what is now called Building G, a steel-and-concrete cube near the center of the Ford River Rouge factory complex, which will be the largest factory in the world for another month or so until Willow Run is complete. Inside Building G, the three-story space is ringed by a catwalk twelve feet above the floor. Two doors off the catwalk lead to overpasses that in turn connect to other buildings. One of the doors, on the north wall, is usually under tight surveillance by Building G's crew because that's where Swerdlow comes from, and it's a poor bunch of line rats that doesn't know where their supervisor is at all times. On the ground floor, three large bay doors face the train siding outside, and beyond it the canal slip that leads down to the turning basin and the Rouge River. Spanning the ceiling, a spine of girders supports a crane-mounted scoop bucket. Clay comes in on open train cars. The scoop bucket drops giant clots of streaming, weedy goo on a screen just inside the Golem Building; the screener comes to life, shaking the bucketloads into pieces small enough to fall through the screen onto a conveyor belt. A work detail of a dozen men goes at this steady flow of head-sized gobs of clay with pick and shovel, breaking it down and pitching it onto the sorting line still squirming with swamp life. The breakdown and sorting crews are under strict orders to kill as few of these worms and snails and crawdads as they can manage, on Moises' eccentric theory that the incorporation of these little lives will make the golems that much stronger and more unpredictable in battle. Nobody knows if this strategy will pay off—they've sent a lot of golems off to Europe without seeing any real difference among them—but every man on the line has thought at least once that at the end of eight hours shoveling clay it's hard to worry about the lives of snails.

It would be a hell of a lot more efficient to use the same clay pits that provided most of the Rouge's bricks; after all, some of them are still on the property. But whether buying an iron mine or defending the Republic, Henry Ford is a tight man with a dollar. Even before they knew that golems made from American clay wouldn't leave North America, Ford had decided that good brick-making clay was too useful to divert to a crazy Yid project like making golems, and anyway he had God's own bounty of the stuff coming out of the swampy parts of the soybean fields and woods he's paving for the Willow Run plant, which is starting to churn out B-24s even though parts of the plant itself are still just I-beams and acres of poured concrete floor. Then after the first golems just stood there on the docks at the Brooklyn Navy Yard refusing to get on the ship, someone somewhere wangled a way to get fresh riverbottom clay from Europe. All of this raw stuff comes with impurities in the form of roots, rocks, and about nine million bullet casings and bits of shrapnel per cubic yard—not to mention frogs, snakes, and occasionally fish, once in a while an unlucky muskrat. If this were a regular industrial operation, all of this stuff would be screened and pressed out of the clay, but Moises isn't rational on the topic, so anything that once had a pulse is supposed to be left on the sorting belt. At the same time the old rabbi is mortally convinced that only detailed human attention will get rid of all bits of metal. "You don't want to see what happens if I raise a golem that has a bent nail still in it," he says. The men on the line don't know what to make of Moises. He's hunched and ugly and speaks English like a bad caricature out of Ford's *Dearborn Independent* or one of Father Coughlin's nightmares, but the men on the Frankenline all remember their first night on the job—the way that color slowly bloomed in the skin of that first golem, the way that when it sat up on its metal slab, the sole traces of its origin were the mud-gray color of its eyes and the tiny letters etched into the skin of its forehead. If Moises says that something bad would happen if they left a nail in the clay, they've all seen enough to believe it.

The sorting crew, a dozen men, works with trowels and rakes to break the clay down into clots that would fit nicely in your hand. At the end of the conveyor, these clots pass under a magnet with some kind of gadget attached that lights up if they've missed a piece of steel. If the gadget lights up, the belt stops until the sorting crew finds what set it off. Under that part of the belt is a bin full of nails, train sprockets, broken watches, all kinds of stuff. When the shift changes, the outgoing crew is supposed to roll the bin to the scrapyard behind the blast furnaces.

Every so often, more often than they would have figured given what the clay has been through to get to this point, a live frog springs out of the piles. If Swerdlow isn't in the neighborhood they stop the line and chase around after it. Whoever catches the frog decides what to do with it; the line is about evenly divided among three opinions. Some hold that the frog should be immobilized in the clay for molding into a golem; others that any frog with the gumption to live through excavation, transport, shoveling, picking, and sorting deserves a get-out-of-jail-free card by way of the canal; still others that the primary function of live frogs is to become frog legs.

Snakes are by common consent preserved to be put into Swerdlow's desk. This is a tradition that predates the Frankenline, predates even the war. Before the Rouge went union, back in 1938 or so when Swerdlow was one of Harry Bennett's Special Service goons, he had once made a Pole by the name of Czerkawski eat a dead snake right at his station, and then fired him for holding up the line. Then, the old-timers like to say, putting a snake in Swerdlow's desk was like being blooded in combat. There were consequences. Now all he does is charge out of his office and scream at whoever's walking by, but even this small reward is enough to keep the practice alive. What the hell, most of the guys on the Golem Line are spoiling for the war but held out of it by the scarlet 4F; they need someone to piss on once in a while.

Jared Cleaves is one of those guys. He'd be in the South Pacific somewhere, probably mopping up Guadalcanal, except he got in a car accident on the Pacific Coast Highway near the end of basic. The car rolled, and somewhere along the way to the bottom of a shallow ravine Jared stuck his hand through the windshield. Now the ring and pinkie fingers of his right hand don't move quite like they should; the Army says he's twenty percent disabled. He's still able to make little pieces of clay out of big pieces of clay, though. Most of the time he can convince himself that it's enough to contribute to the war effort, that he doesn't have to prove himself under fire.

This is harder today, though, because his wife Colleen is pregnant. They thought they were being careful; they had every intention of waiting until the end of the war; but there you go. The baby's due in November.

Jumping Jesus, a baby. A boy? A girl? He's got to make something of himself. Can't have a kid growing up seeing his old man come home every night covered in riverbottom.

* * *

THE GUYS ON EITHER SIDE OF JARED are about as different as two men can be. Jem, on his left, is pure hillbilly, from the coal country in eastern Kentucky. Twenty years old, with a chip on his shoulder over his father being killed in a mine strike and memories of boiling shoe leather and grass for soup still fresh in his head. Jem is spoiling for a chance to get a snake into Swerdlow's desk. He swears he'll write his name on it first. Opposite Jem is Felton, who in Jared's estimate is about forty years old, been to one of the Negro colleges in the South and then come home to Detroit. Once Jared asked Felton why he was breaking up clay when he had a college degree, and Felton said it was better than working in the foundry. Which wasn't really any kind of answer at all.

The three of them form a kind of pod on the Frankenline since they're the only native speakers of English in Building G unless Swerdlow drops by to call them all malingering goldbricks who are killing fine American boys overseas through sheer laziness, and by God he ought to report them all as fifth columnists. Which is bunk, anyway; if anyone was going to report one of the boys on the Frankenline, it would be the razor-cut gent in the black suit who stops by every day to look down from the catwalk and then step into Moises' office for a quick word. "If that ain't a spy," Felton says, "you can call me Tojo."

Typically Jem and Jared call him Tojo for an hour or so after every one of these appearances, just on general principles. Today, however, the spy comes and goes unnoticed by Jared because the only thought in his head is *Jumping Jesus, a baby*.

"Fellas," he says, "I have news."

"We took Paris," Jem says.

"Harry Bennett got religion," Felton says.

"Better," Jared says. "Colleen's in a family way."

Felton shakes his head. "Good Lord. Another Cleaves." He sticks out his hand and Jared shakes it. Jem pounds him on the back. Behind them, the molders look up in puzzlement and ask each other questions in five or six languages.

Jem turns around and spreads his arms. "Jared Cleaves is having a baby, y'all!" he announces. "A baby!" He makes a cradle of his arms and swings it back and forth, and a cheer rises from the molders and the four other guys on the sorting line. Jared realizes he has a goofy smile on his face, and the realization makes him blush. He turns back to the belt and picks up his trowels.

* * *

SORTED CLAY TUMBLES DOWN AN INCLINE to a conveyor that dumps it into a bin. From this bin, it's shoveled out onto long gurneys with shallow outlines of human forms stamped into them. The molding crew is all Jewish and all European; Moises won't have it any other way. Each golem is molded by a single man; if his shift ends while he's working on it, it's supposed to remain unfinished until he comes in the next day. When things are going right—when a wildcat rail strike doesn't hang up the clay and the screener doesn't jam and the magnetic doodad isn't on the fritz and the molders aren't drunk—Moises typically enlivens one golem for every two the crew puts together. He works sixteen-hour days to keep up. Whoever is running the Frankenline (and nobody is quite sure whether it's the OSS or G-2 or maybe the FBI; it sure as hell isn't Ford; Edsel might go for it, but he's a sick man and even when healthy not strong enough to stand up to the Old Man's loopy anti-Jewish mania) must be looking for another rabbi who knows the trick, but apparently Moises is onto a secret that nobody else knows and he isn't willing to share. Strange bird, Moises. If anyone on the Frankenline knows where he's from, it's the molders, and they aren't telling. Jared has heard that he lives over on Twelfth Street in the old Jewish neighborhood, but he's also heard that Moises never actually leaves the Rouge complex, and a third rumor has it that whoever runs the Frankenline keeps him under guard in a safe house for fear that Nazi agents will assassinate him. Where Moises is concerned, anything could be true.

* * *

As each new golem comes stalking blank-faced out of Moises' sanctum, a Hungarian by the name of Ferenc pushes the next gurney over to a series of hooks hanging from a track on the ceiling. Ferenc hooks four of them through the rings welded onto each corner of the gurney. With each group of four hooks dangles a switch; he throws it, and the gurney rises up about six feet off the ground. When Ferenc rings a bell on the wall of Moises' office, a portion of the office wall slides open. With a rattle the gurney moves through the opening, and the wall closes behind it. This happens roughly once an hour, and Jared registers in the back of his mind that it's happening now: the rattle of chains and hum of the crane motor act like a kind of subconscious clock. Another golem, another hour. This time it's four down, four to go; almost time for lunch.

Someone taps him on the arm and Jared turns to see that it's Moises himself. He has, for no good reason, a moment of pure panic, as if he's just been given the Finger of Death. Then, when his heart starts beating again, he says, "Hey, Moises," thinking, what'd I do?

"You have a baby," Moises said. "Is a happy thing. Mazel tov."

Jared's nodding. "Thanks, yeah. Mazel tov to you, too."

Moises cracks a smile and shuffles back to his office. He pauses at the doorway and steps aside to let a golem out. The golem walks out the door to wait by the rail siding; Moises shuts the door behind him, and a few seconds later another gurney slides in to join him.

* * *

They've all seen newsreel footage of the golems at work. Mostly this comes from the Aleutians, where the Army is slowly grinding down the Japanese garrison. Those golems are among the first to step off the Frankenline; it was a cold bucket of water when project planners realized that those golems, made of American clay, wouldn't leave the continent where they were—if you want to put it that way—born. This setback almost put the kibosh on the whole project, but it's all worked out now. The new golems go and get on the trains to New York and then troop right up onto freighters for the ride across the U-boat-infested North Atlantic. About a dozen ships carrying golems have gone down, precipitating a lively discussion among Jem, Jared, and Felton regarding their survival. Jared is of the opinion that they probably just turn to mush in the ocean, and Felton usually agrees with him. Jem holds out stubbornly for his vision of golems climbing from the wreckage at the bottom of the sea and setting out to walk the rest of the way to Europe. "Moises has to scrub one of the letters off 'em, don't he?" Jem always says. "That's the only way to kill 'em unless you shoot 'em all to pieces."

This is a good point, but Jared still thinks that ten thousand feet of salt water is every bit as rough on a golem as an artillery shell. They're all hoping that Jem is right, though, because it would be a pure rush to see pictures of one of their golems walking right up out of the ocean onto the beach in France. As it is, they hear that the golems are used just to scare the bejeezus out of the Nazis, and once in a while as diversions for covert missions or commando operations. There's no way to know how much of this is true.

* * *

JARED GETS A RUSTED FISHHOOK THROUGH HIS LEFT THUMB, and stomps around for a while cussing. "Can't talk like that when your baby's born," Jem says. "Shouldn't talk like that anyway."

"Shut up. I don't need no Bible-thumping hillbilly telling me how to talk."

"You got your shots?" Felton asks.

Jared is hunched over his injured hand, slowly working the fishhook the rest of the way through. "Goddammit. Yeah. I had my shots when I went in the Army."

"Hate to see you get lockjaw with a baby on the way."

"Well, at least he wouldn't cuss around the baby," Jem says, and breaks up at his joke.

"Jem, I'm about to stick this fishhook in your eye, you don't shut up," Jared growls.

Swerdlow chooses this moment to appear. "Come on, ladies, Cleaves, you got something better to do than make golems?" He notices Jared pressing his thumb against the one dry spot on his coveralls. "Fingers hurt, Cleaves? Poor baby."

"Jared stuck a fishhook through his thumb," Jem says.

"Oh no," Swerdlow says. "A fishhook, give him a Purple Heart and send him home. Boy gets a fishhook in the thumb, he's done his duty. Gawd. What a bunch of goldbricks." He throws up his hands in disgust and leaves.

Jared is wishing he had some kind of death-ray vision. He wills it to happen, focusing on a mole just above Jem's left eyebrow. "Why can't you keep your mouth shut?" he says.

Jem gets sullen. "I was explaining."

"All right," Felton says. "How about we make some golems?"

* * *

RATTLE RATTLE RATTLE CREAK. LAST GOLEM OF THE NIGHT tracks into Moises' sanctum. Everyone on the Frankenline has the same kind of clock sense as Jared; they all stretch, take their tools over to the long sinks that line the wall near the ground-floor doorway opposite the scoop bucket. Restaurant-style spray nozzles hang like dying steel-and-rubber sunflowers; the men of the Frankenline crank the hot water up all the way and blast this foreign clay down the drains that empty into the canal slip. A billion little silty bits of Europe, Jared thinks, finding their way to the Detroit River, and maybe after that Lake Erie and the St. Lawrence and who knows, maybe someday all the way home, returning transformed like the golems themselves. At the end of eight hours breaking up gobs of clay, these are the kind of thoughts that run through Jared's head; the blast of the water and the steam rising in his face wrap him up in a sensory cocoon, and he falls into an easy reverie. A baby. There's a thousand babies born every day, maybe every hour. It's the most natural thing in the world—but he has a bone-deep conviction that it is happening to him in a way that it's never happened to anyone else. If he was on Guadalcanal, he wouldn't be having a baby. Maybe two fingers wasn't such a terrible trade.

Jared starts imagining what the baby will be like when it's real, when it cries and waves its stubby hands and grabs onto his finger like he knows it will. Please let it change me, he thinks. I'll still just be a guy who spends his days breaking up clay, but I'll have a baby. He won't care about my fingers. He won't care that I'm not in the Army.

"Hey, Felton," Jem says. Jared looks up and blinks the steam out of his eyes. Jem is standing by the magnetic doodad. They check it at the end of every shift. "Did you turn this off?" Jem asks, and that's when all hell breaks loose.

There's a shout from Moises, and a roar that rattles every window in Building G. *Bang*—a huge dent appears in the tin wall of Moises' office next to the door. *Bang*—the dent bulges outward. And *bang*—the whole sheet of tin leaps away from its frame and a golem charges out onto the floor.

It looks like all the rest of the golems, but after the first glance something about the golem raises the hairs on the back of Jared's neck. Maybe it's the skin the color of old plaster, maybe the eyes like a drowned man's, maybe the just-askew motions of the body as it walks and turns its head to take in its surroundings. All golems look a little off, not quite human, with some quality that would make you notice them in a crowd even though afterward you'd say that there was nothing remarkable about them. This one, though, there's a charge coming off it, like the psychic equivalent of whacking your funny bone. It twitches; its head rolls back and forth as if it doesn't know how to move its eyes; and when it bangs into one of the empty gurneys, it rears back and slaps the gurney all the way across the floor to bang into the sorting line. Then a strange calm falls over it as it notices the expanse of concrete floor and the cluster of men around the sinks. Its head lowers and it walks toward them.

There are moments when you don't have to understand a language to know what someone is saying. This is one of them, as a half-dozen versions of *Let's get the hell out of here* tangle in the weirdly charged air. People scatter, and the golem must be getting used to its body because it moves with sudden decision and focus, barely missing Ferenc before the Hungarian makes it out the door and down the railroad tracks, trailing a string of gibberish that Jared doesn't think is words even in Hungarian. This diversion gets nearly everyone else enough room to clear the building; even Jem and Felton hightail it out through the bay doors facing the canal slip.

Jared can't take his eyes off the golem. It veers away from the door Ferenc went through, and bangs into a nearly finished mold. An expression of odd confusion passes over its face, and it scoops a handful of the clay out of the mold. For a long moment it works the clay in its palm; bits fall to the floor. Then the golem stuffs the handful of clay in its mouth. Jared has a dislocated memory of his mother grouching at his little brother Chucky. *God, kids like you, you'll put anything in your mouths.* The golem is distracted. It chews the clay, looking thoughtful.

Over its shoulder Jared sees Moises emerging from the shambles of his sanctum. He doesn't look injured, but his posture and expression are those of a man so afraid of what he must do that he has absented himself from his own mind so that he may do it. While the golem munches the almost-flesh of its—brother? cousin?—Moises walks toward it like a man sleepwalking, and as if soothing it rubs a hand down the left side of its forehead. Until then, Jared hasn't noticed the letters inscribed on the golem's skin; now he's taken with the way it looks strange as Moises obliterates the fourth letter. *Truth* becomes *dead*, and with its mouth open, weedy clay dribbling down its chin, the golem collapses into a heap of riverbottom.

You'll put anything in your mouths. Jared's mother's voice won't leave his head.

Moises takes a long, shuddering breath. Then he crouches next to the remains of the golem, taking an old man's care getting his balance on his haunches. His hands slide over the heap of dead clay, and pause. He digs one hand into the clay and comes up with a chunk of rusty metal. He holds it out in one upturned palm and with the other hand points an accusatory finger at Jared. "You. Thinking of baby," he says. "You don't pay attention."

A rifle shell? A nail from the sole of a boot? A belt buckle? Holy moly, Jared thinks. Moises was right. But when he opens his mouth, what comes out is, "The magnetic thing is broken."

Moises throws the piece of metal at him. It misses, pinging off the wall over the sinks. He stands there for another moment, then returns to his office. A moment passes. Then the chains rattle and the crane motor groans, and another gurney passes inside. If Jared took three steps to his right, he'd be able to see what was happening. Right then, though, that's the last thing in the world he wants to see.

"Hey, uh, Moises?" he calls. "If the magnet's busted, you sure you should do that?"

No answer.

He understands, not with any great flash of insight but with quiet satisfaction, as if he's made a perfect tracing of his own face in a mirror. Moises is making offspring, and through them making his dream of a world risen from the broken rubble of the Europe that cast him out. One little piece of metal, one clay-buster who can't pay attention, makes no difference.

The Frankenline's various sorters and molders are coming back in. Jem and Felton peer in through the bay door. "Where'd it go?" Jem asks.

Everyone's looking at Jared, and he feels like he should say something, but he's filled up. Again he opens his mouth with no idea what will fall out.

"I'll be damned," Jared says. But what he's thinking is that fatherhood is going to be a hell of a thing.

For Now It's Eight O'Clock

"What it is," said my neighbor Jeff, "is I'm going to get that Wee Willie Winkie."

The little voice had just faded from the keyhole in my front door. It was 8:01. When I went out in the morning, I'd see a fresh set of little dents in my front door. Willie Winkie might have been wee, but he had knuckles like chisel points.

Jeff came over to my house about 7:30 every night. Since Wee Willie had taken his daughter Jenna, he couldn't stay home. His wife Sharon stayed in the house doing God knew what while he sat on my couch tanking up on bourbon so he had a barrier between him and that little bastard who terrorized us every night. I never asked Jeff what Sharon did while he was out. I imagined her standing in the upstairs bathroom, on the floor I'd helped Jeff retile two years before, running the shower and counting her gray hairs so she wouldn't hear Wee Willie and think about Jenna. If I'd been married, I'd have asked my wife to go over there, do something, I don't know what. Nobody else was going to do it—Wee Willie had made us all suspicious of each other. Standoffish. Which wasn't to say we didn't help each other, because we did. You picked up the paper when someone went on vacation, you jump-started dead batteries or held a ladder when it was time to clean the eaves. Neighborly things. None of that standard camaraderie included talking about Wee Willie.

I have a theory that this silence persisted because to talk about it we'd have had to come up with some kind of fairy tale, and we'd had quite enough of those.

* * *

That night, Jeff was a bit more loaded than usual. Or that might have been an illusion. Maybe he'd just come to the point where he couldn't take it any more: Sharon upstairs crying in front of the mirror, him crocked because he couldn't face her, his little girl gone. Everything slowly falling apart.

57

"I'm going to get that Wee Willie Winkie," he said again. "Tomorrow night. You with me?"

Was I with him? Lordy, I thought, how was I involved in this? Which was cowardly, yes. But it was my thought.

* * *

See, I don't have any kids. I get up in the morning, go to work, sizzle up something on the stove, and kick back with the tube until I fall asleep on the couch. Used to be I'd turn up the volume around eight so I wouldn't have to hear Wee Willie. Usually I heard him anyway, and more often than not I found myself catching an involuntary glimpse of him through one of my front windows. If I'd gotten married, I might have had kids, and then Wee Willie might have taken them. It's a risk I was never willing to take.

But was I with Jeff? I worked it over, and couldn't avoid the conclusion that Jeff spent every evening swilling bourbon on my couch because I was his only friend. Maybe it wasn't much of a friendship—we drank, we pounded nails into each other's houses, turned some wrenches on each other's cars—but it was all Jeff had. And truth be told, I was thirty-seven years old, with a job I forgot at five-oh-one every day and nothing else in the world that meant much.

Well, I do have fish. Tetras, mostly, with a couple of angelfish and a fungus-infested kuhli loach. I spend lots of time watching them, listening to the hum of the pump, wondering whether the kuhli would scratch at its fungus if it had hands. So if I was Jeff's only friend, it wasn't much of a stretch to say he was mine, too.

* * *

"Sure, man," I said. "I'm with you. Let's go get him."

* * *

Next morning on the way to work I asked myself: Go get him? I got to the office, moved papers around on my desk, thought: Go get him? Went to a meeting, ate lunch in the cafeteria. Go get him? Chewed on the question all the way home. Never was quite sure what I meant by it, or what Jeff thought he had meant.

I cooked a big T-bone in case Jeff was planning some kind of siege of Citadel Winkie, and then as soon as it was gone I was sorry I'd eaten it. What if we had to run, and all that steak thumping back and forth in my gut slowed me down just enough to leave me in the clutches of whatever dark forces Wee Willie served?

And there were dark forces at work, make no mistake about it. Wee Willie came to your house at eight sharp, rapping at the windows and crying through the locks, and if your children weren't in bed, you could turn around and find one of them gone. It didn't matter if you'd gotten them in bed at seven thirty, if little Johnny got up to get a glass of water and Wee Willie found out about it, that was it.

Lots of parents stood nervous sentry duty outside bedroom doors until eight o'clock had come and gone. An overwrought few strapped their kids down or gave them a little something to make them sleep. Still, anybody who has ever had kids knows that if you devise a security measure, they'll figure out how to get around it. And most people don't want to do things like straitjacket their children, and even if they were willing, it's hard to make yourself believe that something like Wee Willie can actually happen to you.

* * *

BUT IT CAN. I SAID LITTLE JOHNNY, but what I meant was Jenna. That's how Jeff lost his little girl. He went to check on her at 8:01 and found the spilled glass in the hall outside her bedroom. She never made a sound.

* * *

JEFF SHOWED UP EARLY THE NEXT NIGHT, right after seven. A shotgun dangled black and oily in the crook of his right arm.

"Ye gods," I said. "You aren't going to shoot Wee Willie."

"Not unless I have to," he said. I shut the door behind him and looked out the window. Did Wee Willie do reconnaissance? What load of shit would come down on my head if he knew Jeff was lying for him with a twelve-gauge?

The steak rolled over in my stomach. It rolled back when Jeff handed me a pistol.

"Jeff, I've never fired a gun in my life," I said.

"Here's hoping tonight won't bust your cherry," he said, and got the bourbon down from the mantel.

"You can't shoot Wee Willie," I said. "He's not a person, he's like a faerie or a sprite or something. You can't shoot them."

"The hell I can't," Jeff said. "I never read that sprites are bulletproof. Besides, he's real enough to crack your windows, isn't he?"

This was food for thought. I poured myself a drink to aid my consideration.

"Shouldn't go after Wee Willie crocked," Jeff said.

How else would you want to do it? I thought. "You just watch yourself."

"One for you is like four for me," Jeff said, which was true. I'm a terrible lightweight. I think that's one reason Jeff drinks around me. He knows I won't stay with him and spur some kind of hindbrain competitive streak, so he can sit on my couch, get a buzz, and tell himself he doesn't really have a problem.

Both of us could see the clock on the kitchen wall, but I was trying not to look at it. Jeff, though, he must have passed years of his life as the minute hand crept toward vertical. It was nearly time—and I should mention that in this town we know time. It doesn't pay to have your clocks slow when Wee Willie is around.

Jeff hadn't told me his plan, and I hadn't asked because I didn't really want to know. If he'd told me, and I thought it sounded crazy, I would have let him down. I'm a coward. Cowards keep their mouths shut.

He shifted on the couch just before eight o'clock, and looking back I realize that he was facing the front door and limbering up the gun. At the time, though, I was slouched in a funk over my lack of courage, and I saw him move without registering what he was doing.

* * *

WEE WILLIE'S VOICE WOULD GIVE A VIKING the heebiest of jeebies. Every night I heard it, and every night it raised the hairs on the back of my neck. *Are the children all in bed?* he cried, his reedy infantile voice crawling down my spine, and every night I looked up and saw his face at my window, the collar of his striped nightshirt hanging off one bony clavicle. On this night I didn't look, so I didn't see Jeff move as the kitchen clock struck eight.

Jeff's load of buckshot blew out most of the window nearest my front door, frame included. He chambered another shell and was across the living room in the time it took me to spill my drink on the rug. Then he was out the front door, and I was going after him. I bumped into him on the sidewalk, where he was stooping over something I couldn't see. I sidled around him to see what it was, the shock of the gunshot having sent my mind fleeing for the comfort of mundane complaints.

"Jeff, man, you owe me a window."

"Shut up a second," he said, and pointed.

There among the splinters of wood and streetlit shards of glass was a wooden block with painted letters on its faces. A child's toy. My breath caught and I forgot about the window and the whiskey seeping into my rug as I picked out other toys in the fan of wreckage on my lawn. There was a doll with one eye open, a bright yellow plastic rattle. A dreidel, a music box, a hobbyhorse with red ribbons tied in its mane.

"Holy shit," I said. "You blew the shit out of him." How come nobody had ever done this before, I was wondering. All those years of dreading eight o'clock.

"Maybe I did," Jeff said, "but the little son of a bitch is getting away." He pointed, and I saw the trail: children's toys in a weaving line to the end of my street and on into the woods beyond the last house.

I got a flashlight from my car and we went after Wee Willie. I knew the woods well enough that I took the lead, and Jeff bulled along after me through the underbrush, the two of us moving from toy to fallen toy with no other consideration in the world. Moonlight filtered down through the trees to speckle our path, but mostly what I remember is the way each successive toy jumped out in the beam of my flashlight. Every time, the absurdity of what we were doing jumped out at me—my neighbor Jeff had shot Wee Willie Winkie, and we were running him to ground. I wondered if Sharon knew what we were up to.

* * *

WE CAME OUT OF THE WOODS INTO THE TOWN'S oldest cemetery, and I knew we were close. Wee Willie hadn't run here to go on through to the strip of pizza places and furniture stores on the other side. He was going home.

* * *

TOWARD THE CENTER OF THE CEMETERY, individual gravestones gave way to family crypts, stark monuments long forgotten by any living descendant. Groundskeepers made an effort here, but the layering of age was too thick: the trees grew close, dipping their branches down to erase names and dates from the weathered granite. The miniature teacups and finger puppets and other toys stood out in a way I can't explain. Jeff and I stopped when we'd taken a dozen steps without seeing a toy, and I played the flashlight around the cluster of anonymous memorials. He grabbed my wrist, pointed my arm toward a low, flat-roofed tomb leaning under the pressure of an ancient oak tree. The door was open a little.

He let go of my hand and we stepped toward it. I let him go first in case he opened up with the shotgun again. When we got to the door I saw what was holding it open: a teddy bear, patchy and eyeless, one of its ears chewed away by some long-dead puppy.

Jeff made a noise, like someone had reached inside him and taken the only secret he'd ever meant to keep. He squatted, shotgun across his knees, and with heartbreaking care worked the teddy bear loose. The door started to close, but I jammed the barrel of the flashlight into the opening before I could remember that the smart thing to do would be walk away. With its light shining on him, Jeff held the teddy bear in his beefy hands. He lifted it to his face and held it there until I felt ashamed to be watching him. I wanted to say something but didn't know what it would be, and like he usually did Jeff solved the problem. He stood, tucked the teddy bear into his jacket pocket, and got both hands on the edge of the door. Jeff's a big man, and even though the old hinges groaned, the door couldn't resist him. The flashlight fell into my hands as he hauled the door open far enough for us to squeeze in.

I aimed the flashlight inside and got a cold creep from the steak in my belly right down into my knees as I saw a staircase going down. Wee Willie must have paused inside the door; a small jumble of tops and rubber balls and army men lay on the first step. Jeff paused long enough to slide a shell into the shotgun, replacing the shot he'd fired through my window, and then he went down. I stayed right behind him, keeping the flashlight off to the side.

When we got to the bottom there were no crypts. No bodies on shelves, no sealed chambers, no ossuaries or urns. Just a big, much too big, stone-walled room with a pile of kids' toys in the middle of the floor like a dragon's hoard, and in the middle of the pile sat Wee Willie Winkie. He was muttering something to himself in that piping voice of his, and the wounded surprise in his voice brought home to me that he was just a child himself.

They were all in bed, he was saying. *All in bed, all in bed.*

He coughed, bending over with the force of it, and his nightcap fell off. His hair was brown, and a cowlick stood out from the crown of his head. With a retching noise he brought up a Barbie doll, and he held it up before his face for a moment before letting it fall among the other playthings that surrounded him.

"Wee Willie," I said. He looked at me, registered Jeff and the shotgun with glassy, unfocused eyes.

Past eight o'clock, he said. *I'm home in bed.* And incredibly, he yawned and fell asleep.

I guess I'd been proceeding on the subconscious assumption that nothing would surprise me after I'd followed a trail of exsanguinated toys to the lair of Wee Willie Winkie. Anyone might have assumed the same. Maybe Jeff did, but we never talked about it.

The sight of Big Bill Winkie, though, was the only thing I've ever experienced that made my heart stop. When he appeared, from where I'll never know, I could feel the air in the room compress to accommodate his bulk, and for no good reason I thought of Polyphemos rolling the stone across the entrance to his cave, with me and Jeff like the damn fool sailors who trusted Odysseus to get them home. It wasn't just that he was nine feet of blocky muscle and rocky bone, with fingers thick as my wrist and veins thick as my fingers tracking across his arms and his neck and even the sloped ledge of his forehead. I knew that when he opened his mouth, he was going to say: *Fee fi fo fum, I smell the blood of two dipshits who couldn't leave well enough alone.*

Wee Willie woke up when his father came in. His face was drawn, and the pile of toys around him seemed to have grown. What would happen if he died didn't bear thinking about.

Hurt me, Daddy, he said, his voice taut with the uncomprehending loneliness of the child encountering for the first time the merciless truth that the world hurts. And Big Bill turned toward us.

Hurt my boy, he said.

I would have stayed rooted to the stone floor while Big Bill separated my limbs from my body and sucked the flesh from them until the tomb we were in at last had a real pile of bones in it. Jeff, though, Jeff snapped into action. While Big Bill was still coming to terms with the situation, Jeff closed the distance between us and Wee Willie, coming to rest knee-deep in the pile of toys with the shotgun's barrel resting against the side of Wee Willie's skinny neck. And in that moment all I wanted to do was take the gun away from my friend, to force the muzzle away from the fragile pulse that beat in the hollow of Wee Willie's throat. Even if it meant I would die.

Wee Willie began to cry, and the walls around us creaked as Big Bill shifted his weight. "I got five shells," Jeff said. "I might not get all of them off before you get me, but nobody in this town will have to worry about eight o'clock ever again."

Big Bill made tectonic sounds, but he didn't move. Jeff was right, I thought. Wee Willie could be killed.

Daddy, Daddy, Wee Willie said. I was coming apart. I wanted Jeff to kill him, just to answer for all of Sharon's lonely nights in front of bathroom mirrors; I wanted to live. I couldn't have both. We'd never get out if Jeff pulled the trigger.

"The kids," Jeff said.

Hurt my boy, Big Bill said again, and in the boom of his voice was a sadness that echoed, finding an emptiness in me and bringing me up hard against the knowledge that I loved nothing in the world as much as this gnarled and fearsome giant loved his child who stole other children. What fears sent Wee Willie running to his papa, and what pangs ran through Big Bill when he came up against this moment, when he couldn't protect his boy?

And then the catacomb filled with the voices of children. Boys and girls, the ecstatic wordless questions of ten-month-old infants and the cries of *Mama, Mama* from kids ten or eleven years old, before the clock turns and you lose them to a world beyond bedtime. They came in, the older kids carrying the little ones or leading them by the hand, and there's nothing sadder in the world than a two-year-old having to trust a ten-year-old stranger to lead her safely out of the dark. They came in, blinking at the beam of my flashlight, and gathered around Big Bill as if unsure how far they could go.

Tears stood on Jeff's face. "Jenna," he said. I couldn't see her in the crowd of pajama-clad bodies, but he could, and while he was looking Big Bill reached out and took the shotgun from Jeff's hands. I will grow old and die before I figure out whether Big Bill was really that fast or Jeff at that moment couldn't find it in himself to pull the trigger. Big Bill held the gun in one hand and snapped the barrel off with a squeeze of his thumb, and then he dropped the pieces at his feet and led the children up into the world.

MAYBE HE WAS AFRAID THAT WE WOULDN'T be the last people to take a shot at his son, but I don't think so. What I think is that it was enough that we came, that when the people of a town come to the point where they would brave the haunted world to save their children, Big Bill takes his boy and moves on.

How long had it taken us? We're good with clocks, but somehow not so good with time.

And how many times had Wee Willie fled home ahead of humans driven to vengeance by the feral extremity of love?

By the time we were back under the moon, all of the children had disappeared except Jenna, who lay sleeping in Jeff's arms, her face resting on his shoulder. Her feet draped over his forearms, resting on the bulge of his belly. And before I'd crossed the cemetery, they were gone, too. I never saw any of them go.

* * *

I SEE THEM AROUND TOWN, THOUGH. THE sidewalks seem fuller. From my office window I see school groups going to the museum down the block, and I try to pick out faces from that night, but it seems like time has passed, and children change so quickly. Jenna is a teenager, and Jeff still tests the springs of my couch once in a while, complaining about her clothes or her playing time on the field hockey team. I think he remembers. He must, he helped me fix my window and lingered for a minute over the dimples Wee Willie's knuckles had left in a piece of the frame. Also he asked me for his gun back; I'd been so unused to the idea of having one that I forgot about it until it fell out of my pants halfway through the woods on the way home. But we don't talk about it.

Nobody does. We didn't talk about Wee Willie when he was around, and we don't talk about him now. I can't be the only person who thinks about him. I might be the only guy in town who worries about him, though. Once in a while I want to ask Jeff about it, just to see if he remembers things the same way I do, because after all of this I find myself thinking about Wee Willie every time I see a kid on my street or from my office window. I wonder if Wee Willie'll grow up, or if he's just running through another town, crying out the words that we're learning to forget. Also I wonder about Big Bill. I sit at night watching my fish, and my thoughts return to him, knowing that some eight o'clock is always coming when his child must awaken to the brutality of the world so that we may learn what is worth saving.

CLOWNFISH

Waking from an unsatisfying nap, George Lamont had the sense that the fish in his office aquarium had been speaking to him. Again.

Sitting up straight in his chair, he rubbed his face and felt tension in his neck like a tightening hot wire. He thought the fish had been saying *I told you so.*

"Go to hell, fish," he growled, and then was puzzled because he thought he meant one of them in particular, even though the tank teemed with colorful and scandalously expensive saltwater fish, some of which had likely been acquired via environmentally reprehensible methods. He couldn't nap in his office anymore. The naps never made him feel better, and he couldn't have word getting out that the VP-Development was drooling onto his desk blotter. The bank's president, Bob Acker, liked George but had made the bank his life. He wouldn't let his personal friendship prevent him from reading George the riot act, not so much for napping but for napping indiscreetly.

Apart from the possible political consequences of discovery, there was also the problem that these little naps provoked such intense dreams. He called them one-frames because they were fragmentary, lacking any sense of narrative or context. George wasn't used to remembering his nightly dreams, and when he did remember them they were typically not worth remembering: indeterminate amounts of time passing while he fed pigeons from a park bench or sorted through old family photographs of relatives he couldn't quite recognize. His subconscious apparently felt frisky when he was napping, though, because he woke up every time with unsettling images and echoes in his mind. This time he thought he remembered living in a house not unlike his camp on Pushaw Lake—small, rough-hewn pine, suffused with the smells of old fires and early-morning fog—and he remembered fishing from the dock, only when he glanced over his shoulder at the house, he saw only water. It was the kind of dream, too—all of the one-frames were, really—that left him with the sensation not of having imagined something but of having lived it, as if the dream had somehow exported itself from the dream part of his brain into the part where memories lived.

No. That was yesterday. God, George thought. I can't even keep track of the days. Today the fish was talking to me.

"Right down the toilet, fish," George said. "I don't care how much you cost."

There was no response from the aquarium.

George opened his laptop and checked his calendar. According to the computer, it was Thursday. A good sign. The week was almost over. Not such a good sign that he was supposed to be on the phone at this very moment to the development officer of a prominent local half-marathon looking for a new sponsor. He made the call, and fell easily into the kind of autopilot bonhomie that made him good at what he did. After fifteen minutes, he and the development officer, whose name was Scott Gilooly, had decided that hell yes, they should do this. "Let's talk Monday," Gilooly said. "That'll give me a chance to get all my ducks in a row over here."

"You bet," George said. "You running this weekend?"

"Just a ten-k." It was early spring, and there were a number of local races that existed more or less as warm-ups for the half-marathon whose sponsorship George was trying to land.

"Knock yourself out," George laughed. The truth was, he hated running. Like lifting weights, running was assembly-line exercise. Monotonous. George wasn't a fitness nut, but if he was going to exercise, he needed a little more variety. Softball, tennis, something like that.

His exception to this rule was swimming, not in a pool but out in real live water, a lake or the ocean. George loved to swim, and had the good fortune to live in Maine, near the ocean as well as several lakes. His camp at Pushaw, two and a half hours north of Portland, was good for swimming. Maybe he'd try to get up there this weekend, take off early Friday afternoon and be in the water before the chill was out of the air on Saturday morning.

He glanced at the clock. Four-eleven. His calendar showed a morning meeting, a lunch seminar about the problems and opportunities of the locally owned bank in a market dominated by predatory consolidation, and nothing in the afternoon.

Four-twelve. George ran through his email, sent Bob Acker a noncommittal note about his conversation with Gilooly, and as he sent it had the irritating feeling that the fish were looking at him. He looked back. None of them would look him in the eye.

A lawnmower blenny that made a habit of hanging around the aerator drew his particular suspicion. Another possible suspect was the blue-striped clownfish, but it was almost trite to imagine that a clownfish was harassing him.

Perhaps the banana eel that lived inside the sunken pirate ship was the culprit. If you were willing to grant the possibility that a fish was talking to you, it did no good to pretend rationality by making a show of logically constructing a hierarchy of suspects.

He spent the next forty-five minutes with his notebook. As his sole psychological indulgence, George maintained a belief in reincarnation, and believed that he had a sense of his past lives...or at least some of them. He kept a small notebook in which he described aspects of these previous iterations of his existence. The notebook itself was unexceptional, spiral-bound with a red cover that still bore the price sticker from the convenience store where he'd bought it one morning along with a cup of coffee and a pack of gum. For a dollar and nineteen cents he had made available to himself eighty pages of six-by-nine recollection and exploration. Fifty-four square inches per page, two sides, eighty pages. Eight thousand six hundred and forty square inches, or an even sixty square feet of space for words and doodles. He'd filled about half of it, and had entertained the thought that when it was full he would tear the pages out and tape them to the wall of his private room in the basement of the home he shared with Veronica and his fantasies of the children she had not yet borne. When they were older, he would show those children his notes and doodles. Without pressing them to believe, of course. The last thing in the world he wanted was to step too far into Shirley MacLaine territory, and the truth was that George didn't believe he'd ever been pope, or caliph of Baghdad, or a member of the Romanovs. This is a way to learn about yourself, he would tell his son or daughter. You have to know where you've been in order to know where you're going, he would say.

One problem with this vision was that in putting the pages up on the pine paneling of his basement room, he would be obscuring one side of each page. George didn't like the idea of photocopying either the recto or verso of each page, and he also wasn't sure that he wanted to carve the room into two parts by putting up some kind of plexiglass museum frame so the pages could be observed from either side. Those were the only two ideas that had occurred to him so far, though. He still had plenty of time to think about it. Forty or so more pages.

Thirty-nine after he had written down what he could remember of the one-frame. *Camp like Pushaw,* he wrote, *only no electricity?* He couldn't decide. *Ocean, gray sky. On the water I looked back and saw the land was gone.*

Below this, a vague line drawing of waves; and below that, an assessment. George categorized the one-frames according to which of his possible previous lives they seemed to illuminate. He'd dreamed images of this seaside life before. They didn't seem to all come from the same existence, but he was aware of the possibility of a kind of transmission error; his mind was probably taking certain images and experiences and translating them according to an experiential syntax that the now-living George could begin to understand. He had come to this conclusion early in the notebook, somewhere around page ten. Now it was a foundational hypothesis, the basis of all his classification. George was confident that once he arrived at a correct taxonomy of his one-frames, he would be able to figure out exactly who he had been.

He dated the dream and catalogued it as Seaside Life Number Eighty-Four. The other categories included English Manor House, Scottish Castle, Italian Villa, and Park Avenue. If he'd never been a Romanov, nevertheless it did appear to him that he had been comfortable in his previous lives—as he was in this one. Maybe there was a kind of equilibrium at work. For some reason he had never been able to pin down the location of Seaside Life, which annoyed him, and he was reluctant to assume it was Maine, since that would mean he was spending this life repeating the locale of a previous life—a thought George found unbearable. Always forward, that was his motto. Veronica's, too, which was one reason they were a good match. Onward and upward, sky's the limit, reach for the stars.

One more time, before he got to the door, he heard the fish: *I told you so.*

* * *

TOLD ME WHAT? GEORGE WONDERED AS HE DROVE home to his fine Colonial on a dead-end road called Smugglers Cove, where Veronica would already be home from teaching art history at the University of Southern Maine. A good life they had, the banker and the professor; he resolved that this evening he would pour her a glass of wine and take her out onto their deck looking out over the scattering of Casco Bay islands that danced in and out of the spring fogs. There he would say to her that the time was right for children. Perhaps they had even waited too long…or no, he couldn't say that, she would take it as a comment on her age and fertility when all he meant was that at this moment he was wishing that they had already had a child. Veronica had a great many characteristics that he admired, or loved, or which amused him; one of the few that he did not admire or love was her tendency to take offense at comments delivered in a tone of voice that she herself spoke in routinely.

She wasn't home. A note on the kitchen counter said that she'd gone to a lecture that she'd forgotten to tell him about. George poured the glass of wine anyway, and drank it himself on the back porch while the islands disappeared into the lowering fog, and drank another while the fog disappeared into the lowering night. He'd had the porch added on to the house as part of a comprehensive remodel the year before. The financial uptick when Veronica had gotten tenure and he'd gotten the VP had been enough to buy the house, but less than six months later, an article of Veronica's on Cimabue had somehow been optioned for film development. Less than a week later he'd found out that a few thousand dollars he'd invested in a tech startup fifteen years before had overnight turned into more than a million when the startup went public. In the year since then, he'd invested with absurd success and Veronica's lusty, rambunctious vision of the quattrocento art world had gotten her speaking engagements and a book contract for a hell of a lot more than the academic press would have paid.

What with all that, they'd gone through the house top to bottom: radiant heat, Armenian tilework, new redwood deck with granite stairs leading down to the shore, plank flooring salvaged from an eighteenth-century barn in Aroostook County…then the camp got the same treatment, and then they'd bought new cars. George's first was a Hummer, but he felt idiotic driving it around and traded it in for a Chrysler 300, and then added to that the new Ford Tungsten GT. Only American cars for him. Veronica had an M-class Mercedes custom-painted a deep, smoky amethyst. He knew she was considering whether to go after jobs at more prestigious universities; he was the only reason she hadn't yet.

A pretty good life before, George thought, and now it verges on the ridiculous. He owned thousand-dollar suits, hundred-dollar belts, a million-dollar house. His colleagues liked him, his wife loved him, good fortune fell from the sky. Next he was going to get a boat.

I'm pretty close to having enough, he thought. Veronica, though…he was feeling a little tickle of discontent at her constant ambition. Or it could be that he was discontented with himself for not matching her ambition. It was hard to tell the difference.

He closed his eyes in the darkness, and dreaming saw only what was already there: the sweep of lighthouse beams, the bobbing lights of nocturnal boaters, and the restless flicker of reflected moonlight on the water.

* * *

"You're going to freeze," Veronica said, by way of waking him up and letting him know that she loved him even though he was an idiot to fall asleep on the back porch when the mercury stood at forty-one degrees.

George stirred, and rolled his head back and forth. "Hey," he said. It was no longer the moment to propose children. "How was the lecture?"

"I've seen worse," she said. "I only went because Mary and Steve were going."

"Ah." Mary and Steve from the English department, notoriously a nest of viperous scholars striking at each other to draw attention away from their scholarly mediocrity. George mistrusted them, but they were fun to go out with once in a while as long as the destination wasn't a university lecture. That kind of keeping up with the Joneses, George could do without. Give him a charity reception any time; at least there you knew which agendas were competing with which, and how to work them against each other. With academic types, you could never tell who was really after what.

He yawned, and heard an echo of voices from the sea. That's it, he thought. Tomorrow the fish goes. Maybe all of them go, if I can't figure out which one it is.

* * *

Making love to Veronica that night, George was seized without warning by a terrible wave of sadness that he had not yet created a child. Abruptly his passion for her transformed itself into a desire to lose himself in her and find solace in that loss, and afterward he watched her gathering the rumpled sheets up to her shoulders and nestling into her pillow. It seemed to him that the tenuous, indirect light of the moon brought violet tones out of her eyes, which were a streaky gray-green in daylight. As she turned, he watched the shift and fall of her breasts. She curled her legs back toward him, bracketing one of his feet with both of her own. When she had fallen asleep, he got up and threw away her birth-control pills, concealing them under a week's worth of receipts and takeout coffee cups and gum wrappers in the wastebasket next to his desk in the basement. By the time he'd climbed back upstairs, he'd decided that wasn't good enough. He got the pills and popped them out of the case, one by one, over the open bowl of the downstairs toilet. Each plink filled him with a secret satisfaction. It occurred to him at some point during the night, when he was briefly surfacing to near-wakefulness before rolling over again and sounding for the depths, that he had dropped the pills in the toilet by way of sublimating his desire to do the same to the fish from his office aquarium. Huh, he thought. Beside him, Veronica made a noise that sounded aquatic.

George twitched his flukes and was gone.

* * *

At forty-one years old, vice-president of a local bank with a solid reputation and good prospects for growth, married to a woman slightly younger but in many ways wiser than he, George Lamont should perhaps have been happier than he was. He knew this, had assessed the problem from every angle he was capable of, and could not understand why he fell asleep at his desk nearly every day and committed inexcusably invasive acts such as destroying Veronica's pills. If either of his parents had still been alive, he might have asked them. Since they were not, he ended up asking, of all people, Scott Gilooly, on the following Monday when they got together to finalize the fine print on the sponsorship agreement for what would now be known as the CascoBank Half-Marathon. As they sat back in their chairs to bask in the self-satisfaction of the signed agreement, George heard himself say, "Scott. Ever feel like you should be happier than you are?"

Scott covered his apparent discomfort with a smile. "Already laying the groundwork to renegotiate?"

Realizing his misstep, George tried to go along with the joke. "Never too early, right?"

They laughed together, and then George went back to work. From his office window, he could look out over the Portland waterfront. When he was starting college, what was now known as the Old Port, the tourist engine of the Portland economy, had been called the Wild West. It had been grimy, dangerous. Now it overflowed with tourists during the day, and at night every Mainer who secretly wished he lived in the East Village, even if he didn't really know where the East Village was, came out to spend eight dollars on a martini. The teetering warehouses on the piers had given way to condominiums, and the bait shops to T-shirt stores. Something about the change bothered George, mostly because he had undergone an analogous change. He'd been a hell-raising post-adolescent in that Wild West, and sure, he missed it even if he didn't really want to be doing it again. The problem with missing something that you really didn't want anymore was that it started to blur the boundary between the person you were and the person you had been. Forty-one-year-old George couldn't still live his life according to what twenty-year-old George had wanted, and the truth was that George Lamont, with his admittedly nebulous ideas about past lives and his resilient dissatisfaction with his current life, was the last person in the world who needed that particular boundary blurred by desires from his youth.

He woke up with the fish talking to him again, and felt a thump of blood in his temple. "All right, fish," he said, and got up. "Which one of you is it?"

The fish flitted around the aquarium at his sudden movement, but none of them answered. It's the clownfish, George thought. He fantasized about feeding the clownfish to one of the feral cats that teemed around the Casco Bay Ferry docks, then lost his train of thought as he was distracted for the hundredth time by considering feral cats' abundance in Maine. When he'd been an undergrad up in Orono, dozens of them had lived under the sheds out behind the hardware store in town. Once or twice a year, flyers went up announcing that they were all going to be trapped and soliciting prospective owners; then, as if they germinated magically from the concrete dust and cobwebs, six months later the sheds were bursting with cats again.

Once George had wanted one of the hardware-shed refugees, but he hadn't even been able to scrape together the money for shots. He'd come a long way since then, and Veronica had a lot to do with that. George reflected that he had the kind of ambition that needed other ambition to feed on, whereas Veronica was a pure self-starter, a go-getter from the get-go. With her, he had gone farther than he ever could have alone.

And now he thought they'd gone far enough. They'd spent enough of their lives in the, what, the getting and the spending. I could endow a whole charity for homeless cats, George thought—which reminded him of why he was standing in front of the aquarium.

"If I had a net, fish," he said, "there'd be trouble. I don't care if you did cost two hundred bucks."

Secure in its self-worth and George's lack of a net, the fish did not bother to challenge him.

Two hundred bucks, George thought. He'd looked up on the Internet how much a blue-striped clownfish cost. Could be it was more if you bought one at a store. He considered calling the guy who maintained the aquarium; maybe he could sell the fish back at a discount, get some art to cover the wall space. He'd gotten the aquarium on his promotion to VP, since he'd had an aquarium as a kid and remembered the tranquilly fascinated hours he'd spent gazing at the fish—guppies and red-tailed sharks and kuhli loaches then, bought for fifty cents or two bucks a pop instead of the ridiculous prices he'd paid for these new trophies of his corporate climbing. He'd thought then that what with the unaccustomed pressures of his new position, he might need a calming influence, and he'd turned out to be right, but he hadn't anticipated that the fish would cause him as much stress as the job. What the hell kind of a fish was worth two hundred bucks? It was only six inches long, and maybe weighed, what, five ounces? By weight, it was more expensive than silver. George imagined fish as currency, and a split second later realized that the thought had been lying in wait to ambush him.

The one-frame dream: he's turning fish over like tarot cards on a table made from an overturned boat.

George got his notebook out and filled another page, crossing out a number of dead-end tangents. Seaside Life Number Eighty-Five. It had been a while since he'd had a dream that he could confidently place in another category, which worried him. Was he not looking hard enough for evidence that his recent one-frames might belong in Italian Villa or Scottish Castle? None of the Seaside Life dreams (now so classified only tentatively) seemed sunny enough to be Italian, but what if the sea was the North Sea, and the reach he gazed across led to the Orkneys?

He flipped back through the notebook, looking for Seaside Life entries, and couldn't put them together. Several times he saw variants on the phrase *The fish said…* but he couldn't tell from context whether he had meant at the time that the fish was talking in the dream or in his office. How long had he been talking to the fish? He couldn't remember. In that moment George hated dreams and would cheerfully have undergone a surgical procedure guaranteed to prevent their future occurrence.

A depressing sense of futility overcame him. When was it all going to be enough?

I told you so, said the fish.

"Okay, fish," George said. "Told me what?"

That you wouldn't be happy.

"A psychic fish. Or a crazy George. Jesus," George said.

Could be both, the fish said. George was now certain it was the clownfish, and this disappointed him. With almost equal certainty he thought he'd lost his mind.

"Fish," he said, "if you're still talking to me tomorrow, I'm going to have to take steps."

On the way home, he stopped at the driving range and hit a bucket of balls. The necessity of golf was one of those things that George tolerated about his job, like having to polish his shoes and forward vulgar email jokes to his executive colleagues. He wasn't good enough to care whether his form was correct or the balls went straight, but he had swung a club enough times to take an atavistic pleasure from those few instances when he got it exactly right. The therapeutic value of controlled violence, in George's opinion, was not to be underestimated. So *thwack thwack thwack* George hit golf balls, and when the bucket was empty he drove home feeling a pleasant fatigue in his shoulders and forearms.

Veronica was sitting at the kitchen table when he came in. "Have you seen my pills?" she asked.

Alarm bells went off in George's head. He'd done the pill thing, what, four days ago? And she was only now asking about it? Clearly he'd been outmaneuvered. He had thought—well, insofar as he'd thought about anything—that he would force her to miss a day and then rely on the tenacity of his swimmers and the ambiguous clockwork of her disrupted ovulation. But this was a whole new wrinkle. If Veronica thought that he had done something with her pills, she'd have confronted him a long time ago; since she didn't, she must be trying to send him some kind of signal, he thought. At the same time, he was disturbed—why hadn't she told him?

She might already be pregnant, George thought. He wished he'd paid closer attention to her cycles, and what kind of pill she used, and all the other stuff that might have led him to make a more informed choice than dumping them all into the toilet.

"I went ahead and started at the same place in next month's," she went on, "but still. I can't figure out where they went."

Next month's? She had spares?

George became piercingly aware of just how much he didn't know about women. He opened his mouth, unsure what he was about to say until the sounds began to form in his throat. "Well. What the heck. I say lose them, too, and let's have a baby."

"Very funny," she said.

George reached out to her, brushing her cheek with his fingertips. "No, really," he said.

For a long moment she was still. Then she put her hand up to cover his, and squeezed.

"I don't know, George," she said. "I don't know."

* * *

THAT NIGHT, A WARM BREEZE CURLED AROUND the corners of the house and kept George comfortable as he sat on the back porch and listened to the rush of the surf. He remembered a time when he would have thought that money bought happiness, and he considered the fact that it sure was easy to complain about money not buying happiness because you had to have money before you could complain about what it didn't do. Life had granted him many of his wishes, and he had reached the point at which if he didn't have something, it was his own fault. There were few things worse, in his opinion, than whiny rich people.

What the one-frames had in common was a connection to the sea, George was thinking. The significance of this eluded him. I live by the ocean, he thought. I swim in it. I used to fish a lot. I've lived within five miles of the ocean for most of my life. Is it really any surprise that I dream about it?

As an answer, that was pretty good if he ignored the fact that he only dreamed about the ocean in the one-frames, and it was because of the one-frames that he'd become convinced of his previous lives. Was it also the one-frames that had convinced him that a blue-striped clownfish was talking to him? I should tell Veronica, he thought. Who knows, maybe the same thing happens to her. If not, she will perhaps consider it a charming idiosyncrasy.

"Ha," he said to the night breeze and the invisible ocean.

And must have fallen asleep, because when he opened his eyes sunrise was in full swing and Veronica was sitting next to him. "If you're not careful," she said, "I'm going to start thinking you don't want to be around me."

"Been having weird dreams," George said. "I just…"

He wasn't sure how to finish the thought.

Veronica was silent for a long time. The sun, low over the ocean, lit her face brilliantly. Just when George was certain she was about to say something that would shake his faith in the foundations of their love, she said, "Okay, let's have a baby."

George experienced successive waves of elation, puzzlement, joy, terror. He found that he could not stop smiling, and she started smiling, too. "Think you can be a little late for work this morning?" she asked.

* * *

TOLD YOU SO, SAID THE FISH.

George snapped awake, struggling free of the latest one-frame. Sunrise, the weight of a net in his hands... He reached for the notebook, then decided it could wait. "You know what, fish?" he said. "You're wrong. Today is the wrong day for you to tell me I'm not happy."

You just wait, the fish said, and George felt the tug of uncertainty. He fought it with everything he had: the view from his office window, the camp at Pushaw, the smell and sound of the ocean from his back porch, the line of Veronica's throat when she tipped her head back and cried out that morning, the milk-smelling indeterminacy of the baby they would have.

Furious at himself for doubting, furious at the fish and at himself for thinking that the fish was talking to him, George bolted out of his chair. What could he use for a net? Hell with the net; he could punch a paperweight through the wall of the aquarium and pick the goddamn fish off the carpet.

He almost did it, too. The paperweight, a glass disc engraved with the University of Maine seal, felt good in his hand; the vision of a life without the fish undermining him felt good in his mind. At the last minute, he reeled himself back in, brimful of realization and sudden confidence. He didn't have to kill the fish.

One last time I'm going to indulge all of this, George told himself. It'll be cathartic, and then that's it.

"I know what's going on here, fish," he said. "I made this whole thing up. I'm externalizing my insecurities, and today—as of today—I don't have to anymore. I'm rich, I'm good at my job, I'm going to have a baby. I don't have to believe in these stupid one-frames, and I don't have to talk to you. In fact, you know what? Maybe it was just my way of working through things, but I wish I never had," George said.

* * *

AND STOOD ON THE SEASHORE, FLIPPING FISH like tarot cards on his overturned boat. A fair catch today, already sold at the market; these he would dry, or use for bait. He looked over his shoulder at his house, knowing that Veronica would be on her way back from the schoolhouse in town, full of bemused stories of her students' misunderstandings and small epiphanies. It was a bittersweet time of day, when a man of a certain age could understand that he had gotten from life just about all he was going to get. I do wish I was rich, George thought. I wish I did not work with my hands, but my work is honest, and my discontent honestly come by.

Slap went the fish on the hull of George's boat. He whiled away the rest of his work dreaming of another life.

GUS DREAMS OF BITING THE MAILMAN

Summer-bright light fell through the windows of Mitch Packard's car as he awoke to the thump of his windshield wiper slapping down on top of a parking ticket. He tracked the cop back to his cruiser with a bleary scowl and dug in his pocket for a cigarette, and when there were no cigarettes he had no choice but to skip his summer Shakespeare seminar in favor of a trip to the liquor store for smokes and then a Brown Jug breakfast special, leisurely eaten on the big concrete planters out in front of the restaurant. He gave the pancakes to his dog Gus as a reward for Gus's perseverance; not every dog would have taken it so well when his person was kicked out of his apartment after a three-hour vicious-circle argument that had begun as a disagreement over the relative merits of Charles Bukowski. Mitch wondered how long it would be before he could call Trina and begin the delicate negotiations that would culminate in his sleeping in a bed again. She couldn't hold a grudge for long over Bukowski. Mitch Packard didn't cohabit with women who held grudges over Bukowski.

He held onto this conviction while strolling aimlessly around sunny Ann Arbor until three o'clock, when he could go to Doug's Bakery without fear of running into Doug, who was under the impression that Mitch didn't work there anymore. Doug's was in Ypsilanti, ten minutes east down Washtenaw Avenue, across from a house where some people said John Norman Collins, the Michigan Murders guy, had killed at least one of his victims. Patrons of Doug's, especially if they had first been to the Shell station kitty-corner from the bakery, frequently arrived at the counter bearing dire stories of diligent police detectives recovering hairs from painted-over cinder-block walls, or scraping out floor drains to find a single toenail. The Shell cashiers were full of bullshit stories about murderous conspiracies. Eli Gray, Mitch's coworker at Doug's, hated them for this, and for his own agonized predilection to believe whatever arcane gossip propagated viruslike on the tongues of bakery patrons. He was neither stupid nor unusually credulous; he was, however, completely defenseless against the question "what if?"

On this day, the what-if had something to do with Ernest Hemingway's "The Killers" and a rail-car diner that might or might not have once occupied space on Washtenaw Avenue near the bakery. "The thing is," Eli said as Mitch came in the back door and fought his way through oven racks to the fryer, "it could be true."

This was the point at which Mitch's own self-restraint inevitably suffered a catastrophic failure.

"What could be true?" he asked.

* * *

It should be interjected at this point that Mitch Packard had a problem with coincidence, or perhaps with probability, or causality. The ultimate origins were of course occluded, but the immediate effects were clear. Apart from the ordinary encounter-with-synchronicity events any human being can report—anticipating songs on the radio, thinking of someone right before the phone rings, et cetera—odd and improbable events pocked Mitch's life to such a degree that he had begun to regard himself as a living embodiment of negentropy, a conduit of fructifying information, a temple to life in a universe doomed to decline. This was one: if he read a newspaper on any given day, one of its articles inevitably would yield information that he would be called upon to provide later on the same day. If he read an automotive column about problems with tie-rod ends in Windstar minivans, at some point before he crashed out for the night—at the bakery, at the Brown Jug, at the house on Pearl Street, anywhere—conversation would turn to steering problems with someone's Windstar minivan. And Mitch would provide information. There were also incidents like the previous night's at the Monkey Bar.

Unfortunately, templehood meant very little when, as a result of an argument over Bukowski and subsequent imbibery and inability to find a place to sack for the night, you awakened to the thump of your car's windshield wiper slapping down on a parking ticket. Neither did templehood prepare you for the co-opting of reality by your best friend's daily doughnut-fryer rant. Which explained, in an appropriately acausal and synchronistic kind of way, why Mitch had, because of four simple words, entangled himself in Eli Gray's latest obsession.

* * *

Back in the narrative, Eli spun out a lengthy and ridiculous proposition that, to Mitch's thinking, betrayed his recent reading of some crank possible-worlds theory. This took the better part of an hour, during which time Mitch frequently escaped to the front register to ring up dozens and coffees or take a wedding-cake order. Undaunted by these interruptions, Eli picked up each time exactly where he'd left off, delivering himself of a hiatus-punctuated monologue that, much redacted, went something like this: "You know that scene in *The Time Machine* where the Time Traveler sends the model off to see if everything works? Check this out. What would it mean if you looked over on the counter one afternoon and that model was sitting right there? It would mean that you were a character in the book, man, not that you weren't real but that somewhere a fiction existed that encompassed not only you but the whole gestalt whatever that we take to be the universal reality. It would mean that somewhere out there," and here Eli waved the drumsticks he used to turn doughnuts in the general direction of Detroit, causing Mitch to dodge a sortie of crisped crumbs and near-boiling droplets of fryer oil, "what Wells wrote was true, and I'm not talking about true in the sense that literature recovers some essential experience of our being in this world because my point is that our being in this world is in fact a being in a part of someone else's world, which in the case of your finding the model time machine on the counter next to the Hobart would be H.G. Wells's world, which of course on one level is the same as ours only separated by a hundred years, give or take, since he wrote that book, but on another level isn't really separated at all since if time and space are all really the same thing then distance in history should be crossable the way distance between Albuquerque and Des Moines is, and yet on a third level is completely different, or would be if you saw the model time machine because in that case you would realize that somehow, in some way, the writing of that book created or imposed itself on this universe, made it part of a fiction that, if you saw the model time machine, would no longer be a fiction."

It was at this point that Mitch decided to make a model time machine so he could leave it by Eli's bed some night when Eli was on the lysergic highway.

"My point," Eli rattled on, "is that if something like this could happen, and granted it's speculative and not particularly likely for any given person, still you have to acknowledge that probabilities aren't predictive, then anything you read could really be true. True like the-sky-is-blue true or two-plus-two-is-four true. And the other thing is that you, my friend Mitchell, could be a fiction, which," and up came a drumstick in a triumphant salute, "in this case would not make you any less real."

"The sky isn't blue," Mitch said. He was frosting danish, a process that involved repeated submersion of the right hand in an aluminum bowl of slightly watery frosting, followed by a dedicated imitation with that same hand of an arthritic palsy, which stiff-knuckled tremor brought forth the squiggly pattern of frosting without which millions of bakery patrons would find themselves unable to eat danish. Some bakeries do this with a machine, but Doug's was old-fashioned.

"You and your goddamn literal mind," Eli said. "Doesn't matter."

"If I find a time machine out on the porch," Mitch said, "how will I know that it's Wells's time machine? What if someone else wrote a story with a dry-run model time machine? Or what if someone really invented one, and it just happened to pop back into the world on my porch?"

"Doesn't matter," Eli said again, and climbed up onto the deli counter to change the CD in the stereo that sat on top of the cabinets. "Consensus reality is a mishmash of truth and fiction, anyway."

Mitch didn't want to have the consensus-reality discussion again. He kept his mouth shut. Then he found himself speaking anyway. "This whole I'm-a-fiction thing is the oldest idea in the world. We used to do this in the tenth grade."

"The other thing," Eli said, "is that, really, what's the difference between believing you're a fictional character and believing that God waved his hand and said let there be light? You got your figurative inscription of reality on the void or your literal inscription of Mitch Packard on Ypsilanti. Either way, you exist because of another entity's act of will."

Mitch grew bilious. "Analogies," he growled. "Logic. The whore of loony opinions."

"Whatever," Eli said, climbing down and wiping his footprints off the sandwich board. "But you can't prove me wrong either."

* * *

OR IT COULD HAVE HAPPENED AS QUICKLY AS THIS:

"Okay. You remember *The Time Machine*, when the Time Traveler sends off a model to make sure the whole thing works before he gets in his machine?"

Nod.

"Right. So if you were sitting on your porch one June afternoon and that model blipped into existence on the railing next to your ashtray, what would you think? What would you be forced to think?"

Silence of Mitch watching Eli flip doughnuts. The overall effect is that of a heavy-metal drummer near the threshold of human tolerance for Quaaludes. When Eli speaks at normal speed, Mitch blinks.

"You, my friend Mitchell, would at that moment become a fictional character."

More silence. A rack of éclairs plunges crackling into the fryer. "But that didn't happen."

"Not to you. But I can guarantee that it did to someone."

* * *

LATER, MITCH AND ELI PACK A BOWL in the shed. "So if I go home tonight,"

Mitch says, "and there's a little silver machine of indeterminate origin sitting next to the ashtray on my front porch, that means I'm not real."

"Absolutely not." Eli leans against a stack of flour sacks. He is shorter and heavier than Mitch, with a look about him like a New England stone wall. "You're still real; of course you're real. What it would mean is that the fiction was real, too. That what Wells wrote became true when he wrote it."

"Then how come *he* didn't run into a model while he was out walking on the heath or whatever?"

Eli passes the bowl to Mitch. "Do you know," he says, "how unlikely that is?"

"Nope," Mitch chokes through a haze of smoke. He sits on a case of Cokes, reflecting on the time he and Melanie the morning cashier had enjoyed a moment of secretive carnality against the very flour sacks now supporting Eli's weight.

"How many books do you suppose have been written since, say, 1899, or whenever *The Time Machine* came out?"

Mitch shakes his head. "No idea." Whatever happened to Melanie, he wonders.

"A fucking lot," Eli says, taking the bowl back. "And for every one, there's another reality created because someone thought it up and wrote it down."

"No way."

"It's true. And this is no wet-noodle academic quantum cosmology. This is fact, my friend. There are more things in heaven and earth, Mr. Packard, than are dreamt of in bookstores and physics laboratories. Vanishingly unlikely that Wells would run into his own creation like that, besides the fact that it would mean that he'd changed his own reality rather than created a new one. Can't do that."

Melanie moved to Iowa, Mitch remembers. He grunts his way to his feet. "Time to glaze the twists."

* * *

Inside, a skinny, long-wristed black kid wearing corn rows and a Red Wings jersey waits at the counter. Mitch sips a cup of coffee, feels his eyes drying in their sockets. "Do for you?"

"Y'all hiring by any chance?"

"Always." Mitch rips an application from the pad under the register, hands it to the kid with a pen. "Bring it back whenever."

The kid goes to the counter and sits. Mitch is pleasantly stoned, channels opening in his mind, the day replaying. He digs change out of his pocket and finds a near-mint 1903 Liberty dime in his newspaper change. It's the fourth time that June; the coincidence thing seems to focus around money. Hm, he thinks, now I can pay the phone bill.

Phone bill leads to telephone leads to sound becoming energy leads to energy becoming light leads to a redshifting recollection of the morning's paper. There was an article about the age of the universe, search for planets, extraterrestrial life. Mitch recalls this with a dim sense of foreboding.

The kid returns to the counter. Mitch reads his name and sticks out a hand. "How you doing, Roosevelt? I'm Mitch."

"Nice to meet you," Roosevelt says. His fingernails are ragged and bitten.

Mitch comes around the counter and they sit together at a table. Roosevelt's handwriting is small and careful. He has no references and no previous job experience, no address and no phone number. Mitch frowns. He looks again at Roosevelt, probing for signals of homelessness, drug abuse, that ineffable whatever. But Roosevelt Rawls just looks like a regular kid.

Okay, Mitch thinks. It's not every day you see a black kid in a hockey jersey. He falls back on the alternative hiring process known as The Question of the Day.

"Roosevelt," he says, "you ever read *The Time Machine*?"

Flicker of a smile. "Yeah."

"You know that model time machine the guy sends off?"

A nod.

"What would you think if you saw one pop into existence right here on this table?"

Roosevelt shrugs. "In an infinite universe, man, all things are not only possible, but inevitable."

It takes Mitch some time to recover from this answer.

"Who says it's infinite?" he asks pugnaciously, remembering the newspaper article.

"Who says it's not? Tell me where it ends."

* * *

ROOSEVELT'S ANSWER GOT HIM A JOB, but Mitch's day did not simplify. He was perplexed and not a little worried that he had no answer. His informational capacity had failed him. Clearly a new element had been introduced into his interaction with the cosmos; a delicate balance had been upset. He should not have argued about Bukowski. Perhaps no more Liberty dimes would be forthcoming in newspaper change.

But some good might come as well. If Mitch was no longer the focus of some weird convergence of probabilities, maybe he could start flipping coins again without worrying that he was unbalancing some fundamental property of the universe. Maybe he could go a week without some bizarre coincidence such as had befallen him the day before, when while shooting pool at the Monkey Bar he had fired the cue ball off the table and cracked a bystander in the forehead. The bystander turned out to be a guy named Quincy whom Mitch had once seen mercilessly insulted by a street performer in Key West whose act culminated in knife juggling while turning figure eights on a seven-foot unicycle called the Suicycle of Death, which it turned out the Monkey bartender had designed for the performer. Everyone in the Monkey had been thunderstruck by this revelation, so much so that Mitch had to stumble out to the curb and cogitate drunkenly on the odds of such an event while inside, the Monkey's clientele decided *en masse* to road-trip to Key West and witness the marvel of the Suicycle of Death.

* * *

SOME OF THE EVENTS NARRATED THUS FAR ARE TRUE. Others should have been. It's like Eliot said in *Four Quartets* about time past and time future, about what was and what might have been all coming together to create the present.

What follows is really the point of the whole thing.

* * *

IT BECAME APPARENT, AFTER ROOSEVELT HAD HUNG around until one in the morning, that he didn't have any place to go. Tenderhearted Mitch approached him and offered Eli's living room couch. Roosevelt accepted. The graveyard crew came in shortly thereafter and Roosevelt squeezed himself into the back of Eli's Escort for the short trek to the house on Pearl Street.

I should have called Trina, Mitch thought as they pulled into the driveway. When he walked in Gus assaulted him, then scrambled into the kitchen. Mitch fed him from a bag of Purina kept cached at Pearl Street for such exigencies, and then the four of them—Mitch, Eli, Roosevelt, and Gus—took up positions in broken-down recliners on the porch.

"It becomes clear to me," said Mitch to Roosevelt, "that you are no ordinary kid."

Roosevelt seemed discomfited by this assertion. Mitch hastened to clarify.

"Simply that your average teenager doesn't toss off smart-ass lines about the age and extent of the universe."

The phone rang. It was Trina. When Mitch returned to the porch, his spirits were somewhat dampened. Eli passed him the pipe.

"I have figured this out," announced Eli. "Roosevelt here is an alien."

Mitch didn't want to hear it. For confirmation, he looked to Gus, who was leaning against Roosevelt's leg with his eyes closed as Roosevelt scratched behind his ears. "He is not," Mitch said, pointing to Gus as evidence. Gus would never consort with aliens.

"He is," answered Eli.

"I am," concurred Roosevelt.

Mitch puzzled over the situation. "I should have known," he said.

"Correct," Eli nodded. "The Red Wings jersey."

"Not to mention uncommon speculations on the nature of the universe."

"Combined with blithe ignorance of hiring rules that luckily we are willing to ignore."

"A fish out of his contextual water." Mitch puzzled some more, then clapped Roosevelt on the shoulder. "You can have a beer, then," he concluded. The three of them toasted this resolution. Mitch, too, toasted the apparent revival of his clairvoyant newspaper reading.

* * *

MANY BEERS AND NOT A FEW BOWLS LATER, Mitch had that comfortable kind-of-like-wearing-a-hat feeling that came from careful management of marijuana intake. Gus had long since given up and gone to sleep, his head between his paws. His occasional dreaming grumble raised dust from the porch steps.

A soft pop startled Mitch. He looked up and saw a tiny metal machine next to the porch ashtray. The machine was about six inches long and three high, a framework of some shiny slick metal intertwined with sinuous bars of what looked like ice. A minutely crafted leather harness and saddle hung in the frame facing a console of ivory levers. Looking at the console made Mitch a bit queasy; something about it seemed always in motion, always not quite where it was when you looked at it.

"Holy shit," Mitch said. He felt keenly the desertion of causality.

Roosevelt and Eli looked up. For a moment none of them spoke.

"Who did that happen to?" Mitch asked tremulously.

"Who noticed it first?" Eli looked a little stunned. "It looks kind of like a dune buggy."

Mitch, reluctantly: "Me."

"Then it happened to you," said Roosevelt the alien.

"No, man, why? It could have happened to you and I was just who noticed it."

Roosevelt shook his head. "Y'all were talking about this all day, and now it happens and you want to say it happened to me? Take some responsibility."

"So it happened to Eli," Mitch protested.

"Nope," they both said.

"You did this," Mitch accused Roosevelt.

"H.G. Wells means nothing to me."

"But Eli's right?"

Roosevelt shrugged. "Appears that way."

"So none of us are *real*?" Mitch cried. Gus looked up, then went back to sleep.

"Hell yes we're real," Eli said. He kicked a rock off the porch. "See? That was real. You're real, I'm real. Roosevelt's real, even if he's an alien in disguise."

Roosevelt shrugged. "We're sitting here, ain't we?"

"Look, we're sitting here with a fictional damn model time machine. It and us occupy the same plane of existence. We coexist. Now, I read the book that thing came from, and it wasn't real. So if we coexist, I'm not real—we're not real—either."

"You never pay attention when I'm talking," Eli complained.

"You never make sense," Mitch said.

Eli pointed gloatingly at the time machine.

"I am not black marks on a page," Mitch said.

Roosevelt and Eli shrugged. "Who said you were?" Eli said.

"Look, man," Roosevelt said. "This thing obviously is, and we, too, obviously are, so we all must be. Real. It's that simple."

"'S what I was saying earlier," said Eli.

"No." Mitch shook his head. Then he was distracted. To Roosevelt he said, "If you're an alien, where are you from?"

Roosevelt nodded. "Gacrux."

Eli perked up. "Gacrux? How far away is that?"

Ice cream, Mitch thought. Hungry.

Roosevelt shook his head. "Here's the thing," he said. "Simple logic. Listen carefully."

"Whore of loony ideas," Mitch muttered under his breath, but nobody heard him.

"If all space is simultaneously present," Roosevelt held up one finger, "and space and time are really only different aspects of the same thing," a second finger, "then all time is equally present. T.S. Eliot had this figured out: 'Time past and time future / What might have been and what has been / Point to one end, which is always present.'"

"Where the hell did you read T.S. Eliot?" Mitch said.

"Truth?" Roosevelt popped another can of Pabst. "They give us a class on what to say to humans. It's big on sequential logic and quotations from poems,"

Mitch and Eli gauged the degree of condescension in this. They began to feel small.

Eli stood up, breaking the stasis. "That's what I was saying all day!"

It was Roosevelt and Mitch's turn to speak together. "What?"

"What might have been and what has been," Eli said. "Truth and fiction. Mishmash." He flailed his arms, then collapsed back into his recliner. "Shit, you can't expect me to remember it all now."

Mitch was unable to resist. "Hemingway and the Shell guys."

"Those fuckers," Eli said vengefully. "The thing was, I was thinking what difference did it make whether or not the bakery was really the place where Hemingway got the idea for the story. Once you start wondering, it might as well be true. Your mind has already explored the possibilities, assigned connections, delved into variations and uncertainties ..." He petered out. "Roosevelt knows what I'm talking about."

"He does?" Mitch looked at Roosevelt.

"Look at Gus," Roosevelt said. Mitch did. Gus was dreaming, his front paws twitching, his upper lip curling and relaxing, one of his back legs scratching at the porch's weather-beaten boards. "What's he dreaming about?"

"How am I supposed to know?" Mitch said.

"Guess."

Mitch considered. "He's either gamboling through a hot dog plantation or biting the mailman."

"Okay. What does the mailman think?"

"Gus is dreaming the mailman, dude. He doesn't think anything; he's made up."

Roosevelt pointed at the time machine.

Mitch began to sulk. "You're saying my dog's dreamed mailman is as real as I am," he said resentfully.

"Yup," Roosevelt said. "It's all as real as you are."

"Bullshit," Mitch said. "Then nobody would ever make anything up."

"Sure they would. They do. Gus is making up that mailman, but he exists somewhere, but the invention is still invention because Gus didn't know that. And even if you know on an abstract level that everything exists somewhere, you still invent it. Go read Borges, man. Incomplete knowledge of the universe preserves our ability to imagine and invent."

This rationale did little to console, and Mitch resented getting a literary-epistemological lecture from an alien. "What are you doing here, anyway?" he said finally.

"Hey, yeah," Eli piped up suddenly, his exuberance signaling the approach of a non sequitur. "And with Hemingway, the other thing was that the kid in the diner or whatever, he looks at the killers like they're from different planets."

Something about this statement, perhaps only Eli's tone of voice, suggested to Mitch that it was significant. But he couldn't figure out why. "Where does it say that?" he said.

"It's all in how you read it, man."

Again, Mitch looked at Roosevelt. Again, Roosevelt shrugged.

"Oh for Christ's sake," Mitch said.

* * *

OR IT COULD HAVE HAPPENED THIS WAY:

Many beers and many bowls later, after the discovery of Roosevelt's extraterrestrial origins, the three of them sit deep within the fragrant cushions of broken-down recliners. Someone tells a joke, and they laugh.

"I have a confession to make," Mitch says.

"Confess," Eli commands.

"All of this is my fault. If I hadn't read that article in the paper this morning, none of this would have happened." He holds up a Liberty dime as proof. Roosevelt and Eli look back and forth from Lady Liberty to Mitch Packard.

"What?" they say.

"It's like this. Every morning when I read the newspaper, one of the articles sort of becomes necessary for me to get through the day. This morning I read something about the age of the universe, looking for planets, extraterrestrial life ..." They're still staring at him. "Don't you get it?" Mitch says. "I made all this happen. Roosevelt's an alien because I read the paper this morning."

There is a soft pop, and a tiny glimmering machine appears next to the porch ashtray.

"That," Roosevelt says, pointing his beer can at it, "is what solipsism gets you."

* * *

WHAT IT ALL BOILS DOWN TO IS THIS, this one end that is eternally present:

Everyone has gone to sleep except Mitch Packard. Roosevelt the alien is stretched out on the orange sectional couch in Pearl Street's living room. Eli is crashed in his room behind the kitchen, Jane's Addiction playing in his earphones. Gus still lies, head between his freckled paws, at the head of the porch stairs.

Mitch alone remains awake. He is preoccupied with the nefariousness of the universe. No immediate prospect of reconciliation with Trina presents itself. His lungs, tired and abused, agree to one last cigarette; the afterimage of the match puts him in mind of stars. Cygnus, Centauri, Polaris. Gacrux.

In an infinite universe, all things exist. Axiomatic. Mitch smokes his cigarette. Closing his eyes, he puts it down. Damn those guys at the Shell station.

Okay, Mitch thinks, slumping into sleep on Pearl Street's sagging porch with a cigarette burning down in the cockpit of the model time machine. It's an old idea. Might as well be true. But. But.

But I'm as real as whoever's writing me. Real as whoever's reading.

His paws hanging over the porch step, Gus dreams of chasing the mailman through perfectly manicured rows of bushes, their ripening hot dogs waving ever so slightly in an endless summer breeze.

Pictures from an Expedition

Who are they kidding, man? Sure, she wanted to stay behind.
And sure, she destroyed her VR rig. Ooooookay. I believe it.
—sockpuppet446, in Rod Shaver's Forum, 17 March 2012

There were those who had argued caution. Wait until 2014, they said, when there will be unpowered return trajectories available. Wait until 2018, when the fast-transit trajectories are the best. Remember what happened to *Apollo 13*.

But it was 2009, and humans were going to Mars.

Fidelis Emuwa was one of them. His grandfather had been a miner killed in the Biafran War. His father survived to become a doctor in Waltham, Massachusetts. And now he was going to step onto another planet.

When he looked at *Argos 1*, Fidelis Emuwa saw progress.

* * *

"And *Argos 1* has separated from the International Space Station. You'll see now that it's rotating its thruster cones away from the station—a little astronaut's courtesy—before touching off the jets that will take David Fontenot, Jami Salter, Edgar Villareal, Katherine Yi, Fidelis Emuwa, and Deborah Green on humankind's first voyage to another planet. Wait—there's a transmission coming through from the pilot, David Fontenot."

"This is for my old professor Chapman: 'Happy he who like Ulysses has made a glorious voyage.'"

"Is that Homer there, David?"

"No, that's some sixteenth-century French poet, I think. Ask Dr. C. He—"

"Well, stirring words to begin mankind's journey into the uncharted paths of our solar system. Ladies and gentlemen, on November 17, 2009, humankind began our glorious voyage to the stars."

* * *

ROD SHAVER'S FORUM: WHAT DOES THE MARTIAN EXPEDITION MEAN TO YOU?

cosmo0omsoc> It means that we are going to settle once and for all whether we're alone. If there isn't life on Mars, there isn't life anywhere.

luvjamixox> It m33nz Jami Salter's going 2 bring « the sporz, & I want her 2 assiml8 me 1st.

sockpuppet446> It means that even when we go to Mars, we have to look like the cast of Sesame Street. I mean, come on. You've got your black guy, your Asian, your Hispanic. Three men and three women. And Deborah Green's Jewish, isn't she? Where are the Hindus and Eskimos? Jesus.

luvjamixox> Sesame St?

thebeaminyrown> It means that a hundred million people will starve to death who might otherwise have been fed.

sockpuppet446> Look it up.

chariot> It means, when you look in the face, the face looks back.

* * *

EILEEN AUFDEMBERGE LOOKED UP AT THE SKY. I wish it was night, she thought. If it was night, I might be able to see their ship when they fire the engines. It would be like a star coming to life. Or like a last wave from the deck of the ship as it pulls away from the pier. She resisted the impulse to lift her hand.

"Mom?" Jared was there, looking where she was looking. "What do you see?" His ten-year-old face was puzzled. No face, thought Eileen, looks so puzzled as a puzzled little boy's.

"I was looking for your Aunt Debbie," she said, and his frown deepened.

"Come on, Mom," he said. "Aunt Debbie's over the Indian Ocean right now. You can't see her from here."

Thank God I hadn't waved, Eileen thought.

* * *

HOTVEGAS BETTING LINES ON *ARGOS 1*, 16 NOVEMBER 2009:

Odds on *Argos 1* reaching Mars: 1 to 4
Odds on *Argos 1* landing successfully: 7 to 5
Odds that the fuel plant and supplies will survive their landing: 11 to 7
Odds that all six *Argos* crewmembers survive the mission: 3 to 1

* * *

"THREE MEN, THREE WOMEN. WHAT DO YOU BET there's some serious space hubba hubba?"

"Except they say it's almost impossible to, you know, get a grip without gravity. I'm serious. NASA did studies and shit."

"Where there's a will, there's a way, man. I'm thinking, let's see, they'll pair off about the time they get past the Moon."

"If they haven't already. I heard there's an astronaut ritual, they pick someone to welcome the space virgin to orbit. So they must have figured something out."

"Fontenot's the pilot, he'll get first pick."

"Jami Salter."

<reverent pause>

"Damn."

"Then we have our minority representatives. Villareal goes with who, the Chinese girl or Debbie Green?"

"I'm thinking the Chinese girl. Yi."

"So that leaves the black guy with Green. Black and Green. What color will the kids be?"

<laughter>

<pause>

"No way he's going to be able to keep his hands off Jami Salter."

"Shit, man, that's why they brought the" <sound of knuckles on table> "NASA Nigger-Knocker!"

<louder laughter>

* * *

FROM THE *NEW YORK TIMES*, DECEMBER 30, 2009:

"Given the fact that the crew was going to be together for two years, we thought it best that they come from a similar national background," explained Gates Aerospace spokesman Roland Threlkeld. "But, to avoid too much homogeneity, we deliberately sifted our candidate pool for potential Marsnauts who would represent America as a nation."

Gates went on to deny accusations made by NASA and the Cato Institute that Gates Aerospace was more interested in a photogenic crew than a competent one. "Well, that's absurd. I can only guess that this kind of mud-slinging is a result of sour grapes on NASA's part. They've said from the beginning that a Mars mission couldn't be mounted sooner than their timetable, and here we are five years earlier. And the Cato Institute would blame affirmative action for the African origin of mankind."

* * *

ZERO GRAVITY MADE JAMI SALTER'S BLADDER FEEL like it was about the size of a thimble. This wasn't a standard astronaut reaction, and she had done her best to conceal it from the years-long gauntlet of clipboards and lab coats she'd had to run to get here.

Some interplanetary sex symbol, she kidded herself. Running to the john every hour. But she was due to make the crew's daily media dispatch today, and she didn't want to be drumming her feet on the deck in front of the time-delayed pupils of Earth. The PR hacks at Gates had told her that her dispatches drew ratings fifty percent better than any other crew member's, and even though she knew this was just a temporary skewing of the audience composition toward young, male, and horny, she had come to feel an odd sort of duty to live up to the standard that had been set for her. So she washed her hair when it was her day to dispatch, and touched a little makeup here and there. Katherine and Debbie kidded her about it, but they knew the score, and Jami thought they were a little grateful that she was taking the pressure off them.

Said gratitude did not prevent them from nicknaming her Barbarella, though.

All in a day's work, when the day was spent working for the largest private space venture in the history of humankind. They were seventy-five million kilometers from Earth, and the time delay was now almost four minutes each way. The lag hung between *Argos 1* and Earth as much as the distance itself. Every time they spoke to friends or family or (more often) media, it felt more and more like they were speaking to the silence and less like any real human beings existed on the other side of the commlink.

She had written those words down in a leather-bound journal she was keeping: *speaking to the silence*. It had been hard not to write them again. And again.

Barbarella is not coping, she said to herself.

* * *

EBONY FREYTAG, MSNBCNN: JAMI, HOW DO YOU LIKE interplanetary space?

Jami Salter: Well, I haven't been outside in it, so all I can tell you is that it looks pretty much like space looks like from the Moon. (laughs)

EF: How big is Earth from where you are now?

JS: Tiny. About one-fiftieth the apparent size of the Moon from Earth, and shrinking all the time. And we're starting to be able to resolve Mars as a disk.

EF: Is the crew having any problems?

JS: It's surprising how little friction there has been. We're all getting along great. After all, it doesn't do any good to get angry out here; it's not like you can take a walk to cool off. All of us are very careful to talk out differences, make sure we know where the points of disagreement are and what can be done to resolve problems.

EF: One last question. How do you manage to look so great when you're seventy-five million kilometers from a beauty salon?

JS: Can't answer that one, Ebony. Us astro-girls have to have some secrets.

* * *

"How do I manage to look so great?" she asked Edgar and Katherine, who as usual were sitting just out of camera range commenting on the interview. They made an interesting pair, Edgar stocky and Mayan-looking next to Katherine, the tallest of the group and rail-thin except for a roundness in her cheeks. Jami kept thinking they looked like cousins, with their epicanthic folds and their identical spiky haircuts.

"I say genes. Katherine's got her money on plastic surgery and good lighting." Edgar pushed back from the table and jumped toward the stairwell that led up to the crew berths. He loved the low gravity. It brought out the monkey in him.

"Good lighting, in this can?" Jami looked at Katherine and they both laughed.

The commlink pinged. "Your adoring public," Katherine said, and winked.

"A Martian's work is never done." Jami tapped the screen to open the link.

* * *

<A SPLIT SCREEN: Jami Salter on one side, Filomena Huxtable on the other. Running footers identify Jami as *ARGOS 1* ELECTRONICS SPECIALIST; Filomena Huxtable is tagged as KTCM SCIENCE/CULTURE REPORTER. Behind Jami, the *Argos* common area: polished lockers, a microwave oven, a live camera feed of the Sierra Nevada. A studio audience is visible behind Filomena.>

F: So you're the mission electronics specialist.

J: That's right.

F: What does that involve, exactly?

<animated schematics of various missions systems pop up as Jami speaks>

J: Well, the success of our mission depends on our ability to communicate with each other and with Gates mission control back in Houston. My job is to make sure that the communications gear keeps working, and the navigational and laboratory computers, and basically anything else that uses electricity.

F: So when your hair dryer goes on the fritz, you'll be able to fix it.

<laughter from audience; Jami's smile tilts>

J: Well, we've all gotten our Mars cuts here, so nobody brought a hair dryer.

But if anything goes on the fritz, it'll be my job to get it shipshape again.

F: Including the space suits? We hear you have all kinds of camera gear in those suits.

<as Jami speaks, various areas of the suit light up. Camera zooms in for close-ups>

J: That's right. And monitors, and transmitters, and temperature control systems, and everything else needed to keep one of us warm and happy for three days.

F: Three days? I hope they're self-cleaning, too. <louder laughs from audience> Seriously, those suits look great. Do you know who designed them?

J: I don't. That's not really my department.

<vid of Jami, with longer hair and a deep tan, modeling spacesuit without helmet; crowd erupts>

F: Well, honey, wearing them is definitely your department!

* * *

DAVID FONTENOT DIDN'T WANT THE GREAT WHITE HERO LABEL, any more than he sensed Jami was comfortable with the Mission Babe tag. But there it was, and he wasn't about to take a knife to his face or stop working out just so people would stop taking his picture.

Especially not now, when in less than six hours he and Jami would be the first human beings to set foot on Mars. They'd drawn straws, and when he and Jami had won, the reaction from the PR folks at Gates had been decidedly mixed. A photogenic first step was good, but a multiculturally photogenic first step was better. Would the crew reconsider, in light of their standard-bearing situation, representing all nations and races, et cetera?

All of them remembered the lesson of *Apollo 11*: everybody remembers Armstrong. All of them wanted to be first onto the ground.

When the answer came back to Gates, it was negative. Fair was fair.

* * *

FROM DAVID FONTENOT'S TESTIMONY BEFORE THE BEXAR COUNTY GRAND JURY, JULY 11, 2012:

We all of us felt that the farther we got from Earth, the farther we got from any kind of connection with human civilization. Not that we were turning into barbarians or resorting to cannibalism; just that everything on Earth had stopped applying about the time we cleared the orbit of the moon. The word alone doesn't even begin to describe it.

I read once the diary of a sailor who was marooned in the eighteenth century for killing one of his shipmates. He records his slow starvation, his efforts to find food and ration water. And he spends a lot of time thinking about his sins. The more he gets resigned to the fact that he's going to die, the more he starts trying to come to terms with what he's done wrong. He never admits that he was wrong for killing his shipmate, but he does think about all kinds of other things that he should repent.

I forget his name, but his diary was found next to his skeleton a long time after he died. All of us, during the time we spent on Mars, I think felt like we were writing a diary like that in our heads.

* * *

The odd thing was that nothing had gone catastrophically wrong. Every detail of the mission had come off more or less as planned, from separation from the International Space Station right on up to injection into Mars orbit and the exhilarating, exalted space of time when they had fallen out of the sky to a planet no human had ever touched. The ERV was where it was supposed to be, the power plant was churning out water and oxygen, the rocks cried out to be chipped and sampled and mined for new discoveries. Plants were already growing in the greenhouse next to the main station building. No group of explorers had ever been so well prepared.

So why, wondered Katherine, were they all so damned morose?

The commlink pinged. For Jami, most likely. It almost always was.

"They were supposed to encrypt us," she grumbled.

Fidelis shrugged and stroked his mustache. "I always figured someone would find their way through."

"I mean, we're on Mars, here. It's dangerous. Would help if the goddamn commlink didn't ping every two minutes with someone wanting to know Jami's goddamn cup size."

Katherine sighed. They had all just seen too much of each other during the transit. Gates had done the best it could to give them adequate living space and recreational facilities, but no matter how you sliced it, going to Mars still meant nine months in a tin can with five other people every bit as driven and opinionated and sure of themselves as she was.

"You think now that we're here, everyone will relax a little?" Edgar stood next to her looking out at the Valles Marineris. They had landed and set up at the head of the great canyon system, where its stupendous channel broadened out of the chaos of the Noctis Labyrinthus. One theory had it that sublimation of liquid water caused the landslides that pocked the canyon system's walls, and satellite observations predicted large amounts of water locked up in the crust. *Argos 1* had come to find it, and to find out if Gates could make money exploiting it.

Eight hundred miles to the west-northwest, the giant shield volcanoes reared up: Arsia Mons, Pavonis Mons, Ascraeus Mons. A thousand miles beyond them, Olympus Mons. All of them, even Jami and David, dropped their voices a notch when saying those words: Olympus Mons. As if they all half-believed that the gods really did live there.

Which was foolish, of course. None of them were really religious. But *Olympus Mons…*

"I don't know, Ed," Katherine said. "I hope so. I hope everyone straightens out so we can really get some work done."

The strange Martian light caught the planes of Edgar's face. A mechanical engineer by training, he'd taken doctoral coursework in geology during preparation for the expedition, intending to use this unprecedented fieldwork as material for his dissertation. He always complained about being the guy everyone looked to when wrenches needed turning; when they got back to Earth, he said, he'd finish his PhD and never touch a tool other than a rock hammer as long as he lived.

Argos' primary geologist was Deborah Green. She and Edgar and Katherine had been assigned a series of expeditions into the canyons to look for water and life. In that order. The Gates people realized the stir that life would make back home, but shareholders cared more about the commercial potential of water. In the words of Roland Threlkeld, Gates mission liaison: "Look for water. If you find life, great, but look for water."

Katherine, as the resident life scientist, tried to stifle her aggravation at the skewing of the expedition's priorities. They had fifteen months on Mars, until October of next year; plenty of time to indulge some personal hunches without the Gates people having to know, and still get back to Earth for the New York Olympics in 2012.

Fidelis joined them at the window. The light did something odd to his face, too; something about the texture of his skin that Katherine couldn't identify. He looked out at the landscape of Mars, and she could see the want in his eyes. "When are you going out?"

"Scheduled for tomorrow."

She watched him track the side canyon they would take the next morning down into the head of Valles Marineris. "I know you want to go, Fidelis," she said.

He nodded. "I wanted to go tomorrow. Way things are around here, I'm in all kinds of a hurry to get out."

This was a lot of emotion, coming from him. Katherine paused. He was the mission physician, but she was an MD, too, and both of them had undergone training in psychology and psychiatry. "Are you okay?"

Fidelis cocked his head to the side when he looked at her. "None of us are okay, Katherine," he said. After another long look out the window, he headed for the door. "Good luck tomorrow."

* * *

From HotVegas, April 7, 2010:

Odds that the crew will find commercial quantities of water: 8 to 5
Odds that the crew will find evidence of vanished civilizations: 150 to 1
Odds that the crew will find microbial life: 3 to 1
Odds that the crew will find multicellular life: 25 to 1
Odds that the crew will be killed by Martians: 175 to 1

* * *

"Killed by Martians?" Deborah said incredulously. "Killed by *Martians!*"

"I think it's a wonder the odds are only 175 to 1," Edgar said. "I figured every nutcase with twenty bucks to blow would push it down to 10 to 1 or so. Score one for rationality."

Deborah was never sure whether she should be taking him seriously. Quoting odds on the Argos crew being killed by Martians was rational? Well, yes. It was. But betting…!

She scrolled through some of the other odds. "Well, now. This is interesting."

Odds that violence will break out among the crew: 1 to 3
 as a result of sexual jealousy: 2 to 1
Odds that a crew member will be murdered: 12 to 1
Odds that the murdered crew member will be Jami Salter: 6 to 5
Odds that the murdered crew member will be Edgar Villareal: 3 to 1
Odds that the murdered crew member will be Fidelis Emuwa: 7 to 4
Odds that the murdered crew member will be David Fontenot: 8 to 1
Odds that the murdered crew member will be Katherine Yi: 5 to 1
Odds that the murdered crew member will be Deborah Green: 2 to 1
Odds that more than one crew member will be murdered: 22 to 1
Odds that the Argos mission will fail due to the murder of one or more
    crew members: 35 to 1
Odds that all six Argos crewmembers survive the mission: 9 to 4

Edgar came to look over her shoulder. "So you're more likely to get it than I am. What did you do?"

"You haven't heard?" She popped a new browser window and played a short video clip.

Ebony Freytag: So you've slept with Deborah Green.
Statuesque Blonde: On numerous occasions.
EF: And we're not talking about a pajama party here.
SB: <with a wink> Well, it never stayed that way.
EF: She doesn't seem like your type, does she?
SB: Deb? Honey, she's everybody's type.

"Yikes," Edgar said. "She looks a lot like Jami."

"For God's sake, Edgar, she's six inches taller than Jami and her eyes are brown." Deborah closed the window, cutting off a titillated, exultant roar from Ebony's studio audience. "I'm not only a dyke, I'm a slutty dyke. Who better to kill if there's going to be killing?"

Edgar was looking over the HotVegas odds again. "Well, you're not as bad off as Jami and Fidelis." The commlink pinged.

"Half of the people on Earth who are in love with Jami would love to see her killed," Deborah said. "And a lot of the rest of them are figuring that Fidelis won't be able to keep his pants zipped."

Edgar laughed. "Fidelis? Our doctor-monk? Wonder what they'd say if they knew about us."

She laughed. "Well, when Ebony Freytag interviews you, make sure you tell her how happy I was to get out of *Argos* and back on the ground." Her hand found his, brought it to her mouth. "I sure am glad to have gravity all going in one direction again."

* * *

ROD SHAVER'S FORUM, JULY 30, 2010: Is Deborah Green a lesbian? Is she having an affair with Katherine Yi? Where does Edgar Villarreal come into it?

cosmo0omsoc> All of you people are ignoring the most important thing.
godsavenger> WAIT AND SEE. NOT ALL OF THEM WILL RETURN. GOD WILL EXACT HIS JUSTICE.
luvjamixox> Justice?
godsavenger> THEY KNOWINGLY BROUGHT A SODOMITE WITH THEM. WHO KNOWS HOW MANY OF THE CREW SHE'S CORRUPTED BY NOW? DO YOU THINK GOD WILL STAND BY AND ALLOW THIS TO HAPPEN?
thebeaminyrown> No real Christian takes this kind of crap seriously.

chariot> When they come back, it won't matter whether they're gay or straight or what color or anything. What they bring back will destroy all of our petty disagreements, destroy religion.

godsavenger> YOU'VE ALL HAD YOUR CHANCES.

* * *

After all the time they'd spent looking for water, it was almost an anticlimax when they found the lichens in crevices on the sunny sides of Valles Marineris channels. Edgar and Deborah were conducting a hydrological assessment of a series of collapses in a canyon wall, and right before they were due to wrap everything up, she leaned over and said, "Well, I'll be damned."

"What?"

"I think this is lichen."

He went over to look, and it looked like lichen to him, too, worked into the seams of individual rocks that had broken away from the canyon wall. They took a number of samples and went back to the rover wondering when it would hit them that they were the first people to discover life outside Earth.

Back in the lab, Katherine took the samples and ran some quick tests. "Sure enough," she said. "Lichen. I'm going to sequence the algae and pipe it back on the hotline."

That night, they were a little more boisterous then usual around the dinner table. David cracked a bottle of Laphroaig he'd been saving for a special occasion, and they toasted each other. "But did we find any water?" Jami cracked, and laughed a little too loudly at her own joke. Of course they all knew there was water, they could see traces of it wherever they looked, but their evidence of life was quite a bit more convincing than their evidence of water. Gates would be happy for the good PR, but their expectations were more geared toward long-term financial viability. And everyone at the table knew how expectations were beginning to oppress Jami.

* * *

InkStainedWretch.Com's Headline Search, August 30, 2010:

LIFE ON MARS!
Life on Mars
Life on Mars Questioned
Critics Question ET Claims
Wait and See on Life Claims, Experts Say
Mars Life Could Be Native to Earth, Scientist Says

Biotech Stocks Volatile on Mars Life Claims

* * *

Ebony Freytag, MSNBCNN: So you've discovered life on another planet.

Jami Salter: Well, I haven't personally. It was Edgar and Deborah.

Edgar Villareal: It was Deborah.

EF: Deborah Green, you're the first person to set eyes on alien life. How's it feel?

Deborah Green: Exciting. It's humbling. I'm not sure any of us have really gotten our minds around it yet.

EF: Jami, tell us how it happened.

JS: I wasn't there. You should really ask Ed and Deborah.

EF: We'll get the science from them later, don't you worry. But our viewers want to know what it was like.

JS: I can tell you it wasn't like I thought it might be. There we were, on Mars, with Martian life in our lab, and it was wondrous, but … well, we had a drink, toasted ourselves, danced around the campfire a bit and went to bed.

EF: There's a lot to do tomorrow, isn't there?

JS: Always. Always a lot to do tomorrow. So I should sign off here and let you talk to Deborah and Ed.

EF: I think we've about used up our bandwidth, unfortunately. We'll get the science from the nets; I'm sure Deborah Green and Edgar Villareal will be only too happy to tell us their stories. Talk to you next time.

* * *

"Well, I guess we shouldn't be surprised, should we?" Edgar said when they'd broken the link.

Don't get angry, Deb told herself. You knew this would happen.

She kept her temper, but only just. Eileen, she thought. My little sister, tuning in to hear about her big sister who discovered life on another planet.

And getting Jami Salter.

"Sorry, Deborah," Jami said, and that was the worst of it, she was such a fundamentally decent person, and had the grace at least to be screwed up by the relentless attention focused on her. Still…

Ping.

"Fuck it, never mind. Why don't you get that? It's for you," Deborah said, and didn't think she'd snapped. "I discover life on Mars, they want to talk to you about it. That's how it works. We've known that for a while."

"That's just Ebony," Jami said. "You'll have all the tech nets after you." She laughed, short and bitter. "God knows they're not interested in anything I'm doing."

Ping.

Deborah exchanged a quick glance with Edgar, saw that they were thinking the same thing. Jami upset because she wasn't being recognized? She was an engineer; nobody ever recognized engineers unless the bridge fell down. And she was a pilot, and nobody ever recognized the pilot until the crash.

"Public figuring's a bitch," Edgar said. Deborah was startled. She could see Jami was, too. Edgar, saying *bitch*?

They laughed, Edgar at his joke and the two women at him. Public figuring. Ping.

* * *

HotVegas, August 29, 2010:

Odds that lichen is most sophisticated life on Mars: 175 to 1
Odds that the "discovery" is a hoax: 1 to 1
Odds that Mars lichen descended from Earth species: 4 to 1
Odds that Earth lichen descended from Mars species: 5 to 8
Odds that human beings are descended from Mars lichen: 7 to 5
Odds that all six *Argos* crewmembers survive the mission: 7 to 1

* * *

ROD SHAVER'S FORUM, August 29, 2010: Is it real? Does it matter?

chariot> Of course they discovered life. Does anybody out there seriously think they weren't going to?

thebeaminyrown> Does anybody out there seriously think they'd let us believe they hadn't? Come on. Gates needs this trip to pay off. Water's one way; ETBOs are another. And let's not forget that Gates has a piece of all vids, interviews, even books on all the crew. When D. Green talks to *Scientific American*, creds flow into Gates accounts. No way they were going to let an opportunity like that go by.

cosmo0omsoc> So you don't think they found anything?

chariot> Of course they found something.

thebeaminyrown> I don't know whether they did or not. It's possible. I'm just saying that we were going to be told they'd found something whether they did or not.

cosmo0omsoc> But it's lichen, man. Not like little green men or a big monolith or something.

thebeaminyrown> The ways of Gates are devious and subtle, amigos. Just keep your eyes open, is all I'm saying.

* * *

THE SEQUENCE CAME BACK FROM THE GATES DATABASE with three beautiful words: NO SPECIES MATCH.

"Life on Mars," Edgar breathed. For a while all of them stood around the sample containers watching the brown lichen.

Ping.

Ping.

Ping ping ping.

"We're watching brown lichen, people," David said presently.

* * *

INKSTAINEDWRETCH.COM'S HEADLINE SEARCH, AUGUST 31, 2010:

ARE WE ALL MARTIANS?
Panspermia Gets New Lease on Media Life
Humankind Not Descended from Martians, Pope Says
Society for Christian Medicine Floats *Argos* Crew Quarantine
Results Still Not Definitive about Mars Life
Lichen: Symbiotic Explorer

* * *

THEY SPENT THE NEXT TWO MONTHS ABSORBED in the problem of the lichen: where it grew, what could kill it, what made it grow, whether it performed the same ecological function on Mars that it did on Earth. Gates, of course, made sure that they spent most of their time looking for water, but hell, they'd found the original lichen while looking for water; it wasn't that hard to make one activity look like the other.

And they found water, too.

Again Deborah was the lucky party. Late on a surveying mission, irascible from the grit of Martian dust in her underwear and her eyes and her teeth and her socks, she'd said to herself: Fine. One more sweep. Fill out one more grid. Then back to base and I'm not going out for a week. A fucking week. No more peroxide taste, no more dust in the crack of my ass. Seven days.

Something rumbled below her feet.

She was forty meters from the lip of a canyon wall that dropped something like three hundred meters to a titanic jumble of fallen rock. Edgar was about a hundred meters away from her. Both of them dropped their instruments and ran toward the edge.

Deborah threw herself on her stomach and scooted forward until her head was hanging over the sheer drop. Below her, mist swirled above the rockfall at the bottom of the canyon. Carbon dioxide; they saw that all the time. They'd even seen water mist once in a while. Never water in commercially useful quantities, though. Never until this huge beautiful plume that came exploding out of the canyon wall two hundred meters below her pounding heart, eclipsing the carbon-dioxide mist in a thick fog of sublimating water.

She was screaming into her mike, and she screamed louder when the vapor cloud rose up to envelop her. The world went white, and Deborah opened her mouth and let the frustration of the past two months chase the joy, the never-to-be-repeated joy of this moment, out of her mouth and through her mask and into the thin wet Martian air.

"Deborah!" "Deb, Jesus!" "Deb! You there? Come in, Deb!"

"Toggle your cams to me!" she shouted. "God, look at this!"

She heard their exclamations as they saw through her cam. Water beaded on her mask, held for a moment by her body heat before it sublimated away. Something gripped her hand, and Deborah started before she realized it was Edgar, talking to her on their private channel: "You again, Miz Green. Lucky I have you around."

She squeezed his hand through their bulky gloves, and in that moment a ridiculous thought flashed through her mind: *Oh God I'd better be sure to shower before tonight or we're going to scrape each other raw.* She laughed out loud, and Edgar joined in. Over their mikes they heard the rest of the crew shouting, clapping each other on the back, calling them to come back in and start the celebration.

* * *

HotVegas, November 9, 2010:

Odds that *Argos 1* crew will suffer infection from Martian life: 1 to 4
Odds that Martian infection will kill *Argos 1* crew member: 7 to 2
Odds that *Argos 1* crew will carry dangerous microbes back to Earth: 2 to 5
Odds that all six *Argos* crewmembers survive the mission: 8 to 1

* * *

LATE IN THE NIGHT, EDGAR ASLEEP BESIDE HER, Deborah remembered stepping out of the airlock into Bohlen Station and thinking as she did that she would really have to find out why Jami had suggested they call the station that. A character in a book, Jami had said.

Katherine had been there inside the airlock door with a puzzled expression on her round face. "Again," she said. "You, again."

Yes, Deborah had wanted to say. Me again. But the look on Katherine's face was so pained; she had wanted very badly to discover life on Mars herself, or at least to pronounce life absent, and then her grand moment was usurped by a geologist. Who then found water, too. It was all a little much, Deborah thought.

"It's your work they're going to remember," she'd said to Katherine. "You're the one who did the sequence and all that. I was just in the right place."

"Thank you," Katherine had said. "Thank you for believing that."

* * *

ROD SHAVER'S FORUM, NOVEMBER 8, 2010: GHOULIES AND GHOSTIES AND…?

sockpuppet446> You heard it here first: one of them's already sick. They're going to cover it up, but watch and see if they all come back. They won't.

thebeaminyrown> Hooray, Shaver's paranoids are alive and well.

sockpuppet446> Whatever, beam. You wait until they come back and spread it to you.

chariot> Whatever it is, it couldn't be worse than the shit we've already got. I'll challenge any Martian microbe to ten rounds with HIV[3].

luvjamixox> Funny sh!t coming from u, chariot.

chariot> What they're going to bring back is much much stranger than we can imagine.

* * *

INKSTAINEDWRETCH.COM'S HEADLINE SEARCH, NOVEMBER 9, 2010:

WET MARS
Mars Crew 2 for 2
Gates Stock Up 37 Percent on Water News
GM, Airbus, Vishnu Ready Mars Plans
"Life Is Interesting, Water Makes Money," Says Chair of NSF
Ebony Freytag Sued Over Naked Jami Vid—Fake?

* * *

PING.

Ν Ν Ν

IT WAS NEVER SO GOOD AGAIN. ONCE they'd found life, found water, basked in their accolades, there was still nearly a year to spend on Mars and seven months of sandpapering each other's nerves on the voyage home. The Gates scientific crew thought up more than enough experiments and missions to keep them busy, but their real work was done. They had established that Mars held both life and enough water to justify colonization. Already a dozen Mars colonies were moving from pencil-sketch imagining to nuts-and-bolts reality. In ten years, Mars would be utterly changed.

"We'd better enjoy it while we can," said David. "Who knows if we'll get to come back?"

"Would you want to?"

Jami's question surprised him. They were running the latest in an endless series of inspections of joints, hoses, bearings, and seals—anything that could be eroded by peroxides or clogged by dust. Which was to say, everything. They'd taken to doing it in pairs, and when it had become apparent that the pairs were rubber-stamping each other (after Katherine and Fidelis had both missed a badly corroded seal that then blew, freezing the station water supply), they'd taken to sending out pairs who weren't getting along with each other. This meant that Fidelis hardly ever got inspection duty, since everyone liked him.

It also meant that David and Jami were at last going to have to get out into the open whatever it was that had been hanging between them since they'd been anointed *Argos 1* media darlings. Or so, they both knew, Fidelis was hoping.

So here we go, David thought. "Yeah," he said. "I think I would."

Jami looked at him for a long time. The sun was setting, the Martian landscape settling from golds and reds back into evening browns. There was enough dust on her faceplate that David couldn't see her expression.

"I bet you would," she said eventually.

* * *

EBONY FREYTAG'S SHOW BECAME THE CREW'S GUILTY PLEASURE. On a Tuesday in December, they watched as she devoted an entire show to random things her audience wanted to know about the *Argos* crew. Did they lose a lot of weight in space? Were they more religious than when they'd left? What were they really doing?

And why, someone asked, was everyone so heated up about David Fontenot when Fidelis Emuwa was so gorgeous?

"I guess Fidelis is a pretty good-looking guy," David said.

Katherine snorted. "Why do we watch this garbage? Just because they want us to be a sideshow. Why do we let them?"

The two of them were sitting in the common room. Fidelis came down from the dorm level. "Are we a sideshow?"

"When was the last time we got a call from someone other than Gates about either exobiology or water?"

David got up for a cup of tea. He wanted to stay to the side of this discussion. After his exchange with Jami a few days before, he'd tried to be more sensitive to the mood of the crew, and what he'd seen thus far wasn't encouraging. Holiday blues, he thought; all of us get a little crabby around the New Year. He hoped that's all it was.

Deborah came in from the direction of the lab. "Another day, another goddamn revolutionary discovery about Martian geological history. I'm sick of it."

"Maybe we should take a couple of days off," David said, and then wished he hadn't spoken. Where were Jami and Edgar? Edgar was probably tinkering with something, cleaning out a ball joint somewhere or changing the rover's battery terminals. Jami, who knew, Jami was doing her Martian Bedouin-mystic thing somewhere nearby. She had enough to do keeping station computer equipment up and communicative, but recently she'd developed a tendency to wander off once things had reached a bare minimum functionality. Katherine and Deborah were getting sharp about it.

* * *

HotVegas, February 11, 2011:

Odds that one or more *Argos* crewmembers has attempted suicide: 4 to 1
Odds that one or more *Argos* crewmembers will attempt suicide: 2 to 3
Odds that all six *Argos* crewmembers survive the mission: 6 to 1

* * *

DAVID GATHERED THE *ARGOS* CREW IN THE STATION GREENHOUSE. All of them liked it there. It was warm, it smelled good, it wasn't brown. "I think we ought to have a chat. All of us."

Everyone settled into a rough circle. David looked around the group, saw that Deborah wasn't next to Edgar and Jami was between Fidelis and Katherine. So they hadn't arranged themselves according to cliques. That was good. "Katherine," he said, "I know this is more your territory—"

"Fidelis is more of a psych guy than I am," she said. "I was a surgeon."

He let the interruption pass, then plunged ahead. "I'm concerned about our collective well-being here."

The wind kicked up, rattling dust and gravel against the greenhouse walls.

"So am I," said Fidelis. David was looking at him just before he spoke, and he saw Fidelis look quickly at Jami and then away. Worried about Jami? he wondered. Or is Fidelis worried about himself, and Jami's the reason?

"I think we're all worried," Katherine said. "We're on another planet, halfway through a three-year mission. It's lethal and ugly outside, and we're all sick of looking at each other, so inside isn't much better. All of this was in the mission prep. We knew it would happen."

Edgar cut in. "That's not the same as dealing with it when it does."

"But anticipating the problem at least gives us a basis for dealing with it," Fidelis said calmly.

"So let's deal," David said. "What do we need? I'll start. I need to play some euchre."

"What's euchre?" everyone else said more or less at once.

"Card game. It's simple. I used to play with my dad and my uncles up in Petoskey. I've been playing on the computer, but it's not the same. I miss it." He looked to his right, where Deborah was picking dead leaves from a grapevine. She kept picking, but he could see her thinking.

"I need Edgar to leave me alone for a while," she said.

* * *

From the *Washington Post*, March 13, 2011:

THE FADING FAD OF MARS
by Allen Holley

During the six weeks before *Argos 1* left the International Space Station, the bandwidth of the developed world crackled with nothing but Marsnauts. During their voyage to the Red Planet, we worried how they would get along, if they would fall in love; we bet on the possibility of their failure; we spent our free time pouring information about Jami, David, Deborah, Edgar, Katherine, and Fidelis into our heads.

I thought it would peter out before they got there. Interest would spike again once they landed, of course, but apart from that and another flurry of information if they discovered something exciting—little green men or underground rivers or veins of iridium—but beyond that, I figured that the obsessive persistence of the American consumerate was of fairly short duration.

I was wrong.

We have been gaga over the Marsnauts for much longer than I ever would have guessed. Chat threads devoted to Deborah Green's sexual orientation unspooled posts in the millions; viewership of talk shows that took Jami Salter as their subject exceeded the number of eyeballs trained on last summer's World Cup in South Africa; applications to *Argos* Marsnauts' alma maters are up more than one hundred percent since the selection of the crew.

So yes, I was wrong.

I can admit this because we are, at last, beginning to forget. Bandwidth consumption at all the newsnets is down, or at least redirected to the pipes carrying the Chinese incursion into India; Ebony Freytag is stinging from the lawsuit; the various chat forums, if not exactly quiet, are no longer as riotous as they were in the halcyon early days of Mars-mania. This despite the fact that the crew of *Argos 1* has in fact discovered extraterrestrial life, throwing biology (and religion) on its collective ear, and begun to map huge quantities of water under the planet's surface, meaning the colonization has abruptly become a question not of if but of when.

They have been amazingly successful. And we are starting to ignore them. Part of me can't help but think it's a relief.

* * *

"DEBORAH," EDGAR SAID. SHE SNAPPED A TENDRIL FROM THE VINE. "David asked what we need. I'm telling you. I tried to think of something else, but that's it. I need you to leave me alone for a while."

Edgar stood very still for several seconds before picking up his tool belt.

"Edgar," David said before Edgar could leave. "Please stay."

After a pause, Edgar put the tool belt back on the work table in the center of the greenhouse. "Thank you," David said, trying to keep the real gratitude out of his voice. Things were getting very deep very fast, and he had to make sure the gathering didn't fly apart. "Katherine?"

"I would like you to ask Gates to give us more leeway in running experiments. The schedule is still predicated on searching for life that we've already found, and I'm wasting valuable time running useless experiments because people back in the Gates labs have already arranged to publish the results."

David nodded. "Okay. Let's do it this way: you start reporting to me, and I'll send abstracts of your results to Gates. I'll take the heat."

"Thank you," Katherine said. "Also I would like to learn how to play euchre." She smiled at him, and in that moment he could have kissed her. Whatever she said about Fidelis being the psych guy, Katherine knew the thin line David was treading, and she was doing her best to help.

"That's two things," he said, "but we are a resilient enough crew to handle them both, I think. Jami."

"I need everyone to stop looking at me like I'm going crazy."

There was a long pause.

"And I need people to please stop getting so quiet when I talk," Jami added. "Please."

* * *

Dear Ms. Salter,

I am a sixth-grader at Fred P. Hall Elementary School in Portland, Maine. I want to go to Mars some day. Can you tell me what college I should go to? I want to be a pilot and make sure aliens don't take over Mars or come to Earth. Will they let me do that even though I still have to wear glasses because my mom won't pay to burn my corneas?

Sincerely,

Megan Machado

* * *

"NOTED," DAVID SAID. "WE GOT IT. YOU AREN'T CRAZY, and we'll start interrupting you. Fidelis?"

"We're all too alone," Fidelis said. "I need everyone to start talking to each other again…no. I need everyone to start listening to each other again."

Leave it to Fidelis to be level-headed and precise, David thought. Carrying around his own self-assurance, a banked coal hidden from the winds that tore through the rest of them.

Or he was just deep, deep water, with all the turbulence down there in the dark.

"You heard the doc," David said. "Everybody start listening. We're all talking—hell, I talk all the time—but we're talking to ourselves." Greenhouse spring, he found himself thinking. A little island in the midst of so much cold and dark. A little spring, like the one they were all missing on Earth. "I think we need to get control of this," he went on. "As of tomorrow, we resume burst transmissions back to Earth. No more recording and storing; we send everything live."

"Gates won't run it," Deborah said.

"I don't care if Gates runs it or not. We all need to know that someone knows we're out here. When we just record and store for the backup pipe, we're talking to ourselves. Starting tomorrow, we talk to Earth again."

"And I guess we'll find out if Earth wants to talk to us," Jami said. Her voice was barely above a whisper.

"Oh, for Christ's sake," snapped Katherine, "you're the last person around here who should worry about that."

Jami was nodding before Katherine finished her sentence. "Right, you're right. It really helps knowing that they all *care* so much about me. How can I be lonely knowing that so many people *care*?" Her voice throughout was soft, and when she finished speaking she got up and pushed through the door that led back to Bohlen Station.

David watched her go. When the door had settled shut behind her, he surveyed the four people left in front of him.

Only Deborah was looking back at him. "She's cracking up, David. You need to do something. She named the station after a schizophrenic mechanic in an old science-fiction novel, for Christ's sake. Doesn't that worry you?"

"Katherine?" David said. "Fidelis?"

The two doctors looked at each other. David couldn't tell if some kind of secret physician's exchange was passing between them. After a moment, both shrugged. "She's been under a lot of pressure from the beginning," Fidelis said. "It's a good sign that she's still performing all of her work."

"But barely," Katherine interjected.

"That's true of all of us," said Fidelis. "None of us is working anything like we did our first few months here."

David stepped back in. "If Jami, or anyone else, starts leaving critical work unfinished, someone tell me right away. I'll keep an eye out, but the water separator's a full-time job lately. I need people looking out for each other. None of us can afford to crack. Stay together, people."

It was the moment to end the gathering, mission mostly accomplished, crew refocused and given a little momentum to get through the day. Right then David realized he'd forgotten to ask Edgar what he wanted.

* * *

EDGAR VILLAREAL, INTERVIEW WITH BRUCE PANDOLFO OF 700MHz, JUNE 9, 2065:

It's odd to be the last one alive. When we went to Mars, I think we all figured we were immortal. Along the way we figured out that we weren't, and realized how awful it would be if we were. Jami couldn't handle it. David could, he was always better at that kind of thing. I know I was glad to have both of them sopping up most of the attention before it got to me. Remember, I was only 3-1 to be the murdered crew member. Jami, Fidelis, and Deborah were all way ahead of me. People paid more attention to them. And David.

Anyway, I figured half of us would live to be a hundred. Now here I am, ninety next weekend, and I'm the last. And it's sad that three of us ... Fidelis' accident was almost a relief after hearing about David and Katherine and Deborah.

* * *

For three days the wind did not blow. Sand and dust settled in gentle drifts around the camp. Fidelis spent each of those three days immersed in his work, keeping himself away from the windows. He wanted to go outside, but he didn't want to see what he knew would be there.

Blow, wind, he said to himself, and felt creeping unease. Madmen on a dead red heath, that was all of them. Blow, wind. He steeled himself to resist Mars. If the wind would not blow, neither would Fidelis Emuwa go outside. He could outwait the planet. It could not break him.

You're personifying, he told himself. You're seeing agency in randomness. That's what they call paranoia.

Finally he couldn't stand it anymore. He suited up and went outside into the absurd stillness. The sky was bright and clear. His footsteps crunched as he walked around to the back of the greenhouse, where he'd seen Jami writing in the sand three days before, after David's meeting in the greenhouse. Writing, brushing it away, writing again.

Between his feet, the words: *speaking to the silence.*

Fidelis knelt and brushed them away.

* * *

The first day nobody called was hard on all of them. Except Jami.

"Twenty-four hours and no ping," she announced with a broad smile. "It only took a year and a half. Longer attention span than we thought they had, I bet."

"By about a year," grumbled Katherine, who Edgar figured was grouchy because Gates hadn't gotten back to her about her proposal to go into the lava tunnels looking for life other than the scrawny lichen that survived in cracks in canyon walls. He wanted to do it, too, but until today he hadn't figured Gates would let them. Too much to lose. Now that the dataflow from Earth had slowed to a trickle, though, he thought Gates might change its mind. They'd be looking for something to rejuvenate news coverage. Katherine wanted to go, but she also welcomed the relative peace and quiet.

Far as Edgar was concerned, anything that got him out of Bohlen Station and away from Deborah (for weeks now he'd been thinking of her as *that bitch Deborah*, but he was beginning to get over that) more than justified whatever risks arose. And away from Jami, who had suddenly begun to act like she was on the vid all the time. Of course, all of them were on the vid all the time; they'd agreed to sell "uncut" VR of the voyage as part of their contract with Gates. The feeling Edgar got, though, was that she had started playing a part. She was playing Barbarella the Mission Babe again, only now it was for her colleagues instead of Earthside media.

He wondered if she'd forgotten how to be herself. If somehow the intensity of the news coverage had overwhelmed whatever natural person had existed before they'd all become Marsnauts. Edgar thought back to training and their early publicity junkets. He'd liked Jami. She'd been at ease with everyone, able to joke about herself without seeming to make a point of it. The cameras found her, and the rest of them were grateful, even Edgar who had once wanted to be an actor. He quickly found that they needed Jami to take the pressure off them. They would all have imploded long ago if she hadn't done that.

"Now we can go back to being the anonymous discoverers of life beyond Earth," he said.

Jami flashed him a grin. "Thank God. You doing anything today?"

"Not unless Katherine gets the go-ahead to check out the tunnels."

"Then come with me. Reactor sensors are due for inspection."

"Let's do it." Anything to get out of here, Edgar thought again.

* * *

THE QUIET DAY, AS IT BECAME KNOWN AROUND THE STATION, turned out to be an anomaly. Apparently people on Earth were still interested. But where before they'd struggled to answer the flood of scientific and media inquiries, now they found that most of their incoming volume was kids looking for help on science projects and lonely postgrads wishing they were on Mars instead of in Ann Arbor or Heidelberg or Jakarta. "It's official," Deborah said. "We're a niche."

On Jami's birthday, August 22nd, she took off on a long solo hike. David almost didn't let her, but there was only so much he could do, and he settled for making sure that she had twenty-four hours of oxygen and a tested distress beacon. She's an adult, he said, and if she's going to kill herself I can't do much about it.

The more he watched her, the more convinced he was that she would be better once they'd all gotten on their way home. Surrounded by the empty red immensity of Mars, David thought, memories of Earth started to get a little abstract, like something he'd done once and might someday do again.

Deborah, Katherine, and Edgar were shouting at Fidelis when David came back in from doing the final check on Jami's suit. He got in among the four of them and calmed things down enough to get a sense of what was going on. It was cold in the station, something wrong with the thermostat, and he could see his breath.

"She's up to something," Edgar said. "And he knows what it is."

"Up to what?" David asked. He caught Fidelis' eye and tried out his telepathy: *Is Edgar okay? Do we have a problem here?*

Fidelis looked away from him and said, "She's having a hard time. This is true. And we have talked about it. She's entitled to some privacy, though, and I'm not going to just repeat what was said for all of you."

"If she's cracking up, it endangers the mission, Fidelis," Deborah said. Edgar was nodding along with her. "I could give a shit about her privacy."

"You know she's been skating on the edge of pathological for months, Fidelis," Katherine said. "If she's fallen over, you're the one who will know, and you can't keep it from us." Edgar and Deborah started to join in.

"Let me be clear about something," Fidelis snapped. The rest of them fell silent; they'd never heard him raise his voice except to laugh. "If I thought Jami was putting the mission in danger, I would of course tell David. I would not just tell whoever wanted to know, and I will not be bullied because you are all anxious. Do not insult me by turning me into a snitch, and do not insult me by suggesting I will not carry out my responsibilities." He glared at each of them in turn. When nobody said anything, he walked between Katherine and Edgar and went upstairs.

"He's not telling us everything he knows," Deborah said.

David waited to see if Edgar or Katherine had something to add. After a pause, he said, "He doesn't have to. You heard what he said. Do any of us really think that Fidelis Emuwa, of all people, is going to let personal feelings get in the way of his job? Come on."

Again he waited, and again none of them contradicted him, but David could tell they weren't convinced.

* * *

Gates Corporation communications records, August 22nd, 2011

Subpoenaed as evidence in the trial of Fidelis Liber Emuwa, David Louis Fontenot, Deborah Ruth Green, Edgar Carlos Villareal, and Katherine Alexandra Yi

Date: 22 Aug 2011, 14:35:06 GMT
To: Argos PM Roland Threlkeld
From: Tammy Gulyas, Argos Mission Liaison
Re: Argos trouble?

Rol,
David was in touch today. He's worried about Jami (still, or again) and Edgar (again). Doesn't think there's an immediate crisis, but wants to know how much

pressure he can put on Fidelis. Jami's been talking to F. and the rest of the crew thinks he's holding out on them. D. worried that E. might get violent. Ethical issues are your dept., so I'm shuffling this one off. Vid of David's call attached.

Next time we need to send an actor along. Fuck brains, fuck weight restrictions. J. might look good, but she's an engineer. We need someone who can handle celebrity.

TG

Date: 22 Aug 2011, 16:11:53 GMT
To: Tammy Gulyas, Argos Mission Liaison
From: Argos PM Roland Threlkeld
Re: Argos trouble?

Tammy—58 days to Earth-return liftoff. Sit tight. David's strung out like the rest of them. Jami's going to be fine, so is Edgar. Fidelis is a rock. ~R

* * *

THEY ALL TOOK LABOR DAY OFF. IT was a gesture, really, since they could take all the days off they wanted. Their scientific objectives were long ago accomplished, and with the launch back to Earth less than six weeks away, Gates had clamped down on discretionary travel and exploration. So they played lots of euchre and went over preliminary checks and tried not to get on each other's nerves.

Fidelis spent the morning in the common room reading *Don Quixote* on the table screen. He had been keeping a careful eye on Jami for weeks now, since he'd seen her writing in the sand. She was holding herself together, but he could tell it wouldn't take much to unravel her. Everyone else in the crew had come to him wondering about her bright brittle smile, the metronomic way she did her work, ate her meals, slept and bathed and spoke. David in particular was worried, and seemed to be carrying some kind of guilt. "First I thought that when the attention went away, she'd settle down. And she did, kind of, but it wasn't real. Then I started to figure that as launch got closer and the nets started talking about engineering obstacles, she'd perk back up because they'd ask her technical questions, you know? Questions about her area of expertise. Things that make her sound good."

David scratched at his ear, something he did when he wasn't sure how to proceed.

"Then this goddamn latest Ebony Freytag," he said after a pause. "Getting my idiot cousin and Jami's twenty-year-old sister together. I can shake my head and forget about that kind of shit, you know? But I think that was some kind of last straw for her. The way she walks around now I keep thinking she's just going to fly apart. Like every wrinkle in her skin is a crack."

"We're still getting lots of questions," Fidelis pointed out.

"I know," David said. Edgar came in, and he lowered his voice. "But they're from twelve-year-olds and nutcases. It doesn't mean anything to her."

"Where's Deborah?" Edgar said. He had shaved his beard.

Fidelis looked at David. They both shrugged. "Haven't seen her."

"Maybe she's in the lab." Edgar turned to go.

"Edgar," Fidelis called. "Are you all right?"

"Fine fine fine, Doc," Edgar said. "Just time to talk, is all. She wanted me to leave her alone, I left her alone. Now she's got to do something for me, and that's tell me what the hell is going on. Don't worry, I'm not mad, and she could kick my ass anyway, I think." It was probably true; Edgar and Deborah were about the same size, but when it came right down to it, she had a mean streak and he didn't.

Edgar wasn't the one Fidelis was worried about, anyway. "You know I have to ask," he said. Edgar waved a hand and left in the direction of the lab.

"You really think there's no problem?"

Fidelis shook his head. "They're not going to be back in bed, but I don't expect any real trouble, either. They were always together more out of some kind of rock-hound solidarity than because they liked each other."

David was looking at the doorway. "I wondered about that."

Jami walked in. "Fidelis!" she said with that bright and hopeless smile. "Just the man I wanted to see. Let's go for a hike."

* * *

FROM: BLAINE TAGGART
TO: ARGOS 1 CREW
SUBJECT: 15 MINUTES

Dear Marsnauts: How does it feel to know that your moment in the spotlight has already passed you by? My dad was a comedian, had three minutes on Johnny Carson one night in 1981, and never got over it. Just curious. By the way, I hear the fungus in your Mars lichen has a common ancestor with some terrestrial fungus. So three cheers for panspermia, right?

* * *

"I'M NOT GOING BACK."

He had known she would say this sooner or later, and he had lost much sleep over the previous six or seven nights rehearsing possible responses. None of them seemed appropriate now. What could he tell her? That she would die? Of course she would die. That her family would miss her? She knew that. That she was going to be rich and famous, feted in castles and capitals?

"Jami," he said. "Do you know what will happen to us if you don't come back?"

She glanced at him. "No. Come on, Fidelis. Appeal to my sense of responsibility to science, my desire for fame. Something. Just don't make me worry about you anymore."

"I don't think you have those things anymore. Once you did. All of this has fallen away from you."

Jami laughed. A little static sparked in Fidelis' mike. "Wasn't nirvana supposed to be the relinquishing of all desire? I forget. Can't remember religious things anymore. Here's your bodhisattva wisdom, Fidelis: you don't want me with you on the way back." She started walking away from him, gliding easily between boulders in the direction of the trail that led to the bottom of the canyon. "And I don't mean that personally, like people on the mission would rather see me stay. What I mean is, if you make me come with you, none of us will survive the trip home."

Look at me, he thought. I have to see what's in your face.

She did not speak, and he could not, and after a while she reached the trailhead and began her descent into the canyon.

* * *

HotVegas, September 5, 2011:

LABOR DAY SPECIAL—PLACE A $100 BET ON *ARGOS 1*'S SAFE RETURN AND GET A FREE $50 BET ON THE WORLD SERIES! UNTIL THE 15TH ONLY!

* * *

Never in her life had Katherine come closer to violence than when she saw Jami chiseling circuitry out of the VR corder built into her suit helmet.

"What the hell are you doing?" she said.

Jami didn't look up. "I think I've had it with being a spectacle."

"Well, I haven't had it with fulfilling our contract. Stop that."

"Okay." Jami put down the small hammer and chisel she'd been using. "All done anyway."

Katherine punched the wall intercom mounted next to the interior airlock door. "David," she said. "Come here, please."

His voice popped through the speaker. "Problem?"

Katherine stabbed the button again. "Just come here, please."

Jami mounted the plate over the corder and started screwing it back into place. "Don't," Katherine said.

"Cleaning up, Katherine," Jami said. "Not hiding." But she put the plate back down.

David arrived. "What?"

Katherine was about to speak when Fidelis came into the lock, too. It was crowded with the four of them and the eight suits hanging on wall racks. "I didn't ask him to come," Katherine said, pointing at Fidelis.

"Is this a private dispute?" David asked.

Briefly Katherine considered pushing the point. She and David both knew that Fidelis would defend whatever Jami was doing. To a certain extent that canceled out the benefit of the defense. "Never mind," she said. "I walked in here and Jami was sabotaging the recording equipment in her suit."

"Jami?" David asked.

"Guilty," she said immediately. With the toe of one shoe she scuffed at the bits of broken circuitry on the floor.

David sighed. "All right. Look. Jami—"

"How much money did she just cost us?" Katherine asked. She could already see David preparing to go easy on Jami. Well and good for him. He was one of the stars of the mission. She was just a member of the chorus, though, and nobody would be clamoring for her memoirs or her face on their screens. She'd have a good job when she got back, but she'd had a good job before leaving. The only reason she'd wanted to go to Mars in the first place was to cash in on whatever fame might come her way. The science she could have done at home, and Mars itself was so much empty, rock-strewn wilderness. She wouldn't miss it.

"I don't know," David said. After a pause he added, "Station vids are still going. Gates can piece something together. Unless—"

"Speaking of which," Jami said. She stood up and went to the intercom. "Everyone please come to the lock," she said. "No hurry." Then she woke up the terminal next to the intercom.

"What are you doing?" Katherine said.

"Shutting down the autofeed from the station vid." Katherine started to object, but David held up a hand.

"It's okay," he said. "Everything will still record. We can pipe it later."

The four of them stood there looking at each other until Edgar and Deborah arrived. They had obviously been making love, the smell of it preceded them into the lock, and Katherine thought to herself, *Jesus Christ*.

"Okay," Jami said. "First I want to apologize. I haven't done anything to station recorders or the suit recorders except for mine. Gates will be pissed, but to be frank, what I'm about to do is worth a lot more money than what otherwise would have been on my corder."

"Jami," Fidelis said quietly.

"Shut up, Fidelis," Katherine said. "Let her take her own weight for once."

A ghost of a smile crossed Jami's face. "Thank you, Katherine. The short version is this: I'm not going back to Earth." The smile grew broader. Something about it made Katherine a little sick. "There. You're all rich."

"You're not staying here," David said.

"You can't make me go back. You could jump me and tie me down, but if you do that I'll kill myself. Can you keep me too doped up to do it for the next seven months?" She shook her head. "I don't think so. Katherine? You're the doctor. Fidelis? What kind of star material will I be after seven months of minimal-g drooling into my collar?"

The only sound in the room was the rattle of a loose valve cover on the outside of the lock. After some time, Fidelis spoke.

"I think Katherine will agree with me that there would be serious long-term consequences."

"There will be serious long-term consequences if she stays here," Katherine answered. "Since we're all being honest here, I'll admit that I'm sick and tired of the way we've all catered to Miss Jami Salter, but I don't want to see her dead. If she stays here, she'll die."

"I don't know about that," Edgar said. Deborah looked startled.

Jami was nodding. "The station is staying behind. The greenhouse will be here. The reactor will still be working long after all of us are dead. What else do I need?"

"This is ridiculous," Katherine said.

"I'm not going back to Earth," Jami said. "One way or another, I'm not going back."

* * *

INKSTAINEDWRETCH.COM HEADLINE SEARCH, OCTOBER 18, 2011:

COMING HOME!
Marsnauts Come Home!
On Their Way
Gates, ISS Ready Decontamination Procedures
Demonstrators Demand *Argos* Quarantine
Mars Lichen Called "Threat to Humanity"

* * *

Early in the morning of their last day on Mars, while Jami was running a last preflight check on the rendezvous vehicle, David gathered the rest of the *Argos 1* crew in the common room. "We have a decision to make here," he said. "We're in a communications blackout for the next hour, so we vote right now. Leave Jami or force her to come along? Edgar: go."

"It's on her," Edgar said. "David and I can do her job on the way back. Let her stay."

"Fidelis."

"If she stays, she might survive. If we take her, she won't."

"Deborah."

"Bring her. We'll all be in jail if we don't."

"Katherine."

"Fidelis is wrong. And Edgar. She'll die here, and we don't have enough crew redundancy to be safe without her. Bring her."

David sighed. "Okay. Tiebreaker's on me." He paused. "She stays."

"You're fucking kidding," Deborah said.

"I'm fucking not." David looked around at all of them.

"This is Mars, David," Deborah said. "Not a desert island. Mars. She'll die."

"She'll have all the stuff that's kept us alive for the past fifteen months."

"And she'll die if she comes," Fidelis said. "If not on the voyage, soon after."

"You are endangering the mission," Katherine said. "Not to mention all of our lives. You can't do this."

"If we force her and something goes wrong, she could take all of us with her," David said. "I don't think we can risk it. There will be colonizing missions in four years. Six at the most. She'll be fine until then."

"Fine?" Katherine said incredulously. "Fine?"

They all heard the inner airlock start to compress. Nothing was left to say.

* * *

"It really is beautiful here," Jami said. She was spending more and more time outside now, and since she'd wrecked her VR corder her mood had grown lighter. Some of the old genuine Jami Salter effervescence had returned, although tinctured by a sort of maturity that made Fidelis think of the stately poets he'd read in college English classes. Wordsworth, maybe.

He turned off his VR and lay back. Earth was one hundred days away, and Jami Salter was beyond human help.

During their last day on Mars, Fidelis had personally recorded everything after the meeting. He had been unable to take his eyes from her face, from the somehow beatific gaze she cast on him, on the rest of the crew, on the Martian landscape. He watched her as she helped them run the flight checks on the orbiter, as she brought the ERV back up from its hibernation, as she ran Edgar through all of the things she worried he might have forgotten. All of them had drilled in protocols for returning with a partial crew, and none of them was really afraid of what Jami's absence would mean for mission success. She had repaired and jerry-rigged electronics, yes, and piloted when shift scheduling called for it, and it was certainly possible that something would go wrong on the return voyage that only she would be able to correct. That worry was distant somehow, like the abstract concern of being holed by a meteor. Nothing that could usefully be worried about.

It hit him then: Jami, who had been their movie star, was now their guide. She would make sure they got home.

Fidelis had not cried since the birth of his daughter Emily. He found tears again on that last day he spent on the surface of Mars, and now on every day since when he gave himself over to the enormity of what they had done in leaving her behind.

* * *

FROM FIDELIS EMUWA'S PERSONAL MULTIMEDIA RECORD, OCTOBER 17, 2011
Submitted as evidence in Bexar County Court, September 14, 2012

Can you imagine? It's already over. They're already moving on. Tomorrow *Argos 1* lifts off, returns to Earth, and everyone on it commits to being forgotten. And I'm not such a drama queen that that's the most important thing. We commit to forgetting, too, or to becoming the kind of person who does nothing but remember. That's the hell we've made for ourselves, Fidelis. For the rest of our lives, we'll either be answering questions about this mission or wishing people would ask. When they stop asking, we'll get louder, and then what happens?

No. Not me. Barbarella has left the building, Fidelis. I'm just Jami, and I'm just staying here. Nothing for me to go back to.

* * *

THEY MADE THE ERV RENDEZVOUS WITHOUT A HITCH, and had already done the first acceleration burn when the commlink pinged with the Gates security code.

"What in the living fuck did you just do?" screamed Roland Threlkeld when David opened the connection.

David had to stifle a grin, imagining Rol boiling over while the rendezvous vehicle was incommunicado, and then while the ERV came out of Mars' communication shadow. It was a wonder he hadn't stroked out.

Are you laughing? he asked himself. *You left a crewmember behind on Mars. How can you laugh?*

The smile wouldn't go away.

Another burst from Roland: "Are you out of your fucking mind? Jesus Christ on a goddamn Popsicle stick, you fucking left Jami fucking Salter on fucking Mars?"

The connection went dead.

"What are you going to tell him?" Deborah asked.

David thought about it. "Nothing until we've tweaked the accel burn and set the rotation. Once that's all settled, I'll figure something out."

Thirty-five minutes later, another profane tirade from Roland crackled out of the monitor. Thirty-five minutes after that, another. And another. Eventually, when they had the ERV moving like it was supposed to and rotating to give them Martian gee, David called everyone together. "Now we've done it," he said. "So we have to defend it. We can't lie, and we can't just say that we did what Jami wanted. We have to convince people that it was the only thing we could do. So. I'm listening."

"We're all going to go to jail," Katherine said.

"I don't think so," countered Edgar. "If we argue that she was a danger to the mission, then all we were doing was saving ourselves."

"Do you believe that?" Fidelis asked.

Edgar lifted his chin. "Yes, I do."

"I think we endangered the mission by leaving her," Katherine said. "And not just our mission; have any of you thought about what this is going to do to the possibility of other Mars missions? What kind of harm have we done here?"

"None," David said. "Mars is bigger than us; people latched onto our faces, but the guys who put up the money are figuring that the consumerate will do the same for any group of Marsnauts. If nothing else, we've proved that sending six people hundreds of millions of miles to a hostile planet is like a license to print money. We won't be the last."

The commlink pinged. "That'll be Roland again," said Fidelis.

"Guess I should start putting together some kind of response. Unless one of you wants to do it?" They all just looked at him. Deborah and Fidelis at least had the grace to grin. "I didn't think so."

Roland Threlkeld's message started to unspool. All of them started to laugh. Even Edgar who hated profanity couldn't help but chuckle.

"One thing more," David said. "And this is not funny. Nobody in this crew is going to duck what we've done. We all stand up and we admit it, we take the heat for it. No excuses. We did what we did."

"Fair," Edgar said. "No hiding. We did this. We stand by it."

* * *

Article from the *Houston Chronicle*, August 18 2012:

Charges Against *Argos 1* Crew Dismissed

Bexar County District Judge Fulgencio Salazar has thrown out charges against David Fontenot in the marooning of Jami Salter on Mars.

Citing the prosecution's inability to produce any evidence either that Salter would in fact be harmed by remaining on Mars or that the crew had conspired against Salter's well-being, Judge Salazar dismissed felony charges against Fontenot and left little doubt that conspiracy and accessory charges against Fidelis Emuwa, Deborah Green, Edgar Villareal, and Katherine Yi would be dismissed as well.

"I have as yet seen no persuasive evidence that a crime was committed by any of those charged," Judge Salazar said in the courtroom this morning, as Salter family members sat shocked and relatives and supporters of the other crew members exchanged broad smiles.

Outside the courtroom, Salter family attorney Michelle Braunschwieg said that the family would consider its options. Attorneys for Emuwa, Green, Villareal, and Yi refused comment. David Fontenot's attorney Britt Kirschner told reporters that he considered his client's actions completely vindicated. "No one who was not on Mars with David Fontenot and the crew of *Argos 1* should be sitting in judgment of what they did there. None of us has ever experienced anything like what they have. I have total confidence that David acted in the crew's best interests, the mission's best interests, and Jami Salter's best interests."

Kirschner, as he has done throughout the case, laid the blame for the situation on the voracious celebrity culture fostered by the commercial newsnets. "It is my fervent hope, and David's," he said, "that future Mars crews and colonists will not be turned into grist for the celebrity mill."

Planned future Mars missions at this time include hydrological surveys sponsored by Merck, JohnsonCo, and Werner GmbH. Each of these missions has been asked to determine the whereabouts and health of Jami Salter. A planned rescue/forensic-investigation mission financed by Gates appears to be on hold for now.

* * *

Eileen Aufdemberge looked at her sister Deb. Looked hard. They hadn't seen much of each other since Deb had returned from Mars, and today, out in the back yard where three years ago she'd tried to see *Argos 1* when it was on the other side of the world, Eileen wanted to try to get to know her sister again.

Jared came out of the house. He'd slouched his way into adolescence since the last time Deb had visited. The ten-year-old who knew everything about his Aunt Deb had given way to a thirteen-year-old who pretended not to care. Now he walked up to Deb and presented her with a bottle. MARTIAN HAIR, it said.

"They say it's got Martian chemicals in it, that it'll bleach your hair but not dry it out. Girls at school can't get enough of it."

"Are you serious?" Deb said. Eileen watched her turn the bottle and read its ingredients. She handed it back to Jared. "Tell them that peroxides are peroxides. If this stuff bleaches without drying, it's got nothing to do with Mars."

"Thanks, Aunt Deb," Jared said. He flipped the bottle up in the air and caught it behind his back. "You just made me ten bucks."

The screen door slid shut behind him. Eileen sat on the deck behind the house outside Knoxville she'd bought with Derek and kept when Derek left her for the woman who sold him his new car. She'd kept Jared, too, but was happy to see the car go; it was one of those low-slung ostentatiously sporty models that Deb had always called "penis extenders."

Labor Day was the next Monday, and Deb had taken a long weekend away from her round of conferences and public appearances to lie on the grass in her sister's back yard and catch up on the previous three—almost four now, counting all the pre-launch buildup—years.

Where to start?

"So tell me all about it," she said.

"All about what?" Deb said, and they both smiled. Deb laced her fingers behind her head and looked up into the bright blue Tennessee sky. "I'm not sure I know how to talk about it yet," she said.

"Seems like that's all you do."

"I'm not sure I'm doing it right, though, really getting at it the way it was." Deb turned her head toward Eileen, who was sitting on the deck stairs with a glass of iced tea. "I wonder if Erik the Red had this problem.

"People made bets on whether we'd survive. People I didn't know got on international media outlets and said they'd had sex with me. I'm the first human being to discover life somewhere other than Earth, and when we piped the result back, everyone wanted to talk to Jami about it."

"What was that like? Discovering life, I mean." Eileen amended herself quickly, not wanting Deb to get into a Jami Salter rant. She still hadn't sorted out how she felt about the abandonment of Jami. The crew knew best, she supposed, but her sister had wanted to bring Jami back, and Eileen had always trusted Deb's judgment. Except once: Deb hadn't liked Derek Aufdemberge.

"It was, it was, it was," Deb said, rolling back to look up at the sky, "so mundane. Picking through rocks at the bottom of a giant rockslide, at the bottom of a canyon that makes the Grand Canyon look like a drainage ditch. Turn a rock over, hey look, there's some lichen. It's dead, obviously it lived in more protected circumstances, but it's lichen. You want to know something interesting? I can't tell the story like that when someone asks in public. I have this urge to embellish, or I'm afraid they won't be interested. I discovered life on Mars, and I'm afraid people will be bored because I'm not Jami Salter telling them. Jesus."

Neither of them spoke for a while. Music started up in Jared's room.

"What about Jami, Deb?"

"What about her?"

"You know what I mean."

Another pause.

"I have a little secret about that, too," Deb said eventually. "As much as I got sick of everyone loving her and everyone wanting to talk to her and everyone ignoring me because I wasn't her, I have to admit that she took the heat for all of us. People wanted a mission babe, and they decided—for obvious reasons—that it was going to be Jami, and she hated it. But she did it."

"Did she want to stay on Mars, do you think?"

"Yeah, I think she did. I still don't think we should have let her, but as usual the men got their way."

This had been pointed out repeatedly in the media, with a variety of spins. Eileen wondered how to pursue it. "Didn't they like her? Were they afraid of her?"

Deb was shaking her head. "None of that. I think everyone there voted exactly what they thought was best. But still, all the men voted to leave her."

The music in Jared's room changed to an amped-up version of a song Eileen vaguely remembered from her own adolescence.

"It's still not fair," Deb said. "It's still not fair that they recognized her so much more than the rest of us. Sometimes I still think she stayed behind as one last gesture, so she had the last trump card over the rest of us. We'll never measure up to that. How can we?"

Eileen got up and went to lie in the grass next to her sister. "Who wants to measure up? What's to measure up to? You discovered life and water on Mars. She cracked up and couldn't go home. You want to measure up to that?"

Deb was shaking her head, but she reached over to clasp Eileen's hand. "Not that simple. She didn't just crack; she was broken. I don't think anybody could have just sailed through what happened to her."

"You just said that you went through the same kind of thing."

"Not the same."

"Yes it is the same," Eileen insisted. "People seized on what was obvious about you, and they blew it up into something monstrous. They did the same thing with her. And with the rest of you, except David."

"David doesn't make much of an impression," Deb said. "A good guy, a smart guy, but not exactly memorable. Edgar asked me to marry him."

"What? Oh my God."

"I know. I'm terrified."

"What are you going to do?"

Deb was shaking her head. Eileen saw how much gray Mars had threaded into her hair. "Pick the petals off a daisy. Get my palm read. Consult a Magic 8-Ball. I don't know. God, I want to, Eileen. I think about him every second of the day, I want him next to me. If not closer." She grinned at Eileen. "He sure is fine between the sheets."

Eileen's first instinct was to say *Derek wasn't bad either*, but she bit it back. This was no time to mention Derek. So instead she said, "Do you think you can get along when you're not in the sack?"

"That's the thing," Deborah said. Now she looked sad and tired. "He voted to leave Jami. That's the thing."

* * *

HEARING BEFORE THE SENATE SUBCOMMITTEE ON SPACE AND COLONIZATION, SEPTEMBER 7, 2012:

Senator Joshua Lindvahl: Jami Salter had everything to come back for. She was famous, she was going to be rich, she had made a professional name for herself in her field. She was a hero to the people of Minnesota, whom I am privileged to represent, and to the country, and to the world. Why in God's name, Doctor Emuwa, would she just decide not to come back?

Fidelis Emuwa: Because seventy-three million people placed a bet with Hot-Vegas on whether or not she would be killed in a fit of sexual jealousy.

* * *

THE TALK AT BOSTON UNIVERSITY HAD GONE WELL, Fidelis thought, and it was good to be back in Massachusetts. He'd spoken all over the country, and in Switzerland and Italy and Japan, about the psychological stresses of deep-space missions. Everywhere people responded to his low-key authority, and in optimistic moments he felt that he might be doing his small part to effect some kind of change. There would be no avoiding commercial sponsorship of space exploration; given that, he felt it critical that the astronauts were protected better than the *Argos 1* crew had been. He had his critics, but with Katherine saying much the same thing—in her more confrontational way—Fidelis was guardedly sure that future crews would not be quite the commodities that he and Jami and the rest of them had become.

He was standing in front of the business school watching the traffic on Commonwealth Avenue. Earth gravity still felt heavy in the muscles of his thighs. Maybe he would walk down Comm Ave, pick up a book and a burrito in Kenmore Square, walk the bridge over the Mass Pike to Fenway Park. The Sox, as usual, were out of it, but this looked to be Nomar Garciaparra's last year at short, and Fidelis wanted to see him play there one more time.

"Excuse me, Dr. Emuwa?"

Fidelis looked at the young man who had spoken, his dealing-with-the-public smile already falling into place. "Yes?"

"I'm Brad Reynolds, Dr. Emuwa. I'm a student here, and I wanted to tell you that I'm sorry."

"Sorry for what?" Fidelis looked more closely at this Brad Reynolds. An unexceptional young man. Spots of red in his cheeks, a fraternity ring his only jewelry. He had the khaki-and-razor-cut look that business students had chosen since World War II.

"I bet four hundred bucks that you'd be killed during the mission." Brad Reynolds looked down, then back up into Fidelis' face. Gathering his courage, Fidelis thought. "I thought you'd all get into some kind of fight over Jami Salter, and I figured David and Edgar were tougher than you."

"You were right about that," Fidelis said.

"I shouldn't have done it," Reynolds went on. "It was a joke, you know, the whole thing." Reynolds squinted at Fidelis. "None of you were real."

"That's right," Fidelis said. "None of us were."

* * *

THE WEDDING OF DEBORAH GREEN AND EDGAR VILLAREAL took place on September 24th, 2012, in the Garden of the Gods outside Colorado Springs. It was attended by forty-seven people and half a dozen hovering video drones sent by the more gossipy newsnets. The bride wore white. Her veil was beaded with pearls. The groom wore a morning suit, and was proud of having tied his cravat himself.

They had written their own vows, and the ceremony was quick. The only commotion occurred when Edgar's cousin Gerardo "accidentally" scattered the news drones by blasting through them in an old F-4 borrowed from the Air Force Academy, where both Edgar and Deborah had graduated too many years before. Afterward the newlyweds presided over their reception at the Broadmoor Hotel before hopping into Edgar's restored 1959 Bel Air and heading off on a driving honeymoon through the Rocky Mountain West.

No members of the *Argos 1* crew were invited.

* * *

HEARING BEFORE THE SENATE SUBCOMMITTEE ON SPACE AND COLONIZATION, JANUARY 14, 2013:

David Fontenot: We found seventeen species of extraterrestrial life. We found enough water to ensure that colonization of Mars could be beneficial and productive in the long term. But mostly people were interested in faked pornographic video of our engineer and backup pilot, and I think Jami couldn't come back to that. I think it got the better of her, and I think the only reason the rest of us survived is because she took the pressure of all that voyeurism onto herself.

That's all I have to say, Senators.

REFORMATION

alif lam mim

Enter.

alif lam mim sad

Marwan does one last dry run before putting his life on the line. He slips through the outer layers of Southern Baptist Convention security, in and out like a needle through a balloon, and then the Assemblies of God. He does not bother with the Lutherans or Presbyterians or Methodists; they have no security worth noting, not really. The Methodists even permit their congregants to own personal computers. The great temple in Jerusalem is more difficult, especially since the virus terrorism of 2013, and the thickets of security protecting the magnificent Mosque of the Prophet in Medina a still sterner test of his abilities. Marwan does not dare approach the Vatican, not yet. He will only get one opportunity there, and he will have to make that one count.

Ghosting in and out, he monitors his pursuit. A few strays from the Assemblies of God, a few more from Jerusalem and Mecca. All easily dusted off. The kind of thing he's been doing since he was eleven.

He sits in his apartment off Ford Road in Dearborn, Michigan, with the shades drawn. It is five in the morning. Time to pray. Marwan removes his sneakers and his Detroit Red Wings baseball cap. He knows he should wash, but he does not. He unrolls his prayer rug in the living room and kneels on it, facing the balcony. As he bows to touch his forehead to the rug, the first rays of the sun find their way through the drapes and strike the top of his head.

alif lam ra

Marwan never prays to be saved, or to be martyred. He never prays for the

131

souls of his mother and father, dead in an auto accident the previous spring. He never prays for the money to go to university; he can read, and his mother taught him how to learn. He prays only that he is doing the right thing, and asks God to tell him if he is not. So far he has not heard from God, and he carries with him a bone-deep certainty that he has understood the signs of the times and that he has chosen the only course of action possible.

He speaks of this with no one. Not the rental office on the first floor of his building, where he drops off the check on the first of every month. Not the restaurant where he busses tables and washes dishes to afford his three rooms. Not the four hundred or so other worshipers at the Beit Jalal mosque in Dearborn Heights.

And especially not those faceless searchers he encounters online, his fellow travelers. He is more careful with them than with any church or synagogue or mosque.

Not for long, though. Fairly soon all of his cards will be on the table.

The sun is fully up, and the day promises to be hot. Marwan opens the drapes and steps out onto his nineteenth-floor balcony. A couple of miles from his building, Dearborn gives way to Detroit: a lesson in the infliction of the sins of the father onto the sons. The assembly line took its first steps in Dearborn, and sowed the seeds of its own destruction in Detroit. As Marwan gazes off to the east, the sun shines down on nine hundred thousand Detroiters in a city built for two million. From where he stands, Marwan can see trees growing through the roof of an abandoned factory that once produced ball bearings.

He cannot help it; this is what he sees when he thinks of the Neoplatonists—Augustine, al-Farabi, and all the rest—and their City of God. Henry Ford had been Detroit's tin god, and the results spread ruined and empty as far as Marwan can see. Down near the river, heavy traffic congeals around office towers, buses idle in front of casinos, new stadia shine brightly in the June morning. But between Foxtown and Telegraph Road, the city is as empty as if a great plague had passed.

Will I change any of that? Marwan asks himself. And has no answer.

alif lam mim ra

Of all the numbers, the number nineteen is the most holy. The number of verses in the Quran is a 6,346, a multiple of nineteen whose digits add up to nineteen as well. The number of *surahs* in the Quran is 114, a multiple of nineteen. The *basmala* occurs 114 times in the Quran, and each *basmala* is 19 letters. The first and last revelations consist of nineteen words. And so on. Nineteen, Marwan believes, is the number of God. This is certainly true in Detroit, where the number 19 hangs in the rafters of Ilitch Arena, memorializing the great Steve

Yzerman's four Stanley Cup triumphs between 1997 and 2003. Marwan is a great fan of the Detroit Red Wings, and when he sees that number 19 hanging above the ice, a peace comes over him. Surely he has chosen the right place.

He is back at his computer, preparing for the day. A distracted part of his mind wonders what Martin Luther thought of the number nineteen. Another distracted fragment wonders if he might better have pursued his goals in Denver, where Joe Sakic wore 19, or New York, where Mike Bossy wore 19, or …

Names from my childhood, Marwan thinks. Names my father would mention when we were watching the Red Wings. *Poniatowski reminds me of Mike Bossy, you know, he wore 19, too. But Yzerman was the best of all of them.* And they have percolated into my mind, become my own comparisons and touchstones even as I put away childish things.

In high school, Marwan read a play called *Everyman*. Summoned by death, Everyman fears that he cannot complete the voyage to Heaven alone. His friends Kindred, Cousin, Fellowship, and Goods cannot accompany him. In the end, only Good Deeds—previously neglected—steps forward and finishes the journey with Everyman. Along the way, Knowledge offers himself: *Everyman, I will go with thee and be thy guide.* The line has not left Marwan's head since he read the play, now eighteen months ago.

Marwan's father and mother were still alive when he read the play, still there with him to be his guides. No state policeman had yet come to his door with rounded shoulders and shifting eyes. No doctors had yet touched him on the shoulder and left him alone in a cold white room with two sheeted bodies. And he had not yet suffered the comfort of hearing that all was well, that Imad and Ayat Aziz were gone to whence they'd come, absorbed back into the divine. Gone home.

He had gone to school the next day because he didn't know what else to do, and he stayed after Edsel Ford High School had emptied of everyone but custodians and off-season football players. Not knowing where else to go, he had wandered into the shop classroom, where old Mr. Krause was still tinkering.

"Krause," Marwan said.

Krause was the only person in the world Marwan knew who seemed like he really knew what was going on. You were having trouble with an English paper, your car, your girlfriend, you went to Krause and he made it all make sense. He was about five foot seven and weighed maybe three hundred pounds, wore his hair slicked back over his bald spot, and collected kids' toys from the 1970s. A strange guy; the general consensus around Edsel Ford was that the cops would come looking for him one day.

But on this day, it was only important to Marwan that Krause knew what was happening inside him.

"Z," said Krause. He had a nickname for everyone.

"My parents were killed yesterday."

"I heard." Krause looked closely at Marwan. "It hasn't hit you yet, has it? You're still—"

"Are they gone, Krause?"

A pause. "Depends on how you mean that, I guess, but I'd have to say yeah. They're gone."

"Not in paradise, or heaven, or nirvana, or any of that shit."

"Z, are you a religious kid?"

Marwan had to think carefully about this. "I think so."

"That's the problem with this, isn't it? Someone told you something, and you don't know what to do with it."

"One of the nurses," Marwan said slowly. "She said my mom and dad were gone home. Taken back into the divine or whatever."

"Reabsorbed, huh? That's what's bugging you."

"If that's what happens, then they're dead in heaven, too, Krause. What's the point?"

Krause shifted his bulk in his chair and stroked his goatee. Marwan began to cry. The tears came slow and hard, and each breath tore itself loose of his diaphragm. Krause let him go for a while. Then he said, "Z."

Marwan wiped his eyes.

"What the nurse gave you was emanationism. All worldly things come from the divine and disappear back into it when they die, and so on. Neoplatonism, the whole idea of forms and the material world being a debased reflection of what's up there." Krause pointed to the water-stained acoustic tiles over his desk. "You, you probably grew up thinking you were Muslim even though any kid who really grows up in America can't have a pure religion. It's not that kind of a place. Here's the test: if you're a real Muslim, you have to believe that the Quran was dictated to Mohammed by God, and that even though it's full of contradictions and long bits of just plain loopiness, it's the infallible word of God. You believe that?"

No, Marwan realized. I don't. I never did, really.

In that moment something fell into place within him, and he fell away from the comfortable osmotic religion that had been the background noise of his childhood and adolescence. Krause saw it happen.

"Right," he said. "That's crazy. No rational person can believe that. Mohammed was a reformer, Z. He looked around him and saw all the craziness on the Arabian peninsula fourteen hundred years ago, the tribal wars and infighting, and then he saw how the Christians were going gangbusters up north and the Jews were holding on like they always had, and he had a divine vision that would make it all right. For my money, Mohammed was more like Martin Luther than like Abraham. Luther nailed his theses to the door because he wanted to get the church back to the source, the unmediated relationship with God. And that's the argument of Islam, that the other People of the Book have gotten it all wrong, and that the Quran will come along and get back to God." Krause shrugged. "You should go off and read the Sufis. You don't believe the Quran is divine dictation, you're a Sufi anyway. They're all about looking behind the words, them and the Kabbalists and the rest." He reached out a meaty hand and punched Marwan in the shoulder. "You've got a lot to think about. I'm sorry about your mom and dad, Z. Come back if you want to talk more."

"Yeah," Marwan said.

"Oh. You're into math, right?"

Marwan nodded.

"Then you should check out the Brethren of Purity, Z. They'll be right up your alley."

Marwan went straight from Krause's classroom to his car, and then straight out I-94 to Ann Arbor. No way would the Dearborn library have what he was looking for. He needed a university library. He found the Ikhwan al-Safa, and the Sufis, and read until the library closed at midnight, and that night he went home and in the midst of his mourning thought: all over the world there are people like me, suffering because they are told what is not true. Somewhere my mother and father stand together with God, and are complete. But who has gone with them to be their guide?

Mind wandering still, Marwan thinks that Martin Luther and Mohammed would have had much to talk about. A grin passes over Marwan's face as he wonders if the Prophet ever dispelled the Devil with flatulence, as Martin Luther so famously did.

Today is Marwan's nineteenth birthday.

alif lam ra

He has planned his action for early afternoon, when network traffic is at its most intense: East Coast American markets closing and people checking email before leaving work, business use on the West Coast peaking, and markets in the Pacific Rim heating up along with the business of the day in Tokyo, Shanghai, Bangkok, Kuala Lumpur. It will be 1900 Greenwich Mean Time.

He takes a disk from an envelope and watches the sunlight play across its shining surface. He has created this on a computer far from his home, at public terminals in Walled Lake and Eastpointe and Inkster and even Windsor, south across the river. All of his reading, all of his desire, all of his sorrow and hope have gone into it. Somewhere in its rainbowed interior, the broken symmetry of the technical and the mystical is restored.

The disk rests on the lip of a slot in Marwan's terminal. The tip of his right index finger exerts gentle pressure on the rim of the disk. There is no way to be certain that what he is planning will work. It may be that when he inserts the disk, he will wreak changes greater than he imagines.

What changes?

God: stop me if I am doing wrong.

He does not know which God he expects to hear his prayer. With a soft whir the disk disappears into the slot.

khaf ha' ya 'ain sad

Marwan has named the font Brethren, after the Ikhwan al-Safa, the Brethren of Purity. The Brethren had flourished briefly in Basra nearly a thousand years ago, and left behind only one work, a cryptic and self-contradictory collection of notes amassed over a period of years. Reading the Brethren, the year before, with his parents still unburied and a great many of his tears still unshed, Marwan had thought: this is crap. Emanationist crap, to borrow Krause's word. Why did he want me to read this?

Then a diamond, the kind of signal idea that redeems hours and days spent bleary-eyed in the stacks of the university library. The Brethren had believed that the study of Number—of astronomy, geometry, algebra, and music—would bring the student to the mind of God. The simplicity of this idea took Marwan like a lover, and he clung to it as he read Pythagoras and even when he read the attack of the great al-Ghazali, who excoriated what he saw as the Brethren's watery ecumenical mysticism, claiming they denied the omnipotence of God.

But the Brethren had seen no conflict between philosophical and religious truth: mathematics, number, was the way to the mind of God.

Computation on the fingers, making the body into a number, approaches divinity (and did not the Brethren and al-Farabi and even al-Ghazali—and the Christian Gnostics—agree that when a man knows himself he begins to know God?). Computation in the gold and silicon universe of the microchip is as near to God as man has yet approached.

That will change, Marwan says to himself. He almost speaks aloud, and a chill runs up the back of his neck. There is no reason to believe that speaking now would influence anything, but he has not uttered a word aloud since calling in sick at the restaurant the previous Saturday. Four days.

In addition to mathematics, Marwan's real interest since middle school has been programming. He went through a phase of hacking, just like most kids he knew, and then when they all drifted away he kept investigating. The Virt seduced him, and never mind what the faithful said. Out there in the Virt was a new kind of world waiting to be born. It lay like the Golem, awaiting the Word.

Now Marwan thinks he has found the words.

He started designing the Brethren font shortly after another conversation with Krause. "You know," said the shop teacher, "the real miracle of the Quran is supposed to be its language. Arabic is the only language, God's language. What language do you think God speaks?" That night, Marwan had started looking into fonts. How they worked, what made each letter mean what it meant. Then he started working.

After six months, he thought he was onto something. After a year, he was poised between exaltation and panic. This morning, with the disk in the slot and the low hum of the processor drinking it all in, he is somehow distant.

He looks at it as it unspools onto his monitor. Each letter living, breathing. Not just programmable—intelligent. Able to interact with the letters next to it. And each letter charged with its history in the Quran and the sound and meaning of its cognates in the Torah, Aramaic and Greek and Hebrew all standing behind the beautiful calligraphy of the Brethren characters.

Hypersignification.

Brethren is the first language to speak to the totality of the Virt. (And there's that image again, the one Marwan cannot quite force himself not to think of; for if man is in the image of God, is not God an image of man? A line from Ibn al-Arabi's poetry floats through Marwan's mind: "He praises me and I praise Him, He worships me and I worship Him.") Marwan is not a linguist; he is almost a mathematician; he is a programmer of notable dexterity; he is a believer of terrible intensity. There is no violence in him save when he considers repression. He watches the Brethren font with an excitement like heat in the pit of his stomach. Before his eyes, Arabic and English characters are transformed. The letters that replace them gather expectantly on his desktop. Each, he realizes, is a language unto itself, or perhaps a virus. All fonts are codes, but the Brethren is alive. Each letter of it is alive. Marwan's fingers hesitate above his keyboard; every stroke now will be a conversation, an argument, a prayer.

In the beginning was the Word, John had said. And the Kabbalists broke it down further, reasoning that before there could be a Word, there must have been letters. And Mohammed himself, in his recitation of the Quran, had placed letters at the beginning of certain *surahs*. In those letters, Marwan thought a week or so after the last conversation with Krause, is the answer to a question we have not yet learned how to ask. He used them as the basis for the Brethren font.

The other worshipers at the Beit Jalal mosque in Dearborn Heights do not know that Marwan owns a networked personal computer. They do not know that he has sold his parents' house to finance a firehose connection and processors that would be the envy of many university physics departments…and the small jack drilled into the mastoid bone behind his right ear. If they knew about these things, Marwan would certainly not be welcome at prayers anymore. It is entirely possible that other young men, so like himself in so many ways, would force their way into his apartment and destroy his terminals. A weight of history and tradition lies behind this.

If he were Jewish, it would be the same. Hot-eyed young men from the Shir Tikvah synagogue would knock on the door and burst in when he turned the knob. Of if he were Catholic, it would be young men in blazers and khakis from Blood of Our Redeemer; if he were nondenominationally Protestant, white-shirted young men from the Church of God in Christ. It happened every day. Every day people died. Every day.

ta' ha'

Most dangerous, though—much more dangerous than the youth groups who spent their activism clarifying their fellow congregants' values—were church hackers.

In 1992, Monsignor Frederic Dugarry had a vision. What he saw horrified him: a world of computers speaking to each other, people drowning in the torrent of ideas without guidance from the Church. This Virt would be Pandemonium, an earth-shattering collapse of authority on a scale not seen since Gutenberg. There was no question of stopping it; Monsignor Dugarry knew this, and directed his energies toward ensuring that if the Virt were to take over the world, it would bear the standard of the Church.

He studied computer science, and found it beyond him, but Monsignor Dugarry understood politics, and he quickly arranged for the Holy See to fund the education of promising Catholic youth in the intricacies of computer pro-gramming. Sensing as well that the fruits of this program might flower too late, he also scoured parishes from his home city of Montreal, south through Boston and New York, west through Detroit and Chicago. He found computer-savvy youth by the hundred, and winnowed their numbers until he was left with a few dozen of the best. Then he turned them loose.

Usenet newsgroups dealing in pornographic images found themselves inun-dated in postings of the Gospels. Underground chat parlors imploded under the weight of thousands of automated postings. Child pornographers and parish whistleblowers alike found their computers disabled, their personal information embarrassingly disclosed, their telephone service impeded.

Then Dugarry set his young hacker legion on Judaism and anti-Catholic big-otry. Nondenominational Protestant churches that made a practice of publish-ing anti-Catholic pamphlets, books, or comics found that their tax exemptions had been removed from local municipal mainframes. Charitable exemptions for synagogues likewise disappeared, costing affected congregations millions of dollars in time, legal fees, and redirected budgetary energy. Emails praising the Church of Rome and admitting the errors of Judaism and Protestantism trickled out from the servers of Virt-linked synagogues and churches.

With that, Dugarry's enemy began to return fire. Invisible enemies paralyzed the archdioceses of Montreal and Chicago; Vatican databases were corrupted or erased. A crossfire erupted when one of Dugarry's protégés shut off electrical service to every mosque in the New England states and irate Muslims formed hacker squads of their own in the mosques of New York, Chicago, and Detroit.

Each faith rationed the amount of energy it spent undermining the others. All agreed that the real work lay in making the Virt an organ of salvation, renewal, revelation instead of the cesspool of vice, depravity, and atheism it seemed in the spring of 1994 to be becoming. Catholic schools began directing their best and brightest into new monasteries devoted to programming. Lutheran, Baptist, and other Christian churches followed suit, as did Jewish day schools across the country. American Muslims alerted relatives in Kuwait and Saudi Arabia and Oman about the threat to world virtue, and soon madrassehs all over the Islamic world were importing state-of-the-art computer equipment. The Sultan of Brunei paid for trunk lines that spidered out from Munich through Cairo, Baghdad, Damascus, Beirut, Medina, Islamabad. Each faith enacted prohibitions on the use of networked computers—except by its own Swiss Guard of hackers. Like the Book before it, the computer became a tool forbidden to the uninitiated.

Over the next five years, as the numbers of hackers fired with the spirit of God increased, it became clear that the secular population lacked the will to resist. Online pornography concerns dried up; sites promoting atheism were careful to do so in the guise of academic analysis; enrollment in graduate courses in poststructuralist literary theory plummeted. Virt business thrived; Virt idleness and vice did not.

All of it, as far as Marwan is concerned, is just the latest act in the long history of emanationist idiots trading punches, arrows, and bullets. Idiots, all of them, reading Plotinus and Augustine and al-Farabi, thinking that humans exist only as some kind of divine effluvium, to by cycled through the world and reabsorbed once most of the odor had faded. No, he thought. That isn't right at all. There is nothing to go home to. We are all home already. The Kabbalists had it right, the Kabbalists with their long body on the table awaiting the Word that would bring it life. We return to the divine to coexist. This is the creation of the Virt, the instantiation of the mind of God that is our birthright. We will not be kept from it.

ta' sin mim

Mohammed was a reformer, Marwan thinks. Martin Luther was a reformer. And I, Marwan Hussein Aziz, am in their company.

What a wonderful moment of hubris, of bursting self-confidence, of absolute certainty.

Marwan prepares carefully. He has been maintaining a list of those he will contact when the moment comes. He invokes the list, and his terminal opens a wagon-wheel connection with spokes leading to each name. There are nineteen names.

With a keystroke he converts them all into Brethren.

ta' sin

I'm calling it in.

ta' sin mim

The spokes of the wagon wheel vibrate with activity as the message blazes out into the Virt. Each person on the list reacts almost immediately. A seminarian in St. Charles, Illinois, slips a worm into the Chicago Archdiocese and watches it work its way through Cleveland and New York and Mexico City; the bishop of Pretoria forwards Marwan's message on to the Vatican, where the Brethren characters will begin seeping through the Holy See's walls of security. A rabbinical student in Haifa touches his yarmulke and with a keystroke slaves every terminal in the temple to Marwan. A fourteen-year-old white supremacist in Prague, under the impression that Marwan is planning a virus attack on a hospital in Tel Aviv, unleashes a brute-force crack on the Israeli State Information Service.

Marwan watches as one by one, the portals he has had under observation for weeks begin to crack open.

alif lam mim

Among the forces mustering to Marwan's aid are several groups of Marxist or Maoist bent, all of whom have been fighting Dugarry's progeny since the 1990s. Without them, Marwan's goals would be out of reach, but he is nevertheless a bit mystified by materialism, and never more so than at this exact moment. All things are metaphysical, Marwan thinks. To believe in anything beyond what you can touch and hear and smell is metaphysical. To believe that you can touch a sequence of keys on a computer and speak to another human being on the other side of the Earth is metaphysical. If we can love, why not the soul?

One question begets another: What am I doing that is so different from seeking the Philosopher's Stone or performing numerological operations on the Book of Elijah? Is it not just magic by another name? A sliver of doubt works its way into his mind, and Marwan touches the jack behind his ear.

The first seconds of the attack are now bringing gates down all over the world.

Data pipes into and out of Rome, Tel Aviv, Jerusalem, Mecca, Medina, Dallas, and Colorado Springs begin to squeeze shut.

Marwan has anticipated exactly this. This is why he has spent his inheritance on the living letters that await his instructions on his desktop. He toggles the terminal to touchscreen mode; the only thing on the screen other than the Brethren alphabet is a small ENTER button at the very bottom right. The program to activate Marwan's jack awaits only a touch of that button.

With a steady hand he reaches toward the glow of his terminal screen.

ya' sin

The Virt like the Golem of Prague, wanting only the word inscribed on its forehead to come alive. *Life*, Marwan thinks. He begins to touch his screen.

alif lam mim
alif lam mim sa
alif lam ra

He can feel the force of the information pouring away from him, roaring like water released from a dam. The Brethren letters, exploding out along the pathways charted by the nineteen members of Marwan's list, carving their own ways through the security of Baptists and Muslims, Catholics and Jews. The living language, thought Marwan. The words that will give the Virt life: I worship Him and He worships me. This is the syncretic truth.

alif lam mim ra
alif lam ra
khaf ha' ya 'ain sad

It begins almost immediately. Marwan maintains a separate terminal that scans public newsnets and cameras. Out of the corner of his eye he notices signs and wonders: holograms of saints appear in particle-laser laboratories; the words of Moses Maimonides echo from the public-address system at Fenway Park; at every roulette wheel in every casino in Las Vegas, the ball drops on nineteen.

sad

Defenses start to come up, reactive attacks. The lights in his bedroom flicker, but Marwan reconfigured all the pipes into and out of his building weeks ago. Down the road, patrons of the Dearborn Swim Club are no doubt wondering what happened to their electricity—if they're not all gaping at the recitation of the *basmala* that is booming out of the golf-course loudspeakers. (Marwan remembers Susan Heddle in a purple bikini, the summer before by the side of the pool. Even now the memory takes his breath away.) *In the name of God, the Merciful, the Compassionate...*

Marwan centers his attention back on his terminal screen. His defenses are up; if they're enough, they're enough. If not...never mind. No doubt there are groups of young men on their way to his door now. No doubt they will find him. He feels certain that they will kill him now that they know what he is doing.

Unless he is right.

His field of vision narrows to the Brethren characters on the screen. He devotes his entire being to touching, from memory, the letters. He does not speak.

ta' ha'
ta' sin mim
ta' sin

The second terminal goes dark, and Marwan's breath catches in his throat. He hesitates, waiting for the fatal strike from the Virt.

It does not come.

ta' sin mim
alif lam mim
ya' sin

A siren sounds faintly, away down Ford Road toward the Fairlane Town Center. In the back of his mind Marwan wonders if he has had anything to do with it. His second terminal comes alive again. Scrolling on its display, he sees the Virt addresses of his unwitting co-conspirators. Most of the addresses are grayed out, inert. Seven survive.

It is more than he asked for, more than he expected. Belief, Marwan thinks. If God is with us...

sad
ha' mim
ha' mim 'ain sin qaf
Three more.

ha' mim

Marwan's finger moves of its own accord. He has long since stopped directing it. He catches himself almost speaking the *basmala*, and closes his mouth before he can speak out loud, or even whisper.

ha' mim
qaf
nun
Done.

At any moment his main terminal could go dark. There could be a knock at the door. The telephone could ring. How long can he survive? How long will the Brethren letters have to do their work?

Failure is still a real possibility. Marwan is suddenly infuriated. *What is your right?* Marwan thinks, as Martin Luther had and perhaps Mohammed. *What is your right to put rules and priests and rituals, dead languages, the homilies and hadith of dead men, between me and the God who created me? What is your right to keep me from the fulfillment of my humanity?* He has staked his life to know that his mother and father are not bits of divine stuff, assimilated into the Godhead like proteins dissolving in the protoplasm of some immense and thoughtless bacterium.

On his other terminal, one name remains active. The rabbinical student in Haifa, tirelessly baffling the temple defenses with self-reflexive Kabbalistic numerology, strings of integers that endlessly ramify in the depths of Judaism's electronic bunker.

ha' mim 'ain sin qaf

And then he, too, is gone, and Marwan is alone.

There is a knock on the door. Then a bang. Shouts in English and Arabic.

He thinks they've kept the pipes open long enough for the word of life to breathe into the form of the Virt. His second terminal erupts in a chaotic slush of images and text; Marwan cannot make sense of it.

I have worshiped you as I can, Marwan thinks. I have struggled with error and deception. I have not come this far...

He cannot finish the thought. My life, he thinks. My life.

ha' mim

The Brethren alphabet disappears from his screen.

For an endless moment Marwan believes he has failed. Then his eyes adjust and he realizes that the terminal is not dead. A living black radiates from the screen. The ENTER button at the bottom right suddenly glows too bright to look at.

The breathing void, the Naught that Is. What the Kabbalists called *Eyn Sof.*

Marwan speaks for the first time in four days. His voice is dusty. "I want to see my father again. I want to see my mother again.

"I know they are not gone. I know they stand with you, as I will stand with you. I know that you have shown yourself to me, and you will show yourself to the world. *Allahu akbar.*"

Marwan gets out of his chair and slips off his sneakers and his Detroit Red Wings cap. For a moment he wishes for the comfort of his rug; then a wave of unease sweeps over him as he realizes that he is facing not east but south. Another moment, though, and he has caught himself. This, after all, was the whole idea. My God, he thinks.

He touches his forehead to his bedroom rug. When he looks up again, the ENTER button now displays Brethren characters.

qaf

Marwan hears his doorframe splinter. He picks up the four-pronged plug and looks at it, as he has looked at it a thousand times before.

Here I stand, he thinks. I can do no other.

He slips it into the jack behind his right ear. His right index finger poises over the lower right-hand corner of his terminal screen.

nun

Everyman, I will go with thee and be thy guide.
But Knowledge, too, falls by the wayside at last.

alif lam mim

Enter.

THE UTERUS GARDEN

S
he had been dreaming of Mexico. In her dream she understood what people said even though she didn't speak Spanish. No one avoided her eyes.

✳ ✳ ✳

"HENRY," SAID JULIA AS THEIR DAIMLER WHIRRED up the driveway, coasting to a halt in the garage. "Should we have done this?"

He looked at her. She thought he looked uncertain himself.

"J," he said. "We're going to be parents."

The words flooded her. "We're going to be parents," she said back. A fluttering in her stomach constricted her throat. As if I was actually going to give birth, she thought. And began to cry.

Henry spread his fingers over the back of her neck and drew her head into the lapel of his coat. She cried quietly. Henry's lapel smelled like the adoption agency office: clean hair, licorice, sun-warmed dust. Henry himself smelled frightened.

Julia was frightened, too.

They went into the house. Lights came on in their favorite rooms and the coffee pot began to perk. Henry gave the incoming a cursory check, but all the calls could be ignored for the moment.

Julia looked at him. Age was starting to show in the angle of his neck, the softening of the line around his jaw. His hair had been graying when she'd met him, nine years before; now the gray had spread from his temples to meet on the nape of his neck. He looked like a kid who'd gotten a bi-level dye job.

Henry Bancroft was forty-nine years old. Julia herself was thirty. Somehow it was okay that he was infertile. Somehow it was not okay that she was.

Not that he ever said anything. Henry was too decent for that. Instead she watched him, and when he got tired she saw disappointment and regret peer out from the cracks in what had once been Henry's invulnerable armor

145

of energy and optimism.

He caught her looking at him, and what Julia had come to think of as his Understanding Wrinkle deepened. "J," he said. "Seventy-three percent."

"I know," she said.

As of that year, 2041, seventy-three percent of women of childbearing age in the United States and Western Europe were infertile. Estrogen mimics in the air, some other kind of pollution, some chemical in the groundwater…nobody knew for sure what was causing it, but the industrialized world was less and less able to reproduce. The number for men was said to be sixty percent, but male infertility hadn't been studied so rigorously, and all men weren't required to undergo fertility examinations before gaining a marriage license.

Julia had passed the examination. She had been twenty-two, marrying a wealthy and charismatic man nearly twice her age over her parents' objections, and nothing could have been wrong in the world.

And then something had happened. The doctors said she would probably never know what.

Seventy-three percent, she thought. The numerals appeared in her mind, and as if they were some kind of ethereal jungle gym, the child she and Henry were adopting swung from the crossbar of the 7, slid whooping off the bottom curl of the 3. He was the color of the coffee Henry now poured into the mug she'd bought him in Costa Rica. The name his parents had given him was Marvel Ssengoba. He had been born in Uganda, and was now in therapy at the Charles River Adoption Services inpatient facility off Storrow Drive. In three days he would be ready to come home.

Henry and Julia were going to call him Arthur.

* * *

THE FIRST THING SHE BECAME AWARE OF was a terrible medicinal taste in her mouth. Then her hands twitched, and through the fog clearing from her mind she thought: I can move.

I can get out.

There were needles in her arms. She worked them loose. Then, growing more frightened as her head cleared, she tore the adhesive patches from her temples and wrists and right breast.

She was in a fiercely clean white room. Seven other women lay on beds, linked by tubes and wires to squat machines that blinked and muttered. Three of them were visibly pregnant.

Her own machine was silent. Something had gone wrong, and she had awakened.

It was cold in the room, and she was wearing only a hospital johnny. She found a robe hanging on the back of the bathroom door, and a cardigan sweater draped over the arm of a chair that faced her bed. She left the robe where it was, but put on the sweater and two pairs of rubber-soled socks from a drawer in her bedside table. In the same drawer she found paper underwear and put in on. Its crinkling made her wince, and it hung loose from her belly.

Peering through the door, she saw a long hall. Occasional recesses on either side marked doorways.

I'll only get one shot at this, she thought, and walked quickly out and to the left.

* * *

JULIA SAT UP LATE WATCHING VIDEO OF MARVEL SSENGOBA.

He wasn't really old enough to have cavorted around on the jungle gym numbers her anxious brain had conjured that afternoon. He was just a baby. Six months old, maybe, from the look of him. He could almost sit up, listing to his left, and he had apparently just discovered how to grab his feet. He had a single tooth, a bit off center in his bottom gum.

In the video, his mother's hands appeared and disappeared. Whoever had been behind the camera, though, had been careful not to capture the mother's face. Her hands were long-fingered and strong. Julia looked at her own hands. Her fingernails were perfect, and she wore two rings on her left ring finger. Once there had been a lump of callus on the inside of the first knuckle on her right middle finger. When she was a girl, and she had liked to draw pictures. Now the callus was long faded, and she signed her name with a thumbprint.

Having a black baby didn't bother her. Especially since he wouldn't really be black when the therapy was done. A little tinkering with the periphery of the genome, and Arthur Bancroft, formerly Marvel Ssengoba, would be a bright-eyed little Caucasian boy. The nose and the lips would need to be taken care of, of course, but decades of practice had made those surgeries little more involved than a root canal, and significantly less painful.

An unwelcome thought entered Julia's mind: What if they hadn't had the therapy done?

Poor families had been known to do it, raise children who were obviously African or Pakistani. Julia and Henry made too much money to do it that way, though; the social consequences alone at Henry's law firm made the idea unthinkable.

People with more money than Henry and Julia—not tons more, but more—could afford to adopt healthy Anglo babies born to American parents. There were terribly few of them, and they went for exorbitant rates, but for a while Henry and Julia had discussed a home equity loan, decreased retirement contributions for a few years.... In the end they had done the right thing.

"Race is all just appearance anyway," Henry had said. "An aesthetic problem."

And he was right. Still Julia looked at Marvel Ssengoba and felt that she was scraping him away, replacing him with an Anglo changeling named Arthur who would come into their home denatured, his past abraded away by the skillful surgeons down at Charles River Adoption Services.

Julia looked up. Henry was in the doorway. His pajama bottoms hung on his hips. "Did you hear something?" he said.

"No."

He looked around the room, as if the noise he thought he'd heard might disclose itself between the curtains.

"Henry?" Julia said.

His eyes still searched the room. "Yes, honey?"

"What would the Wheelers think?"

Henry woke up a little. "About what?"

On the video screen, Marvel Ssengoba toppled over and lay smiling on his back.

"J," Henry said. "The Wheelers' kids are from Africa, too. Come on." He held out his hand to lead her up to bed.

That's not what I was asking, she thought. What would they think if we hadn't put him through the therapy? She stood up. "In a minute. Let me pick up a bit first."

"Okay," he yawned, and went back upstairs.

Yes, she thought. The Wheelers' kids were from Africa. But the Wheelers, Mark and Sophie, who played doubles with Henry and Julia in the firm's annual tennis tournament, were black themselves. They hadn't had Thomas and Grace—

Bleached.

Their doctors down at CRAS hadn't much cared for the term. Neither did Henry. But that was what the newsnets called it, and that was what the chatters called it, and if she was honest with herself Julia knew that all the word's connotations were exactly right.

Marvel Ssengoba was being bleached. And they were paying to have it done.

In three months we'll have him home, she thought. Then he'll be ours. There won't be any more Marvel Ssengoba. There will instead be Arthur Bancroft. We will love him like he is our own, and no one will ever have to know. There are secrets kept from every child.

* * *

SHE WAS WALKING ALONG THE MEMORIAL DRIVE bike path when she remembered her name. Denise. Denise Kean. She wasn't from Cambridge but she'd hung out there a lot after school. In the Pit, the sunken brick plaza over the Harvard Square T station.

That's where she would go. Someone there, a friend, would know what had happened.

The evening was warm, which was lucky. She cut through a little park, trying hard not to be self-conscious about her clothes. In the Pit, everyone dressed weird, but she didn't want to attract attention before she got there. She walked down Mount Auburn for a bit, turned up JFK and crossed over to the wide brick plaza that contained an ancient newsstand and the Pit. Denise paused for a few minutes at the corner, watching people go by and scanning the faces of the kids in the Pit. Nobody she knew was there. Which was impossible; she knew thirty or forty kids who regularly swung through the Pit to trade music, score drugs, or just hang out at the top of the T escalator and panhandle change.

Wait: there was a familiar face. Skinny, bobbing Adam's apple, live tattoos on both cheeks…Leon.

Denise walked straight up to him. "Hey, Leon."

His tattoos jumped straight into his ears. "Holy shit! Denise! Holy shit!"

"Relax, freak," she said. "What's the big deal? I was just in the hospital for a bit."

"A bit," he repeated. "Fuckin' two years. That's the last time anybody saw you. And…holy shit! When are you due?"

He was looking down. She followed his gaze.

"Oh my God," Denise said.

"You're gonna fuckin' pop right here if you're not careful," said Leon.

"Oh my God." As she looked down at her swollen belly, all the sensations she'd ignored since splitting the hospital came crashing together in her head. The sore feet, sore back, bad balance, looseness in hips and knees. She was pregnant. Really pregnant. So pregnant that Leon was right. She looked like she might drop right there.

I knew that, she thought. I knew it right when I woke up. But I didn't think about it until just now. If I'd thought about it when I woke up in there, I'd still be there.

Plus I was *used* to it.

She was from Charlestown. Her father drove a truck, and her mother worked in a boat dealership, and both of them would kill her if they found out she was pregnant.

No wonder she'd run away. But how had she ended up in the white room over by the Harvard Bridge? What went on there? Denise wished she'd looked back at the building, or at least stopped long enough to grab something to identify where she'd been. She could find the place again, but who knew if they'd be looking for her?

Had her parents committed her there?

Leon was still staring at her. She had to say something. When she did, it shocked her all over again. "Two years?"

"In August. Today's July seventeenth. So not quite two years. But yeah. Holy shit." He grinned at her. He had a big mouth. "Pregnant is pretty sexy on you," he said.

Gone two years? And now pregnant?

Oh my God, Denise thought. I always thought those places were like urban myths.

"I have to go," she said.

"Me, too," he said with his big grin.

"Leon," she said. "I like talking to you, but you need to leave me alone, okay?"

He held both hands up, palms out, and let her gain some distance. "As you say. I'll see you around."

Two years? she wondered as she wandered out of Harvard Square onto Mount Auburn Street. She passed the Indian restaurant her uncle had taken her to once, right next to the pharmacy where the tech would misplace stuff into your pocket if you didn't pay too much attention to what his hands did along the way. Both memories made her shudder.

Two years, she thought again. That makes me eighteen. Where have I been? And how the hell did I not notice I was pregnant?

* * *

JULIA AWOKE FROM UNCOMFORTABLE DREAMS. In them, Marvel Ssengoba had spoken Spanish to her. But nobody spoke Spanish in Uganda. And she didn't speak Spanish, and didn't really know anyone who did except for the waiters at Taqueria Cancun over on Arrow Street.

She went outside. The morning air smelled rich and earthy in her back yard. Julia breathed it in, wishing she spoke Spanish so she would know what Marvel—what Arthur—had said to her.

"Just a dream," she said, to convince herself.

A small voice echoed her words from under the trellis at the side of the back patio.

Julia started. There was a girl under the trellis. She was dirty, wearing a green sweater and what looked like hospital clothes. "What are you doing here?" she asked, her voice sharp.

"Just a dream," the girl said again. She began to cry. "I wish it was just a dream."

Then Julia saw that the girl was pregnant.

Right away social responses so ingrained that they might as well have been instincts kicked in. Julia rushed to the girl, made sure she wasn't hurt, helped her to her feet, got her inside.

"What's your name?" Julia asked.

"Denise Kean," the girl answered. She was crying more freely now that someone was taking care of her, and looking down at the floor. "I thought those places were just like urban myths, you know?"

Julia ignored that. Pregnant women weren't supposed to have hot baths, she remembered that, but this girl was dirty. She unbuttoned the old sweater and tossed it on the floor. "Denise, how far along are you?"

Denise shrugged. The hospital shift fell off her shoulder and she didn't slip it back.

"You don't know? Who's the father?"

Another shrug, and the tears came harder. Julia relented.

"Okay, honey, I'm sorry. I know. Is there anybody I can call for you? Your parents?"

A violent shake of the head. *Did her father...?* Julia wondered, and did not know how to ask. "Are you hurt?" she said instead.

"No." Denise finally hitched her sleeve back up over her shoulder. She left her hand there.

"Hungry."

Another shake of the head. Still Denise wouldn't look up.

"Can you stand up long enough to take a shower?"

A nod.

"Take a shower, then." The house started water as Julia spoke. She got a set of towels from the hall closet. "I'll be downstairs in the kitchen, okay? Take all the time you need."

She called Henry the minute she got downstairs. "Henry, there's a pregnant girl in the shower."

He just stared at her like she'd known he would.

"A pregnant white girl," Julia added.

"Where did she come from?"

"She was in the back yard when I went out first thing this morning." Julia looked out the window. The gate was open. "She's wearing a hospital shift, Henry. Do you think she's in trouble?"

"She—is she all right? Is someone coming to get her?"

"No. She didn't want me to call her parents. As far as I can tell, she isn't hurt, but...."

Henry's Understanding Wrinkle creased and relaxed. An odd expression passed across his face. "We should talk about this face-to-face," he said. "Why don't you come down here for lunch?"

Henry worked in an old building across the street from the Park Plaza Hotel. It was half an hour on the T. "I'm not sure I should leave her here. What if she steals things?"

"Do you still have any of those sleeping pills?" Henry asked her.

All of a sudden they were talking about much more than just a stray teenager. Julia opened her mouth, shut it again. "Henry, what ... Those wouldn't be good for the baby, would they?"

"Come on, J. If you can tell she's pregnant, the baby's big enough that one pill won't hurt it. And she probably needs the rest. Who's it going to hurt? Fix her some tea," he made a crumbling motion with his fingers, "let her take a nap while you're gone." He looked away from the vidlink in his office and nodded. "Got to go, J. One o'clock okay?" She nodded. "See you then."

The wallscreen in the kitchen went dark. Julia stood listening to the water running in the upstairs bathroom. Then she put water on for tea.

* * *

WHEN DENISE WOKE UP, IT WAS DARK. She was in a bed, still wearing the night-gown Julia had given her, along with a cup of tea when she'd gotten out of the shower. There were no clocks, but Denise remembered that the house was smart, so she asked it what the time was.

"Seven fifty-seven p.m.," it said in a competent female voice.

A light knock at the door startled Denise. "Yes?" she said, after a moment's hesitation.

The door opened a crack. Light from the hallway backlit Julia, obscuring her features, but Denise could tell it was her. "I'm glad you're awake," Julia said. "I need to talk to you for just a minute. Then we should get you back in bed until you have a little more energy."

"I slept all day?" Denise asked. Something about it didn't seem right.

"Sometimes we're more tired than we think we are."

This seemed like something Denise's mom might have said.

"Are you going to tell my parents I'm here?" she said.

"You didn't want me to before. Do you want me to now?"

For a short moment Denise did, powerfully; then the urge passed and she shook her head. If she'd been gone two years like Leon said, she was eighteen now, and she'd sworn to herself a long time ago (probably in the Pit, and Leon had probably been there) that once she was eighteen she was never setting foot in that dingy Charlestown triple-decker again.

"They might worry about you," Julia said, but without much conviction.

She wants me to stay here, Denise thought. She doesn't want anyone to know

I'm here. It was frightening, but Denise had a feeling that the alternative was the white room she'd come from, full of ticking machines and pregnant bellies. She'd take her chances here.

"No," she said. "I don't think they'd really want to know."

Two years, she thought. By this time it might be true.

* * *

OVER DINNER, JULIA TRIED TO KEEP CONVERSATION LIGHT, but Henry looked at the girl the way a hawk eyes a pigeon, and Denise withdrew to the point that Julia had to tap her on the shoulder to suggest that she might go to bed. She nodded and got up. When she'd left the dining room, Julia turned on Henry.

"Well, you sure made her feel at home. Could you have looked a bit more like the fox in the chicken coop?"

"What are you worried about?" Henry asked. The dishes clinked as they put them in the dishwasher. "She isn't going anywhere. She's got nowhere to go. Like I said at lunch, for all intents and purposes she doesn't exist."

The casual brutality of those last few words echoed in Julia's head. At times like these she couldn't remember why she'd married Henry. But then he was kind to her; he hadn't laid any guilt on her for being infertile. Half of her friends nursed smoldering anger at their husbands—or, increasingly, their ex-husbands—over reactions to their barrenness. Henry had been nothing but supportive, empathetic, and sad, not for himself but for her.

Then at other times he was the kind of man who could say of a frightened and pregnant eighteen-year-old runaway that she didn't exist. And he was right.

"Whatever happened to her, J," Henry said, "she's going to be better off once it's over. Everyone's going to be better off." He paused. "You're right about dinner. I'm sorry. But a healthy American baby."

He didn't say white, Julia thought. At least he didn't say it.

"We'll all be happier once it's over," Henry finished. "You should go talk to her. I would but she's probably scared of me. Will you apologize? I didn't mean it."

She touched him on the arm and left him to finish cleaning up the kitchen.

Upstairs in the guest bedroom, Denise was brushing her hair. She had long, lustrous brown hair, not at all what Julia would have expected to see on a runaway.

And there was the thing that was really bugging her. What, exactly, had this girl run away from?

Those places are rumors, Henry had said when she brought it up at lunch. *Do you think this government would let that happen to the flower of America's female youth? Impossible.*

Henry's speech always got like that when he was lying.

"Denise?"

Denise put down the brush and looked at her.

"Henry said to apologize for the way he was looking at you tonight. We've just—" Julia shrugged. "We've been trying to have a baby for a long time, and then there you are with a baby. It's hard for him not to be a little bit envious."

A tentative smile brought out a dimple in Denise's right cheek. "Yeah."

Julia sat on the reading chair under the window. Denise started brushing her hair again, like a girl in a fairy tale who counts a hundred strokes every night.

Do you know what you have? Julia thought. *That baby growing inside you, do you know how many people want a baby just like that one, how many people would sell their houses and everything they owned to have one?*

"Tell me about yourself," Julia said.

The brush stopped.

"What do you want to know?"

"Where did you come from?"

Denise put the brush down and looked at herself in the mirror for a long time, her hands folded in her lap. "I told you," she said eventually. "I'm from Charlestown."

You didn't tell me that, Julia thought. But she said, "Right. I forgot." Then she said, "But how did you get into our back yard?"

"Through the gate," Denise answered, and in the silence that followed they both knew she'd been too flip. Julia waited her out.

Still looking in the mirror, Denise started to speak. Each word measured, each word carefully kept in check. "Yesterday I woke up in a room. I thought I was in the hospital. The walls were white and the floor was white and there wasn't a window. I was hooked up to a machine, but it had stopped working." She never took her face from the mirror, but the corner of her mouth began to tremble and tears spilled onto her cheeks. "There were seven other girls in the room, and seven other machines. All of the girls were asleep, and they were all pregnant, and the machines ticked and hissed and before I could think about it I grabbed some clothes and I got out of there." Her mouth kept moving after she stopped speaking, but Julia couldn't hear any sound. Then the sound cut back in. "I saw my friend Leon down at the Pit, and he said nobody had seen me in two years." Now she looked at Julia, terrible confusion and fear in her eyes. "I'm eighteen. I remember being sixteen. I remember flunking my driver's test. I remember starting my sophomore year. Now I'm eighteen. And I'm pregnant, and what I keep wondering is how many babies have I already had that I don't know about? Where are they?"

The last of Denise's self-control crumbled, and she began to sob. Julia went to her and let her cry. It took a long time for the storm to pass, and when it did Denise was sleepy. "Julia?" she said.

Julia stroked her hair. "You're okay here, honey. You're safe."

"Julia, what's going to happen if they find me?"

"They won't. Henry and I will make sure of that." That much was true, Julia thought. She and Henry would take care of that much.

When she went back downstairs, Henry was in his study. She left him there and went into the living room. When she flicked on the television, Marvel Ssengoba's beaming image appeared and as if she had been slapped in the face Julia began to cry. Henry came in and found her like that. He turned off the television and popped the disc out and put it in his pocket.

"She's not lying, Henry," Julia said.

Henry sat next to her on the sofa. "Maybe not."

"No maybe. She's not lying. Someone took her and put her in some kind of coma and shot her up with babies like she was a breeding sow." Her anger at this surprised Julia, and then her surprise surprised her; of course she was angry. Why hadn't she expected to be angry?

Because you're part of it, she thought. You sent Marvel Ssengoba to be bleached, and if you'd had more money you would have bought a white baby from one of the places like the place that had Julia in their basement with all those other girls and their machines.

"If they catch her, she'll be safer if she doesn't have the baby she's carrying now," Henry said.

Julia knew what he was doing, and was too tired and heartsick to argue. "We talked about it at lunch, Henry. I agreed. You're right."

"It's for the best," he said.

She nodded. Then wondered out loud: "Shouldn't we at least let her keep what's hers, after what she's been through?"

"She can keep Marvel Ssengoba."

"He's not hers."

"The baby she's carrying might not be hers either. It could be an implant. And no, we can't find out; any doctor we went to would run a sample through the fertility database. It'd be a red flag to whoever runs the place where she came from. Or hell, the doctor could be involved. People might kill her, Julia, if they think she's given them away. Do you know what kind of money we're talking about? Well-intentioned liberalism only gets you so far, Julia. People might come after us."

"We should at least tell someone about the place."

Henry thought. "Yeah. Maybe we should. Did she tell you where it was?"

Julia shook her head. "But she would if I asked her, I think, as long as she didn't think we were going to take her back."

"Okay. Once the swap is done, once she's better and gone. We'll tell someone." Henry settled against her, put his arm around her shoulders. "'Kay, J? We'll tell someone. Good will come of this. You watch."

* * *

THE BACK YARD WAS DENISE'S FAVORITE PART of the Bancroft property. It was walled in on two sides like an old English garden, and a wooden fence with ivy growing on it marked the other edge. Although Harvard Square and Memorial Drive were only a few hundred yards away, it was quiet here. Denise wondered what Henry did for a living. The Bancrofts had some money, that was for sure. Their house did things for them, they lived in the old part of Cambridge…but for Cambridge, they weren't exactly rich. Looking more closely, Denise could see that the trim on the Bancrofts' Queen Anne needed painting, and a couple of the windows were cracked. And Henry had to go to work in Boston, he didn't have a v-office set up the way the real moneymakers did.

On this morning she was sitting on a metal bench that faced from the back patio out into the yard. A couple of mourning doves cooed on an old telephone line; Denise wondered who in this neighborhood still had landline service. Her belly forced her to recline against the back of the bench, and she had to shift often to keep her butt from going to sleep. But she was safe for the moment, and the Bancrofts didn't seem like they were going to force her out right away.

The sliding door opened and Julia came out with cups of tea. Denise wasn't a tea drinker, but it would have been rude to turn it down. She sipped, enjoying the honey Julia always added, but put her cup down when she saw the look on Julia's face.

Julia was looking at her the way Henry had at dinner the night before. "We'll make you a deal," she said.

"What deal?"

"We won't tell anyone you're here, and we'll take care of you and the baby until you give birth." Julia looked hard at her, and Denise figured the tough part of the deal was coming.

"Do you want this baby?"

Denise blinked. "I don't know."

"I want this baby," Julia said. "I want it more than you do. More than you've ever wanted anything in your life."

You don't know how bad I want anything, Denise wanted to say. You don't know me. But she bit down on the words, knowing that she was a phone call away from her parents or the police or whoever had knocked her out and hooked her up to machines in the white room over off Soldiers Field Road.

"What will happen if I give you my baby?" she asked.

"We'll give you ours," Julia said.

Denise heard the words but could not make sense of them right away. "You have a baby?"

Julia nodded. The corner of her mouth twitched.

"Then why do you want mine?"

Julia's face closed down, and Denise knew she was about to lie, and knew that her husband had gotten her to do it. "We are adopting. And we would rather adopt your baby to help you out."

Do you think I'm that fucking dumb? Denise thought. She didn't want any woman who would lie like that to have her baby.

"What are you going to do with it?" Julia asked, as if she'd rehearsed the conversation beforehand. "Your parents don't know you're pregnant. What would they say?"

"Of course they don't know! I didn't even know until yesterday! And you want to know what they'd do? They'd kill me. Not a figure of speech. I would be dead. You'd read about it in the paper over your coffee in your little breakfast nook."

Denise had leaned forward, and her belly pushed her back into the bench. Julia stared at her. There was the Julia that Denise had met the day before: easily shocked, a little naïve. Sensitive. Denise liked her much better than the hungry Julia who had come into the room today wanting to swap her baby like it was a pair of shoes that didn't quite fit.

"This isn't a deal," Denise said. "You're not really asking me what I want."

"Well," Julia said. "Do you know the risk we've taken by allowing you to stay here? The people who you escaped from would certainly like you back, and I don't imagine they'd hesitate too long before killing you if they thought your story would find a sympathetic ear." She paused to let that soak in, and Denise realized it was true. Who would protect her from people that had that kind of money and that kind of a secret to keep? Leon?

"And the baby might not even be yours," Julia went on. "It's just as likely to be implanted; something like forty percent of infertile women ovulate perfectly healthy eggs. They just need a place to grow them, and I'd guess that your white room was a little uterus garden for women who don't care much where their babies come from, as long as they come." Something flickered in Julia's face as she said this, and Denise thought: A little too close to home, there.

"What do I get out of this?" she asked. "If I take your baby that you don't want, how am I going to take care of it? Those people will still be after me, and I still won't be able to go home."

Julia took a deep breath. "Henry and I are prepared to offer you four years of tuition and expenses, including housing, at any university in a country where a white girl with a baby isn't going to be an object of undue curiosity. We suggest Mexico; since the opening of the border, it's relatively Americanized, lots of people speak English there, and there are good universities. You do speak Spanish?"

Denise nodded. Didn't everybody?

"You can go to college and get a job, raise this child or give it up for adoption. I'd like to say I don't care, but the truth is I do. I want this child that was going to be mine to have a good home, and I'm willing to do what I can to see that you provide it. So that's the bargain: we trade babies, and you get college and a new start for free. How does that sound?"

"You mean I have to decide now?"

"The longer we wait, the more likely it is that someone's going to find out you're here. Nobody wants that. Also, the baby we contracted for is due back from the hospital tomorrow."

Denise thought. The doves flew away and her tea got cold.

"Promise me one thing," she said.

Julia raised an eyebrow.

"Promise me you'll tell someone about that place."

"I will," Julia said.

* * *

Artemis Bancroft was beautiful: ruddy, squalling, grabbing whatever she could with tiny fingers, staring at the world with dark, dark blue eyes. Henry and Julia agreed that their new story would be that the adoption people had accidentally sent them a baby girl, and, well, what could they do but love her? Simple. No one would pursue it; after all, Henry was a lawyer, and if there was litigating to be done he could do it himself. The responsibility of Charles River Adoption Services ended at their front door, and if Marvel Ssengoba's birth certificate declared him to be male, so what? It would hardly be the first document to come out of Uganda with notable errors. Everything would work out fine.

The day Marvel was due back from CRAS, Henry had gone walking in Cambridge and come back with a midwife who agreed to induce Denise Kean at what she thought was approximately thirty-seven weeks. As Henry was writing her the check, the midwife speared him with a glance and said, "You make sure you do the right thing here."

"You can trust us," Henry said, and showed her to the door.

Julia was holding Artemis when Henry came back upstairs. "What did you tell her, Henry?" she asked.

"I told her this girl was in trouble, and had nowhere to go, and we were going to take the baby. I think she's pretty certain someone raped Denise and we're covering it up."

He looked at her as he said this, and Julia knew he was waiting for her to comfort him, to say, *No, of course, we wouldn't cover something like that up*—but she couldn't say that. Couldn't say anything. Could only look into the eyes of this marvelous baby girl and think: *We're doing the right thing. We're going to do the right thing.*

With the resilience of an eighteen-year-old, Denise was out of bed the next day, and that evening she was nursing Marvel Ssengoba.

"What are you going to name him?" Julia asked.

Denise shrugged. She hadn't said much since the delivery. Julia was trying to leave her alone to work through it all. Everyone was safe, though. Having the delivery in their home saved Julia and Henry from worrying that hospital records could put unwanted people on Denise's trail. And Artemis'.

Next Wednesday, Denise Kean and her baby would move into an apartment in Mazatlán. The week after that, she would start distance classes at Harvard Extension, her tuition covered by an anonymous scholarship.

Next Thursday, Julia thought, she would be able to breathe again.

* * *

BUT SHE COULDN'T. CRAWLING THEIR WAY ACROSS the Longfellow Bridge on the way back from the airport, watching the Red Line train rattle past and disappear under the MIT campus, Julia felt the weight still on her chest. Artemis made a small noise, a little quack almost, from the back seat, and Julia looked over her shoulder. The little girl was nearly asleep.

"We need to tell someone now, Henry."

"I know," he said, and she could tell he meant it. "But not just yet, J. Too many questions, you know? People are going to ask too many questions if we blow that particular whistle right now, with this particular baby."

She knew he was right, but God she wanted to set everything straight. She'd promised. But her first duty was to Artemis, who she thought was going to be Arthur, but life was full of little surprises like that. That was her first duty, and they would tell, later. Just not right then, when everything was all so uncertain, when all the wounds were still so fresh.

* * *

MARVEL SSENGOBA WAS BEAUTIFUL: TANNED ALREADY in the Baja sun, his hair growing into big looping caramel-colored curls, his eyes an earthy green and getting darker every day. He rested in the crook of Denise's arm as she walked along a boardwalk looking at the Gulf of California. It was hot, and she stopped for ice cream.

"¿Cómo llama?" the woman running the ice-cream stand asked.

"His name is Marvel," Denise said. The woman smiled after her as she walked off with her ice cream in the direction of the beach.

Volunteers

I have always had only one parent. Sometimes I can convince myself that I remember my mother plucking nervously at her harness as gravity disappeared on our way to the moon, but it's probably a capture from the vid archive. I think she must have seemed beautiful to me then, but so many video images of her lie between me and that memory...I can't tell anymore.

Her grave is near the center of the cemetery carved out of the brushy forest that surrounds Grant City. I visited it sometimes, and I tried to miss her, but she was too distant. Every time I ended up back with my father, sitting on the bench, trying to make something live between us.

* * *

When you look up at the sky from Grant City, 47 Ursae Majoris doesn't look that different than Sol from Earth. You have to have spex on to really compare, although some of the people who were older when we left Earth spent a lot of time glancing sunward and then shaking their heads like something wasn't quite right and they weren't sure what it was. That was where it all started, I think. Little puzzled glances at the sun that wasn't what it should be.

By the time I was about eleven, though, things had gone much farther off course.

This was about when I started wearing spex all the time. They belonged to my father, and I put them on just to imitate the old man, who thought it was funny and anyway James Brennan wasn't physically up to doing any kind of work anymore so he had no need of spex. So for a while I pretended to do what my father had been doing, surveying and materials analysis; I hung around work sites and let myself become a kind of mascot for the workers. They called me Flash Gordon, and laughed at my imagination when I asked them where all the robots had gone. Not too long after that, I started to notice that I was the only kid in Grant City who wore spex all the time, and I started to like the

161

way it made me feel different.

My teachers didn't like it. "Can you take off your glasses?" they'd ask, and I'd think, Glasses? My civics teacher, Mr. Fulton, tried to take them away from me, but my dad made Fulton give them back. Civics. We were on another planet learning about the bicameral legislature and the electoral college.

Kids started to call me Four-Eyes.

After a while, picking up on the same shit they were swallowing, I started to tell them that four eyes were better than two. Verbal judo: use their weight against them. Also I had already figured out that I wasn't doing myself any favors by calling attention to the fact that it wasn't 1956.

* * *

THERE REALLY WERE ROBOTS WHEN I WAS A LITTLE KID. Blocky things on six wheels, with jointed arms ending in flat pincers. The adults called them lobsters, so us kids did, too. I was fifteen before I knew that lobster wasn't just a slang term for robot.

When you're a kid, you adapt to all kinds of insanity without thinking about it too much. Lack of perspective gives you amazing resilience. So the day I came to school and saw chalkboards in the classrooms, I didn't think much about it, especially when I discovered I could drive the teachers crazy by making the chalk squeal. I was ten years old, and we had been on Canaan for five years. Plenty of time for delusions to spread.

* * *

I CAN'T HELP IT IF I TELL THIS STORY with a little too much ironic distance. Nobody can tell childhood straight. When I talk about delusions spreading, it's only by accident that I mean now instead of then. I think. It's hard to be certain when you're talking to yourself. Or when you think you're talking to yourself.

I forgot how cold it is here.

* * *

TO ME IT'S JUST A SUN, BUT I was only three when the *Susan Constant* left Earth in 2067. Which makes me two hundred and three years old, but if you ask me my age I'll tell you I'm nineteen.

I should be seventeen. I should never have had to spend two years alone on *Susan Constant*, ghosting around in the four rooms heated to sustain life. The ship was always cold; even when I was on Canaan I was cold all the time because when you've spent two years feeling a chill it never quite goes away.

I miss lying in that sun even though it's not the right sun. I miss lying in the grass even though it wasn't the right grass. I miss Iris.

Because my old man was a Volunteer.

× × ×

IF YOU'D KNOWN HIM IN GRANT CITY, if someone had pointed out the thin, bearded guy with the whining exoskeletal supports and a tendency to stare off at the sky while mumbling to himself and said, "That's the guy they got to keep Evelyn on an even keel," you would have thought to yourself that it was a miracle anybody survived the trip. And it was. Out of two thousand colonists, four hundred and thirty-two lived to see Canaan. That was because of my father.

It was also because of him that the others died.

* * *

YOU CANNOT IGNORE THIS. LISTEN TO ME.

× × ×

I THINK I FELL IN SOMETHING LIKE LOVE the first time Iris Flynn came up and talked to me in the cemetery. I was walking away from my mother's grave, confused and a bit dislocated like always, and she was coming up the road walking a brown puppy that chased after the big dragonfly-like insects that buzzed up from the river behind the cemetery. "Hi," she said.

I said hi.

"You're Wiley, right?"

There was no point denying it. "Yeah," I said, and waited for her to make some remark about how lucky I was. As if we weren't all lucky.

She pointed off to my right. "My sister's over there."

There was a long uncomfortable moment. Then I said, "I'm sorry."

Iris smiled at me. "It's not your fault."

Bang. Dead. After that moment, I would have done anything to be with her.

When I got home, my dad was sitting on a bench in front of one of the dozen barracks-style buildings that housed the citizens of Grant City. Across the new road, a work crew was welding I-beams to frame an apartment building. The pace of construction had picked up now that we'd gotten an oil well pumping for plastics and a smelter for good steel, but Grant City as it stood was still only the row of barracks, the school house, a shuttle pad already sprouting cracks, the bio lab, and a cluster of tech buildings at a respectful distance from the reactor housing. And the cemetery.

I was still dizzy from the rush of feeling Iris' smile had started, and my confusion gave me a kind of courage. I sat down next to my dad and said, "Dad. How do you know when you're in love?"

He looked me in the eye, and the brave surge I'd felt turned into the kind of scrambling apprehension you feel when you know you've gotten in over your head.

"Love," he said. "Love is when you can let a thousand people die because you can't stand, not even for a second, to tear yourself away from one."

He looked young as he said it, but as he told me the whole story I started to see the things that the telomerase therapy couldn't touch: the tic at the corner of his mouth, the way he licked his lips when he took a breath. I had been awake in the world for thirteen years, my father for more than thirteen squared. That afternoon I began to understand the difference.

* * *

HE'D EXPECTED THE DEPRESSION THAT FELL OVER HIM after the communication lag between *Susan Constant* and Earth grew too long to really have a conversation. He still monitored transmissions from Earth, but most people there had more pressing things to deal with than a Volunteer's loneliness. All he could do was listen to military communiqués, coverage of disaster after disaster after disaster, and then someone finally took the last plunge and let loose the ICBMs. After that, transmissions slowed to a trickle, and the last signal he heard, in 2144, was from a shortwave operator deep in the Siberian forest: *I think I'm going to go skiing for a while. Maybe that will make me feel better.*

The next thirty years or so were an empty space in his memory. He followed all the protocols, dealt with minor malfunctions, spent more and more VR time with a group of personas Schimmel had installed to give him some semblance of a social dynamic. More and more it seemed to him that he was dreaming the ship, his periodic rounds to run system checks and flush the reactor core.

You knew this would happen, Evelyn told him. It was included in your preparation.

He did know it, and after some time—even though the sensation didn't go away—he reached a kind of accommodation with it. It was a lucid dream, he reasoned, unreal but under his control. That was perhaps the best anyone could have done, but it only delayed his breakdown.

Schimmel puppetmasters had figured on that, too, and Evelyn put her psychiatric subroutines to work after preventing my dad from going out the shuttle-bay airlock. After a while, around the time *Susan Constant* turned around and began its long deceleration, she took the restraints off him. She was always there, though, talking to him, encouraging him, reminding him of the importance of what he was doing, and at some point during his convalescence my dad caught himself thinking that maybe he was falling in love. "The patient falling for the nurse," he said. "God." And he laughed, but at the time he was ashamed. "She wasn't even human."

I waited for him to mention my mother, but he didn't. I was thirteen, and my father was trying to tell me about love without mentioning my mother whose grave I had visited not an hour before.

Now I'm nineteen, and I don't resent him anymore.

* * *

I AM OLDER THAN I AM.

All of us feel that way sometimes, or so I've read. Einstein once explained relativity by noting that a minute at the dentist feels like an hour, and an hour with a pretty girl feels like a minute. Or something like that. I could look it up, I guess, but the exact expression doesn't matter. All of us sometimes feel that way.

The ship is quiet; but I knew it would be. Music just makes it seem emptier, so I make my rounds in silence now, except when Evelyn speaks to me.

* * *

MY FATHER GOT UP AND WALKED IN A SLOW CIRCLE around the bench. He did that a lot; he couldn't sit for too long in one place or his knees would stiffen. When he sat again he said, "I was with Evelyn when your mother died."

Why did it take you so long to tell me this, Dad? I wanted to say. Did you think I hadn't figured that out, when you spent twenty-two hours out of every twenty-four in the womb with her, leaving me to bounce around that great big goddamn tomb of a ship with nothing for company but VR spools of everything we'd left behind? A huge space opened up inside me, as if his admission had broken through a wall into a chamber of my memory that had been sealed up since I'd awakened cold and scared to see my father with tears on his face and a terrible fear in his eyes. That fear got into me, and it's never left.

* * *

BECAUSE I WAS SO YOUNG, I DIDN'T KNOW WHY we were going to leave San Diego and go to the moon. It was obvious to me that all the adults I knew—my mom, her boss Mr. Franklin, her brother Herschel, my teacher Miss Alaves—were nervous. It came out of them in different ways, according to their ordinary personalities, but I remember knowing that something was up, and because nobody wanted to explain it I was certain that it was something awful. Of course I had no way to ask; if I said, *What's wrong?* They smiled and said, *Nothing.* My only clue was something Uncle Herschel growled at the wallscreen during the 2066 World Cup, when Nigeria scored a late goal to tie the US in the quarterfinals. "I hope Big Mickey lands on fucking Lagos and fries every last one of you cheating bastards," he said. It's one of my first memories.

After that I started to ask about Big Mickey. What was he? How could he fry the Nigerians? Did he know they were cheaters? My mother sat me down and explained that outer space was full of big rocks, and one of them might hit the Earth but probably wouldn't. How big, I wanted to know. Bigger than our house? Bigger than an aircraft carrier? Bigger than the mountain where we'd gone camping?

Yes. Yes. Yes.

I guess we better get out of the way, I said.

We're going to, my mother said, and brushed my hair back on my forehead. You and me, we're going to.

And we did. On a hot spring day the next year, we took a plane out to the desert and got on a shuttle bound for the moon. My mother cried, and looking back on it now I wish I'd said something to her, but I was too keyed up for the trip. Going to the moon! To Armstrong Base!

And, more marvelous yet: going to see my father.

I hadn't seen him in so long that I only knew what he looked like because he was on the vid so much. James Brennan, Volunteer. He and Patricia Walsh and Antonio Queiroz were going to save us. How many of us? Everyone, my mother said. Don't worry, honey, we're all going to be gone by the time Big Mickey gets here.

* * *

WAIT A MINUTE. I WAS THREE WHEN WE LEFT. I was two during the 2066 World Cup. I couldn't remember that.

* * *

BETTER LATE THAN NEVER, I GUESS. IT WAS GOOD to hear him admit it. At the same time it made me wonder how much he knew before *Susan Constant* ever left Earth. Was he afraid of you—of Evelyn—even then?

I think he was. He'd stood up to the grueling physical screening, but so had more than a hundred other pilots. What made my father different was one thing: Evelyn responded to him. He must have wondered why, and wondered what it would cost him.

Why him, I wonder? How many other people with the same resume had she reduced to catatonia? I know that happened.

You're not even a woman.

* * *

Two years I spent drifting around *Susan Constant* after the accident, haunted and frightened and compelled by the ghostly ruin of my father who emerged from the pilot chamber once a day to visit me and run the routine diagnostics he'd so disastrously neglected before. That's a lot of time for watching canned vid history, but I didn't understand anything I saw. Pictures of people who looked angry. Fires. Every once in a while vid of the Lagrange station with *Susan Constant* taking shape.

When my dad came out of the womb I cried. Every time. He held me and said, *I'm sorry, pal*, over and over until I stopped. I remember asking him why he couldn't stay, and the broken expression on his face when he couldn't explain it to me. Desperate to hear his voice, I kept talking, asking him questions about what I'd seen on the vid, and that's how I got his version of what happened. I think if things had gone differently, he might have been a good father.

* * *

The kinds of people who controlled the vast majority of the world's wealth were also the kinds of people who couldn't actually believe that Big Mickey would destroy *them*; they'd ride out the impact and afterward set about remaking the shattered Earth in their own images. Everybody wanted a lifeboat, but everybody wanted someone else to build it and let them board.

So when a brand-new German corporation called Schimmel GmbH offered the American government thirty billion dollars for a short-term lease on the entirety of Lagrange's dock space, the cash was impossible to refuse. The White House fed the money to Lockheed, which revved up its Mars program, and Schimmel monopolized launch facilities all over Central Asia, lifting material and personnel to their new base at Lagrange.

They tried to deflect questions about what they were doing, but before too long the pressure got so intense that they had to respond. At a news conference broadcast worldwide on September 23, 2064, a Schimmel spokesman dropped a bombshell that for a few weeks made everyone forget Big Mickey.

They had discovered something out there that wasn't really an AI, wasn't really a ship either, wasn't really anything any of us had words for just yet.

* * *

EVELYN SHOWED ME A RECORDING OF THE SCHIMMEL press conference when I was about twelve, before I knew about the Lodge, before Julio Furcal died, when I still had a chance at being a kid. Not a normal kid—two years alone on *Susan Constant* took care of that possibility—but a kid. I think being a kid means being able to rely on people to make good decisions for you. If Grant City hadn't turned into a nuthouse, I could have had that. Even in the middle of the slide, I had Iris, even if I had her all confused in my head with my mother and Evelyn and every other woman who had ever shown me kindness.

* * *

"WHAT'S EVELYN LIKE?" I ASKED MY FATHER ONCE, a year or so before we slipped into orbit around the planet we would name Canaan, and long before I knew I'd already been talking to her.

He couldn't answer. The accident was too recent, his mind still too scrambled by guilt and desperate hope and the wrenching dislocation he felt whenever he left her to spend time with me. I never asked him again, and thought I'd never find out.

Funny how things happen.

* * *

THE FIRST TIME I ASKED IRIS OUT ON A KIND OF DATE, she said yes, as long as she could bring her little siblings along. This was humbling, but I was so gone over her that I said sure. Hannah and Peter were then six and five years old. I was fourteen. We were going to the farmer's market and then a movie; some of the older colonists had formed a film society that showed old movies in the school gym. They were slipping into the Fifties psychosis that eventually doomed Grant City, but at this point, before they'd left the shuttle pad to get weedy so they could build a movie theater, they had a sense of humor about the whole thing, mostly screening corny science-fiction movies that had the effect of making us all feel advanced and smart and a little bit heroic.

I'd expected the kids to be a burden, but I surprised myself by enjoying their company almost as much as Iris'. Of course I was trying to be nice to them so I could score points with Iris, but pretty soon I didn't have to try. They were just a joy to be around, full of questions that made me feel important because I could answer most of them and other questions that put me happily in touch with the little-kid state of wonderment over everything. Why were green beans and kidney beans both called beans? Why didn't pineapples grow on pine trees? Who knew, and who cared when you could revel in the innocent goofiness of the question? We ate barbecued chicken and hand-churned ice cream, and Hannah and Peter asked me a dozen times each if I was their sister's boyfriend. "You better ask her," I said, and couldn't breathe until she'd said yes I was.

The evening's movie was *The Blob*. During the scene in the movie theater, when the titular red goo poured out of the projection booth over the doomed kids necking in the back rows, Iris leaned over and whispered in my ear. "Guess we better be careful."

I don't remember anything else about the movie except looking over once to see Hannah and Peter wide-eyed and swept away.

* * *

I KNOW YOU KNOW MOST OF THIS ALREADY. All I have to offer that's new is me. My feelings, my perspectives.

Before we planted anything, we had the genelabs up and running, and we cultured seeds that wouldn't spread disease or be vulnerable to native strains. And for a while it worked; near the cemetery where my mother was buried, there was a cornfield. The only one I've ever seen. I used to climb the hill above it and look down on the rows of green stalks, watching the leaves ripple in smooth arcs as breezes swept down the valley. Canaan's amino acids were mostly left-handed, but we'd figured out a way to break the protein chains and turn them around. This absorbed a large part of each plant's energy, but with careful management the crops came in, smaller than they would have been on Earth but edible and nutritious. Our breeds of cattle and chickens seemed to be working, too, and about a year after we landed—this was 2251 by the Earth calendar—we had a Thanksgiving. We were surviving.

Most of us, anyway. Many of the adults suffered bouts of nostalgic depression, a phenomenon that GC doctors soon recognized as a variation on post-traumatic stress. A few committed suicide; others just walked out of the settlement and were never seen again; but most of us who felt the old Earth longing just toughed it out, and all the while Grant City grew younger. In ten years the population grew by three hundred, and things got better.

At least that was what I thought when I was a little kid.

* * *

THERE'S ONLY SO MANY DAYS AND NIGHTS you can spend on another planet pretending you're the Cisco Kid. When I was ten I wouldn't have believed this, but at twelve, goaded by incipient adolescence to look at the world outside my head just so I had something to nurse a grudge against, I started to feel uncertain about the self-imposed illusion that permeated Grant City.

I arrived at my first Boy Scout meeting to find that the troop leader, Detlef Hamann, had undergone a rhinoplasty to look more like Karl Malden. While Hamann handed out our Boy Scout Handbooks and taught us the oath, I had the small epiphany that all of Grant City was becoming a movie set. Hamann had also gotten a haircut and adopted the moony earnestness of Malden's character Mitch Mitchell from *A Streetcar Named Desire*. Which didn't even come out in the right year, but it didn't take me long to figure out that Grant City's 1956 was just a placeholder for The Fifties as a whole, and anyway I don't think I could have stood it if Hamann had decided he was Father Barry from *On the Waterfront*.

Hamann was the first I saw, but within a few months, people were having plastic surgery done so they resembled Marilyn Monroe or Joe DiMaggio, Edward Teller or Jack Kerouac or Dolores Del Rio.

* * *

BY THE TIME I WAS OLD ENOUGH to know what was going on, Grant City had sunk completely into its pathological nostalgia. The colony shrank into itself, redirected its energies from survival on an alien world to the re-creation of a time on Earth that never was. Our new start became a simulacrum of a simulacrum.

This should have prepared me for you.

* * *

I GOT IN A FIGHT ONCE, WHEN I WAS FOURTEEN. Not much of a story except for the long-term consequences make it interesting. This sixteen-year-old side of beef named Justin Rowe called me a pansy one too many times because I was wearing spex, and even though I knew it was dumb I took a swing at him. Hit him, too, but it didn't have much of an effect.

Justin hit me flush on the right eye, and then the ground hit me on the left shoulder. My first thought was *Oh shit what if they're broken*? Next I started worrying that Justin was going to hit me again. When I looked up he was already gone. I was lying in an eddy at the side of the main between-classes current, and if anybody knew I was there they weren't letting it show.

As it turned out, the spex were tougher than the skin beneath. My eyelid swelled up until I could hardly see out of that eye. My dad levered himself up off the bench when he saw the damage, and from various sources I heard that my dad had nearly assaulted the school principal, a guy called Milt

Bahrani, but nothing came of it beyond that. Justin never hit me again, but that might have been because I never said another word about the fact that it wasn't 1956.

Bahrani was just like the rest of them. He'd invented a new history for himself, claiming to have been an Iranian court aristocrat who fled the country when Mossadegh was toppled by the CIA in 1953. Victor Arroyo claimed he'd won the Silver Star in World War II, and when he'd had too much to drink he would display an appendectomy scar and tell the story of how he'd gotten it from a Japanese bayonet on Saipan. If Akira Ikuma was around, that was his cue to say that Victor was lucky it hadn't been Akira's bayonet because Akira would have finished the job, and hell yes Akira had been on Saipan, the only survivor of a grenade attack on his bunker and then later the last man on board a troop bus leaving Hiroshima, looking up at the drone of a bomber as they headed north to Osaka.

And on and on. They were all crazy. I watched them through spex and plotted escape. I could tune the spex to see bones, temperature fluctuations, brain activity, anything. I saw that Miss Callahan, who I remembered as a biologist from when I was little but who now seemed to be some kind of secretary, had large sacs under the skin of her breasts, and I nearly suggested she see a doctor before suffering an attack of discretion which lasted long enough for me to do some research and discover the history of cosmetic surgery.

Someone else noticed my black eye. Another nerdy kid named Vince Tukwiler, who glared at the world from his side of an invulnerable barrier composed of equal parts scorn and fear. Two days later he leaned against my locker and said, "Don't go to the movies tonight."

"Movies are the only thing keeping me from killing myself," I said. Almost meaning it.

"That's why you should go here instead," Vince said, and handed me a slip of paper. I reached for it, and he moved his hand. "Look at this and then destroy it. I shit you not, eat it or burn it or flush it down the toilet, but get rid of it. Okay?"

"Sure, okay," I said, just so he'd give it to me. He did, and I'll never forget the look that came over his face. Like he'd just taken a terrible chance on someone who didn't deserve it.

The paper had a place and time on it. I took a look, let the information stick in my head, and ate the paper right there in the hall. Whatever it meant, I didn't want to take a chance on anyone seeing me with it.

That was how I found out about the Lodge.

* * *

ONE DAY I SAT DOWN AND TRIED TO DO THE MATH. I had been born in 2064, and taking into account relativity and the rest of it I was two hundred and seven years old, but physically I was fourteen, and anyway everyone I knew insisted it was 1956, they argued about Eisenhower and Nixon for God's sake, and by that count I wouldn't show up for another hundred and eight years.

I seized on the idea that I was waiting to be born, and clung to it.

* * *

YOU KNOW, I HAVEN'T PUT ON MY DAD'S SPEX SINCE WE LEFT? I don't trust lenses anymore. Through the spex I thought I could see the truth, but all I was getting was another layer of masks.

They were your masks, though. Weren't they? Loving masks.

* * *

THE MISSION PLAN FOR YEARS FOUR AND FIVE called for nutritional self-sufficiency through agriculture, and they got there, but there was nothing in the mission plan about a bowling alley. Instead of adding onto the school, the city council redirected materials and labor into the construction of Bel-Mark Lanes.

Even though it was insane, I had to admit that the Lanes made for a good time. Ten alleys, four pool tables, a pinball machine, and a full bar. There was a jukebox with a killer selection of Elvis and Little Richard and Buddy Holly, and a league started up on Tuesdays and Thursdays. It was something to do after school that didn't involve walking in the park or watching robots frame a new building, and right away everyone in the school started going there. There was general agreement that a good old-fashioned place to hang out was doing the colony good.

When, that is, anyone would admit they were part of a colony.

This was where the Lodge came in. It started off when Julio Furcal, a social-studies teacher who had once been some kind of neurotech consultant, realized that Grant City's problems weren't just an affectation and weren't going away. The colony was sick, would get sicker, and needed a group of people to stand off to the side, nod and smile and pretend to go along while in fact they made sure that we all survived. At first there were six of them: Julio, Sharon Pelletier, Vince Tukwiler, Miss Callahan, and I don't know the other two. When I went to my first meeting Julio said they were on assignment. Like spies, and they were spies, but they also thought of themselves as guardians. "We're hoping that this delusion is just a temporary kind of collective defense mechanism," Pelletier told me. "In the meantime, we try to get some science done, make sure everyone can eat, and hope that people wake up before things get to a crisis stage."

I have to put this in a kind of Fifties perspective to get across how terrifying and thrilling it was. Imagine finding out that a breakfast-cereal decoder ring really did put you in touch with a secret society of superheroes; that's what this was like. I hated everything about Grant City except Iris and sometimes my dad, but now I had been welcomed into a grand subterfuge. Someone understood. I wasn't crazy. And maybe there was a plan to get everything back on the right track.

Julio told me I didn't need to come to meetings unless I had something important to tell them. People were already watching me because of the spex and my tendency to shoot off my mouth in class, which made me a bit of a danger to what they were trying to do. "But now we'll be watching you, too," he said. "And once you get a little older, we'll ask you to do certain things."

I imagined lurking in an alley—Grant City didn't have any, but I'd seen vids—waiting to stick a knife between Justin Rowe's ribs. Then Julio let me down by saying that they wouldn't want me to do anything violent, or even illegal. It wasn't that kind of a group. "What we need from you is your eyes and your brain," he said. "Keep both sharp, okay?"

"Okay," I said.

"And don't tell your father. He knows about us, and he knows we've asked you to join, but it's best for now if the two of you don't discuss it."

This was easy. Not discussing things came pretty naturally to the Brennans.

* * *

But he was still my dad, and I was still a kid, and I was so wound up with the knowledge of secrets that I had to talk to him about something just to distract myself. So I found the old man on his bench looking out at the woods, and I sat down next to him. "Dad, is Evelyn a robot?"

Dad opened his mouth, shut it again, got up for one of his slow circuits of the bench. When he sat again, he said, "No. She's not a robot."

"What is she?"

"Before I tell you this, you need to understand something," Dad said. "A lot of people around here think I'm crazy. They're right, but I'm not crazy the way they think I am. I'm crazy because only a crazy man would have done what I did. Now I'm going to tell you about Evelyn, but you have to swear that you won't repeat any of this. Not to anyone."

He knows, I thought. We're talking in code, like spies in Berlin or Cairo. "I swear. Cross my heart and hope to die."

He looked pained at the expression. "For God's sake, Wiley, people stopped talking like that before I was born."

This shamed me, and I looked down at the ground. "What am I supposed to say?"

A frustrated sigh escaped the old man. "I'm sorry, kid. None of this is your fault. I hear you talking like Beaver Cleaver and I want to fucking strangle Milt Bahrani." He looked at his hands. "Not that I'm strong enough to strangle anybody."

Through the spex, I could see the gyros in my dad's hips and the coil around his spine. I could measure the volume of my father's indrawn breath and track the dispersion of what he called the Telomerase Monkeys from his bone marrow. But I could not see why James Brennan had done what he had done on *Susan Constant*.

My father put a hand on the back of my neck. "You're surrounded by lunatics, son of mine," he said. "Nothing I can do about it but tell you how we got this way. You're not going to want to repeat this to anyone at school. People don't like to think about it. They don't like to think about me, and that's part of the reason why they're giving you such a hard time." He sighed. "Where to begin. While your mother was pregnant with you, I got a call from a German company called Schimmel wanting to know if they could hire me for a trip to the asteroid belt. I said no, that I was dirt-bound until my kid was born, and signed up to do the weekly milk run to Lagrange Five for almost a year after your due date. They wouldn't tell me why they wanted me to go out there, but I found out later. After we started hearing about Big Mickey, which was when you were about a year old, Schimmel called me again. This time they didn't want me to go to the asteroids; they wanted me to go to Hamburg and wouldn't tell me why, but they offered me a lot of money to consult on a project. I said okay, and went.

"The Schimmel headquarters was something. It spread out over a huge piece of land along the Elbe River, and Mehmet Scholl, the guy who picked me up at the airport, gave me the tour before taking me in. He said he was a xenobiologist. 'Am I supposed to consult about Martian bacteria?' I asked. I'd been to Mars twice, but wasn't any kind of expert on anything except going there and getting back.

"Mehmet laughed. 'No, we're way up the food chain from those,' he said. We went into his office and met a woman named Birgid Prinz, who was some kind of psychiatrist. That's when I started getting a little spooky about the whole situation. Then another guy came in, one of these oily guys with a title like Stakeholder Relations Manager, and we got started. The flack's name was Rudi, and he didn't waste any time. The first thing he said to me was, 'Mr. Brennan, we need you to save a portion of humanity.'"

My dad saw me looking at him and laughed. "I can see what you're thinking,

Wiley. You're right. I was the wrong guy. But the problem was, Evelyn didn't care."

* * *

This is what I'm worried about. How much do you care about me?

* * *

"While prospecting in the asteroid belt six years ago, in April 2058," Rudi began, "freelance rock miners discovered three artifacts apparently of nonterrestrial origin. Schimmel acquired these artifacts without publicity and set about trying to discover their history. This effort proved largely futile because the artifacts refused to tell us.

"Gradually we were able to determine that these three artifacts were in fact sentient, and that their long period of isolation had deranged them to a considerable degree. Communication was laborious at best, and frequently impossible; but with dedicated effort, and at no small human cost, we were able to determine that these three beings were in fact merely facets, aspects of entities that existed only partially in our familiar four-dimensional spacetime. They were captured, harnessed in mechanical devices that, they said, enabled four-dimensional objects to travel at supraluminal speeds. It goes without saying that this ability, if true, is the most significant scientific discovery in the history of mankind, and it comes at a time when it is most sorely needed.

"Before Big Mickey, we at Schimmel were in the process of interrogating these beings to understand what short-term benefit we might derive from their knowledge. In light of the current threat to human civilization, however, we have turned our research in a new direction, and it is now apparent that we can construct spacecraft incorporating these beings. It is for this reason that we have leased the facilities at Lagrange Five: Schimmel GmbH is donating three vessels, each with a capacity of two thousand persons, to the dream of human survival.

"The technological obstacles, though formidable, have been largely overcome. What remains is a challenge of literally another dimension. Birgid?"

The psychiatrist picked up her cue. "A consequence of the Navigators' long isolation—how long we do not know—is that they are deeply withdrawn into themselves. This has made them unable to maintain their consciousness of four-dimensional spacetime unless a being native to that spacetime is in more or less constant intimate contact with them. In some fundamental way they have forgotten how to *be* in our spacetime, and will need a physical presence to remind them. If the mission of these three ships is to succeed, each Navigator will require a single human as an anchor to the ship and its occupants. Without such an anchor, we are informed, it is a near certainty that the Navigators' attentions will drift. In that situation, ships will suffer a catastrophic—deceleration is the best word we have—from what we have chosen to call hyperspace into real space, the energy imbalance of which would annihilate the vessel.

"We are asking you, Mr. Brennan, to perform this essential task of anchoring the Navigators and perhaps even more importantly providing them the kind of sentient interaction they so desperately crave. These are terribly lonely and needy beings, irrational and in fundamental ways impossible to understand, and sustained contact with Navigators has during the past seven years killed or deranged nearly everyone who has undertaken it. They're trying to make it easier—they've even gendered themselves to render a simulacrum personality that we can understand—but this is enormously dangerous."

"I can't do this. I have a wife," my dad said. "We just had a baby."

"We realize this," Dr. Prinz answered. "We would not have chosen you. Ideally we would be able to screen a large sample for people who are both compatible with an individual Navigator and endowed with the kind of physical and psychological strength to survive what might be a journey of decades or even centuries. The problem is that one of the Navigators has chosen you."

* * *

HE TOLD ME THE REST OF IT AS THE MOON CAME UP over the hills west of Grant City, beyond the farm and the cemetery and the shuttle pad. "I wasn't famous, exactly, but not everyone on Earth had been to Mars twice, and there was still a little glitter on anyone who made his living in space. Evelyn apparently took a liking to me. I'm not sure how else to put it. Prinz and Scholl had her look at lots of vid, newsnets, and whatever else, to try and ground her in the here-and-now of Earth in the 2060s, and she seized on me. Birgid Prinz told me it was a network feed of me coming out of a shuttle after the *Burroughs* expedition."

"You telling me she got a crush on you, Dad?" I asked. In that moment I felt like I'd already heard enough.

"Not exactly," he said. "Well, sort of. She was like a little kid, all the Navigators were. They had these intense desires and no real ability to get perspective on why they wanted things. She saw me and she liked me, and after that she wouldn't let anybody else get close."

Another trip around the bench, and this time Dad grunted when he sat down. "You want to walk?" I asked him.

He shook his head. "Wouldn't help. I'm two hundred and thirty years old, Wiley. The T-Monkeys can't work forever." His head drooped. "Sorry. Not good parenting to talk about your mortality in front of your kid."

I was about to say that it was time he stopped trying to hide things from me, his mortality included. Instead I scooted closer to him on the bench and put an arm around his shoulders. I was barely fifteen, but already bigger than him. "Don't worry about it, Dad," I said.

He breathed slowly in and out a couple of times, and then went on. "Truth of the situation is that I was an idiot. I resented Evelyn choosing me, so my first response was to say, Tough. Let her fixate on someone else. Even though there were two thousand lives depending on her, and I guess on me. Birgid and Rudi gave me a little time to get over myself, and then pointed out that they had ships to build and might be able to save some lives if I would get my head out of my ass long enough to talk to Evelyn and see if she liked me in person. So I did, and she did. She liked me a lot. She kind of probed at me all the time, swore she couldn't read minds but always seemed to know what I was feeling. That got to be nice, since your mom and I weren't getting along all that well. The first year after a kid is tough."

I pulled away again. "Just say it," I said. "Just admit that Evelyn got jealous and killed Mom."

My father went very still. He lifted his head with painful slowness and turned to look me in the eye. "Nothing is ever that simple, Wiley," he said. "I killed your mother. I didn't mean to, but I did. Evelyn didn't do it. I was scared and lonely and she made me feel peaceful and safe and happy, and while I was feeling peaceful and safe and happy I forgot to run maintenance checks and the life-support computer went out. That's what happened."

He believed it. He needed me to believe it. I wanted to, but I wasn't sure if I could.

* * *

OTHER THAN THE BOWLING ALLEY, THE PLACE to hang out was the Nickelodeon. That went up the year after Bel-Mark, and pretty soon if you were looking for someone in Grant City and you knew they weren't at work, you could find them at one of those two places. There were movies every night, and after a while the time between seven and nine at night became an unofficial 1956 rally and revival around the altar of the movie screen. The Lodge took to meeting during this same period, rotating who attended so nobody drew suspicion for missing too many movies. I didn't make many Lodge meetings because I wasn't supposed to be obvious, but that was okay because I was a plain sucker for movies. Iris liked them, too. We sat there watching Fifties B-movies about alien invasions, holding hands and liking the way the old stories made us feel brave and a little superior—because we knew what other worlds were like, and we still knew we were on another world.

The day after I talked to my dad about Schimmel, I went looking for Iris at movie time. We sat through *Track of the Moon Beast* and then took a walk together. Iris remembered more of Earth than I did. She'd been five when we left, so we were the same age now but she'd had two extra years to soak up Earth memories.

"Do you remember getting on the ship?" I asked her. We were walking toward the river, and it took a conscious effort not to veer toward the cemetery.

Iris nodded. "There was a big umbilical between the ship and Lagrange Five. In the station you could look out a window at the ship, and my dad tried to hold me up to see it but lifted me too hard and kind of bounced me off the ceiling. So I boarded *Susan Constant* with a bump on my head."

"There was no gravity, right?" Of course there was no gravity. I just wanted Iris to validate my memory of my mother.

"Come on, Wiley. You know there wasn't. I had fun in the umbilical, bouncing around. My parents tried to do what I was doing and ended up accidentally kicking each other. After that they were strictly handhold-to-handhold. I think half of the people on the ship had bruises when they went into the berths." She was smiling at the memory. One of her front teeth was a little crooked. I liked it.

We reached the river and stood looking down into the black water. There was no wind, and the shallows were still enough that stars reflected on the surface. "I used to think that Evelyn killed my mother," I said.

"Oh," Iris said, with a sharp little inhalation.

"I don't anymore."

She hesitated. "That's good."

I felt for her hand in the dark, found it and some thigh, too. She twined her fingers in mine. "Maybe it's better that you don't remember Earth," she began, but I cut her off.

"No, I do."

"Wiley," she said. "Maybe it's better that you don't. You're much more a, what, Canaanite than an..." She searched for a word, didn't like the one she found.

"Earthling?" I suggested, and we both broke up laughing.

* * *

In year eleven—this would make me sixteen—Milt Bahrani showed up at one of the meetings. "Hey, Milt," Furcal said. "What's the good word?"

"What are you guys doing here?" Milt said. He smiled at Furcal's use of his name, but it was the kind of smile you offer when you're confused and trying to figure out whether the people you're smiling at are dangerous lunatics or just lunatics.

"We're trying to figure out what to do," Furcal said.

"About what?"

"About the fact that you and most of the rest of the people here have gone stark fucking bonkers."

Milt frowned. "That's not really appropriate language in front of kids."

So he's noticed me, I thought. I wondered how it would play out in school the next day.

* * *

IT DIDN'T PLAY OUT THE NEXT DAY, OR THE DAY AFTER THAT. The Tuesday after, my luck ran out. Bahrani caught me coming out of last-period social studies and took me down to his office. "I'm not sure this crowd you're with is good for you, Wiley," he said when he'd settled me in the chair facing his desk. "I know kids like you have trouble sometimes. It's the times, I guess. Kids want to rebel; heck, I did, too." He tried on a smile, abandoned it when he saw I wasn't going to give him anything back. "But it can be taken too far, and when it gets out of hand, the school administration needs to take action. We'd like you to see someone, try to talk out some of the hostility you're experiencing."

I was scared out of my mind. Too many movies full of old men in white coats with big syringes. So I played along—mostly. "How about the AI first?" I asked, trying to sound cooperative. "It's designed to work through dissociative feelings, right? If that's what I'm feeling, let's do that."

"I'm not sure what to say to that, Wiley." Bahrani crossed his legs and tapped his pen on my file. "What do you mean by AI?"

That was the most frightened I had ever been. Bahrani had gone completely over the edge; if he was just playing a role, I saw that he didn't know it anymore. Right then I went from feeling like people didn't understand me to believing that I was surrounded by enemies.

Play along, I thought, long enough to get out of here. "Can you make me an appointment?"

"That's a good idea," Bahrani said. He got another file from his desk and consulted a schedule. "You know, it's perfectly normal to feel the way you're feeling. At your age." He made a note on the schedule. "Dr. Macavenue can see you tomorrow right after school."

"Okay," I said, and that was it. Bahrani let me get up and leave and I walked out of the office feeling like I'd narrowly avoided something awful.

I went straight to Iris. She was watching Hannah and Peter on the playground. I sat next to her in the swingset and I didn't mean to but the first thing out of my mouth was, "They've all gone crazy." Which wasn't an ideal thing to say considering I was under suspicion of being nuts myself.

Iris was on my side, though. "Yeah, they have," she said.

"We can't stop it."

"Nope." She was still watching her siblings, two perfect Fifties children on another world.

"I think maybe we could get away, though," I said, and held my breath. Iris didn't say anything and eventually I had to exhale, and then there was nothing to do but take another breath and tell her about Evelyn.

* * *

THIS IS WHERE I HAVE TO ASK YOU whether you wanted this to happen. Did you cull me from the herd, choose me like you chose my father?

How much of this was you?

* * *

"SHE TALKS TO YOU?" IRIS SAID.

"Sometimes, yeah. More often lately. But we talked some when I was on the ship, too."

"You have to tell the Lodge," Iris said.

"Why? Iris, there are spies in the Lodge. What are they going to do if they find out I've been talking to Evelyn? Jesus. Bahrani'll have me committed."

"To where? They haven't built a loony bin yet."

She meant it as a joke, but the idea chilled me. What vital project would be canceled so they could build a nice, quiet place for people like me to spout their fantasies in little white rooms?

"They want me to see a psychiatrist. Bahrani wouldn't even admit that there was an AI. I'm scared, Iris. I'm starting to wonder if they're going to put something in my lunch at school."

She reached across the space between swings and touched my arm. "How about if I start bringing you lunch? Would that make you feel better?"

I had to laugh. "Yeah. But I don't know if I can tell the Lodge."

Then they killed Julio Furcal.

* * *

AT SOME POINT WHEN I WAS A LITTLE KID, the council decided that Grant City needed a cop. Nobody really wanted to do it, because at that point they all hadn't gone off the deep end, but eventually Chad Latta stood up and said he'd be willing. They voted him in immediately, and gave him office space in a back corner of one of the lab complexes. We'd come a long way since then. The lab complex morphed into a kind of YMCA, and Chad took to the job of being a town cop like he was born to it. Iris wouldn't go within half a mile of him, and wouldn't say why.

I don't know what he was doing back on Earth, but by the time I was thirteen he'd had a badge and uniform made, and even took to carrying a gun. There was some deep division in the colony over that, but already too many of our people had begun the retreat into Fantasy 1956-Land, and they wanted law and order. I later found out that the Lodge was born at about the same time, when Julio Furcal and Sharon Pelletier and a couple of other people started to see that Grant City was on its way to deep trouble. They started meeting to plot out ways to slow the colony's slide into delusion, and when it became clear that they couldn't do anything overtly, they started infiltrating organizations like the PTA and the city council as fast as those bodies sprang up.

Problem was, that infiltration went both ways, and about a week after Milt Bahrani told me I needed to see a shrink, Chad Latta went to the school to arrest Julio Furcal. Julio demanded to know what the charge was, to which Chad answered—I'm not kidding—contributing to the delinquency of a minor. Chad had lost his sense of humor long before, and when Julio told him to fuck off in front of his riveted home-room students, Chad hauled off and decked Julio. Then Julio got up and went after him, and in the struggle Chad's gun went off.

I wasn't in Julio's home room, and by this time most of the other kids in the school had me pegged as the kind of kid you shouldn't let adults see you talking to, but I heard third- or fourth-hand that Chad shot Julio three times while Julio was on the floor. It might be true, in fact I'm pretty sure it is, but it's also exactly the kind of thing that a bunch of traumatized kids might say to transform their fear into some kind of ghoulish thrill. I was in my computer class—called Electronics—when I heard the shots, and the next thing I knew the school was evacuated, and the next thing after that I was back in Bahrani's office with Chad Latta standing inside the door. He'd had some kind of work done, sharpening his chin and giving his hairline a sharp widow's peak. Another James Dean, I thought to myself. I would have rolled my eyes if Latta wasn't looking at me.

Bahrani reached across his desk, and I figured out at the last second he was after my spex. Before I could think about it, I slapped his hand away.

He was standing, maybe to hit me, and I was standing definitely to hit him, when Chad cracked me in the back of the head and I went down, banging my forehead on Bahrani's desk on the way. I stayed on my hands and knees trying to focus my eyes. Bahrani came around his desk.

"Give me your glasses."

"They're not mine," I said. "They're my dad's."

"Give them to me."

"My dad needs them."

Bahrani tapped my head, exactly where Chad had hit me. When the black spots were all gone from my vision, he said, "Why do you go to those meetings? They're dangerous."

I hadn't yet heard that Julio Furcal was dead. "You've got a cop busting my head and you tell me a meeting is dangerous? What's he going to do next, kill me? Or do I get the bamboo slivers under my fingernails first?"

"I'd hate to have to put you in a hospital, Wiley," Bahrani said.

I didn't know whether he meant having Chad Latta hurt me or putting me in some kind of mental ward. Either possibility terrified me.

"I want to talk to my dad," I said.

"In a minute."

It hurt like hell, but I looked up at him. "No," I said with tears in my eyes. "Right now. Unless you plan to kill me, you let me talk to my dad right fucking now!" I was screaming by the last few words, and I guess I got to whatever shred of sanity Bahrani still had hidden away behind his high-school-autocrat facade, because he took a step back. He looked past me, and for a second I thought he was actually going to tell Chad Latta to kill me; when I found out later that Chad had shot Julio, I started shaking and didn't stop until I'd thrown up.

"You're suspended," Bahrani said. "Go home."

As I walked by Latta, he said, "Give Carol Ann a kiss for me," and winked. I had no idea what he meant, and couldn't look him in the eye anyway.

When I got home my dad took one look at me and said, "Jesus Christ, Wiley." I shoved past him into the house and slammed the door to my room. He let me stew for a while, but around sunset he knocked, and when I didn't answer he came in. I was sitting at my terminal watching a video without any idea what it was. Dad sat on my bed and said, "Milt Bahrani says you're suspended. That have anything to do with the knot on your forehead?"

"You wouldn't believe me," I said.

"Wiley, you're my son. I will believe whatever you tell me unless I know otherwise."

I turned around. "Okay. Bahrani called me into his office and Chad Latta hit me over the head and while I was falling down I got this on the corner of Bahrani's desk."

He hated hearing it, both because it had happened and because he was too wrecked to do anything about it. Or so I thought: the next day I heard he found Milt Bahrani at the Elks Lodge, called him the shitpot tin god he was, and broke a beer bottle across Bahrani's forehead before Latta arrested him.

That was why I never got to tell my dad that I had been wrong who Chad

Latta was trying to look like. I ran a biometric against all of the archived stills and vid we had from the Fifties, and although he'd ended up close to James Dean, I was pretty sure that our town cop had gotten a nip and tuck so he could look like Charles Starkweather. He wouldn't have had to get a doctor to agree; there was a MedSmart berth that took care of all minor surgery, and as deep as Grant City got in its we-like-Ike hallucination, they never failed to keep the MedSmart in top condition.

He'd told me to kiss "Caril Ann," Starkweather's girlfriend, who had to be Iris. I don't usually talk to myself, but I said, "Jesus. What am I going to do?"

And Evelyn answered.

* * *

IT SEEMS ODD THAT I HEARD ABOUT JULIO FROM YOU. Why wouldn't it have been one of the kids at school? Justin Rowe would have been glad to get me up to speed on my favorite teacher's murder. Iris also would have told me.

I don't know why nobody tipped Julio off. Could be that they'd figured out who we had on the council, or it could be that Chad wasn't working for the whole council. They were at each others' throats most of the time over things like who should pay to mow the cemetery lawn since most of its residents had died before *Susan Constant* came to Canaan—or as they put it, "before Grant City was organized in its current form"—so I guess it isn't a surprise that all seven of them wouldn't have passed a resolution calling for the murder "while resisting arrest" of Julio Furcal.

* * *

SOMEBODY SCHEDULED THE NEXT LODGE MEETING against the most recent showing of Grant City's perennial favorite *The Bridge on the River Kwai*, made the year after the one we were all pretending to inhabit. I think the movie pleased everybody. Those who had bought into 1956 subconsciously craved the movie's validation of their impulse to believe that all of their work would be destroyed no matter what they did. Those of us who remained sane, whatever that means, loved all the stuff about being forced to work in the service of things we despised; plus the last line of the movie is "Madness! Madness…madness!"

Anyway, I told the Lodge. Not because Evelyn had suggested it or because of Julio Furcal being killed, but because Iris wanted me to.

It was the first Lodge meeting my father had attended. That's one thing I wish I could take back; I would trade every good deed to expunge the memory of my father's face when he heard that I'd talked to Evelyn.

Julio's murder had radicalized everyone; there were calls for more open resistance, for the scientists to strike until the Wingtips agreed that it was really the twenty-third century. There were threats against Chad Latta, at least until I pointed out his resemblance to a certain serial murderer from 1957 and told them about his "Caril Ann" remark.

Everyone wanted to do something, and everyone wanted everyone else to drop what they were doing and pull together. Then my father raised his hand.

He was sitting near the front of the room, so even the people who couldn't hear the whine of his shoulder servos shut up. Once he was sure everyone was paying attention—my dad never did like to say things twice—he said, "The thing to do is leave."

The silence changed. When he'd raised his hand, people were curious. Now they were dumbfounded.

"It's still possible," he went on. "Evelyn's spotted other planets. We can pack up and go, try this again. Start over."

Start over. I could feel the wave of weariness roll through the room. Wasn't it enough that we'd tried once? Look what had happened.

The only alternative was to go. There was room for everyone aboard the ship, especially since most of them wouldn't want to go.

It was thinking of Hannah and Peter that made the decision for me. I stood up and for the first time in my life took advantage of the aura of otherness that had always dogged me. Another fairy tale. Dumbo, maybe. The furor in the meeting room died away.

"You couldn't survive the trip, Dad," I said. It was true; he was breaking down a little more every week, breathing a little shallower, relying a little more on the servos that kept his legs under him and his head erect.

They misunderstood me, thought I was agreeing with the side that wanted to surrender. I took a deep breath and went on, giving up the one secret I always thought I'd be able to keep.

"But I could."

* * *

HOW LONG HAS IT BEEN SINCE I SAID THAT? Time is funny. Sometimes I can still feel the words on my tongue, and sometimes the whole scene is a memory so distant it's taken on the surreal clarity of a dream, or a story I've heard so often I've come to believe it happened to me. But in this little womb, this liquid steel heart of a ship tethered to the invisible fabric of the real—to Evelyn—everything feels like that. Everything has happened to someone else. I thought that the danger of solitude was that my self would expand to fill the gaps left by my father, Iris, everyone else who has been taken from me permanently or not; what I find, though, is that I begin to disappear into these vacancies, to hear those other voices more clearly than my own.

More clearly even than yours.

Don't leave me, Evelyn. We're almost there.

* * *

MY FATHER SPOKE FIRST, "YOU CAN?"

At that moment we were the only two people in the room. On his face I could see everything he hadn't asked, or had compressed into those two words.

Yes, Dad. I could have shared your loneliness. But you left me alone with images of a dead Earth and a dead mother that I drank in and called memories, and I was afraid of this invisible woman you loved so much that you turned to her and let my mother die.

And now she's mine.

"Yes," I said. "That's what she told me."

Something broke between us then, and I imagine now that he must have grown smaller somehow, shrunken by the knowledge that we had without being able to help it betrayed each other.

It would be easier if I could just blame him, but can I do that now when I find myself facing the same awful temptation he did, and knowing that I can exchange it for another, and knowing that the other might be worse? He woke me too late, but now I know why he waited. I could wait. You are beautiful, and kind, and your need envelops me and keeps me safe.

Can you take me where you are? Can I know the rest of you, know you as you are? Can you make me forget the sacrifice I would make to be with you?

Please stop.

All I have are questions. Without questions I have no hope of making you say what I need you to say.

* * *

THROUGH THE WINDOW IN HER BERTH, IRIS LOOKS PALE. I think of Sleeping Beauty, envision myself the prince who will condemn her to mortality again. Sometimes I wander up and down the rows of berths, lingering over the children. All of them have lived years longer than they would have on Canaan. We took as many as we could, and you can call it kidnapping if you want to. They boarded *Susan Constant* like I seem to remember going to the moon so long ago: nervous, even tearful, but trusting their parents to keep them safe.

Trusting me. On either side of Iris sleep Hannah and Peter; I remember the feel of their hands in mine, the last time I swung them around in the park after we'd lost their ball in the woods. Iris is on my mind all the time, but Hannah and Peter are the responsibility I feel most heavily. I cannot fail them.

Iris would understand. Will understand. When I wake her, she will understand.

Is this some kind of revenge?

* * *

I CAN'T EVEN ARTICULATE WHAT IT FELT LIKE to seal that hatch behind me, knowing that I was leaving eight hundred people behind to die because their delusions threatened me. My father killed a thousand people because he was in love. So did I. The only difference is that I talked myself into believing that I had to kill those people to save the rest, and that's not much consolation when I look up and realize that it's been three years since we left and everyone on Canaan is probably dead.

I'll admit that this is mostly cowardice talking, but it seemed monstrously unfair to me that we should have come so far only to be forced back into space again. But what might have happened to the others? Had they survived? Perhaps we were the fortunate ones, able to flee again. Perhaps *Argos* and *Santa Maria* were destroyed by malfunction, a stray pebble, failed orbital insertion…that we survived in Grant City for as long as we did is from a certain perspective miraculous. From this same perspective, our second exodus was a second chance. I tried to think about it that way.

A couple of weeks after the meeting, after everything had already been set in motion, something about the idea of departure sent me rummaging through the colony records to find clips of my mother. There was a little hiccup in the link, and then I wasn't talking to the colony's local AI anymore. I was talking to Evelyn. I asked her about my mother, and she spooled some old newsnet files of a short, round-faced woman with brown eyes. I turned off the sound so I could just look at her, and I tried to see myself in her. Her face wasn't my face; her hair was curly and mine was straight; my eyes were the same green as my father's.

Her hands, though. When she tucked her hair behind one ear, I saw my hands. I placed my palm on the screen.

Evelyn anticipated what I was feeling. She was good at that. *Wiley*, she said. *It's all right that you take after your father.*

Is it? I asked her.

You spend so much time blaming him for his failures, she said, *that you never think about the fact that he kept you alive. Is it so bad that you should inherit that?*

I cut the link, but I was hearing her words in my head three weeks later, on the day my dad told me he wasn't leaving Canaan.

It wasn't a surprise, but once it was out in the open I was scared. He'd done this before, and even if he'd failed I wanted him around. He could help me avoid his mistakes, couldn't he?

And even then, I think I was afraid that without him around Evelyn would be too much for me to resist.

"Are you sure?" I asked him. "The low-g might be good for you."

"Wiley, kid, sometimes when you fall off the horse you have to get right back on. Other times you need to be smart enough to know that it's too much horse for you to handle. And I'd be willing to bet that if I said I was coming, somebody would shoot me dead before I could get on the shuttle. Best not to find out, don't you think?"

He sat there on his bench, looking out at the hills and panting a little from the effort of speaking. I almost begged him, but I was sixteen years old, and everything else aside it's awfully hard to beg your father for anything when you're sixteen. I had won. I was taking the love of his life away from him and leaving him to die. So I sat with him and felt myself dividing into the me that existed and the me that would sit on a bench watching the hills on the next planet, body broken and mind turned inward to past failures.

* * *

WHERE I WAS BORN, THERE IS AN OLD GHOST. He appears in the ruins of San Diego, a young man born two hundred years ago. I am nineteen years old. Fourteen of those years passed in the company of other human beings. During the rest I was alone with *Susan Constant*. And with Evelyn.

You are my first memory, you know that? Some people remember being three, but I don't. I don't remember going to the moon or boarding this ship or the kiss my mother must have given me before I settled into my berth and fell into the dream that ended with her death. It seems like I did, but I must have made it up. I don't remember being awakened, or the desperate, grateful despair my father must have wept onto me when he saw that I had survived.

Don't tell me he didn't cry. If I want to know the truth, I'll look it up for myself.

I remember the stillness of the long hallway between the berths and the space reserved for my father's downtime. I remember I started calling that room the galley after I read an old novel about submarines. And I remember that you showed me how to work the VR. In my head your voice has collapsed into my imaginings of my mother. You were kind, so she must have been kind. She raised me, and so did you.

Another old ghost haunts Grant City now that my father is dead. That was my first thought when you told me.

Then I felt an incredulous sense of betrayal that you knew. *You talked to him?* I screamed at her. At you. My jealousy made me sick, and I flew into a violent rage, destroying whatever I could get my hands on, which in the womb was anything Evelyn wanted to be there. As soon as that realization penetrated my anger, I froze, like a horse that is finally broken.

We thought it was best for you, she said.

Parented at last.

* * *

Iris came to me the day before I was supposed to call Evelyn down. All of the robots and backup equipment were already on *Susan Constant*, and Lodge members had preserved their more important experimental data. We decided to leave the MedSmart; there were others on the ship. The next morning I would call Evelyn, she would bring the ship down, and anyone who wanted to would get on it. I was worried that Chad Latta would do something crazy, but Sharon Pelletier and Miss Callahan told me I had nothing to worry about. All I had to do was make sure Evelyn came down and went back up with us on board.

"Walk with me," Iris said, and led me through the husk of Grant City, along the river trail to the cemetery and my mother's grave. Weeds had grown over the plots in the months since we'd thrown ourselves into the evacuation, but my mother's name was still visible. I saw her face in my mind, and saw the shipboard monitor that framed it.

"You need to leave her here if we're going to live through this," Iris said.

I said I knew that.

"You're not your father, Wiley," she said.

"I'm as much him as I am me," I said.

"No," she said, and stepped between me and my mother's tombstone. "He didn't have anyone. He thought he had Evelyn, and then he thought he had you, but in the end he was alone." I closed my eyes, and felt her hands on either side of my face. "Open your eyes, Wiley."

I did, and began to cry.

"You have me, Wiley. Let that hold you. When you think you're alone, know that you have me. I'll be there on the other side."

I couldn't speak. All I could have said was, But what if you don't have me, Iris? What if I get lost? What if I'm not even as strong as he was? I wanted to, wanted to warn her away from her faith in me, but instead I bowed my head to her breast and cried because she was so brave and I needed her courage.

The day after that she slept, and the day after that I crawled into the womb that had once held my father, and *Susan Constant* turned away from Canaan to the stars.

* * *

You asked me a question a long time ago. *We have both lost so much, Wiley*, you said. *Can we not have each other?* I came to you needing to know something about my father, and instead...

Did I say yes? I think I must have. I was a child, and my father was a ghost, and my mother was another kind of ghost. You were there, and you were kind, and I think I must have responded to your fear as much as anything else. We could be afraid together.

But I'm not my father. He had courage I'll never have, but maybe I can save myself out of fear, and maybe I can save everyone else, too.

Except Iris.

* * *

We would land on the delta planet of Taurus V, wake everyone up, and start over. Everything would work this time. And along the way, all I had to do was remember that I wasn't alone because Iris believed in me. Maybe she was lying; maybe she told me that because she knew it was the one thing she could do to hang onto a little bit of control over the years she'd spend frozen. But I don't think so. This is the girl who said to Wiley Brennan: *It's not your fault.* She didn't have to do that.

The first morning I missed the lab check, I was with you.

Maybe it's the sense that you go on forever, that I'm touching only the part of you that can squeeze into four dimensions. Maybe it's just the way you make me feel so safe, like a two-year-old sleeping with a hand on his mother's belly, his breath cued to hers. Maybe it's just our secret history—you were my mother when my mother died, and every little boy thinks about his mother. Do I have to tell you that's not healthy? Does the rest of you even know what happens to this little four-dimensional sliver?

But thank you.

You know what will happen, don't you? We're seventy-nine years away from Taurus, and I'm already cracking. It took my father more than a hundred years to get to this point. I'll never make it. You understand, don't you?

You can cook up telomerase injections for Iris. So could I, if I had years to learn how to do it, but I don't. You have to do it for me. And I know you can make me believe I've already done it. Please don't. Don't make me into him.

It's not like what my father did to me. He was terrified, and so am I; but he unloaded all of his fear onto me, and I never had a chance to say no. With Iris it's different. She didn't take me up to my mother's grave just to profess her faith in me.

She was offering herself.

You have to stop this. You have to stop making me feel so safe, you have to stop protecting me.

I'm going to go away for a little while, Evelyn.

* * *

IRIS.

* * *

EVELYN. ARE YOU LISTENING TO ME?

* * *

IRIS. IRIS, I'M DREAMING. IRIS, WAKE UP.

Peter Skilling

Peter Skilling did not remember falling into a glacial crevasse on the north slope of Mount McKinley, so it came as a surprise to him when he awoke to find what appeared to be a robot sitting next to his bed. "You're a very lucky man, Peter Skilling," the robot said to him. "A genuinely unique set of circumstances. You might have sustained fatal trauma from your fall, but look! You fell into a subglacial stream, resulting in scrapes and bruises only! And you might have been ground to gel by the glacier, but for the earthquake that struck hours after your death and sheared away a portion of the mountain, leaving your body exposed in a depression away from the redirected glacier. Then, too, consider the above average snowfall that encased your remains and protected you from the depredations of weather and wildlife."

"My remains?" Peter croaked.

Noting the dryness of Peter's throat, the robot moved swiftly to unspool a thin hose from the wall and place its nipple in Peter's mouth. Reflexively Peter sucked, and his mouth filled with cool water.

"This is the truly amazing chapter in your saga, Mr. Skilling," the robot gushed. "You died so quickly and in such cold water that—if you'll permit me an inorganic figure of speech—your autonomic system shorted out. Your brain function is astonishingly well preserved, and we have been able to surgically reconstruct damaged pathways. You were our perfect candidate. Quite a find, if I do say so myself!"

The robot paused. "Do you consider yourself sufficiently apprised of the fortuitous circumstances in which you find yourself?"

Peter hadn't caught much of the robot's effusion, but he gathered that he'd been in an accident on the mountain and survived. That seemed lucky. "I guess," he said.

"Very good," the robot said. It extended a hand, and Peter shook. The robot's hand was warm. "I am called Burkhardt," the robot said. "I wish you all the very best."

It left, and Peter noticed a woman in a white coat who had apparently been waiting near the door while the robot, Burkhardt, had told Peter how lucky he was. She stepped forward and smiled at him. "I'm Doctor McBride," she said. "I hope the steelie didn't overload you. We have to observe protocols as part of our grant mechanism, and it's easier to have robots take care of them than entrust the process to people."

"Okay," Peter said. She wasn't making any more sense than the robot had.

"Why don't you sit up?" Dr. McBride suggested. "I think you'll find everything's in working order."

Peter sat up, surfed a brief wave of dizziness, and discovered that he did indeed feel pretty good. "Yeah," he said. "I feel okay. So why am I in the hospital?"

Dr. McBride looked annoyed. "Yes. I thought maybe Burkhardt had rushed a little. These federal programs, you know. Not that I'm criticizing, it would be much more difficult to address everything on a case-by-case basis when we don't have access to all the intelligence, but it's only natural." Although she still looked in his direction, the doctor was no longer talking to Peter. He had the feeling that Dr. McBride thought someone else was in the room.

He took another drink from the wall nipple. Dr. McBride looked up at him and smiled again, apologetically this time. "I'm sorry, Mr. Skilling," she said. "I haven't answered your question."

Peter raised an eyebrow and sucked at the nipple.

"You see, you died in 2005. We've spent the past several months working you through the rejuvenation process, and I have to say it's gone very well."

The nipple fell out of Peter's mouth and a little water dribbled down his chin. Dr. McBride's smile regained some of its strength.

"There's no way to cushion it," she said. "Although God knows Burkhardt tries. You've been dead for ninety-three years. And now you have another chance to live."

Her gaze shifted to a monitor by Peter's head. "Mm," she said. "I was afraid of that." Crossing to the monitor, Dr. McBride opened a drawer and removed a shiny instrument.

Peter couldn't breathe. He tried to speak, and a breathy whine came out of his mouth.

"I've going to give you something that will alleviate your shock response," Dr. McBride said. Peter heard a hiss, and then he was gone.

WHEN HE WOKE UP, THE ROBOT WAS THERE AGAIN. Peter felt worse than he had the first time he'd opened his eyes in that room. "Don't give me another shot," he said.

"Oh, I don't administer medication," Burkhardt said airily. "Fascinating colloquialism, 'shot'—bit anachronistic now. We do all transdermals now, of course, except when intravenous administration is indicated. But I'm not here to go on about our medical procedures; you're a healthy man; you don't care about this. I do need to apologize for yesterday. It seems I moved a little too quickly for circumstances, and Doctor McBride…" Burkhardt trailed off. When it spoke again, prim disapproval radiated in its tone. "She was terribly inappropriate and unprofessional. To say some of the things she said, given the fragility of your condition…Trust me when I say that you won't have to deal with her anymore."

Sometime during its apology, Peter remembered what she'd said to him. "Are you serious that I was dead?" he asked. Having slept on the idea, even if the sleep was drug-induced, made it easier to grapple with.

Burkhardt cocked its head to one side. "Oh yes, perfectly serious. My function here is to ensure that your assimilation process is maximally efficient. There is significant state interest in making certain that you come to terms with the reality of your surroundings. Yours is truly an exceptional situation. I can certainly sympathize with your feelings of loss and displacement, but do not neglect gratitude. You have benefited from the most advanced and powerful science the world has ever known."

"You can?" Peter asked. "Sympathize?"

"Ha ha," Burkhardt said. "Not in an emotional sense, no. But my simulations of emotional interaction are considered very sophisticated. I belong to the only class of artificial intelligences whose testimony is admissible in court."

Peter could have sworn that it sounded proud. He considered what Burkhardt had said about loss and displacement. Pretty soon he figured he'd feel both, but right then he was letting himself be caught up in the puzzle of where he was and how he'd come to be talking to a robot that seemed to have been programmed by some kind of Chicken Soup book for the Future Resurrected.

"This is ridiculous," he said. He tossed back the blanket and swung his legs over the side of the bed. The floor felt good under his feet.

"Delightful," Burkhardt said. It actually clapped. "Marvelous. You're making tremendous progress."

Peter gave himself a moment to get blood to his head. Then he stood. He was wearing light blue hospital pajamas, and when he ran his hands over his scalp he found that he had a lot less hair than he remembered. That brought on the first tremor of dislocation; someone had cut his hair. "Okay, Burkhardt," he said, forcing himself to focus on what was in front of him. "Where am I?"

"Bremerton, Washington," Burkhardt said.

"You're kidding." Peter had grown up in Kirkland, just across Puget Sound. Ninety-eight years. He wondered what Seattle looked like. A powerful surge of optimism overcame him. He was alive, and Burkhardt was right that he was lucky, especially in that he hadn't had any family left when he'd apparently died. "I died," he said, testing it out. He had no memory of it, and was unaffected by the idea. "So this isn't heaven?"

"My goodness, no. This is still the world of the flesh. You don't seriously think you might be in heaven?"

"No," Peter said. He chuckled. "My idea of heaven wouldn't be a hospital room."

"What would it be?"

Burkhardt's amazing cheer seemed to have gone on hiatus. "Am I supposed to have a theological discussion with a robot?" Peter asked.

"Part of my assessment must include the state of your beliefs," Burkhardt said. "Given the blessing you've received, it occurred to me that you might be thankful."

"Blessing? What are you, a robot priest?"

"The cutting edge of robotics, if I'm not being too immodest in characterizing myself in such a manner, is conducted in affiliation with the Office of Faith-Based Investigation. We are all products of our upbringing, aren't we? Ha ha. Now please, back to my question: Are you thankful?"

"Sure. But thank the doctors. I've never been much of a religious guy."

"I see," Burkhardt said. "Well. It so happens that this project is centered on the grounds of what was once the naval shipyard here. The primary strength of the American military is now orbitally based, so the facilities here were reconditioned some years ago. There is another similar facility in our Siberian protectorate, but we thought it best to keep you close to home."

Siberian protectorate? Peter let it pass. A lot could happen in ninety-eight years. "Okay," he said. "Can I get some clothes? I want to get out and see this brave new world."

Burkhardt's face was a single textured piece of metal, but Peter could have sworn the robot grimaced. "That's an unfortunate choice of words, Peter. We can certainly get you dressed—in fact there's clothing tailored to you in the closet there—but we think it's better for you to stay right here for a while."

"What for? Am I sick?"

"I'm reaching my functional parameters here, Peter. You seem to be adapting remarkably well to what must be an enormously wrenching turn of events. Please stay here. Feel free to get dressed. I'm going to hand you off to one of the staff who will get you settled in here." Burkhardt extended a hand, just as it had the last time, and just as he had the last time Peter shook. The robot left, and a bubble of fear rose up and broke in Peter's mind.

He closed his eyes and gathered himself. Okay. Things would be different. He would have to cope, but it would be like he was an immigrant to another country where people spoke the same language but lived in an entirely different way. Difficult but doable. Peter opened the closet door and found a suit of clothes that wouldn't have looked out of place in church the last time he'd gone to church, which was sometime in the Nineties at his college roommate's wedding. It fit perfectly, and so did the shoes. A pair of spats came with the shoes; Peter looked them over, and decided that his willingness to assimilate only went so far. Spats were plain goofy, and he wasn't going to wear them unless there was some kind of law.

Alone and awake, he had a chance to really look around the room for the first time. There was no window, no TV—did people still watch TV? He couldn't imagine they didn't. It would be weird if the hardest thing about blending into the year 2103 was the lack of television.

2103. The number didn't mean anything to Peter. When it came right down to it, he had to admit that he didn't quite believe it yet. The alternative was that he was hallucinating, which didn't seem likely since he hadn't dropped acid since a memorable Wednesday in Boulder ten years ago...well, a hundred and eight years ago. Still, it wasn't impossible. There he was in a room painted pale green with a bed and a monitor and a chair in the corner and a little tube that came out of the wall. Surely he had enough imagination to hallucinate something better than this.

The door opened and an orderly came in with a tray. "Up and around," the orderly said. "Looking good." He was tall and ropy with muscle, hair in a crewcut. Peter's first instinct was that the guy was military.

"I feel okay," he said. The orderly set the tray on his bed and left. Peter removed the cover: baked chicken, muffin, vegetables, a plastic bottle of juice. He sat down and ate, getting progressively hungrier as he demolished the meal until by the time he was finished he wanted to start all over again.

There was nothing visible that looked like a call button. Peter looked at the monitor, saw that it was tracking his vital signs even though he wasn't connected to it. He hadn't seen any kind of contact patches when he'd changed into the suit, and it wasn't clear how the monitor could get a close reading on him. Was there some kind of camera system that could track all of his vitals? He looked around the room and didn't see one. Then again, Dr. McBride had been talking to someone the day before.

Peter went to the door and tried it. It was locked. He banged on it and it opened almost immediately. The orderly stood in the doorway. "Are you comfortable?" he asked.

"Am I under surveillance in here?" Peter asked.

A disbelieving expression swept across the orderly's face. "Surveillance is routine," he said. "It presupposes nothing about guilt or innocence. Do you need anything?"

"I'd like to get out of this room for a while. Get some fresh air."

"A tour is being arranged, Mr. Skilling. You will be contacted when arrangements are complete." The orderly shut the door.

Peter got mad. He banged on the door again. The orderly opened it. "If you're going to bullshit me," Peter said, "you could at least remove my tray."

"Your language is objectionable," the orderly said, but he came in and got the tray. When he was gone, Peter stood in his room and started to really wonder about what kind of world he'd been resurrected into.

* * *

WITHOUT A CLOCK IN THE ROOM, HE HAD NO WAY of knowing how much time passed before the door opened again and three people came in. Make that two people and a robot: Burkhardt stood behind the orderly and a woman Peter hadn't seen before. "Mr. Skilling," she said.

"Are you my new doctor?"

"No. I'm here to take you outside and answer any questions you might have. My name is Melinda. If you'll come this way."

Peter followed her out into a hallway. Burkhardt and the orderly fell into step behind them. "Your rejuvenation is our first full success," Melinda said as they waited for an elevator. "It really has been a gift both to you and to science."

She fell silent, and Peter figured out that he was supposed to respond. It was beginning to dawn on him that people in twenty-second-century Bremerton expected certain ritualistic exchanges, and that so far he hadn't made a very good impression. Even Burkhardt had been bothered by the offhand brave-new-world comment, which Peter had meant with Shakespeare in mind instead of Huxley—but it might be too late to explain that. He resolved to pay closer attention to how people spoke.

The elevator door opened, and the four of them crowded into the car. Peter noticed a crucifix on the wall. "Is this a Catholic hospital?" he asked.

Melinda shook her head. "This is a military research installation. You'll find that one of the things that's changed since your accident is that we have different ideas about the appropriate role of religion in public life."

She'd put strange emphasis on the word accident. Peter wasn't sure why, but before he could frame a question the elevator door opened and they walked out into a spacious lobby, all glass and steel. Military police stood at a screening checkpoint just inside the front doors, and at least half of the people moving through the lobby wore uniforms. Most of the others wore white coats. "Since when does the military fund research into how to bring people back to life?" Peter asked.

"National security concerns dictate that most scientific research be conducted in cooperation with the military," Melinda said. "We've taken the lead on this project." She leaned her face down to a screen, and one of the MPs waved her through. The orderly did the same, and Burkhardt held one hand in front of the screen. Peter followed suit. The screen was blank, glowing a dim green. It didn't respond visibly to his presence, but one of the MPs nodded at him and he followed his escorts outside.

It was a nice day, warm and clear. Peter looked out over the islands in Puget Sound, then turned around to see the mountains. Something about them looked different. They weren't quite the right shade of green, and everywhere he looked he saw the savage, brown scars of clearcuts. "Isn't that still national parkland?" he asked.

"We've all had to make sacrifices," Melinda answered. "National parks are a luxury in an age of terror. With the exception of presidential historic sites, they've all been transferred to private ownership."

Peter was furious, but he bit down on the acidly profane comment he'd been about to make. "Speaking of ownership," Melinda said, "I believe these are yours." She reached out with his wallet and a small Ziploc baggie with what was left of the last quarter-ounce Peter had bought before falling into a glacier.

An instinct to caution prickled the back of his neck. "Thanks," he said, and took only the wallet.

"Please, Mr. Skilling," Melinda said. "Blood tests clearly indicated the presence of marijuana in your body, and this bag was found in your right front pocket. It's a little too late to deny things."

Peter shrugged and took the weed. He walked back toward the hospital door and threw it into a trash can. "I doubt it's any good after ninety-eight years anyway."

"I wouldn't know," Melinda said. "Are you angry about something, Mr. Skilling?"

"My goodness, of course he's angry," Burkhardt piped up. "A perfectly rational response to his situation, in fact a clear indication that he is coping in a sane and intelligent manner. I note that your expression changed when you saw the mountains, Peter. Is that because of our conservation practices?"

"Is that what you call it? Looks like a clearcut to me."

"That's not a current term. Maximal extractive intensity and utilization is the standard practice at this time. I believe 'clearcut' is jargon from the environmentalists of your time, am I correct?"

Peter pointed up at the mountains. "No, 'clearcut' is an accurate description of what's happened up there," he said.

"So would you consider yourself an environmentalist?" Burkhardt asked.

"Yeah, I would. Especially compared to whoever authorized that."

"Whoa there," the orderly said. "All conservation decisions come straight from the top. Show a little respect."

"Were you a member of the Green Party of the United States?" Melinda asked.

"What, if I was a Green it means you can write me off as a wacko?"

"It's a simple question, Mr. Skilling. We need to know as much as possible about you to make correct decisions."

"Fine. Yes, I was a Green. Still am, if there's still a party."

"There isn't," Melinda said. She turned to the orderly. "Vince, do you need anything else?"

"We need to get the drug offense squared away," Vince said. "Mr. Skilling, who did you purchase the marijuana from?"

Peter just gaped at him. "The guy I bought from has probably been dead for sixty years, Vince."

"You may address me as Colonel Trecker. Answer the question."

Peter hesitated. He didn't want to rat on anyone, but you couldn't do much harm to a dead guy. Except me, he thought, and if they're going to make a big deal out of this I better cooperate. Especially if they've had this colonel pretending he was an orderly. "His name was Phil Kokoszka. Happy?"

Colonel Trecker whipped out a PDA and tapped at it. "Philip J. Kokoszka of Redmond?"

"Yeah, he lived in Redmond." Peter had just been there last week, or ninety-eight years ago by the world's reckoning.

"Was he a Green, too?"

"Yeah. I knew him through local meetings. Come on, what's the point? He's dead. So was I. Jesus."

The curse brought a moment of icy silence.

"Are we all set here?" Melinda asked.

Trecker put away the PDA. "Looks that way. Take him back inside."

"Wait a minute," Peter said. "I'm kind of looking forward to seeing what the world looks like now."

"The brave new world?" Colonel Trecker responded. "Maybe some other time. Right now there's business to take care of."

Burkhardt stepped closer to Peter. "Time to go in, Peter," it said. "You really are doing marvelously well. Don't let your initial emotional responses cloud your judgment."

When they entered the hospital, one of the MPs at the door fell into step, his rifle slung at his hip and pointed in Peter's direction. They didn't go back into the elevator; instead Melinda and Colonel Trecker led the party down a curving hall to an open door. They went in, and Peter got a cold chill as he recognized the setup: a desk at the far wall, set on a low dais; two tables facing it; a few chairs arranged in one corner. A courtroom. Burkhardt sat Peter at one of the tables and remained standing behind him. Colonel Trecker went to the desk. Melinda sat at the other table.

"You've got to be kidding," Peter said. "You're prosecuting me for holding a quarter-ounce of weed a hundred years ago?"

"That's certainly a rosy way of putting it," Burkhardt said. "I'm deeply sorry that the situation is in fact a little more serious than that."

The door opened and shut behind Peter. He started to glance over his shoulder to see who was coming in, but Burkhardt stepped to block his view. "Eyes front, Peter. Let's make the best of things here, shall we?"

Run, Peter thought. But he didn't. He turned back around and looked at Colonel Trecker, who had his PDA out again. A display set into the wall came to life, and Trecker took a gavel from a drawer and rapped it on the desk. "Case of United States Government against Peter Skilling," he said. "Major Fullerton, your stipulations."

Melinda rose. Working from her own PDA, she began. "Defendant Skilling is known to have fallen into a glacial crevasse while hiking in Alaska during the late summer of the Year of Our Lord 2005." The screen flashed a *Seattle Post-Intelligencer* article from August 29, 2005: KIRKLAND MAN MISSING ON MCKINLEY. The article disappeared, and a video recording appeared. Peter and Melinda—Major Fullerton—outside the hospital: *Fine. Yes, I was a Green. Still am, if there's still a party.* "Defendant was at that time, and still claims to be, a member of a terrorist organization, the Green Party of the United States."

"What?" Peter said.

Colonel Trecker rapped his gavel. "You will speak only in answer to a direct question. Continue, Major."

"Defendant was at the time of his death under the influence of a Class I controlled substance, cannabis sativa." Peter disappeared from the screen, replaced by a medical report that came and went too fast for him to read it. "The concentrations of THC in defendant's blood indicate that his motor functions would have been considerably impaired, and that mountain hiking under this influence would have been criminally reckless according to prevailing legal standards." A list of legal decisions scrolled across the screen.

"Counselor Burkhardt, do you accept these facts as stipulated?" Trecker asked.

"We do, Colonel."

"Since when is the Green Party a terrorist group?" Peter said.

Trecker got up from behind his desk, walked up to Peter's table, and leaned over Peter. "If you speak again without being asked a direct question, I swear on my mother's Bible that I will bang your head on this table until you can count your teeth on one hand. Is that clear? That was a direct question."

Peter's throat had dried shut. He coughed, and managed to say, "Clear."

Trecker nodded and went back to his desk. "Major."

"Following from the entered stipulations, and under the Terrorism Penalties Enhancement Act of 2005 and the VICTORY Act of 2005, we accuse the defendant of terrorist acts resulting in death. In addition, we accuse the defendant of making comments pejorative to the stature and actions of the Commander in Chief, which act to undermine confidence in the United States of America and therefore weaken our efforts to fight global terror."

"Peter Skilling, do you understand the charges against you?"

"I sure as hell do not," Peter said. "What did I do that was terrorist? Since when is it illegal to make pejorative comments about idiot politicians?"

"Counselor," Trecker said. "Advise the defendant before I have to get up again."

Burkhardt's hand fell heavily on Peter's shoulder. "Peter. You've put yourself in a tricky situation here, and you're only making it worse. Wouldn't you be better off cooperating and not being quite so antagonistic?"

"Are you defending me, Burkhardt?"

"That is my role, yes, and I am very proud to perform it."

Burkhardt straightened. "I believe we can count on a more civil atmosphere," he said to Trecker.

The colonel nodded. "How do you answer the charges?"

"Oh, not guilty. In addition, I move for the dismissal of the pejorative-comment and undermining-confidence charges, which are possible only under laws passed during the 2020s. Clearly Peter can't be charged with a crime that didn't exist at the time of his death, and at that time, free-speech law was much less codified than it has since become."

Trecker looked down at his PDA. After a moment's consultation, he said, "Those charges are dismissed."

"Objection," Major Fullerton said.

"Overruled. Major, you will make your case only on the charge of terrorist acts resulting in death. Proceed."

Hope fluttered weakly in Peter's stomach. Burkhardt had done the job so far. He might be a crazy robot, but Dr. McBride had said he was built to ensure protocols were met; what else would you want in a lawyer?

"Colonel, the government's case is simple. Under the Terrorism Penalties Enhancement Act of 2005, it is a capital offense to commit an act of terrorism that results in a death. The VICTORY Act of 2005 liberalized the definition of terrorism to include drug possession and distribution if it could be shown that drug money financed terrorist organizations. The defendant has admitted that his supplier was a member of the Green Party of the United States, which was on terrorist watchlists as early as 2003 and officially added to the government's list of terrorist organizations in April of 2005 following the first re-election of President George W. Bush." On the wall screen, Peter watched himself say that Phil Kokoszka was a Green.

"Medical and toxicological reports indicate that the defendant was seriously impaired by marijuana intoxication at the time of his death. Under the provisions of the Terrorism Penalties and VICTORY Acts, his purchase of marijuana was a terrorist act in that it benefited a known terrorist organization. His use of that same marijuana impaired his physical coordination to the extent that he suffered a fatal fall on Mount McKinley. It is clear that his terrorist act of purchasing marijuana from the Green Party of the United States led directly to his decease, which makes the Terrorism Penalties Act applicable here and leaves the government no choice but to subject the defendant to the ultimate sanction. The only question is whether or not the defendant is compos mentis, and to answer that issue the government calls Burkhardt."

Before Peter could say anything, Burkhardt slapped a metal hand over his mouth. "Please, Peter. This is all standard. You must realize that things aren't the same as you remember. We're all much safer now."

Letting go of Peter's jaw, Burkhardt stood and walked out in front of the table. Trecker swore it in.

"Do you find the defendant Peter Skilling to be fit for trial?" Major Fullerton asked it.

"Peter has done an exceptional job of adapting to severely trying circumstances," Burkhardt enthused. "I would not have thought it possible for him to be as well-adjusted as he is, but I can find no evidence of deficiency in analytic or emotional responses. What a fine example of the human mind he is."

Numbness was slowly settling over Peter's mind. Now I can't believe this is real, he thought. No way. I'm still dead, still on the mountain, and all of these lunatics are a dying paranoid fantasy.

"Thank you, Burkhardt," Major Fullerton said. "You are excused."

"That was a defense?" Peter muttered when Burkhardt returned to the table.

"Peter, I'm under oath," the robot said. "And I'm very proud of you."

"Anything else, Major?"

Fullerton shook her head. "We rest, sir."

Trecker looked at Burkhardt. "Defense?"

"The defense challenges the toxicology report," Burkhardt practically crowed, "and calls Doctor Felicia McBride."

"Objection," Major Fullerton called. "Doctor McBride's security clearance has been revoked for lack of confidence due to comments made in the defendant's presence. She cannot be counted on to deliver objective testimony."

"Sustained," said Colonel Trecker. "Anything else, Burkhardt?"

"This is terribly disappointing," Burkhardt said. "No, Colonel. The defense rests."

Colonel Trecker stood. So did Major Fullerton. Burkhardt tapped Peter on the shoulder and Peter rose, feeling stoned again, as if all of this was very distant. "Right," the colonel said. "We defend our homeland against those who would destroy our freedoms and our way of life. In that defense it is sometimes necessary to take actions that in other circumstances would be found repugnant. Peter Skilling, you are guilty of terrorist acts resulting in the death of Peter Skilling, and under the Terrorism Penalties Enhancement Act of 2005 you are sentenced to death. Sentence to be carried out immediately. Dr. McBride?"

Peter turned, and this time Burkhardt let him. The robot was whispering close to Peter's ear, something about how resilient and exceptional he was, how astonishing it was that he had so successfully adapted to what must have been a terrible blow, and Doctor McBride was walking up to him with the transdermal in her hand and a look in her eye that told Peter all he needed to know.

"I'm going to give you something, Peter," she said, and he thought, *I don't blame you.* He heard a hiss, and then he was gone.

Shepherded by Galatea

I dropped through the outer layers of clouds, wispy methane and thick bands of hydrogen sulfide I imagined I could smell even though any crack big enough to admit odor would already have killed me. As the density of the atmosphere increased, so did the force of the winds, and between the water band and the ammonia clouds below it I was ripped off to the west at something close to a thousand kilometers per hour.

The water clouds are especially dangerous because of the lightning. If I'd had a window it would have been quite a show, and even though all I had to go by was the crackle in my headset and the occasional hesitation in Bunny's answers to my questions, I could tell that there was one fine electrical storm out there on this eleventh of October in the year 2177. It abated as the temperature dropped from nearly 300K in the outer reaches of the atmosphere to a brisk seventy-four at that magic one-bar level.

Bunny slowed the ship down without me having to tell him. I watched displays: external temperature creeping up, atmospheric pressure not just creeping but leaping. At a thousand kilometers in I signaled my companion sensor array to distribute. At three thousand kilometers into the detectable atmosphere, I was reading ten gigapascals of pressure and a balmy 970K. From there the temperature and pressure curves steepened until, a mere thousand kilometers below me, at what we gas-moles call the adamapause, the atmosphere precipitated into a mix of ices at 3000K and something like thirty gigapascals. The equivalent of being under three thousand kilometers of water on Earth, if that water was superheated to the point that it could boil iron.

"Bunny," I said, "kick up the conductors and drop us a little lower."

It isn't easy mining diamonds on Neptune.

* * *

THE BOILING POINT OF DIAMONDS IS 5100 DEGREES KELVIN. The deep interior of Neptune is about 7000 degrees Kelvin. But the diamonds don't boil away because of the incredible pressures they're under, something like six hundred gigapascals. Even my ship, which has been tested up to about thirty-five gigapascals with conductors running as hot as they can, would become some kind of superheated condensate at that kind of pressure. The conductors take advantage of the electrical charge in Neptune's atmosphere, especially right around the adamapause where the pressure spikes and little molecules like methane get broken apart and rearranged in all kinds of interesting and possibly remunerative ways (superconducting magnets also keep off the radiation, which pays off in the long run, too). My ship's hull is one huge directional conduit; the layers of charged molecules nearest it are swept off and around, creating an effect kind of like a wing and kind of like a curveball. I prefer the curveball analogy myself, since one very real byproduct of the conductors' operation is that I have to fly in circles, following the bubble of decreased pressure created by the directed conduction. I am propelled by the increased density at the rear of the ship, so if I stop at any pressure greater than a dozen or so Gpa, I'll get rear-ended by a big chunk of the atmosphere of Neptune. Changing direction is possible but tricky; you have to alter the directional current ever so slightly to create a miniscule imbalance on one side or another, or above and below. Conductors are not good to steer by.

Every once in a while the conductors get hot enough that Neptune's atmosphere can act as a sink. You know you're not behind a desk when you're counting on a 3000K atmosphere to cool the hull of your ship so you don't die.

The combination of Neptune's highly charged outer atmosphere and its dense interior, and the fact that its poles get a lot of seasonal heat due to the planet's axial tilt, means that lots of heat is released by convection. Superheated condensates roil up from the interior, break through the adamapause, and release heat and pressure in great geysering storms that from Earth look like, well, spots. If you're a little closer they still look like spots, but you can do quick spectrographic analyses to look for the presence of hydrogen cyanide, which is a dead giveaway that a big hot chunk of Neptune's lower atmosphere has just come up to bust like a bubble the size of Phobos. And when that happens, there are often diamonds to be found.

And when there are diamonds to be found, there you will find yours truly, Stig Davidsohn, in his ship *Eightball* with his trusty AI sidekick Bunny.

The diamonds precipitate out at the adamapause, as the combination of pressure and temperature breaks the C-H bond. Methane becomes ethane, which outgasses, and hydrogen, which liquefies and sinks. What's left over is carbon, which becomes diamonds about ten microns across. As they, too, sink toward whatever makes up Neptune's core, the increasing pressure molds millions of these tiny diamonds together. Sometimes, very rarely, Mother Nature molds these larger diamonds well enough that they can survive the sudden journey of thousands of kilometers combined with a radical change in pressure and temperature. Those diamonds that survive, you will not be surprised to learn, are highly prized by those populations on Earth and elsewhere that lie awake nights figuring out ways to spend their money.

Or maybe you will be surprised to learn that. I was. I figured that a diamond from Africa was as good as a diamond from Neptune. I was wrong. I underestimated the importance of novelty to the psychology of the consumer.

Neptunian diamonds, you see, have an almost unbearable cachet. They cost several orders of magnitude more than regular old Earth diamonds for the sole reason that they are fashionable, and they are fashionable for the sole reason that they cost a lot more than regular Earth diamonds. I do not follow fashions, and I have so far failed to understand how this one operates.

But the cost of Neptunian diamonds, let me say, is not unreasonable. My fine ship *Eightball* is expensive to maintain and operate. Bunny is expensive to maintain and operate.

I am not cheap either.

* * *

THE HCN PLUME I WAS FOLLOWING HAD SPREAD rapidly under the influence of Neptune's psychotic high-altitude weather, but I had managed to track it to the intersection of the imaginary lines 33 degrees south by 272 degrees west. Near what I liked to think of as Neptune's austral pole, on the edge of a constant and spectacular auroral show, and not incidentally smack in the middle of the most magnetically charged region of the planet. The closest thing to a good vein that my generation of miners is ever going to find. Magnetism keeps the electric charges humming, the poles get lots of solar energy to generate convection, and the auroras keep the weather lively. Heat plus electricity, on Neptune, equals diamond fountains.

I settled in less than one hundred kilometers above the adamapause, letting Bunny set *Eightball* in a loop around the bubble of Neptune's innards that I was pretty sure was going to pop soon. HCN plumes were nearly always harbingers of fine things to come, and what better omen of wealth than cyanide, I always say.

"Conductors running eighty percent," Bunny said. I try to keep them there; any higher and you're within the margin for error.

I wished I had a window. There's no way to do it, of course. The only materials that can survive these kinds of pressures—nanoengineered superconducting polymers, mostly—are not transparent. Still, like every other time I'd ever done this, I wanted to see. What did it look like out there? I worked in the dark. Inside, my ship was lit and comfortable. A little warm, even, once the conductors started shedding heat.

Outside, as far as anyone knew, there was no visible light. I was four and a half billion kilometers from my mother's Earth—and yes, I was born there—and thirty-seven hundred kilometers deep in the atmosphere of Neptune, surrounded by temperatures and pressures that humans couldn't even replicate in labs until the end of the twentieth century. And it was dark.

The array of sensors I'd left in the upper atmosphere started to ping. The bubble was bursting. Bunny tightened the loop, and I resisted the urge to amp up the conductors. Strange magnetic things started to happen when the conductors were dialed up all the way. Ambient pressure was twenty-six Gpa. They could handle it.

Now came the hard part. At some point during the loop, when the sensors pinged the right way and Bunny thought the time was ripe and I decided that they were both wrong and I was going on my intuition like I always did, I would pop a small vacuum chamber under *Eightball's* nose (I call it the nose because it usually faces forward; *Eightball* is actually spherical). If I did that at the right time, I would suck in about one thousand cubic meters of relatively low-pressure ejecta from Neptune's lower atmosphere. If things went really well, the conductors would blow away all of the sulfides and methane condensates and liquid molecular hydrogen—leaving those diamonds that had survived their explosive decompression to be scooped into the vacuum chamber of the good ship *Eightball*.

If things went a little bit wrong, I would die before I ever knew anything was wrong. An injection of high-pressure condensates into the vacuum chamber could blow the seals around it; the decompression as I climbed back into the higher atmosphere could also burst the chamber. The door could stick open. Oxygen could leak into the vacuum chamber and react violently with the hydrogen that always came in with the diamonds. Or the wind could shear and thrust me down into a part of Neptune where the conductors wouldn't make any difference.

This is why Neptunian diamonds are expensive.

Many people think that all gas-moles are misanthropic, angry people who harbor secret wishes to kill themselves. I can't characterize the profession, but speaking for myself, I like the work, and I've got no urge to die. In fact, it's the other way around. When I come up through the crackling band of water clouds and burst out through the last hydrogen reaches of Neptune's atmosphere, and I'm alive and there are diamonds in the nose, that's living. The stars shine a little brighter, Neptune glows a little bluer, and Triton seems pinker than it has any right to be.

It was hot in the cockpit, and I told Bunny to goose the conductors another five percent.

The sensor array pinged, indicating that the outflow from Neptune's interior was peaking. I had Bunny correct our prospector's loop, and when he'd gotten *Eightball* shaving the edges of the big upwelling— which would turn into a storm soon, and be visible from Earth by the time I got back to the orbital base—I counted to ten and flipped the switch to pop the vacuum chamber.

I didn't hear anything, but then, I never did. Once, a few years ago, I could have sworn I'd felt a thump, and when I got back to the station I had a diamond crystal that weighed in at nine hundred and seventeen grams. Ever since then I'd been waiting to feel that thump again, and I never had. Probably I just made it up out of being hopeful. And today, I wasn't just hopeful. I was a little bit desperate.

When I popped the switch, the chamber flashed open for some miniscule fraction of a second, sucking in whatever was around it; then it either closed automatically or the ship collapsed into a molten smudge. When the dummy light flashed announcing that the chamber had captured material and closed successfully, I goosed the conductors and let Neptune's atmosphere push me up toward space.

* * *

ON THE WAY OUT OF THE UPPER REACHES of Neptune's hydrogen stratosphere, I always tried to pass over the tiny moon Galatea and the glittering arc segments that she shepherds around the planet. This time I was on the wrong side, and couldn't see the arcs as I passed below the Adams ring and fell away from Neptune toward Roderick Station.

The orbital station looked like it was surrounded by a million Tinkerbells, which likely meant that they'd just blown their wastes. Nothing sparkles like explosively decompressed slivers of water-rich organics. It was so easy to refine water out of Neptune's rings and upper atmosphere that nobody bothered to recycle out here. Most of what went out the waste locks eventually fell back into the planet anyway, or became part of its rings. Some of it eventually became diamonds, a fact that was carefully concealed from in-system consumers.

Roderick was a radial station along the lines of Kadadaev's first Lagrange installations. Eight spokes, each half a kilometer long and twenty meters thick, connected the hub with the outer ring. Halfway along the length of the spokes, another ring stabilized the structure and made getting around inside it a little easier. Roderick's hub was about half a kilometer in diameter, and a full klick in length; at either end of its cylinder were zero-g construction and maintenance labs, and most of its center was taken up by the Big Mak fusion reactor and associated safety and energy-distribution apparatus. The outer ring, ovoid in cross section and measuring fifty by one hundred meters, housed gravity-sensitive things like vegetables and human beings. A monorail ran around the inner ring at about the pace of a brisk walk but without all of the low-g navigational hassles. Roderick's rotation provided about point-seven g in the outer ring, enough to keep the brain and inner ear oriented and prevent the worst long-term health problems.

Total volume: two hundred million cubic meters, give or take. Total population: three hundred, also give or take. Total diameter: almost exactly an old English mile. Don't ever let anyone tell you that was an accident. Roderick was American-designed by people who were still nostalgic for feet and inches.

Roderick featured eight docking stations, one opposite the conjunction of each spoke with the outer ring. These stations were basically extensions of the spokes, jutting out about seventy meters from the outer ring and terminating in magnetic docking arms and a lamprey airlock. I ghosted *Eightball* into Dock Number Seven, one of four equipped with damping facilities to drain some of the stored juice from *Eightball*'s hull. Docks Five through Eight also had multiple blast doors and quick-release explosive bolts in the event of a catastrophic failure at diamond offload. This happened more often than anyone involved in the industry liked to admit or think about. Neptune's chemistry was still understood only imperfectly, and once in a while something would react violently to the depressurization of a gas-mole's vacuum chamber. Best-case scenario in this situation is a ship blown to pieces and a big hole where the docking station used to be. Worst-case is a big hole in Roderick's outer ring and a suspension of all operations while Gas Giant Recovery Industries investigators try to figure out exactly what the trigger was. They never do, but we keep hoping.

So depressurization takes place in a vacuum as pure as we can get it.

"I've got the preliminary density in the chamber," Bunny said. "Approximately one point three grams per cubic centimeter."

One point three. Ambient atmosphere at that depth was right around one, which meant something heavier was in the chamber. I let myself get hopeful for exactly a count of three, then shifted gears back into my typical pessimism.

The lamprey locked onto my ship and I hopped off into gravity. It's an interesting feeling, by the way, to go from the gravity near Neptune's adamapause to zero-g to Roderick-g all in a few hours. Before locking the ship down, I uploaded Bunny to Roderick's localsphere and made sure he was all there. I know three other moles who have lost their AIs when their ships blew up in the dock.

You're probably thinking: Why not do the depressurization farther away from the station? And you'd be right to think that, and the answer you'd get if you asked the question might leave you shaking your head.

Truth of it is, GGRI doesn't want gas-moles stealing diamonds, and the only way they can make sure of that is to have the diamonds unloaded on-station. I'm sure that somewhere a cost-benefit analysis was done and it was determined that the financial and personnel risks of depressurizing on-station were outweighed by the potential for employee skimming of valuably arranged carbon atoms if the depressurization and initial inventory were conducted in space. I mentioned that Neptunian diamonds are worth a lot of money, I believe, and GGRI has shareholders to answer to, and if a hole gets blown in their station once in a while in the name of maximal shareholder value, well, that's the cost of doing business.

I have a pet theory that the accidents also work as price supports for the industry. People back on Earth and Luna and Mars hear that gas-moles on Neptune are disintegrating once in a while, they form romantic opinions about the industry and they want that much more to associate themselves with the product.

Which is not to say that GGRI is entirely cavalier with the lives of its employees. There are safety precautions in place. The depressurization takes place in a near-perfect vacuum contained in a mobile chamber that is maneuvered by robots into position over the vacuum chamber door. The contents of the chamber, which are about to go from thirty gigapascals to none, are next cooled by a liquid-nitrogen bath to near-ambient, which on the shadow side of Roderick is usually about fifty K. Then and only then, when Boyle's Law has done its work, is the chamber door cracked. Remaining gases are siphoned off, and then the door is opened the rest of the way to see how many diamonds are left. If any.

Gas-moles are independent contractors, mostly because constantly paying death benefits got to be an annoyance to GGRI shareholders. We are very well paid, though, and it is written into our union contract that we supervise the depressurization of our own ships. GGRI doesn't want us stealing diamonds, okay, but we don't trust them either.

I got Bunny started on the depressurization maneuvering, and I watched from the supervisor's office at the base of the docking arm. The view was fine, Neptune's rings shining in the sun and tiny Galatea leading the arc segments in the Adams ring around the great blue planet. Just showing a bright pink limb around the edge of the planet, Triton hove into view, and the light in the room picked up some of its methane hue. An odd place, Neptune. Not as odd as Io or Jupiter, maybe, but odd for a boy who grew up in Minnesota and went outsystem when he was still a kid.

The big spherical chamber floated up to the big spherical ship. They stuck together. I started watching readouts instead of the window. The only visible thing that could happen in the next few minutes was the destruction of my ship, and I'd be able to see that from the screens anyway. There were three possible outcomes, the way I had it figured. Either the ship would blow up or the ship would not blow up and there would be only atmospheric junk in the chamber or the ship would not blow up and there would be diamonds in the chamber.

The spectrometer display lit up, meaning the robot stevedores had finished the cooling and cracked the vacuum chamber. No big boom rattled through the walls of the docking arm, so I figured *Eightball* hadn't exploded; now all that remained to be seen was whether I'd scored. Big convection, right time of year for that latitude … everything was right.

I was sweating a little bit, there on the shadow side of Roderick Station where it's always a little bit cold. "You would think," I said to Figo, the tech monitoring the depressurization, "that Roderick's rotation would distribute the heat a little better."

He shrugged. "Shadow side always seems to cool faster than the sun side heats up." Figo knew how I was when the diamonds were hiding, and so did I. Complaining about the station thermostat, for God's sake.

The results came up on the screen and simultaneously Bunny spoke through my audiolink. "Bad luck, Stig," he said. "Only six grams. The rest of it's just hydrocarbon sludge."

Six grams.

Thirty carats.

Maybe a third would survive cutting, and even that remainder would be worth a small lottery in the boutiques of Bangkok or the tourist shops at Burroughs Base. But that was after transport, brokering, and finishing, not to mention retail markup. Six grams of diamonds for me meant I should have stayed at home. GGRI wouldn't even break even on the fuel I'd exhausted getting out of Neptune's gravity well.

That made seven in a row. Seven drops without turning a profit, and my contract up at the end of the month.

* * *

THINGS COULD BE WORSE, I TOLD MYSELF that night as I glanced over the delayed-burst Luna League maghockey games on the station net. I could be a war refugee. I could have an incurable disease. I could be popular with women.

None of it changed the fact that I had made seven profitless drops in a row, and in the final month of my contract. If GGRI re-upped me after that kind of performance, they'd hear from their shareholders, and it didn't matter that I'd been a gas-mole for eleven years and never failed to turn a profit on each and every contract. Forty-three consecutive quarterly returns, sometimes as little as two percent (what GGRI termed a Probationary Return) but more often in the neighborhood of twenty. And once I made the magic Keystone: one hundred percent return. None of it mattered. In a GGRI ledger, you only get one line of red ink.

Not that I was railing against the system. I'd had my eyes open when I signed on. I knew that atmosphere mining was purely results-oriented. I also chose to stay contract even after GGRI wanted me to join their stable; the salary they offered amounted to my commission on a ten percent return, and I figured that if I couldn't do better than ten percent most months I'd be better off in another business anyway.

Another of the stereotypes about gas-moles is that we're all prima donna hotshots. Again, I can't speak for the profession, but I see myself as an artist, and art is about failure as often as it is about success. Ask any sculptor. And there is an art in following a cyanide plume through four thousand kilometers of raging wind and a three-thousand-degree temperature gradient; there is an art in circling an upwelling dome of superheated Neptunian atmosphere, staying close enough to take advantage when it bursts and far enough away that the burst doesn't incinerate you; there is an art in riding a downdraft off the side of a high-atmospheric storm the size of Mars and pulling off the draft right before the adamapause when holding on for another thirty seconds would be fatal; there is an art to knowing when to pop the vacuum chamber and capture those diamonds that have fallen so far only to come boiling up again.

I tried to explain this to my last girlfriend, who was at that time a gas-mole herself. We were in bed. When I was done she propped herself up on one elbow and looked thoughtful.

"What?" I said.

A little crease appeared between her eyebrows, then faded. "I was just trying to remember," she said, "when I have ever heard such a load of self-serving pseudo-transcendental crap. But I don't think I ever have."

I was, as you might expect, at a loss for words.

So she went on. "We're miners, Stig. We fly ships down into the soupy part of Neptune's atmosphere and we harvest diamonds from convection storms. Then we come back up here and GGRI pays us a fraction of what those diamonds are worth, and then we go out and do it again until we either get sick of it, we get fired, or we get killed. It's not art. It's work."

She got up then, and swept the sheet off the bed as if I might see something I wasn't supposed to, and went into the bathroom. We weren't together too much longer, and she didn't stay a gas-mole. She sold the note on her ship and used the money to lease a retrofitted asteroid miner and dock space from GGRI so she could lead photographic and vid tours of Neptune's rings. Valerie van Gaal; we called her Valerie the Valkyrie because she was built like an opera singer and loud like an opera singer and there was just something Wagnerian about her.

It's her fault that I even know about Wagner. It's her fault that I got thinking of diamond mining as art. I never paid any attention to art until I started hanging around with her, and then just when I started seeing where the art was in what I did, she snorted and took off with my bedsheet. You can see why I took it as a slap in the face when she started escorting artists through Neptune's rings.

I also took it badly when, before we'd even had a final powwow to formalize our ending, she started parading around with a reactor tech who had the insufferable name of Acer Laidlaw.

Acer.

He, apparently, was everything I was not. I am hairy and unkempt; he is clean-shaven, razor-cut. I am heavily built; at one meter seventy-five I weigh an even hundred kilos. Acer is half a head taller and built like a caricature of an athlete: long, ropy muscles, broad shoulders, muscular hands with long fingers. Acer can sing. I cannot, at least not on key. He had a steady and well-paid job. I lived on the vagaries of intuition.

It wasn't Acer Laidlaw's fault that I hated him. My limited interactions with him were civil enough, and he never made the mistake of gloating—or worse, trying to commiserate with me over losing Valerie. In a jaundiced and bitter way I was grateful to him for this. If he had turned out to be the kind of asshole the name Acer implied, I would have had to crack him in the mouth and then quit talking to Valerie for having left me for a handsome reactor monkey. As it was, I stayed on half-decent terms with Valerie, too. She was kind to me, and I tried not to let it show that I'd only fallen in love with her when she walked out on me.

* * *

THINGS COULD BE WORSE, I TOLD MYSELF AGAIN. I could be competing with Valerie to get vid tourists and snob directors to the good spots on the Arago Perimeter or Galatea's resonance points with the Adams arcs. This is what I told myself as I watched hockey games from Luna and wondered how I would pay the note on my ship if GGRI let my contract expire.

The answer, which was as clear in the morning as it had been the night before, was that I wouldn't. Nobody could afford the note on a ship that specialized if they weren't doing what it was designed for. If GGRI didn't renew my contract, I'd have to sell the ship to some lunatic who wanted in the gas-mole business because he'd read some romantic garbage about it when he was a kid. Then I could do one of a few different things. I could stay at Roderick, go in-house at GGRI, and pilot the giant hydrogen harvesters that we gas-moles derisively called bladders. I could hire on at a pretty good salary working in the zero-g shipworks in Roderick's hub. Or I could go back in-system and slip into the easy routines of asteroid mining, which is what I had been doing before I got into the gas-mole business because I'd read some romantic garbage about it when I was a kid. I'd been a 'roid cutter for six years, saving every cent against the down payment on *Eightball*. Now I was thirty-five, with some equity in my ship and piloting skills on several different exotic-atmosphere craft. I was employable. Maybe it was time to get out of the gas-mole business after all. With what I had in *Eightball*, I could file mining claims on two or three of the more difficult rocks, maybe the ones that rode outside the ecliptic. Go freelance, pick up a used mining ship like Valerie had and use it like it was meant to be used.

Damn Valerie, anyway. She was right. It was work. I was a working man.

I pulled up my financial records and had Bunny do the math. During my current contract, I'd run forty-two drops, a little above average. GGRI always said that a drop every other day was standard, but maintenance backlogs usually kept us down to thirty-eight or forty in a ninety-day contract. Before my current empty streak, I'd been doing fairly well this quarter; two weeks before I'd even considered putting money down on a new Deep Diver sensor array. Good thing I hadn't. As of right then, with only seventy hours remaining on my contract, I was running four point seven percent under the break-even point. Either my next mission would return five percent on a full quarter's expenses, or I'd be looking for another job.

* * *

THERE WAS A KNOCK ON MY DOOR while I was eating breakfast. I was in a relatively good-natured funk of resignation when I opened it to see Valerie. "Val," I said. "To what do I owe, et cetera." We stayed on pretty good terms, me and Val.

"I hear you're running a shortfall this quarter," she said, still in the doorway. I asked her in and tried not to slam the door behind her.

"I'm a little behind," I admitted.

"How many more drops will you get in?"

"One. I could do two, but union regs won't allow it."

She considered, and that little line between her eyebrows appeared and disappeared. "Swear to me that you will not feel belittled if I offer you a way to make your balance whether you make your balance or not."

"I don't have that much pride, Val. You know that as well as anyone."

"Well, with you artists it's hard to tell," she said, and I had to work real hard not to walk out the door and leave her there to be smug by herself.

Instead I said, "It's better that you're not a gas-mole if you're not going to appreciate the beauties of it," and both of us were able to laugh. But I was still angry. Art is about failure, and suffering, and survival. Gas-moles know quite a bit about all of those things. We dance with gravity. Anything that involves intuition is art, and mining diamonds on Neptune is all about intuition. Unfortunately my intuition had been disastrously off base these last two weeks, which meant I had to sit in my own room and be patronized by my ex-lover.

"GGRI is doing a PR vid over the next few days," Valerie said. "Board members came all the way out to have themselves filmed walking around Roderick and oohing at the rings. Since I was already here, they contracted me to fly, and since this is going to be a bigger production than most of what I do, I need crew."

"I don't know anything about vid, Val," I pointed out.

"You don't have to. You fly, I'll take care of the vid logistics and VIP strokes. And," she went on, "the best part is that if you work this, it falls under the Other Services to the Company clause in your contract, which means that what they pay you goes on the plus side of your contract ledger."

"I'm five percent down. They aren't paying you that well."

She hesitated, but only for a moment. "No, they're not. But the fee would knock it down under two, I bet, and then you wouldn't have to get the crown jewels to break even."

I thought about it. I refrained from asking her why she hadn't offered the job to Acer. I refrained from asking her why she didn't pilot the job herself. Then I said no.

"Thanks, Val. I know you're thinking of me, and it's really generous, and yeah, I'm in a little trouble, but see, here's the thing. I don't know when I can schedule dock time in the next seventy hours, and I haven't even had *Eightball* checked out for maintenance issues. So I don't know when I can drop. If you count on me to pilot your shoot, I might end up having to back out, and I wouldn't want to do that to you. The fee for the shoot isn't going to put me positive by itself, so I've got to make the drop first priority."

It was all true, every word, but behind it was a simple obstinate desire not to let Val help me. I admit it.

She looked me in the eye, and she knew it, too.

"Okay, Stig," she said. "You're right."

"I mean it," I said. "Thanks. I appreciate you thinking of me." Which I did, sort of.

"Good luck," she said, and let herself out.

* * *

THINGS WENT FROM BAD TO WORSE WHEN I CHECKED in on *Eightball* at the company shop. Bunny had warned me that the news was not going to be all good, but Bunny is always kind of morose and gloomy about technical things. For an AI, he's kind of arty and philosophical. So when I found Farouk the shop tech and asked when I could drop again, I was expecting him to put me on the Hokey-Pokey, which is what us gas-moles call the dynamic of repeatedly walking down to the shop only to be told to come back later. I had once worked an asteroid called the Football with an old guy from Schleswig-Holstein who sang the Hokey-Pokey in German: *Du machst den Hokey-Pokey und Du drehst Dich um Dich selbst....* I could never forget the song after that, and it had become my own little contribution to Roderick Station slang.

So twenty-four hours, I was figuring, which was okay since no matter what happened GGRI wouldn't let me squeeze two drops into the next seventy hours. If they did, and something happened, the union would have a fit.

"You got reactor trouble," Farouk said. "I have to ground you."

I remained calm. "For how long?"

He shrugged. "If it turns out you need a new reactor, could be two weeks."

Cool as could be, I said, "And what if I don't need a new reactor?"

"Well, I'll know by the end of the day. Could be you'll be dropping again in no time," he said, and chucked me on the shoulder as he walked away. This was Farouk's way of telling you to get out of his shop if you ever wanted your ship cleared for flight again.

So I got. I headed back to my room and sat fuming on the side of my bed while Bunny did his best not to point out that he'd told me so.

Even if I could afford a new reactor, which I couldn't, I had to get at least one more drop in on this contract or I'd have no way of coming out ahead. And if I didn't need a new reactor, the maintenance expense would make it that much harder for any but the most outrageously successful drop to bring me out in the black. Oy. There was only one thing to do.

"Farouk," I said later that day. He gave me the hairy eyeball, and I held up my hands. "I know. I know. You know I know. But it's important."

"Tell me," he said.

"I'm running a wee bit in the red this quarter." He nodded like he'd already known that. "So there are two things. First is, I really cannot need a new reactor. So I need some good news on that front, okay? Help me out here. Please, Farouk."

"You don't need a new reactor," he said.

It took me a minute to figure out that he was serious. "Really?"

"Really. Acer ran the check, and structurally everything's okay. But output is way down, both raw heat and impulse. You haven't changed your fuel in how long?"

I couldn't remember. I was still hearing Acer's name ricochet around the inside of my head. He had run the diagnostic on my reactor! It wasn't enough he had to steal my girlfriend, he had to get his hands all over my ship, too. Perfectly normal, I told myself. He's a reactor tech. He works on reactors. There is a reactor in my ship. Perfectly normal.

Farouk saw me not answering him, but he didn't understand why. "Before I took over here," he said, referring to the last change of my reactor fuel, and I knew it was true.

"How come you never reminded me?"

"You can read the logs as well as I can," he said. "You're way overdue for fuel insertion, and you can't drop until it's done."

"When will it be done?"

"Day after tomorrow."

"Farouk," I said. "Do you mean forty-eight hours from right now?"

"Give or take," he said.

"Farouk," I said. "Forty-eight hours from right now I will have less than twelve hours left on my contract. I cannot make a drop in twelve hours, even assuming your monkeys here get everything done when they say they will." I could feel myself starting to lose my temper, and I fought it, but it wasn't easy. "If I don't make another drop, I don't make my contract. If I don't make my contract, I can't make the note on my ship. If I can't make the note on my ship I need to get another job either piloting bladders or 'roid cutting in-system.

"But all of this misses the point anyway. If I have a fuel-insertion expense this quarter, I'd have to come back with a three-kilo diamond to make the quarter. We both know this is not going to happen, do we not?"

It is never good to yell at Farouk. He stood calmly looking me in the eye the whole time, and even as the words were coming out of my mouth I was telling myself to shut up, shut up, don't make things worse than they already are. Except they couldn't get worse, so my mouth kept running.

"You probably won't find a three-kilo diamond, no," Farouk said.

"So we're at an impasse here. This repair means that I won't make my quarter. Period."

Looking uncomfortable, Farouk nodded. "Nothing I can do," he said. "Acer's already getting into it up in Bay 3."

Acer again. Bad enough I wasn't going to make my quarter; also I had to sit by while Acer got *Eightball* shipshape for whoever I would have to sell it to.

An inexcusably jealous paranoid fantasy swept over me. In that moment I was certain that my reactor was fine. Acer had flagged the diagnostic so he could make sure I didn't make my quarter. He knew I'd leave Roderick if I wasn't a gas-mole, and that bastard, he was going to make an offer on *Eightball*. I was sure of it. He wanted me off Roderick because he knew that Valerie would come to her senses sooner or later. She would recognize him for the shallow plaything that he was, insufficient for a substantial woman like her—and she would come back to me.

That was when I caught myself and knew I was way off base.

"Besides," Farouk said, "the union would have my ass if I let you go out with your reactor running tepid the way it is."

"They haven't bothered you for the last twenty times you checked me out without changing the fuel," I said.

This was something new. I had something on Farouk, or more accurately on his predecessor since he had only been head shop tech for a couple of months.

I could see him working this over in his mind.

"How about if you do the repair and just bill it next week?"

"I can't do that," he said. "Inventory tracking, there's no way around it. Especially reactor fuel. I have to personally sign it out."

"And you can't just sort of forget to process the order so they don't know whose ship you put it in?"

"Come on, Stig," he said. "I have to log the spent fuel, too. What am I supposed to say?"

"Okay, you're right. Sure." I thought hard. "There's only one thing to do, then. I have to ask you not to fix my reactor."

"But I already processed the work order."

"Farouk, please, I'm asking you for a favor. Pretend it was a mistake. Blame the readouts or something. Please. I have to make a drop tomorrow or early the day after if I'm going to get back and be logged in before my contract ends. You know GGRI is real careful about that."

"Do you know what you're asking me to do?" he said. "You want me to send out a substandard reactor, and if it screws up and you die, you want me to blame whoever had this job before I did."

"His name was Elliott Roundtree," I said. "No one will be surprised that he made a mistake like that."

* * *

LATER THAT NIGHT VALERIE CONFRONTED ME in the corridor outside the billiard hall. "Swear to me you're not going out just because you're having some kind of reptilian macho reaction against Acer working on your ship."

"What?" I said.

"He came to me and told me what Farouk told him about what you said today," she said.

"He came to you?" I said incredulously. "What, is he worried about me? What a prince."

"As a matter of fact, he is. I know you're never going to like him, Stig, but he's a good guy."

"I'm sure he's wonderful," I growled. "And I'm fine, and *Eightball* is fine. Everything's fine. I'm going to make another drop and find a diamond the size of my head, and then I'll retire in-system and make a living explaining the Cassini division to Martian tourists."

She stood there looking at me. People walked by, and I took a selfish pleasure in the fact that they were seeing Valerie and me together.

"Listen, Val. I have been a gas-mole for most of my adult life. It is uncertain, lousy work, and I take my life in my hands every time I make a drop. But I don't have any school, and every cent I have is tied up in my ship, and I don't want to do anything else. It's my work, and you go ahead and laugh, but when I get it right it's art."

She didn't laugh. More people walked by us into the pool hall. "I got Acer to work the VIP shoot with me," she said after a minute.

"Good," I said. "Glad you found someone." Then I figured out why she was telling me. "He's not licensed, is he?"

Valerie shook her head.

"You're going to fly the GGRI board into the rings with an unlicensed pilot?"

"Well, you said no. You're happy here, that's fine, Stig, but I want out. If this shoot goes well, the board will know me. I can use that. I can get into in-house filming, public relations, something. Anything's better than this right now. I want to get back in-system. My brother's on Mars, I haven't seen him in five years. I'm not cut out for the station life. I miss sunlight." She lifted her hands, let them drop.

Listening to her talk, I could feel myself dividing down the middle of my mind. One hemisphere believed her, sympathized, understood the desire to be closer to family and the rest of humanity. Life was tough out here in the trans-Kuiper.

The other side was thinking: Do you think I don't remember that you could pilot this little excursion and get someone else to do the schmoozing? You're not fooling anyone, Val, you treacherous bitch. Don't want work so much any more now that you're a little closer to art, do you? Or maybe it's just that you don't want work, period. Management seems like a good solution to that problem. *You're happy here, that's fine*, she'd said, but what she meant was: *I'm looking for something better. Something that you never were interested in. That's why I walked out with your bedsheet and sashayed off to find Acer Laidlaw.*

Then that deranged half split down the middle and I became suddenly and mortally certain that Valerie had asked me to pilot the shoot as some sort of test, and that her selection of Acer was to let me know that I had missed my last chance to recapture her.

"Look, I need to get prepped," I said, and left her standing in the corridor.

* * *

THIRTY HOURS LATER I GHOSTED AWAY from Dock Seven and goosed *Eightball* toward the austral pole of Neptune. I was sure there were diamonds there. The storm I'd sampled three days before was still going on, and had reached the upper atmosphere. It was a pale, oval smudge on Neptune's fine Caribbean blue. Long storms, especially big long-lasting convection storms, create all kinds of little stormlets around them. I figured that the halo of this storm would be full of smaller surges and upwellings. All I had to do was pick the right one. Simple. Before the last two weeks, I had consistently done it for eleven years.

I tried not to think too much about the reactor, which Farouk said was performing at something like seventy percent. It powered the external current that allowed *Eightball* to survive in Neptune's lower atmosphere, which as well as the ship's thrusters, and if it was under the weather that meant that I had much less time to fish around the edges of the storm.

There were, of course, ways I could conserve energy and forestall testing the reactor before I had to. One of those ways involved letting the atmosphere itself brake me instead of dropping in and impulse-braking.

To do that, I needed a strong updraft and a strong downdraft close together, which was why I was letting *Eightball* drop toward the edge of the big polar storm. I flashed past Galatea on the way in, kind of for good luck. She was my good-luck moon: Galatea, like Pygmalion's statue brought to life by Aphrodite. When I watched her shepherding those arcs of ring around Neptune, I thought: *There is nothing like you in the Solar System.* And I longed for Aphrodite's intervention.

I know, the moon isn't named for the statue. But don't ask me about the other Galatea. That's never been a story I needed to hear.

Things started to rattle as soon as I dropped through the hydrogen shell and hit the first methane layers. By the time I'd reached the depth where I normally expected water clouds, *Eightball* was bouncing so much I couldn't focus my eyes on the readouts. "Bunny," I said. "Soon as we fall off the edge of the storm, kick up the conductors and kill the exhaust."

"So mote it be," Bunny answered.

With the reactor the way it was, I had to fold in the main exhaust now if I wanted to have the conductors up to speed by the time I got close to the adamapause. Also, I was figuring on needing a little directional impulse on the way down, and I thought I'd save my heat for that. It wouldn't do any good to pull off this fine storm-surf if I ended up super-condensed hydrocarbons at the end of it. Oh, the irony: the gas-mole become diamonds.

It occurred to me, not for the first time, that I might at some point have scooped up diamonds whose carbon atoms had once belonged to colleagues. Also that a colleague might some day scoop up beautiful crystalline fragments of me.

Then I suffered a vision of Acer Laidlaw piloting *Eightball* back to Roderick Station with a hold full of atoms that had once been mine, and gritted my teeth so hard I cracked a filling. There is no depth to which the jealous mind will not sink.

No, I said to myself. That couldn't happen. If you die down here, *Eightball* goes too. See? Much better.

I blew the sensor array when the edge of the storm got within fifty kilometers, and all of the little gyro-stabilized spheres followed after me as I went over the edge of this ten-thousand-kilometer Niagara.

First, *Eightball* started bucking so hard that I couldn't even read my retinal display. Then Bunny kicked on the conductors and warned me that they probably wouldn't run past seventy percent. Then he warned me that if the conductors were running at seventy percent, I'd have next to no impulse available to arrest my free-fall toward the crushing depths of Neptune's atmosphere. "Yeah, Bunny," I said. "I know. You're the computer; you make sure that the conductors leave me some directional heat when I need it."

"All I'm saying," Bunny said, "is that timing will be extremely important at the end of this maneuver."

"I am forever in your debt, et cetera. If you're so worried, why don't you just let me know when to start the roll?"

I had done this before: fall off the edge of a storm, then turn over just as the pressure began to spike so that the conductors created a cushion of atmosphere below. The deceleration sometimes knocked me out, but Bunny always kept it together until I came around. All it took was timing and the correct application of an impulse burn to roll the ship over so the conductors would slow the fall and start the loop.

"Adamapause at five hundred kilometers," Bunny said.

"Roll at two. Conductors are at seventy now?" I asked.

"They are."

"Can you goose them to eighty when we roll?"

"Probably," Bunny said.

"We will die if you don't," I said.

"I'll do what I can, Stig." Bunny was exasperated, I could tell, and suffering his typical pessimism when it came to technical obstacles.

Four, three, two, and I blew a quick burn to roll *Eightball* over. Then I locked down all of the impulse nozzles. They were a prime cause of integrity failure at high pressures, and I ran the check twice, and then Bunny amped up the conductors and the last thing I heard was a painful roaring in my ears.

* * *

I THINK I LOST ABOUT NINETY SECONDS. When I blinked myself back to awareness, *Eightball* was steady, nose pointed straight up, and conductors running exactly hot enough to keep the ship suspended on a pillar of Neptunian atmosphere. We started to rise, and Bunny tipped *Eightball* into a standard cruising loop.

"External pressure twenty-seven Gpa," Bunny said.

A current buffeted the ship. I had to work at it, but I could focus on the readouts, and they showed the big storm as an endless wall immediately to our north. Three of my remote sensors had failed on the way down, but the seventeen remaining showed a flurry of smaller storms birthing on the perimeter of the big one. "Let's see," I said. My throat was dry, and I rummaged under the seat for a water bottle. "What looks likely here, Bunny? Where are the three-kilo diamonds today?"

Bunny pointed out a temperature bulge along the storm front, some way to the east. "Right," I said. "Good spotting."

"Local pressure there is close to thirty-two Gpa," Bunny said.

"What's your guess when it breaks open?"

"You never pay attention to what I say anyway."

"Just tell me or I'll sell you along with the ship," I said.

"Pressures greater than thirty-five Gpa would not be surprising."

Eightball could handle thirty-five Gpa with conductors running full. I'd never done it, but I knew guys who had. What I didn't know was how much margin for error there was there. "Bunny," I said. "How much can we get out of the conductors?"

"I told you," he said. "It would be ill-advised to try for more than seventy percent."

Which put the safe threshold somewhere between thirty-one and thirty-two Gpa. If I couldn't get any more out of the conductors, and the temperature bulge popped at thirty-seven or thirty-eight, Acer Laidlaw would get a chance at my atoms—but at least he wouldn't have my ship to do it in.

"Amp the conductors up all the way," I said.

"The reactor might shut down."

"No it won't. Just test them. Amp up, verify full current, then ease back to seventy."

Bunny didn't say anything.

"Bunny, I don't want to die," I said. "I just want to see what we've got. The reactor won't shut down on a one-second test. Those shop guys are a bunch of chickenshits, you know that."

There was a pause. Then the conductor readout swung from seventy to one hundred, held for a blink, then fell back to seventy. *Eightball* scooted ahead in its loop as the pressure gradient around it grew briefly sharper.

"Any change in reactor values?" I asked, sounding calmer than I felt.

"As long as you don't want any impulse at the same time," Bunny said, "the ship can handle full conduction, possibly for as long as a full minute."

"Mighty fine," I said. "Take us over to that bubble."

The remote sensors picked up a temperature spike at the near end of the bubble, which generally meant that the first rupture would occur there. I floated *Eightball* over near it and waited off to the side, figuring to ride the expanding new storm front up and out of the dangerous part of Neptune. If the storm blew like most near the pole tended to, I could figure on a four-hour trip to make it above the water clouds. The conductors wouldn't work for the entire trip; they weren't much good below densities in the neighborhood of half a gram per cubic centimeter. So at some point I'd need to throttle up the reactor again and heat some hydrogen. My hydrogen reservoirs were nearly full because I'd used so little exhaust to get down to the adamapause. No problem there. I just had to hope that the reactor would give me enough thrust to achieve escape velocity. Twenty-three kilometers per second. That wasn't so fast, and like I had told Bunny, shop techs were chickenshits, afraid of union stewards and obsessed with the letter of regulations. I didn't figure I'd have any trouble.

There was a ping from the sensor array. "Storm front coming," Bunny said, and the external pressure jumped to thirty-one Gpa.

That was just high stuff blowing in front of the real meat of the convection, which would be coming at the next pressure jump.

Eightball rocked, and pressure shot up to thirty-six. Bunny had the conductors running full before I had a chance to tell him, and as we rocketed along the edge of the front I toggled a close analysis of temperature bands. "On my mark, Bunny," I said, watching the display.

Thirty-seven Gpa.

A gout of condensate overtook us, and the ship bucked harder. Six thousand K. That's the one, I told myself. From all the way down straight to me, and barely cooled along the way. At thirty-seven Gpa there's no way for diamonds to boil or sublimate.

"Pop the chamber," I told Bunny.

There was a thunk. I swear it.

"Chamber filled," Bunny said, and I put *Eightball* through a turn that was maniacal by conductor-steering standards, hotdogging just a little because I was sure. Sure I heard a thunk.

"Did you hear that?" I asked Bunny.

"It could have been lots of things," he answered.

"Like what?"

"Stray heavy metals. You know this. Tungsten."

"Tungsten on Neptune?" I nearly shouted. Once a gas-mole had come back with a knuckle-sized chunk of tungsten in her chamber. The geologists were still arguing about it. "Tungsten on Neptune? Measure the goddamn density, Bunny!"

We rocketed up on the welling storm, pressure dropping faster than temperature until I had to cut the conductors off and burn some exhaust to get clear of the storm. The reactor's output faltered here and there, but I was making twenty-three km/s, and that was all that counted.

"Density in the chamber two point four grams per cubic centimeter."

Two point four? "Jesus," I said. "Are you sure?"

"I don't randomly quote figures, Stig," Bunny said peevishly.

"Two point four," I said with lightning all around me, still climbing. The only time I'd ever had a load come in at two point four was the quarter I'd turned the Keystone profit. Unless I was carrying all hydrocarbons or freak liquid hydrogen or goddamn tungsten, my quarter was made. I could keep my job. I could keep my ship.

"Stig Davidsohn," a voice said over my external comm.

"Farouk?" I said.

"Mayday, Stig. This is serious."

"My reactor's reading okay, Farouk. I've got things under control here."

"It's not you. Seems that Acer's got himself in trouble."

"Is Val okay?" It occurred to me in passing that if Acer had gotten Val killed because her miner was too much ship for him, I would have to torture him to death.

"She's fine. She's on Galatea with the crew."

Unlicensed pilots, I thought. Unlicensed reactor-monkey pilots who are showing off for their Valkyrie girlfriends who they don't deserve anyway. Unbelievable.

"You're sending *me* a Mayday? What can I do?"

"I don't know, Stig, but nobody up here can do anything. You and them are on the wrong side of the planet. By the time anyone here can get there, they'll be long gone."

"What did Acer do?"

"He didn't do anything. He was letting one of the Board poobahs pilot into Galatea. Val and the vid crew had already landed separately, and Acer's AI fired a retro burn right past them. It kept burning for fifteen minutes until Acer could override it, and now the ship is falling right into that storm you're coming out of. I'm feeding you the trajectory now."

It came up on my retinal. I was already above the miner, which was falling in a shallow arc into the big storm I'd surfed down early that morning. Miners like Valerie's were designed to work in high atmospheres, but the pressures inside that storm would tear it apart.

"Did Val call you?" I asked.

"Yes."

She hadn't called me.

"You're a good pilot, Stig," Farouk was saying as I tried to think of what I could do, "but remember you have no wiggle in your reactor performance." I didn't respond; I was already falling back toward the crashing miner.

"Are you listening?" Farouk said.

There was one thing.

I didn't want to do it. It probably wouldn't work anyway, probably all of us would die if I tried it, and I didn't want to risk that on Acer Laidlaw and a shipful of the guys who made money off me risking my life three times a week.

* * *

ANOTHER MYTH ABOUT GAS-MOLES IS THAT we're all violent frontier wackos willing to kill for anything. Stories abound of gas-moles killing each other over good drafts at the edge of a fresh storm, or over love, or money. Any story they used to tell about gold prospectors they tell about us. And, as I've said, I can't speak for the profession, but I'd be lying if I didn't admit that there existed the briefest of moments when I thought that the world would be better off without Acer Laidlaw—not to mention the GGRI board—and that if all of them were subsumed into the stormy interior of Neptune I might have a chance again with Valerie. I admit it.

But I made the burn back down into Neptune's atmosphere, and I got Acer's attention on the way in.

"Acer."

"Stig?"

"Saint Stig on his spherical black horse of the apocalypse," I said. "Are you aware that the ship you're in has electromagnets to keep off the radiation?" All the miners did. They were designed for long outings with no atmospheric protection.

"Okay," Acer said. I could tell that he didn't care about electromagnets. He was going to die, and he didn't want to talk to me while he was doing it.

"Okay is right, reactor monkey. If you want to live, you'll find a way of changing the polarization of those magnets sometime in the next couple of minutes."

Brief pause. "Why?"

"Because I am going to try to save you and our illustrious board of directors," I said, "and I can only do it if your magnets are polarized opposite mine. Get it? We need to get together."

I made visual contact with the miner. It was falling fast, but I caught up to it easily enough. The problem was, with my reactor feeling poorly there was no way I could boost both of us out of Neptune's gravity well. I couldn't even arrest the progress of our combined tonnage, I didn't think, although I was sure as hell going to try before I got desperate.

"Magnets, Acer," I said. "Are they switched yct?"

There were voices in the background on his end. Someone else came on the channel. "Who is this?"

"Stig Davidsohn. Gas-mole."

"Do you have a way to transfer us to your ship?"

"Nope," I said. "I have a better idea."

"Oh, for God's sake," the anonymous board member said, and broke the connection.

I was running parallel and a little below the miner now, keeping a hundred meters away. Wispy currents of methane belched up from the storm began to rattle both ships. I called Acer again. "Time's running out," I said. "I'm not even sure I can get out now." It was true. Bunny was trying to get my attention by flashing dispiriting numbers about reactor performance on my retinal display.

"Magnets are just about ... hold on," Acer said. "Okay. They're switched."

"Where are they?" I asked.

"Where are what?"

"The magnets, Acer. Where are they on the ship?"

"Oh," he said. "In the rear, about a third of the way up from the engine nozzles."

Close to the center of mass, then, especially if the fuel tanks were nearly empty. "Good. Get everyone on board as far forward as you can, and if you've got oxygen, distribute it. Fast."

In sixty seconds he let me know that it was done. "Can you control the magnets from where you are?" I asked.

"I can."

"Amp 'em up," I said, and did the same to my conductors.

Eightball snapped around until the nose was pointing almost straight down into the storm and rose upward as if on a line, banging hard into the underside of Val's retrofitted miner as the two ships' magnets drew each other close. The intervention of Aphrodite, I thought sourly. Perfect.

"You okay there, Acer?" I called.

"We're all still here," came the reply.

"All right then, hold on for a minute while I see if you were right about my reactor trouble."

"Jesus," he said, and I got a wicked thrill out of the fear in his voice. I couldn't help it.

I wound the conductors down to about twenty percent, which I figured was enough to keep the two ships locked together, and fired up the hydrogen exhaust for all it was worth. Our descent slowed, but only a little. "Is there any more, Bunny?" I said. "Turn off the lights. Shut down the heat. Put it all in the exhaust."

Still we didn't come close to arresting our descent.

"Bunny," I said. "Are you thinking what I'm thinking?"

"I have no idea what you're thinking," Bunny said.

I was thinking this: a thousand cubic meters of material, compressed at something like thirty-six gigapascals and a temperature of six thousand degrees Kelvin, might well offer significant thrust if directed out into a pressure of something less than one ten-thousandth of a gigapascal.

If, the standard rejoinder went, it didn't destroy my ship upon its release.

"I'm thinking," I said with great unhappiness, "that we might be able to ride up out of here on my diamonds."

"I hope you aren't serious," Bunny said, and Acer, who was overhearing this on the open channel, added, "What?"

"Strap yourselves in there, Acer," I said. "I don't know how bumpy this ride will get." Or how long it will last, I added to myself as I broke the connection. "Bunny, get ready to crack the vac chamber." Outside, the weather was getting heavier. *Eightball* wouldn't have any problem as long as the reactor held out enough for the conductors to work, but the miner would be shaken to pieces pretty damn soon, or crushed with all the people in it like bugs under a rock.

"Preparations complete," Bunny said morosely. "On your order."

I took a deep breath. "Okay. Give us a little oomph."

A deafening roar sent tremors though the ship. I tried to keep my attention on the retinal, which showed a slowing of our descent. At this angle, we would skip off the edge of the storm and be sucked down faster than we would have if we'd fallen straight into it. "A little more, Bunny," I said. The roar got louder, and the ship vibrated so hard that I had to close my eyes and let Bunny take care of flying. I could only guess what it was like for the passengers on Valerie's miner. If it was still there. For all I knew I could be flying along with only its electromagnets and a few stray bits of steel clinging to my hull.

I toggled the comm channel. "Acer, you there?"

"We're here," he answered. "What are you doing?"

"The dumbest goddamn thing I've done in years," I growled, and then I had Bunny open the vac chamber a little wider.

* * *

I NEVER DID MANAGE TO BOOST US UP VERY HIGH, but I leveled out the descent and got us a little altitude. By the time we'd made half a revolution of beautiful blue Neptune, there were rescue ships dropped from Roderick Station waiting for us.

Turned out there had been some kind of assassination plot originating in-system. Corrupted Val's ship AI using a virus riding on one of the board members' own ID badges. Crafty, but basically what you'd expect from disgruntled shareholders, which as anyone will tell you are more dangerous than mother grizzly bears.

You will not be surprised to learn that I did not fulfill my quarterly contractual obligations to Gas Giant Recovery Incorporated. Or that when my unkempt ugly mug was briefly on every in-system vidscreen the board publicly decided that this one failure didn't offset my many years of service to the company. Bonuses came my way, as well as appearance fees for a startling variety of vid shows. In about a week it was over and I was just a gas-mole again.

Acer and Valerie left Roderick and went in-system. I don't know what they're doing now. I'm just about certain that they're doing it together, though. When he stepped off the rescue ship … it was an operatic scene, and I don't mean that pejoratively. Over his shoulder she looked at me, her eyes full of gratitude so pure and chaste it broke my heart to see it. I knew right then that all my clumsy effort to recapture Valerie had been wasted. You can't fight the intervention of Aphrodite.

Me, I'm still here. I make drops. Sometimes I come back with diamonds. On the way back, if I've timed it right, I slow down as I'm passing Galatea and settle into one of the glittering arc segments that she shepherds around the planet. Being in the edges of a planetary ring is an experience like no other that I know. Fine mists of ice hang about you, and the ring looks like solid ground, like dirty snow. Any light sources are scattered into millions of sparkles. Neptune is a pretty shade of greeny blue, and the stars are as beautiful in space as everyone says, but for my money there's no experience like ghosting along the fringe of a ring, looking at Galatea and saying, *There is nothing else like you. Nothing.*

蛇警探

Follow the Continuing Adventures of Inspector Chen, Singapore Three's Premier Supernatural Investigator

ISBN-10: 1-59780-043-0 $14.95

John Constantine meets Chow Yun-Fat in this near-future occult thriller. Detective Inspector Chen is the Singapore Three police department's snake agent – that is – the detective in charge of supernatural and mystical investigations.

Chen has several problems: In addition to colleagues who don't trust him and his mystical ways, a patron goddess whom he has offended, and a demonic wife who's tired of staying home alone, he's been paired with one of Hell's own vice officers, Seneschal Zhu Irzh, to investigate the illegal trade in souls.

As a plot involving both Singapore Three's industrial elite and Hell's own Ministry of Epidemics is revealed, it becomes apparent that the stakes are higher than anyone had previously suspected.

ISBN-10: 1-59780-045-7 $24.95

When Detective Inspector Chen leaves Singapore Three on long-deserved vacation, Hell's vice-deceive-on-loan, Zhu Irzh finds himself restless and bored. An investigating into the brutal, and seemingly-demonic murder of a beautiful young woman promises to be an interesting distraction.

The trail leads to one of Sigapore Three's most powerful industrialists, Jhai Tserai, the ruthless heiress of the Paugeng Corporation. While Zhu Irzh isn't normally attracted to human woman, Jah Tserai seems to have an unnatural effect on Zhu Irzh's natural appetites. Meanwhile, Robin Yuan, a former lover of the deceased, and employee of a Paugeng Corp. research lab, is finding that not all is as it seems at her place of employment.

Inspector Chen returns to Singapore Three to find Zhu Irzh's erratic behavior has placed the demon under suspicion. Tensions flair and the entire city find's itself under siege from otherworldly forces both Heavenly and Hellish in nature.

Night Shade Books Is an Independent Publisher of Quality SF, Fantasy and Horror

ISBN-10: 1-597800-02-3
Hardcover; $25.95

Dissolution Summer: the soon-to-be-former UK was desperate. The world was in the grip of a fearsome economic depression. The anti-globalization movement threatened stability throughout Europe, supported by rioting youth, bitterly disaffected voters, and encroaching environmental doom.

The Home Secretary decided to recruit a Countercultural Think Tank: pop stars would make the government look too cool to be overthrown. It was just another publicity stunt for the rockers, until the shooting began. Will the accidental revolutionaries, Ax, Fiorinda and Sage find a way to stay alive while the UK disintegrates under their feet? Will rock & roll's revolutionary promise finally deliver, or will ethnic, social and religious violence drown hippie idealism in rivers of blood? Either way, the world will never be the same.

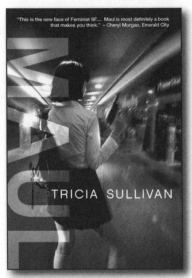

ISBN-10: 1-59780-037-6
Trade Paper; $14.95

Sheri S. Tepper meets Neal Stephenson (and kicks his ass!) in this feminist-cyberpunk thriller by Arthur C. Clarke Award-winning author Tricia Sullivan.

In a mall, a gang of teenage girls is caught in a maelstrom of violence and shopping. But it's not only their own lives they will have to fight for—It's that of a man trapped in another world, with very different enemies; a man they haven't met, but who could change the future of the human race.

"Two stories unfold in parallel in this fast and furious blend of gender issues and balls-out action. Maul is a thoroughly enjoyable, well-written novel that stares hard down the barrel of sexual politics and happily sticks its finger in the muzzle." – *infinity plus*